CW00860495

Hiding Cracked Glass

Hiding Cracked Glass

Perceptions Of Glass Book 2

James J. Cudney

Acknowledgements

Writing a book is not an achievement an individual person can accomplish on his or her own. There are always people who contribute in a multitude of ways, sometimes unwittingly, throughout the journey from discovering the idea to drafting the last word. *Hiding Cracked Glass*, the second book in my *Perceptions of Glass* contemporary fiction / family drama series, has had many supporters since its inception in the fall 2019, but before the concept even sparked in my mind, others nurtured my passion for writing.

First thanks go to my parents, Jim and Pat, for always believing in me as a writer and teaching me how to become the person I am today. Their unconditional love and support have been the primary reason I accomplish my goals. Through the guidance of my extended family and friends, who consistently encourage me to pursue my passions, I found the confidence to take chances in life. With Winston and Baxter by my side, I was granted the opportunity to make my dreams of publishing this novel come true. I'm appreciative to them for inspiring me each day to complete this book.

Hiding Cracked Glass was cultivated through the interaction with and feedback from several talented alpha and beta readers. I'd like to share a special call-out to Shalini for supplying insight and perspective during the development of the story, setting, and character arcs. I am indebted to her for countless conversations helping me to fine-tune every aspect of this tale. Shalini went above and beyond to find as much time as I needed, and I'm humbled at how generous this woman has been. Thank you.

I am also beholden to the talented author, Didi Oviatt, who has become a close friend in the last year. So close that we have recently finished co-writing a book that will release in 2021. While editing *Hiding Cracked Glass*, I asked Didi if she would read a draft and point out all the areas that needed more emotion and pop. Didi very quickly turned around her thoughts on twelve scenes and provided valuable suggestions—that's when I knew our partnership as authors on other projects was going to be a phenomenal experience. Thank you so very much.

There were also several amazing members of the team who volunteered to read an early draft of the book. These amazing nine readers and friends found most of my proofreading misses, grammar mistakes, and awkward phrases. I couldn't have completed this wonderful story without Misty, Nicole, Anne, Laura, Lisa, Anne, Mary, Valerie, and Nina. A major thanks to them for encouraging me to be stronger in my word choice and providing several pages of suggestions to convert good language into fantastic language. I'm grateful for their kindness and bigheartedness to play such an integral role in catching the things my eyes and mind completely overlook.

Thank you to Next Chapter for publishing *Hiding Cracked Glass* and paving the road for additional books to come. Their support and focus on my novels in the past three years has been a key reason I'm able to keep on writing more. I look forward to our continued partnership.

Perceptions of Glass – A Contemporary Fiction Family Drama Series

My debut novel, *Watching Glass Shatter*, was published on October 8th, 2017. After its successful release, I committed to writing a sequel. Once the *Braxton Campus Mysteries* grew more popular, this sequel suddenly took a bit longer to write. As I thought of title options for the book, two clear choices stood firm. In the end, I chose one of them as the name of the series: *Perceptions of Glass*. The second book in this series, which will be published on the third anniversary of the debut, October 8th, 2020, is called *Hiding Cracked Glass*.

I recommend reading *Watching Glass Shatter* before you devour *Hiding Cracked Glass*. While it isn't necessary, as I provide a summary of the key events in the first chapter of this second book, you will grow to love the characters more if you've read the books in order. Both revolve around Benjamin and Olivia Glass, Olivia's sister Diane, and the five sons, Teddy, Matt, Caleb, Zach, and Ethan. In *Watching Glass Shatter*, a secret letter is revealed during Ben's will… it's no spoiler that the book opens with his death. *In Hiding Cracked Glass*, which takes place several months after the end of the first book, a courier delivers a new secret letter. And this time, it is unclear to whom it belongs.

It's shocking to realize this is my ninth novel in three years… that said, I hope you enjoy your extended journey with the Glass family. You never know… there might just be more stories to tell with these amazing people, so stay alert for various treasures buried along the meandering path in *Hiding Cracked Glass*.

-Jay

Chapter 1 – 10:00 to 11:00 AM

Memories of a forty-year marriage undoubtedly pale in comparison to the visceral experience of loving sand supporting another human being throughout an entire lifetime. Awakening to the familiar rhythm of a husband's beating heart as her head rests gently on his rising chest is steadfast and comforting. Clutching a pillow with an unrelenting grip because it contains the faintest hint of his woodsy scent becomes a feeble consolation prize. Death in all its glory knocks the strongest to their knees, naked and raw, in search of a tangible identity, especially once accepting widowhood is the most recognizable facet of her remaining years. It is Destiny who ensures these hidden truths will trigger stumbles in our finale.

Shoulder-length wisps of striking gray hair scattered across Olivia's rosy cheeks as a serpentine breeze hugged the curves of the cemetery's solemn pathways. Her lazuline-blue eyes sparkled from the sunlight blasting through a gathering of thick, frost-covered oak trees. Its dense canopy temporarily comforted and sheltered Olivia from the outside world. She sat perched against a mossy gravestone, a determined hand tracing the etched inscription of her late husband's name.

Benjamin Glass: Husband, Father & Friend. 1947 – 2017

A little over eight months had passed since Ben's fatal acci-dent, yet the memory of audibly witnessing his car's collision with the impenetrable steel of a Connecticut overpass struck far more primal than any pain her husband endured during the same event. At least Olivia believed so. The police and ambu-lance crew had assured her that Ben and his driver died instanta-neously. She replayed the incident in her mind daily, pondering whether Ben suffered any last-minute regrets or relived fond memories as life slipped from his body into the dark ether sur-rounding them. Olivia had come to believe that loved ones lin-gered behind only to suffer an indulgent exacerbation of grief and nostalgia.

Unrepentant February winds continued to flog the surround-ing tombstones. Though startling and chilly, it refreshed and awakened Olivia. When a limb snapped from a stalwart ever-green several rows away, a surprising comfort settled inside her as though she were no longer alone. "Are you trying to console me, Ben? I miss you more each day, my darling." She imagined her late husband hovering nearby, conveying his concurrence with all her major life decisions since his death.

Immediately upon Ben's passing, Olivia had channeled every waking moment toward reminiscing about their life together, repeating and overenunciating his full name, Benjamin William Glass, to all five adult sons in the hope it would keep his mem-ory alive. Not just floating in their minds but inside the lone-liness of their family home. Their unremarkable yet intimate town where history always triumphed. The dewy air they un-consciously breathed and smelled while the rest of the world prospered without him. Although the remembrances reinforced Olivia's confidence and composure, sometimes they crippled her ability to visualize a future without Ben.

During the reading of her late husband's will, a deeper layer of darkness unexpectedly descended upon Olivia—a secret reve-lation Ben left behind that nearly destroyed the family. Ben had unleashed two explosive letters in his attorney's care years ago, inadvertently playing Russian Roulette with the Glass family's bonds—emotional and blood. Few knew of their existence or the damage they could incite had those troubling facts fallen into idle hands. Olivia morphed into an aging matriarch ravaged by secrets, loss of faith, and a desire to hide from everyone. She concealed the newly discovered information for months until pressed into obligatory action. Not only had she lost a treasured partner, battled waterfalls of tears that left her body brittle and dehydrated, and clung to a sense of hope for at best a tolerable future, but the *Eternal Creator* beseeched the widow to offer penance beyond Ben. Destiny craved more. Someone else to be sacrificed because of Olivia's past failure to become the mother she'd always yearned to be.

Olivia considered sharing Ben's confession with their children. She wanted to tell them that she'd given birth to a baby who died minutes after greeting the world sans a single cry or laugh, offering only a handful of insufficient breaths. That Ben switched the infant with another, one whose mother wanted to secure a loving home for her son because she had lost the father and couldn't care for a child on her own. But Ben had never even told his own wife. And now, in his death, he challenged her to bring the truth full circle. Unfortunately, Destiny intervened and insisted Olivia reevaluate such instincts.

Ben's two letters, a pure but painful deceit, changed every trajectory of Olivia's future life. One letter was hers. The other Ethan's. Ethan was the boy who'd been switched at birth. Only Ethan never received his copy of the letter. Destiny delivered her final blow to Olivia by demanding Ethan's return to her intimate fold. Ethan would be the price Olivia paid for her mistakes. When Ethan informed his mother that he only had months to live, she refused to eviscerate his remaining days and hours with the truth. Olivia begged for mercy, citing alternative ways to make her suffer and to ameliorate her errors, all the while re-membering the harsh realities of life.

Derelict addicts survived intentional overdosing. Vicious murderers avoided prison death sentences. Innocent souls frequently perished young. It was a fact, not an observation. All too often the case for darkness made its presence known in the world encompassing Olivia's existence. The bad outweighed the good, and the best hope one could cling to involved staying slightly ahead of Destiny's tormenting game. Life was rarely fair to those who had earned a reprieve or a temporary moment of tranquility.

Before he passed away inside the Glass family home, Olivia tracked down and granted Rowena Hector the opportunity—no, the privilege—of meeting the son she'd given up. Rowena, a more selfless mother in those few moments than Olivia had been during her entire lifetime, agreed to conceal the secret. Olivia saved her letter from Ben as a keepsake to remind her of the past when she was egocentric, aloof, and neglectful. All those behavioral tendencies had begun decreasing as the tumors riddled Ethan's body into a mere shadow of its former glory. Ethan tragically left the world at twenty-three-years-old, clueless that he was not the biological son of Benjamin and Olivia Glass. His last excruciating gasps for air, like the only breaths of Olivia's infant who died, marked a life-changing event.

Confident a lesson was buried somewhere in the messaging, Olivia accepted blame for all the drama and tragedy affecting her family. Throughout the preceding years, she'd transitioned into someone she never intended to be, and only via the senseless catastrophe had she summoned the courage to alter the course of her future. Last fall, Olivia buoyed her surviving sons when they each faced and conquered significant problems in their own lives. She'd finally put her children first. Once confident they navigated the complex road to recovery, she committed to addressing her own healing process.

"I've learned surprising facts about myself in the last few months. Family means everything to me now, Ben," stated Olivia, her voice searching for the proper balance between confidence and wishful thinking.

During her recovery, Olivia's sister functioned as a prodigious and necessary limb, an extension of a broken soul clawing its way into the remaining corporeal bond between two siblings who couldn't be more different. Diane had always admired and loved Olivia—never once jealous of all the blessings bestowed upon her sister—and bolstered the unexpected widow during the chasm opening upon Ethan's death. Olivia and Diane embarked on an extended vacation to Italy to experience *La Dolce Vita*, the sweet life. A second honeymoon she and Ben had hoped to take that summer, rendered impossible once the accident interfered in what should have been their jubilant golden years. While on the trip, Olivia relied on Diane for everything, and they eagerly embraced the intoxicating culture, divine beauty, and mouthwatering food of a country so magnificent, it effortlessly lifted their spirits.

Yesterday, she arrived home from Europe and moved back into the Glass family estate. She would temporarily occupy her old family home, the one she'd entrusted to her surviving sons before leaving the country. After the initial shock of stepping foot into the house she and Ben had built, Olivia struggled to summon the strength to hold her head high. It instead hung low and waffled between rage and relief. Accepting Ethan's and Ben's deaths would demand a much lengthier commitment than she anticipated.

"I'm proud of them, Ben. All our boys are making better decisions." Flurries anxiously descended at her sides, trapping Olivia in her very own picturesque snow globe. Fear of someone absentmindedly shaking the tenuous symbol, whirling her life upside down for a moment's pleasure, still lurked furiously in her bones. Olivia interpreted the wet snow as Ben's tears of happiness, for if she thought they were anything else, the delicate balance she maintained on a fragile existence would crumble into oblivion.

She'd escaped that blustery morning to visit Ethan's and Ben's graves for the first time in months. No one knew she'd disappeared shortly after dawn for a cathartic walk around the neighborhood. Once ready, she reserved an Uber, requesting a drop-off and return pickup one hour later. An hour that had already passed, though it felt like seconds since her wobbly feet initially stepped on the frozen ground and instinctively walked toward the final resting places of her husband and son.

"They have a new maid, Ben. Our housekeeper retired when I left. It's best the boys find their own help. We all need a fresh start." Olivia brushed away persistent snowflakes from congregating atop the headstone, narrowing her eyes to minimize the sentimentality overwhelming her emotions. "I don't like her very much. She's… too friendly, too eager."

Olivia had once attended law school and worked side by side with Ben before retiring from the firm to raise their five sons. When the boys were old enough, she involved herself in countless charities and organizations, which meant the Glass family home required more than just a nanny. After several failed attempts to handle it all on her own, she hired a maid who understood her role in the household—neither to be seen nor heard. While that's what Olivia's parents had always advised about their own children, Olivia felt it more aptly applied to staff. For years, she was deemed cold and shrewd toward others, but Ben's and Ethan's deaths had shattered the previous iteration of Olivia Glass. Upon reassembly, she should've emerged a changed woman. What was taking so long?

Not that she didn't trust the new maid's cleaning abilities or felt uncomfortable by another woman's presence in the last place she'd seen Ben alive. It was that the girl frivolously hummed and sang, played with the children in all the wrong rooms, and flitted about the home as if she owned it. Olivia warned herself not to behave as snobby or persnickety as she'd once been. Perhaps she struggled with adjusting to change now that she no longer headed up the household. Maybe the maid was simply too young and inexperienced but would grow into her role. Nonetheless, Olivia kept her mouth shut the previous day, promising not to get involved. Her son's wife, Margaret, had hired Pilar, and if Pilar proved to be an unreliable housekeeper, Margaret would be the one to reprimand and fire her. Managing and disciplining people taught a woman how to mature gracefully into the leader she was destined to be. Olivia also assured herself that exhaustion from the flight home could've led to misjudging the situation. Age made certain people ornery and blind. It educated and reformed others, like Olivia, under normal circumstances. But nothing was typical for her anymore.

Amid the desolate cemetery's shrub-lined passageway, the Uber driver nonchalantly waved to notify his fare of his arrival. Olivia held up her hand to request another five minutes, suddenly distracted by a new mourner admiring various marble statues and ornate benches on the opposite side of her section. Olivia thought the person's frame and stance looked familiar, but she couldn't capture a clear angle of his or her face. Before she knew it, the figure disappeared behind a hearty grove of rhododendron bushes. Had she imagined the individual, or was he or she truly watching her?

Although she'd visited Ethan's grave earlier, Olivia wanted one last goodbye before leaving Ben's plot—her future plot, where she'd reunite with her husband for all eternity. In the distant future, as her life was far from over, per her most recently putative opinion. Navigating through three rows of brittle yellow-brown grass that crackled as she firmly trounced on its decaying life, Olivia arrived at Ethan's permanent resting place.

Two manicured mugo pines adorned either side of the immaculate headstone—nothing was too good for her baby who would never be granted the privilege of fathering a child of his own. Upon reliving his death all over again, a piercing stab of torment ricocheted inside Olivia's chest as if an overloaded electrical system had shocked her core mercilessly. She covered her lips to prevent a primal cry from escaping, but nothing could contain the heartbreak and utter sense of loss that had broken her. To die at the beginning of his career in medical school as a newlywed to a beautiful college sweetheart, magnified all that was wrong in the world.

When doctors diagnosed Ethan, his girlfriend had just graduated from Boston University and accepted her first professional job. He followed through with his plans to propose to Emma, keen to attain a myriad of goals before Death plucked him from her life. Rather than run from a fiancé being issued a death sentence, Emma dove headfirst into caring for Ethan. She delayed the start of her new position as the choral director at a private school in Boston and moved into the Glass family home in Brandywine, Connecticut. Emma nursed her new husband morning, noon, and night, taking turns with Olivia and Diane during the last two weeks of Ethan's life. She held his hand as he passed to the afterlife early one October evening under a crimson and lavender sky. Emma likened the lost tension in his final grip to releasing one's childhood into the vaporous air, accepting that a blind belief in miracles was humankind's most fatal mistake.

After the funeral and spending a few weeks with her inlaws, Emma returned to Boston to surrender the apartment she and Ethan shared, declaring a gaping inability to live there any longer. She hinted to Olivia that memories of the past, before learning of his disease, were too difficult to handle once seeing what he'd been reduced to in the end. They agreed to disagree regarding Emma's best next steps, especially with

Olivia's intention to leave on her trip. She surmised Emma was too shocked and naïve to accept Ethan's death, supposing her daughter-in-law had run off to recover from her trauma in private. Once Emma had settled into her new position in January, she regrettably began avoiding the Glass family. As far as Olivia understood, Emma had spoken with no one else since the holidays. Olivia attempted to contact Emma from Italy, but the voicemails were never returned.

"Your wife and I need to connect, Ethan. She grieves as much as I do. Widows must support one another. I have a duty to protect her from a life of solitude and depression." Olivia tapped the top of his headstone twice, once for the past and once for the future—always a future with her son, even if it was a connection no one else understood.

With a heavy heart and shallow breath, she recalled the day Ethan skinned his knee on their front patio while trying to skip rope faster than his brothers. Deflated by the thought of never again drying his tears or fixing his booboos, Olivia shrank inside herself and concentrated on happier memories. Ethan seemed to speak to her from beyond his grave, soothing her apprehensions and disillusions. She often sensed his presence, as if he stood behind her, looking over her shoulder with his trademark goofy smile plastered on his face. *I miss you, Mom… You were always good to me. Even then, I forgive you for all that you've done.*

As Olivia shuffled to the main pathway, she unsuccessfully searched for the stranger who'd been watching her. Bewildered, she instead reflected on the party her family would throw that evening—the first time the entire Glass clan assembled since Ethan's funeral three months earlier. Olivia and Diane had vacationed in Italy. Theodore and Sarah had reconciled after her one-night stand with his brother, Zachary. After Matthew had returned home from the rehabilitation facility, he and Margaret prepared for their newest child's arrival. Caleb and Jake had become parents to an adopted son in Maine. Zachary had won custody of his daughter, Anastasia, from his ex-girlfriend. Although Ethan had died, Emma promised to visit the Glass family whenever she could.

The promises people made during their initial bereavement period were often forgotten, cast off as nonsensical or whimsically trivial. Would Emma attend Olivia's grand birthday celebration tonight or snap the most brittle limb from the family tree? Time had become so precious to Olivia. Nine months ensured a mother's readiness to give birth to her child. Could nine months also convince a widow to transition beyond her husband's untimely death, assuming she allowed herself to conquer the essential obstacles?

The melancholy matriarch of the Glass family unlocked her phone and smiled at a photo of her and Diane from their recent trip. *What's going on with you lately, sister?* Diane had behaved strangely the last few days, even seemed nervous about their return home. Determining it had something to do with a surprise for the upcoming birthday party, Olivia sank into the backseat of the Uber and sighed heavily. She slipped the phone into the outer pouch of her purse and rummaged through its inside pockets in search of Ben's secret letter. She'd stored it inside her handbag for safekeeping before leaving Rome's Leonardo da Vinci-Fiumicino airport the previous day, at least she'd thought she had. After hurriedly dumping the contents on the leather seat, Olivia whispered in a tremulous voice, "Where could it have gone?"

* * *

Chasing three young girls in a feverish game of hide and seek, Pilar raced through the center hallway, passing Ben's former personal study. Still decorated with an air of old-world allure, historic splendor, and treasured photos—she'd been asked not to touch anything. On the left, a sprawling seating area congregated around a magnificent stone fireplace under twelve-foot cathedral-domed ceilings. On the right stood an inspirational oak desk abutting a set of grand bay windows and boasting an antique Tiffany lamp.

Melanie and Melissa were Matt's two oldest daughters, at five and three respectively, and Anastasia was Zach's five-year-old girl. Melinda, Matt's one-year-old daughter, napped upstairs with her mother and the new baby, Madison, who had arrived only four days ago. Matthew and Margaret insisted on sticking to the fanciful theme of all their children's names beginning with the letter M. Pilar found it both amusing and terribly Waspy, but she dared not express her opinion.

Anastasia ducked under a vintage pewter and smoked glass table in the octagonal entrance hall, motioning to her cousins to follow her into the secret hiding spot. "She won't find us here!" Wild and unruly red curls bounced effortlessly against her shoulders as she crouched low to the ground with a precocious smile.

"You're all too fast for me!" Pilar crooned as she rounded the corner into the foyer, halting to catch her breath near the front door. "I think it's time you had a morning snack, girls. I need a break."

Once Olivia had turned over all her charity obligations to her daughter-in-law and departed for Italy, Margaret knew she needed live-in help. A modern woman with more organizational skills than most, she resisted the solution at first. A stranger in her house, someone else giving orders to her children was frightening and concerning. How could she surrender her control, one of the only ways she felt alive and strong enough to conquer the world? But Margaret acquiesced when she recognized the benefits additional help might bring: a solid night's sleep, uninterrupted quiet time for herself on occasion, and clean sheets she didn't have to strip from the bed and wash every week. After interviewing and hiring a nanny for Madison's arrival, she and Matt also offered the role of temporary housekeeper to Pilar. Using the money her husband had inherited from Ben, Margaret hoped both women could keep the house in order while the Glass family recovered from the previous year's invasive ordeals.

Pilar, who turned twenty-five the previous month, had only worked at the Glass estate since the week before Christmas. She was one of three women the agency sent over, and Margaret advised Pilar they'd chosen her against better judgment. Although the other two candidates offered more experience, Margaret shared concerns that both would tire of all the young children in the house and exit the job too hastily. At least that's what she'd informed Olivia, who stubbornly insisted someone with decades of qualifications was the correct hire, in an attempt to justify the decision.

Melanie and Melissa, radiant glee emanating from their pudgy cheeks and alert eyes, screeched in unison. Anastasia, the more reserved and analytical of the cousins, sluggishly crept across the braided rug and shrugged at Pilar. "If you say so. I was having so much fun."

Pilar affectionately cupped Anastasia's wrist, chuckling at the young girl's response. Anastasia's freckled cream skin contrasted Pilar's mocha-infused tones, a perfect artisanal cappuccino symbiosis of art in the making. Although Margaret had suggested a proper maid's outfit during the interview, Matt interceded and permitted Pilar to wear whatever she felt was most suitable for her role. Having just been released from the rehabilitation center, where he'd kicked a nasty habit of balancing uppers and downers to deal with his anxiety issues over money, Matt desired less formality and more creativity in his surroundings. Pilar's dark, low-rise jeans and long-sleeve Henley fully covered her body, but they flaunted each of her dangerous curves. Sable hair and high cheekbones added a feminine, exotic charm, but Italian ancestry was all she could claim.

"Remember. It's your grandma's big birthday party this evening," Pilar announced, instructing the children to follow her into the kitchen.

Once everyone settled at the nook, Pilar divvied up the juice boxes to all three girls. Anastasia preferred strawberry while Matt's girls requested grape juice. Both kinds were all-natural and contained no extra sugar, per Margaret's endless file of detailed instructions. While the girls devoured three peanut butter crackers and a handful of carrot sticks, Pilar studied a to-do list to confirm her impending chores. The day churned much more quickly than she expected, and with the party that evening, everything had to be in proper order before Olivia Glass returned home.

Pilar wasn't fond of the woman, especially after Olivia scanned her from head to toe in petulant judgment the previous day. When Olivia traced a finger along the fireplace mantle and blew dust into the air, Pilar realized things would change drastically in the Glass home. She'd heard various stories while Olivia was away and researched the family many times before accepting the job. Experiencing Olivia Glass differed from hearing about Olivia Glass through the perception of a stranger or one who claimed to know her well.

"I need to load some towels in the dryer. Please stay in the kitchen until I get back here, okay? You're in charge, Anastasia." Pilar knew Anastasia was the most responsible of the group, even though Melanie was a few months older. When the girls nodded like a trio of wide-eyed porcelain dolls, Pilar descended to the basement to swap the last load of laundry.

As soon as Pilar disappeared, the girls devoured their snacks and deposited their plates on the counter near the sink. They weren't allowed to arrange them in the dishwasher without adult supervision, in fear they'd inadvertently break something while trying to fit each item between the metal prongs. Anastasia hadn't finished all her juice, so she carried it with her as they approached the main hallway. A few drops of red liquid oozed out of the straw and coated the girl's sticky fingers.

As Melanie tut-tutted, her eyes bugged out like a doe caught in headlights. She prevented her younger sister, Melissa, from following Anastasia. "Pilar told us not to leave the kitchen. What are you doing?"

"We can sit on the stairs and wait for her, that's all!" Anastasia pushed through the swinging kitchen door, unable to hold it for her cousins because the juice dripped into her hands. "Yuck!"

"I guess."

All three girls sneaked into the foyer just in time to hear a commotion outside the door. "You check on it," Anastasia directed at her cousin, frowning at her messy hands.

"We're not supposed to talk to strangers," Melanie nervously stuttered, cocking her head aside.

"But maybe it's a new toy for us to play with?" Anastasia suggested as the younger girl, Melissa, strutted to the front door and turned the knob with fearless curiosity.

"No, I don't want to get in trouble," cautioned Melanie, but it was too late.

Straining the limits of his sloppy uniform's brown fabric, a portly visitor dawdled on the porch, breathing heavily and squinting from the sun's direct glare. "Hello, children. Is there an adult home? I have a letter for someone in the Glass family."

Anastasia placed her juice box on the nearby table, unaware it dripped strawberry liquid on the surface. "Pilar is downstairs. She's our maid. I mean our friend. My daddy is working today. Aunt Margaret is upstairs with the baby. Everyone's busy. At least that's what they always tell us."

The deliveryman perused his watch in haste. "I don't have a lot of time. Could you give this to Pilar—*improperly pronouncing it Pilluh*—or another adult in the house? Tell them it's important. There's a name on the envelope. That's who it belongs to, okay?" He eyed the girls quizzically, evaluating whether he should trust them to deliver the parcel. The overworked and underappreciated man had other stops to make and had already gotten a late start to his day. Upon deciding they would follow his instructions, he fiddled with his scanning device and marked the item received.

Melanie rushed to the door and yanked Melissa back. "Yeah, okay. We need to go." After she grabbed the letter from his hand, her eyes zeroed in on the juice box on the table. Melanie shut the front door and yelled to Anastasia in a silly voice, "It's leaking everywhere!"

Anastasia snatched the envelope from her cousin and placed it on the table as a buffer, then put the juice box on top of it. "All better. I hear Pilar coming back. Let's play hide and seek again. Maybe she won't find us this time!"

Melanie and Melissa eyed one another, giggling in innocent delight and speaking their own secret language. Melanie then said, "Hide in the library! She'll never find us."

As all three girls trod up the stairs, the juice box dribbled onto the envelope. Four viscous drops landed directly on the first name of the person to whom the letter was addressed.

Having finished transferring the laundry, Pilar strolled into the foyer. "Was someone at the door? Where are you girls?" She wandered across the hall into the study but couldn't find them. As she approached the vintage table, she heard a distant snicker from the second floor and knew where they had gone. "You're in trouble. If I find you again, you're gonna help me clean for the party tonight."

Pilar raced up the steps to collect the kids, unaware there had been a deliveryman at the house or an envelope idling on the foyer table. An envelope whose recipient was no longer known because the juice had blurred the writing so badly, any name other than Glass was sadly indecipherable.

* * *

Elsewhere, someone startled when a nearby phone vibrated and played a few bars of haunting organ music. A jittery hand placed a steaming cup of coffee on a silver tray, retrieved the device, and scrolled to the next message. Upon learning the package had been delivered, the individual cackled at great length and noted assuredly, "You deserve every bit of my revenge. Only one of us will win this battle, and in the end, you'll beg for mercy. Once a brittle and feeble glass begins to crack, it can never be repaired again."

Chapter 2 – 11:00 AM to 12:00 PM (Olivia)

"Happy Birthday, Olivia," Diane bellowed as her sister joined their cozy table in a delightfully bespoke Italian restaurant on Brandywine's west side. "You left so early this morning I couldn't give you my card." Diane, two years younger than Olivia, grasped the edge of the table to balance her aging frame as she stood and presented a gift to her sibling. Her wobbly, liver-spotted hands dropped the card into Olivia's, then she moaned loudly, "Don't neglect me now, body!" Years of arduous work, a failed marriage, and an unfulfilled desire to have children had imprinted permanent worry lines on every inch of her round face.

"You shouldn't have," replied Olivia, her thin lips curling in amusement on her patrician countenance. After hugging Diane and offloading her coat to the hostess, she selected the hard, straight-backed chair across from her sister. "But I'm glad you did." Olivia ordered two glasses of Prosecco, a dish of garbanzo beans drizzled with olive oil and red chili flakes, and several wedges of Parmigiano-Reggiano cheese.

"It's like we never left Italy." Diane watched as Olivia slit open the red envelope, her sister's favorite color, and bounced on the bench's plush cushioned seat. "Nothing big, just a memento of our trip." Diane had recently trimmed her long braids, abandoning the murky gray-brown colors she usually ignored. Now, she kept her alabaster white and thinning hair in a shorter style, often adorned with clips or barrettes, in an effort to appear a tad younger and more fun, should she ever choose to date again.

La Villetta, the most savory and charming of all the local eateries, reminded the sisters of the cozy *little villas* they'd visited during their trip. A bellissima gem hidden beyond a sizable copse of birch trees, with less than twenty checkered tables snugly pressed against the patterned walls, elegantly curtained windows, and the immensity of everyone's personalities, it echoed the warm and inviting kitchen of an authentic Italian home. The owner, a personal friend of the Glass family, treated them like royalty, remembering everyone's names and special days. Diane admitted she knew that's where Olivia would relish spending time before facing the family and accepting the momentous occasion of her sixty-eighth birthday.

Olivia read the inscription on the card, smiling at the vibrant photo of them taken atop the breathtaking Terrace of Infinity in Villa Cimbrone, Ravello. The most scenic of all the panoramic views, often called the *mountain pearl*, resembled a Garden of Eden on Earth where the pleasures of life existed for only those present in that moment of bliss. She recalled their trip to the famous plateau, the day when Diane had suspiciously escaped for an early return to the Hotel Marmorata.

"Thank you. I will always cherish our time together." Olivia gently brushed her hand over Diane's, pausing while the server dropped off their drinks and an amuse-bouche. She clinked her flute to Diane's and toasted to their most recent experiences. "So… have you heard from him?"

Diane unexpectedly swallowed a large bite, and her cheeks reddened at Olivia's inquiry. Any response, caught in the base of a newly parched and burning throat, stumbled to appear initially. "I… I'm not sure what you're talking about." Diane expanded the menu as a blockade to prevent Olivia's penetrating eyes from singeing her exterior.

"You could recite that menu from memory in both English and Italian. Put it down and answer my question." Olivia pressed a firm hand against its backside until Diane's eyes peered over the top, blinking and darting back and forth to the tablecloth.

Upon returning to the Hotel Marmorata post an afternoon of sightseeing weeks ago, Olivia craved one of their signature luxurious cocktails. As she strolled through the lobby, Diane's voice carried across the damp and perfumed air. Olivia hid behind a tall and leafy lemon tree, eavesdropping on her sister's conversation with a distinguished gentleman. Diane appeared to be laughing, almost flirting with the man seated next to her. Olivia had never seen her sibling smile so wide, her eyes glimmering from the candlelight lining the bar's smooth veneer surface. Though Olivia had arrived too late to understand his intentions, she watched Diane accept a napkin from him and discreetly stuff it in her pocket. That evening before they went to sleep, Olivia rifled through her sister's coat and learned the man's name and phone number. Diane later invented several errands and unplanned side trips during their last three weeks in Italy, and Olivia was certain they were excuses to meet with the dark and mysterious charmer named Nate.

"I'd rather not. Isn't today about you? It's your birthday, after all." Diane released the menu onto the table and scooped a wedge of pungent parmesan between her salivating lips.

"Nate, I presume? Have you two continued exploring the realm of transatlantic possibilities since we've returned home?" Olivia's smug expression looked more natural than coaxed, though it often appeared to be intentionally doled out in the most opportune of times.

Diane was eagerly awaiting her final divorce papers. After thirty years of marriage, she'd informed her husband, a life-long car mechanic and recent owner of a profitless service station, that she no longer wanted to be married to an insolent aggressor. Though George had never physically abused her, his verbal lashings and passive-aggressive tendencies finally forced her to present the man with his walking papers. For some reason, George had held up the final decree and Diane avoided discussing the topic. Olivia never learned why but had ceased pressuring Diane in the preceding weeks, hoping her naïve sibling would volunteer the information once she was ready.

"How do you know about him?" Diane tensed against the back of the bench, equally shocked and worried over the direction of the conversation. "Nate and I are… were… friends, that's all."

Olivia sipped more Prosecco before insisting Diane tell her the truth. Given Olivia's overpowering personality and George's demonstrative ways, Diane had consistently relinquished her own identity throughout most of her life. Olivia firmly believed that marriages were complicated, and husbands fell into two buckets. Some men, like George, were the wrong choice. They forced their wives to wait on them hand and foot. Dinner promptly at six every night. A house must be sterile and clean each week. Lovemaking once per month and only if George initiated it. No children because they only sullied people's lives. In unions on par with George and Diane's, the wife's blessings manifested only when the husband died. Diane had never been a lucky woman, not once in her life, and she'd graciously accepted such an unforgiving lot. Until Ben's death, when something changed in her, and she began to prioritize her own needs first. Diane had finally decided to sell the house she and George lived in, then use the profits to buy something new without him. In the meantime, she'd kicked him out while the divorce was in process.

Other men, like Benjamin William Glass, were the right choice but made dreadful decisions. Olivia had loved Ben since the moment they met at the opera, yet it took months to forgive him for switching babies in the hospital. Ultimately, despite all the lies, Ben had given her a gift—the temporary reward of twenty-three years with Ethan. Nothing would ever erase their time together. Ben's mistake had led to Olivia living the blessed life of a mother to a fifth son, one that lasted many decades. Until Ben's death, when the lives of the entire Glass family shattered, and all Olivia could do was watch it disintegrate piece by piece, nicking her limb by limb.

Once the waitress captured their orders and sauntered away, Olivia pressed further. "You deserve happiness. Why hasn't George agreed to the divorce? Can I do anything to help?"

Diane begged to change the conversation's topic. "Another day, we can discuss it. We only just returned home, and I'd rather enjoy my afternoon. Nate was a wonderful man, but he was just a passing fancy. Please leave it at that for now." She gulped a generous portion of Prosecco and tore a slice of bread from the basket. Drenching it in olive oil, salt, and balsamic vinegar was her only prolonged defense to limit the discussion.

Olivia reluctantly nodded. She recognized her sister's growing distress, including Diane's inability to divulge the source of the anxiety or pain consuming her thoughts. Olivia would permit the conversation to pass, focusing instead on her birthday, and resume it the following morning. Ben's death had taught her never to ignore an issue with someone you loved. Delaying the confrontation, altering routes to elicit the truth, or applying pressure through other means was necessary to resolve the situation. Another twenty-four hours would cause little harm. Timing was everything, and Olivia *would* obtain the answers she sought.

"How do you expect this evening's festivities to go?" Olivia checked her watch to confirm the time. Less than six hours before all her sons would be home again for a celebratory dinner and drinks.

"Matt and Margaret seemed exhausted last night. I can hardly believe they wanted to throw this party for you." Diane unlocked her phone and clicked on the photo app, sharing the newest picture of baby Madison, who'd arrived a few days earlier than expected.

Diane and Olivia had timed their trip to return home before Olivia's newest grandchildren would be born. When Margaret went into unexpected labor, Olivia couldn't secure an earlier flight. They instead flew home and met Madison when she was three days old. Teddy's wife, Sarah, was also due this week, adding another new baby to the family. Olivia had sensed something was wrong with her eldest son, yet none of her other boys expressed any concerns about him.

"I tried to reason with Margaret. She assured me the nanny would look after Madison, and Pilar agreed to help with the kids and plan the party." Olivia and Margaret had grown closer after Olivia confronted her daughter-in-law about all the unnecessary burdens she'd previously placed on her husband. In the past, Matt had climbed mountains to keep up with his wife's spending on their home renovations and children's daycare and future education. When Matt turned to pills as his relief and developed a nasty addiction, Olivia stepped in to redirect the trajectory of a death sentence bound to happen.

"Margaret is calmer than last fall. Remember her nutty panic? I think being away from you might've relaxed her," Diane teased. She'd always been the warm, generous aunt to the five Glass boys, in opposition to their frosty, more indifferent mother, Olivia.

"You're hilarious. We worked out our differences. Margaret and I no longer quarrel over the insignificant things." Olivia wanted to believe she'd convinced her daughter-in-law how to properly care for a husband like Matt, but she was hardly home long enough to verify her advice had done its job effectively.

"Have you heard anything from Sarah? She must be due any day now," asked Diane.

Olivia gently shook her head. "Sarah's confined to bed rest with no visitors. Theodore told Margaret weeks ago that the doctors were worried about Sarah's health." Olivia hadn't heard much from her son. Every time she'd checked in from Italy, he declared all was fine and that he had no news to report. Knowing Sarah was in her early forties, the pregnancy was ripe with risk. Olivia was also grateful the baby turned out to be Theodore's and not Zachary's. What a foolish plan Sarah had concocted to circumvent Theodore's low sperm count. In the end, Theodore had impregnated his wife, and Sarah's sexual encounter with his brother had evaporated before anyone else became privy to the news.

For a fleeting moment, Olivia worried that her son had regressed to his former self. For most of his life, Teddy had absorbed the incessant pressure to follow in Ben's footsteps and run the family law firm once his father retired. After Ben died, Teddy finally spoke out, sharing his secret desire to become a painter. The Glass family sold their majority interest in the law firm to the remaining partners and accepted the unknown future placed before them. Teddy's facial tics and nervous twitches had disappeared, but his lack of communication during Olivia's lengthy trip to Italy stirred old concerns.

"We can ask Teddy tonight. I'm sure Sarah won't make it, but Teddy will put in an appearance for his mother's birthday." Diane rested her fork and knife on the plate, then thanked the busboy when he cleared the appetizers from the table. "Caleb is driving down today, right?"

"Yes. He and Jake and the baby should arrive shortly. I'm so proud of the man he's become." Olivia reflected on the progress between them since learning the previous fall he was gay, married to a man, and adopting a child. He'd moved to Maine a decade earlier, avoiding his family except for major holidays and important family events. Even then, he'd conveniently forgotten to tell them about his husband, Jake. Ben's funeral had brought them together, lifting the veil of darkness over his seclusion.

"Of all the boys, you and Caleb patched your relationship most successfully." Diane reminded her sister of the weekly calls Caleb and his mother shared while Olivia was in Italy. Between video chats to track the baby's growth and the home renovation to build a nursery, Olivia had savored being side by side with them at every step.

"Caleb is the happiest these days, true. His life is complete, content, where he's always wanted to be." Olivia was thrilled and comforted when all the secrets were brought to light. In all her relationships with her sons, a nasty truth festered under the surface, threatening to destroy any minuscule connection. One by one, as her visits with each son occurred, she'd rebuilt the bond and guided them in the proper direction. Now she needed to figure out what remained in her own future.

"Zach's close to achieving his goals too. Anastasia is a smart little girl, and she loves her new school. Your rebellious son has turned his life around." Diane had a soft spot for Zach, the renegade of the family. While his parents had given up on him, Diane never strayed too far. She babysat his daughter when he had to work and offered advice to help him realize his lifestyle endangered his future.

"I'm shocked at how much he's forgiven me. Of all the boys, Zach never seemed to need his mother." Olivia hadn't seen him on her return the prior day as he'd remained in New York City to promote an upcoming concert. He had moved into the family house the previous fall, agreeing to let Anastasia attend the same schools as her cousins. He spent a few days each week in New York and the rest of his time in Connecticut raising his daughter as a single father. Zach's ex-girlfriend, Katerina, had finally lost custody and backed off from interfering in her daughter's life.

"Has Emma been in touch since we returned?" Diane inquired, absentmindedly nibbling on her third slice of bread.

"I don't think she's planning to attend tonight. Margaret never heard from her, and Emma has been difficult to catch with the time difference." Olivia thought Emma would have been ecstatic to return to the Glass house this weekend, a retreat to be closer to her husband who died weeks after they exchanged vows. "I suppose being around us might still be too much for her to handle. I wonder if she'll remarry in the distant future."

Diane coughed loudly for an extended length of time, then sipped from her water glass before focusing on the waitress as she delivered their entrees. "Let's eat. We'll deal with whatever the evening brings us later. You deserve a memorable night, sister. For now, it's time to enjoy our meal."

A half-hour later, after skipping dessert—assuming there would be a delectable birthday cake at the party that night—Diane and Olivia departed the Italian restaurant. Diane had driven them in her car, so she brought Olivia back to the Glass family home. They both planned to stay in guest rooms for a few weeks until agreeing on what to do next with their lives.

While pulling into the driveway, Diane's phone vibrated in the top of her handbag. Olivia glanced at it, noticing a new message from an unknown number. "Someone's asking if you mailed or received something? It's cut off, I can't read the rest."

Diane stepped heavily on the brakes, jerking the car to a stop. "I love you, Liv, but we are two different people. Must you nose into every part of my life?" After putting the car in park and turning off the ignition, she grabbed the phone and her purse and bolted out the door.

Olivia smirked and followed her. "You're very touchy today, Diane. That message wouldn't happen to be related to another birthday present for me, would it?"

Diane quickly turned before entering the house and sneered at her sister. "I suppose you'll find out soon, won't you?" She promptly volunteered to check with Pilar on the evening's plans and made a right from the mudroom into the kitchen. "I'll see you a bit later. I have some things to take care of for tonight. Off you go!"

Waltzing through the central hallway, Olivia acknowledged Margaret and Matthew's lack of any substantive changes to the family home. Given the move, a new baby, Matthew's recovery, and the unknown circumstances of where Olivia planned to live, it made sense. Why rock the boat until you had to? Olivia still owned the house but had surrendered responsibility to them during her absence.

The original plan was to buy something smaller with the money Ben had left her, sharing a lovely home with her sister on the other side of Brandywine, where life would be quieter and less stressful. Olivia wasn't prepared to move into a retirement complex, no matter how elegant the options. The thought of dating again had also never crossed her mind. At sixty-eight, she'd experienced a lifetime of love, and the rest of her days would be focused on bonding with her children and sister. Being a grandmother was the most important task in front of her. She'd begun dreaming about their poolside cannonballs, braiding each girl's hair, and reading stories before naptime. All the priceless moments she'd neglected with her own boys but promised to concentrate on now that she was free from commitments. Imagining their innocent smiles and boisterous laughter as they matured into beautiful young ladies would make up for the anguish Olivia still carried over Ethan's death.

When Olivia entered the octagonal foyer, she searched for the girls but found no one else present. Margaret was likely romping upstairs with the baby and children. It was too early for the rest of her sons to arrive for the big event.

Olivia leaned against the only wall with no paintings or art, her back arched and hands wrapped around herself in a moment of nostalgia. All the memories of kissing Ben goodbye each morning before he took off for work… all the moments when the kids returned home from school and raced up the stairs toward their bedrooms… all the times she let life pass her by without stepping in to show everyone how much she loved them. It was essential to make amends for the past, and if there were anything she had an excess of these days, it was time.

Before Olivia ascended the grand staircase, Anastasia's juice box on the antique table caught her attention. Olivia scrambled toward it, her instincts comprising an amalgam of frustration and acceptance over the new order of things, and attempted to remedy the situation. When she found the blurry envelope under the juice box, she wrinkled her brow and wondered to whom it belonged. A birthday card for her? Should she wait to open it until later in the day? Slightly annoyed about the abandoned juice box, yet eager to smile over the contents of the birthday card, she traced her finger across the unreadable name. "Must be for me."

Olivia carefully sliced open the envelope, excited to learn who'd left her a surprise. She unfolded the parchment, curious why it wasn't an actual birthday card but a handwritten note. As she read its contents, her body stiffened. Blood rose up to her face, then drained away. Heartbeats accelerated. Sweat puddled on her brow. The letter, inches away from her dumbfounded face, called to her in a way she hadn't felt for months. A woodsy scent emanated off the parchment and lingered between Olivia's nose and hands, haunting her like a ghost from the past. The smell was one of her favorite colognes. Full of aromatic citrus head notes, a dash of sandalwood and pine. Ben's scent. The one he wore every day for the last decade of his life before the car accident had ripped him away from Olivia.

It couldn't be. Who had written this letter to her? Ben was gone. What did this person want? Trapped in a trance as she reread the letter's contents, Olivia failed to hear Pilar enter the foyer.

"Oh, ma'am, I didn't realize you were in here." Pilar cringed at the juice box in Olivia's hands. "One of the girls must have left that behind. I'll take it." Olivia proffered her shaky wrist to Pilar and released the juice box too soon. It landed on the tiled floor, its contents pooling in a Rorschach shape. Pilar immediately dropped to her knees and yanked the rug away from the spillage. "Don't move. I'll get a wet cloth."

As Pilar rushed to the kitchen, Olivia partially stuffed the letter into the envelope and scaled the staircase in a daze. With the correspondence held loosely in her hand, she misjudged the location of the thirteenth step and tripped forward onto her stomach. Olivia used her hand to break the fall, dropping the envelope invariably, and moaned at her clumsiness and near slip down the entire staircase. Noticing a few drops of blood beading on her forehead, she gasped, grabbed the envelope, and shoved it into her purse. After clomping up the last few steps and reaching the second-floor landing, she turned to the left hallway, where the master bedroom resided, then realized it no longer belonged to her. Matthew and Margaret had taken over that room. She turned to the right hallway, where she'd slept the night before in one of the guest rooms, and trudged slowly through it in a nearly catatonic state.

Before Olivia reached her room, the last door in the furthest corner, a loud noise from the opposite end of the hallway startled her. Matt exited one of the other rooms and enthusiastically waved. "Where did you disappear this morning, Mom?" He briskly walked toward her, bending in for a hug, but she unexpectedly stopped him.

Olivia shook her head, unable to find the words to respond, then shielded her lips to ensure nothing could tumble out. She needed time to think, to process what just happened. In the awkward near embrace, both were unaware of the mysterious handwritten threat plunging from Olivia's purse and gently wafting through the air. It landed on the polished wooden floor, face down, waiting for someone to discover it. "I… your father is… not—"

Matt leaned in to steady his mother, but she jerked further away. "What's wrong? Did you hurt yourself?" He wobbled his head at the blood and waited for her reply, oblivious to the letter lurking just inches from his feet. When Margaret called his name from behind, Matt paused and rotated his frame to address his wife.

During the tense moment, Olivia escaped and shuffled into the bedroom, where she closed the door and hid from yet another unwanted secret. No one could hear her speak her next words as they were muffled among her pain, memories, and fears. "Someone else discovered the truth, Ben. And they plan to hurt me with it tonight."

Chapter 3 – 12:00 to 1:00 PM (Caleb)

Caleb and Jake crossed the border from Massachusetts into Connecticut on I-84, making excellent time since their departure from northern Maine five hours earlier. They only stopped once to feed Ethan, who'd been named for his late uncle, Caleb's brother.

"Ready to pull over? Let's get some lunch at this rest area," Jake suggested while twisting around to the back seat to check on their son. "The little guy's uber restless. I think he needs a new diaper." Having recently swapped his trademark blond hair to experience the dangerous side of a seductive ginger, Jake lowered his Clark Kent glasses and pointedly stared at Caleb.

"Totally your turn. I changed him earlier. I warned you not to give him smashed peas this morning." Caleb flashed a wicked grin at his husband, then winked dramatically to hit home his point. They usually alternated parental duties, but Jake had volunteered to play the lead during their extended car trip that day, assuming Caleb drove the eight hours to their destination. A few strands of wavy inky hair fell against his olive skin, prompting Jake to reach forward and lovingly brush them back in place.

"Ah, my little mess… just wait until we get to your mother's place. With your family around, we won't have to change a diaper for days." Baby Ethan would turn six months old in the coming weeks. Though biologically he shared DNA with neither Jake nor Caleb, he looked like both of his fathers. From Caleb, he'd inherited a mischievous smile, and Jake's brooding emerald eyes were a standout trait.

When they pulled into the parking lot, Jake opened the car door and inhaled a gulp of biting winter air. " '*Once in his life, every man is entitled to fall madly in love with a gorgeous redhead.*' Guess who said that famous quote. It's your first test for today."

Caleb closed his eyes and thumped the steering wheel repeatedly. "Ah, now I understand why you dyed your hair this particular shade. It's got to be Jessica Rabbit or Ariel from *The Little Mermaid*. You do love your cartoon vamps."

"Apparently I'm still not done educating you on *The Greats*. Lucille Ball, darling, one of our original queens. Must I explain everything all the time?" Throughout the years, Jake had been compensating for Caleb's lack of any knowledge about all the icons who either paved the way for or celebrated gay culture. "Let's go inside. You're buying lunch since you failed the easiest of quizzes. Every time you share one of those inexcusable guesses about our famous divas, it stinks to high heaven. Unless that odor is coming from Ethan!?"

"We share all our expenses. What difference is it if you pay?" Caleb shrugged melodramatically before exiting the car, careful to avoid the muddy puddles from the previous night's rain. "And that smell is most assuredly from your son. I already told you not to give him smashed peas!"

"You have no imagination anymore, chickadee. It's like I'm dealing with a lump of clay sometimes. And not the sexy kind from *Ghost*. Mmmm… Patrick Swayze was a snack in his day."

After devouring lunch, Caleb tossed away their leftover detritus and flung the keys at Jake. "You guys head back to the car. I'm gonna use the bathroom before we leave."

Jake bundled the baby into his warm coat and furry fox hat, a Christmas gift Olivia sent them from Italy, and packed up the carry-on bag. "Do you want your phone, babe?"

Caleb told Jake to carry it to the car, then strolled through the rest area and listened to the myriad of strange voices and dialects. After living in rural and isolated Maine for a decade, he'd forgotten how multi-cultural other parts of the nation had become. Although his career as an architect had taken him all over the country, he rarely spent more time than necessary in those places, mostly because his priority dictated being home with his son as much as possible. After washing up in the restroom, he swung by the doughnut shop to buy two of Jake's favorite kind. The lunch crowds had emptied out of the building, leaving him the only customer in the line.

A twenty-something guy with slicked-back platinum-blond hair and closely shaved sides that had been dyed lime-green called him to the counter. "What can I get for you? With a body like yours, I wouldn't have guessed you'd eat anything we sell." He paused to observe Caleb's interpretation of his salacious greeting, then continued. "I'm not used to seeing scrumptious eye candy this early in the day."

Caleb smiled awkwardly, blushing from the shop worker's forward nature. Was he flirting or being super chatty and friendly? Though he was a nearly decade older than the kid whose name tag read Austin, Caleb hadn't yet lost his baby face and often passed for someone much younger. "Good metabolism. Occasional sweet tooth. Couldn't resist coming by."

"To tease me or buy a doughnut?" Austin smirked, licked his plump and crimson lips, and leaned forward so he hovered only a few inches from Caleb's face. "You look like a model. I'm picturing you on an underwear billboard in Times Square, right? Tell me the truth, are the packages always as big as they appear?" He stared directly into Caleb's sea-blue eyes, then down to his crotch, and sighed exaggeratedly. "My luck's never been this good. So, what brings you to Connecticut today?"

Okay, he *was* flirting. Harmless. Caleb had done nothing but hibernate and be a new daddy for months. Every shirt had vomit, purees of nasty baby food, or worse types of unmentionable stains. His eyes were often red-rimmed and swollen from lack of sleep. His energy levels dipped lower than the San Andreas fault lines. Then again, everyone deserved a little pick-me-up, regardless of how worn out they appeared. Maybe this moment served as a reminder that Caleb was an attractive dilf who still had a playable game.

"Aren't you direct? While you'd certainly be a delicious treat, I think today I'd prefer the one that'll cost me a few extra calories. Two glazed jellies, please." Caleb sucked his bottom lip into his mouth and gnawed on it. "But thank you for making my day, Austin."

Caleb always hated having unreliable gaydar, as in Halley's-Comet-once-every-seventy-five-years gaydar. It'd been a curse since he was a teenager and stuck in the closet with six different kinds of professional-grade locks. Mostly, he had wannabe gaydar, the kind where he wished every hot guy he saw was interested in jumping his bones. It rarely worked out. What happened in the movies and on television never occurred in reality. Well, almost never.

His initial encounter with Jake six years ago had been a steamy assignation that left him weak in the knees and a believer in love at first sight. Now, after months with a new baby who viewed sleeping as optional, his mind had systematically blocked those memories. If he and Jake didn't reignite their passion soon, he'd succumb to something regrettable. For some inexplicable reason, today, his gaydar was in full swing. There was no way he'd misinterpreted Austin's come-ons. A mini magnifying glass would've found them buried behind every single one of Saturn's moons.

"I'm sure we could invent a way to work off those calories," Austin teased while dropping the doughnuts in a bag and scurrying around the counter. He scribbled something on a piece of receipt paper and approached his weakening customer, a confident hand brushing against Caleb's thigh. "I'm due for a break if you'd like to… you know…."

Please say "Grab a cup of coffee" and not "Follow me into the storage closet."

When Caleb reached for the bag, their sweaty hands briefly touched. A wave of heat cascaded up Caleb's arm as dangerous thoughts set up shop inside his cluttered and reckless mind. "Flattered, but I've got someone waiting outside. How much do I owe you?"

"Management permits me to dole out a few freebies at my discretion. Consider yourself in my top three this month." Austin retracted his hand and rubbed the back of his head seductively, his bicep flexing as he sashayed behind the counter. "Such a shame. Hope the little devil knows how lucky he is."

Caleb stepped closer to the counter, then leaned in to whisper, "How did you know we're on the same team? What if I were some homophobe who created a scene?"

Austin giggled in an immature but alluring way. "For one, you're too sizzling to be straight. For another, you looked hungry and wanton when you sidled up to the register. I saw the once-over you gave me. Kinda like you needed a tantalizing… X-rated adventure? Plus, I'm pretty much never wrong."

Caleb thanked Austin for the sassy attitude, bevy of compliments, and bag of doughnuts before exiting the store. When he glanced at the receipt, curious why he even had one if he hadn't paid for the treats, he chuckled. Austin had written down his phone number along with a list of things he wanted to do to Caleb when they met up. Caleb hadn't even heard of the last item on the list! Was he that ancient?

Get ahold of yourself, fool. You're just horny, and this is ridiculously uncool.

As Caleb traipsed back to the car, he convinced himself the conversation was merely a reminder that he and Jake needed to spend quality time together, pronto. Months had passed since they'd found the opportunity to be more intimate than sharing a prolonged kiss or halfhearted attempt at a back rub. Perhaps they'd carve out a few hours alone in Brandywine while one of his brothers, sisters-in-law, or aunt could watch the baby.

Caleb adjusted his jeans to hide the obvious tent he began to pitch, opened the car door, and slid into the driver's seat. He tossed the bag on Jake's lap and swung his head around to confirm the baby had fallen asleep. "A gift from someone who loves you."

"Thanks. So… who's the mystery guy?" asked Jake, cocking his head and persistently studying his husband as a detective would his suspect.

Caleb flinched. Had the receipt with Austin's number fallen out of his pocket? No, it couldn't have. What was Jake babbling about? He looked up to find Jake staring at his phone. "Is that mine?"

"Yep. You got a text message from someone named Airport Guy. It says, *'Great chat. I look forward to meeting again very soon.'* I only read it because I thought it was my phone, then realized it was yours. Got mixed up when I put the baby in his car seat." Jake handed the device to Caleb and fiddled with a dashboard button to raise the heat. "Hurry up, it's as frigid outside as Leona Helmsley before she got herself incarcerated and consented to turn slightly nicer than a pit of vipers."

Jake wasn't the type of guy to snoop. Neither one of them had given the other a reason to suspect anything in the past. Even now, Jake's tone was more curious and less concerned. After almost six years together, they'd been committed, monogamous, and honest with one another. Everyone flirted with a cute stranger occasionally, kept a secret from their lover or partner. It didn't automatically imply you'd crossed a line or tainted your relationship. Then again, Caleb had never intended to indulge in something that would hurt his husband. It just happened one day—a chance encounter, kind of similar to what happened with Austin, only it failed to end after a single, quick interaction.

"A recent client," Caleb lied as he shifted the car into drive and joined highway traffic. "Someone referred to me by another firm. We're supposed to get together to review his design ideas before I draft initial plans for a new house."

"Oh, I thought you kept your work and personal phones separate. Did you finally decide to embrace the dark side and commingle your two clandestine lives?" Jake smiled as he pressed a button on the GPS to continue navigating, then popped a donut in his mouth.

Caleb choked, blanching at his husband's inquiry. Did Jake know what he'd done? "Huh? What? No… he was recommended by a colleague, and I unintentionally saved his info on my personal phone."

Jake rested a hand on Caleb's jittery quad, squeezing it twice. "Relax. You look like you've been caught stealing from the cookie jar. I'm just making conversation. Yeesh! *'I suppose when they reach a certain age some men are afraid to grow up.'* That quote is your second test for today."

Caleb barely hesitated before spitting out a response "Mrs. Cookie Monster? Was she a gay icon? I'd be shocked if she—"

"That was really lame. I don't think I can speak with you again until we get to your mother's." Jake withdrew his hand and slapped his forehead. "Elizabeth Taylor. Oh, the horror of it all. I wonder if I married the wrong kind of homosexual. Whatever is a boy to do when he's been handcuffed to a lovable newbie who confuses cookies and divas?"

Caleb encouraged himself to calm down as he resumed his course to Brandywine. Jake had bought his excuse about the text message and abandoned the conversation. How much longer could he keep up the charade? This was the second time Jake had almost caught him in a lie, and if his husband applied enough intelligence, he could easily discover the truth.

Shortly after he'd returned home from Ethan's funeral last fall, Caleb drifted into a somber place. Not only had he lost his father and become a father within a few months' time, but his brother had tragically died at an early age. Caleb and Ethan had been close when they were younger, but once Caleb ran away to Maine, they lost touch. When their mother had broken down at Ben's seventieth birthday party, a posthumous celebration for the husband and father who died, to tell everyone about Ethan's disease, Caleb's unstoppable descent into anger, frustration, and fear blossomed like wildfire.

For too long in his youth, he'd hidden from the people who meant the most to him. Although he and Jake had found one another, gotten married, and adopted a son, it was as if he lived two distinctly separate lives. Avoiding his family was the only way he knew how to live, and when his world combusted upon Olivia's surprise visit, where she discovered Caleb's secret husband, he had no choice but to merge his competing identities.

After a few weeks of opening up to his family, he even hosted Thanksgiving following his brother's death. Once Olivia left for Italy, things changed drastically. While Caleb was alone with Jake and their new baby, he realized how much was missing from their lives. Ten years had passed since he lived at home… ten years wasted without building more solid relationships with his family. Caleb worried whether he could truly be a model father to his son.

At that most inopportune moment of his life, Caleb received an urgent request from a client in the Midwest to resolve a catastrophe with a building renovation. After three days away from

Jake and their son, also three days of arguing with various people about the viability of the architectural plans, Caleb drove to the airport to fly home to Maine. Due to a snowstorm, air traffic control delayed his flight for six hours. He was stuck at the terminal. He called Jake to convey the news, then ordered a drink at the bar. His desperation and angst led to another drink, and by the third, he met another traveler who'd also been trapped by the weather.

Whether it was all the drinks he consumed or the distress settling inside his weary body, Caleb bonded with the stranger. He divulged his entire life story, including his current despair and worry over the future. The stranger who introduced himself as Warren shared his own life story. It was a tale of worse heartbreak. Warren had grown up in a hostile family who viewed one another as mere punching bags and obstacles to individual success. When something bad happened in school or at work, you took it out on your family, whether it be your parents, children, brothers, or sisters. Warren was the middle child, sandwiched between four older and four younger siblings. At thirty-four, he was a handful of years older than Caleb but like Caleb, had a good complexion, exercised, and ate well; he could also easily pass for someone in his twenties. When Warren had revealed to his parents that he was gay, everyone exploded in a blind fury. His religious and homophobic family had no tolerance for such deviance—Warren's curt summary of their tirade—and immediately renounced him.

Warren and Caleb forged a friendship during that venting session at the airport bar. By the time the weather turned favorable, they agreed to stay in touch. They only shared first names and phone numbers, nothing more. Caleb added Warren as *Airport Guy* to his phone, a running joke between them. To Caleb, it was the first legitimate gay friend he'd made in years. It hadn't even crossed his mind to think about the impact on Jake or whether others would assume the random encounter odd. It wasn't about attraction. It was about recognizing things could've been a lot worse for Caleb, had his family reacted in the same manner as Warren's.

A week went by with no further conversation. Caleb decided it wasn't worth mentioning to Jake. Had Warren wanted to become better pals, Caleb would have informed Jake, so they could both be friends with the itinerant computer programmer who needed someone to lean on. A week before Christmas, Warren had unexpectedly called him. He would be traveling to Boston in a few days for a training seminar. Was it close to Caleb's place? In an odd coincidence, Caleb needed to visit Boston that week for a client meeting.

Both agreed to share a meal the first night of the training seminar. Caleb called home to tell Jake about the guy as he preferred not to hide things from his husband. It was strictly a platonic friendship; there was no reason to worry. Jake never answered the phone. Caleb later learned that the baby had been fussy and Jake opted for a nap. Caleb went to dinner with Warren, and during the course of the night, things radically changed between them. When Caleb returned to his hotel room after barely nibbling any food, imbibing several more drinks at the bar, and taking an unplanned trip to Warren's room, his head had been bombarded with so many new and complicated emotions, he could barely focus.

Unsure what to tell Jake, he texted his husband that he loved him and would call the following day. Caleb still needed to process what had transpired in Boston. Destiny must have arranged Warren and Caleb's original meeting at the airport as no other explanation presented itself for why they'd also been brought together again several weeks later. Caleb had a decision to make, and he knew it wasn't one he could easily render.

While en route to Olivia's birthday party in Connecticut, Caleb studied his sleeping husband. Jake looked peaceful, at ease with his identity. Jake was happy with their cozy little family, and he claimed that was all he ever needed or wanted in life. Caleb's treasured spouse was genuine and caring. His words, though direct, were thoughtful, showing his sensitive side. Jake never concealed anything. He loved his life and drew a line in the sand once he and Caleb met. Jake had always bragged, "The day I met you was the day my life began."

Caleb gently rested a hand on his husband's knee and whispered, "I hope you'll forgive me for what I've done. I don't know how I let things get so out of control, my sweet, sweet Jake."

Chapter 4 – 1:00 to 2:00 PM (Matt)

"I'll never get back to a size four!" Margaret dangled two dresses in front of the mirror, debating which was the more appropriate one for her mother-in-law's birthday party. "Any preference? I can't believe I still don't fit in my pre-baby clothes."

Matt stopped mid-crunch and cranked his head one-hundred-and-eighty degrees, observing Margaret half in frustration, hiding the amusement half to avoid further angst. "Ah, my beautiful wife. You gave birth less than a week ago. You've spit out four children in five years. No one expects you to achieve your fighting weight anytime soon." When Margaret scowled as though he called her a heifer in a muumuu, Matt retreated both in action and words. "But you'll always win the Miss America pageant for me no matter what you wear."

"Nice save, player. Maybe I won't keep you on the sidelines for a full month while I heal." She tossed a red wrap dress on their king-size bed and selected the black ruched elbow-sleeve one for the party. "It's more slimming. I suppose it'll do. Your mother just had to tell me how simple it was for her to shed the baby weight right away. Ugh!" Margaret's button nose wrinkled with obvious dismay and disillusion.

"She never meant to worry or insult you. Please don't stress me out today of all days, hon." Matt checked his phone for the third time in the last ten minutes. He was waiting for a call about his impending return to the law firm. Although the Glass brothers had sold Ben's majority interest in the practice to the two outstanding partners, they agreed to let Matt remain onboard after his initial recovery period.

"One day at a time. Remember your new mantra, Matt. Wittleton and Davis promised to call today with a proposal." Margaret opened the jewelry box on her dresser and hunted for her diamond teardrop earrings. "Why do you think your mother scuttled into her bedroom like that an hour ago?"

Matt shook his head, uncertain himself. Although the lighting in the hallway was dim and the giant oak trees had cast a shadow through the window, he was certain his mother had been crying when she'd avoided him. "It's after one o'clock. Davis told me they'd decide before lunch. As for my mother, who knows. This is the first weekend she's been home since the trip. Maybe the memories of my father overwhelmed her." As soon as Olivia had shut the door earlier, Matt retraced his steps back down the hallway to find out what Margaret had wanted. He'd also waved at Diane, his aunt, when she passed by too.

"True. I can't imagine what she's going through these days. For how long do you think she'll move back in? Your aunt told me earlier they planned to meet with a real estate agent on Monday to search for a new place," said Margaret. Although Margaret had brokered a truce with her mother-in-law before Olivia departed for Italy, they'd only spent a few days together, primarily discussing responsibilities for the charity organizations Olivia had once led and turned over to Margaret. As a supportive wife, she wanted to build a healthier relationship with Olivia, yet as the new female head of the household, she was reluctant to accept that her mother-in-law would truly relinquish control.

"Not sure. I gotta get some fresh air. Be back in an hour. Just gonna walk around the estate, wander over to the garage and tinker with one of my woodworking projects." Matt kissed his wife's dimpled and rouged cheek, then hurried down the front staircase. Although the temperature hovered marginally above freezing, the nip in the air might do the trick to jolt him from the haze.

As he passed Pilar, she smiled and told him the girls were with the nanny taking baths. "Everything's ready for tonight. The caterer arrived a few minutes ago and is in the kitchen preparing several tapas. Light dishes, Tuscan. Nothing too heavy, per your mother's request."

"She's trying to keep Italy alive and kicking. Ah, maybe I need a real vacation too." Matt snatched his heavy winter coat from the hallway closet, detaining Pilar before she returned to the kitchen. "Have there been any calls for me today? You've listened for the phone, right? There's a really important one I should've gotten."

Pilar squinted and lowered her gaze toward the floor. "None since you asked an hour ago, sir."

Matt sighed expressively, repeatedly blinking his chocolate-brown eyes. "Call me Matt. Please, for the sake of my sanity, don't call me sir. I'm barely five years older than you." Once Pilar nodded cautiously, Matt grunted and stomped out the front door.

After three months of in-patient and out-patient therapy focused on relieving his anxiety, depression, and addiction to pills, Matt had received approval to return to work at the end of the month. While he understood that his condition had no official cure, he refused to accept he had a disease. Psychiatrists and psychologists threw words and expressions around like candy to kids on Halloween. Idioms like ruthless invasive diseases, cognitive regression, intentional denial, and defense mechanisms. Whatever happened to the plain and simple rationale, "I want something more than I should have it, so I guess I have to stop before I die." Matt recognized the extent of his unhealthy actions, specifically ignoring his daughter's injury while he got high in the bathroom as well as stealing tens of thousands of dollars from the family law firm. He deemed them mistakes brought about by stress, promising to seek treatment for his *minor ailment.*

The counselor had suggested Matt would struggle with urges for the rest of his life, but Matt insisted the problem was a dilemma of the past and not a disease to monitor every day. Margaret convinced him to secure a sponsor, participate fully in the program, and search for friends who would understand what Matt had gone through and who could be available to stop it from happening again. She told Matt that their future was too important to let a solvable situation derail their joy and success. Given nothing was more important than his family, whom he adored more than anyone ever could, Matt consented. He selected a well-established survivor named Maude who reminded him of his mother, even joked with his counselor that his Oedipus complex was burgeoning to explode. Maude, nothing at all like his mother, had been off pills and alcohol for twenty years and went back to a high-powered job as the Chief Financial Officer of an expensive New York City retail chain.

After pumping out a dozen push-ups and jogging in place for a minute, Matt dialed Maude's number and waited for her to pick up, eager to ask her an important question. One that had been on his mind for weeks but never seemed appropriate until now. She answered just as he smirked at the reflection of his bulging arm muscles in the window.

"Hey, Matt. I'm heading to lunch with a friend. What can I do for you?" Maude's cheery voice sprinkled through the phone like fairy dust meant to soothe a worried soul.

Brushing tense fingers through his thick chestnut hair, Matt hesitated at first, then pushed himself to sound pleasant and healthy. No harm in a little exaggeration to convince others he was on the right track. "Things are outstanding. We're throwing a birthday party for my mother tonight. Madison is a happy little baby. I'm a lucky guy."

"Excellent. Anything stressful going on today?" Maude asked him that question every time he called, not because she thought he would revert to his old ways but because she wanted to present an open door whenever he needed one.

Matt crossed the front lawn to the side of the house, one hand holding the cell phone to his ear and the other rubbing his temples in deliberate circles. The wind was calmer near the house, its cedar-shake facade protected by tall evergreens and firs. When he reached the side pathway, he meandered along the route toward the garage. Matt had never told Maude about the big decision happening this week. He wasn't hiding things from her so much as he was waiting to determine the most suitable moment to inform his sponsor that he would return to work—a place that had caused him excessive stress and worry nearly every day, ultimately leading to his interminable major life crisis.

"I had a thought this morning. Actually, it was something I dreamed about last night." Matt cringed over his impudent lie as the thought had been nagging at him for weeks, not just the night prior. "I've been researching the company you work for. It seems stable. Maybe I could come work for you. We could take our connection to new levels, yeah?"

Matt had started out as a junior accountant at Ben's law firm. After a few years, his father and the two other partners turned over the day-to-day financial responsibilities to him. He managed client accounts, the partners' portfolios, and the annual bonus and weekly payrolls—everything that played a role in the firm's billing and investments. When Matt began suffering from financial problems at home because of the renovations on his house and his fourth child on the way, he stole money from the practice to support his drug habit. Once his brother Teddy and the other partners discovered the theft, they forced him into rehabilitation. No charges were filed as the partners had been close friends with Ben and his family. After the firm transferred to Wittleton and Davis, they learned exactly how much Matt had screwed up.

Maude sighed, an eerie mix of despondent angst and nervous concern. "This has nothing to do with your skills or talent, Matt, but do you really think we should mix business and pleasure? Not that being your sponsor falls into either category, but we have a solid relationship today. Let's leave it at that for a while longer, okay?" Maude knew nothing of Matt's financial fraud or that he'd stolen from the family firm. He'd kept the incendiary source of information to himself when they first spoke about his anxiety, money troubles, and addiction to uppers and downers.

Matt's chest tightened. A vitriolic doubt descended upon him upon hearing the news. If Wittleton and Davis were taking this long to confirm his return to the firm, they probably planned to renege on their promise. Anger built up inside his diminished body. He'd done his penance. He would never steal from them again. They had to offer him his job back. Maude had to help him. He was feeling lost and needed an anchor in addition to his family, to keep him focused each day.

"I thought about it a lot today," Matt noted, a confident tone overtaking his wavering skepticism. "If I need to step into an associate role, that's fine. I'm eager to get back to work, and change is the best thing for me right now." Matt reached the side entrance to the garage and gripped the door handle. He'd only been inside once since they relocated, on moving day, to tell the delivery workers where to store some boxes. He'd led Margaret to believe that he'd initiated various woodworking projects in there, but it was an outright lie. Matt felt helpless every time he approached the building, drowning in the disappointment his father would've felt over what became of his son. Instead, he went for long walks and read the newspaper in a hidden lounge chair by the property's far corner. His daily need to check the game scores and track the stock market became a new vice; it seemed his body always craved the next high.

"Listen… this isn't the best time to discuss working together. How about we schedule a chat next month when I get through our quarterly reporting period? You'll have had some opportunity to make a few inquiries, update your resume… decide what's best." Maude paused to let Matt respond, yet he remained stoic. "I'm not saying we can't figure something out down the line, but you need to focus on *you* right now. My organization demands long hours, and I want to ensure you're at the top of your game before we negotiate job prospects. Fair?"

After clenching his fists several times, Matt entered the garage and attempted to prevent himself from excessively lashing out. He bit his tongue, both in anger and frustration, to stop what seemed inevitable. A steady stream of blood pooled along his gums, a salty metallic taste filling his mouth. Roadblocks in his every which way resulted in words exploding too quickly to contain. "You're supposed to help me get back on track. Dammit! I don't understand why you won't do me this one favor. Come on! My family is hurting right now."

Maude's reply was swift and direct as if he'd hit a well-concealed nerve. "We all go through rough times, Matt. The Glass family isn't unique, and they don't hold the marker on grief. I know what it's like to lose someone you love. My husband died last year due to someone else's negligence, but I never shared that with you, did I? Every single day I fight the urge to get revenge. I'm not always lucky enough to stop myself, though."

"I didn't know. I'm so sorry. What happened to him?" Matt's chest fluttered with a mixture of sorrow and confusion. How could she keep something important from him?

"That's not the point. I've struggled to accept his loss. Sometimes I want to take a handful of pills to forget everything. But I don't. Instead, I focus on setting things right. Fixing what happened in the past so I attain the future I deserve. That's what you need to do, not sulk or beg for help." Maude explained she was being rough on him to instigate a wake-up call as he was heading down the wrong path again. "Be stronger than what you were."

Matt was about to apologize when an incoming text message buzzed on his phone. Could it be Wittleton or Davis with an offer? He thanked Maude for her consideration and hung up, compressing unbridled energy and fervent uncertainty deep inside his body. He'd call Maude later to express regret for pushing her on the job front. He needed to be a better team player, not a reactionary loose cannon.

When Matt perused the text, his body jolted at the words. It wasn't a job opportunity. It was an offer of a different kind from a familiar phone number he should've been ignoring.

Quinn: *Haven't heard from you in a while. We got some good stuff coming this weekend. In need, bro?*

Matt shoved the phone in his pocket and hoisted himself onto a bench in the garage. When he'd checked into the rehab center, one of the other patients had chatted about signs guiding his life each day. The sun rising every morning was a sign that another day had dawned, a chance to start afresh and focus on all the wonderful things in life. The people who visited him were signs that his loving friends and family wanted him to heal. The prayers they shared each evening, about believing in themselves and trusting in a higher power, all signs that a positive outcome was only moments away.

Matt had passionately searched for these illustrious and mysterious signs since coming home. He stumbled upon a few in the immediate days, but it never convinced him of his rightful path. The sign of returning to the law firm where he'd once been a hero, the star player who helped them rise to the top in their industry. He waited forever for the call. The sign of Quinn, his drug dealer, being carted off to prison for two months after a bust in the neighborhood, ensuring the temptation was moved further from reality. Matt had cried out in gratitude when it happened. The sign of his daughter's birth, when he looked into her eyes for the first time and recognized hope for a bright future. An enormous family who loved playing sports and competing with one another, motivating his hopes and dreams for the best life possible.

Then one day, all those signs disappeared. No matter how hard Matt tried to persevere with a claw-like grasp, an implacable enthusiasm, and a powerful thirst, things grew worse. It seemed finding a new job would be extraordinarily difficult. His daughter cried every time he held her, but she was an angel for her mother. Margaret had roused tension about Olivia's return to Brandywine. Quinn had been released from prison and contacted him with news of fresh products. Were these the actual signs? The last one he refused to accept. It was one he kicked, punched, and beat down every morning after nightmares ravished his body for hours without end; they'd threatened to conquer his sanity and kill any hope for a better future.

One day at a time. I am stronger than each of these individual items. I will survive.

Matt fetched a scrap of wood from the corner shelf, then plugged in the table saw. He clamped the wood to the device, tossed on a pair of goggles, and flipped the switch. An abrasive, powerful grind blasted through the air. Matt cut the wood in half to a manageable size, so he could begin tracing a pattern on the top. He'd promised his girls a dollhouse, and it was time he acted. If he couldn't help himself, he knew he could make his family proud and happy with something beautiful and useful.

In ten minutes, he shaped out the rough beginnings of the roof, scalloping the edges as a test of his carpentry skills and the wood's flexibility. His imagination took front and center stage, driving his energy and concentration as he plowed through a desire to finally commit to the project. He'd just turned off the saw to view his handiwork when his cell rang. For the briefest of moments, Matt had forgotten his worries. When he saw the firm's number, they flooded back with unrelenting, fiercer vengeance.

"Hello, Mr. Wittleton. I'm so glad to hear from you. Can't wait to discuss next steps." Matt inhaled a deep breath, ready to accept their positive decision.

"Good afternoon, Matt. Ms. Davis is here with me. We've finished our analysis, and I, unfortunately, have some tough news for you." Wittleton's voice, nasal and resolute, sliced through the air with more precision than the wood saw.

Matt's stomach sank. The signs were all around him. Like shooting stars. Rebounding off the bare scraps of confidence and hope he desperately clung to, growing stronger and more penetrating with each blast. "I swear, things will be better this time. You promised me I could return to the firm. My father wouldn't—"

Davis interrupted, ensuring she conveyed their troubling decision with ease and proper consideration. "Matt, please don't make this any harder than it already is. We were prepared to offer you a part-time role, one that would enable you to prove yourself again, let you slowly acclimate back to a regular work schedule."

"That's great. When can I start?" Matt begged, though certain their decision was final.

"Then we received some additional information this week. Do you remember working on a case involving a tricky patent? The one where two partners were suing each other over who had created the innovative infrastructure that ran their business?"

Matt swallowed heavily. Of course, he had. Matt had been tasked with analyzing all the company's expenditures, sales, and investments. He'd skimmed money off the top of the settlement to pay part of his mortgage. He'd completely forgotten about that incident before entering rehab. Although he'd attempted to repay all his debts, using the inheritance from his father and the proceeds from the sale of his house, it left him and Margaret with just enough to address his recovery costs and the girls' education. That's why he had to get back to work soon, to cover daily expenses and save for their future. His children and wife meant the world to him. If only he could stop craving chemical relief.

"Yes, I do. I must've neglected to fix that before I left the firm last fall." Matt slammed his fist on the delicate dollhouse roof he'd just finished, cracking it in half. A fissure that could not be repaired. He'd have to start the project over again. A pit formed deep in his gut. "I can repay you. This shouldn't stop us from proceeding." He'd find a way to remedy everything. If he remembered correctly, it amounted to just over ten-thousand dollars. Unfortunately, he couldn't be sure anymore, especially since his last few weeks at the firm had been a humongous blur of inescapable highs and lows.

Wittleton coughed awkwardly. "The missing money isn't the problem now, son. The clients found out what happened before we could intervene, and it's blown up to epic proportions."

Davis explained that the clients had reached a settlement after working with an arbiter to agree on shared patent ownership and future profits. Unfortunately, during the final review of all the paperwork, it became apparent someone at the law firm had stolen money. "The clients trashed their agreement, accused one another of hiding money, and now they refuse to settle."

Wittleton added, "On top of that, they fired us and are suing for damages. We simply cannot risk bringing you back into the firm right now. We have nothing but respect for your late father, and we understand you have a disease that led to these complications, but—"

Unable to control his irritation, Matt screamed into the phone, "I don't have a disease. I made a mistake. Why doesn't anyone believe me!?"

Davis interjected, "There's no reason to get emotional. Let's have a civil discussion. We've scheduled a meeting with the clients next week. It's possible we can correct the entire ordeal, but under no circumstance can we jeopardize the future of this firm."

"Where does that leave me? Am I out for good now?" Matt sunk to the floor, clutching the phone to his ear and gritting his teeth. He couldn't disappoint his family again. It'd kill him.

"During my initial conversation with one of the two partners, Warren Payne clarified that any deal we agree to must include termination of the responsible party. I'm sorry, Matt. Even if we can save the firm's reputation, you will not be permitted back to the offices. Warren was extraordinarily adamant. You are to be fired, or he will not back down from seeking a monstrous amount of damages." Davis clarified that the other partner wasn't as insistent as Warren when it came to firing Matt. That partner had acquiesced to merely collecting his share of the missing money and subsequently moving on, but Warren wanted the guilty party to suffer severe and memorable punishment for his misdeeds. Davis directed Matt to take the weekend to let the news settle in, and she'd arrange a follow-up in a couple of days.

Matt chucked his phone across the garage, seething as it landed on a pile of blankets rather than smashed into smithereens. His entire life was ruined because of one man. All he knew was the client's name, Warren Payne. He'd spoken to the guy on a few calls but had never met him in person. Matt had stolen the money, moved a few balances between accounts, and hid his role for the last month he'd been in the office before they forced him to take a leave of absence. But foolishly, he'd forgotten that once he was gone, the replacement accountant would find traces of his deceitful actions.

Matt's immediate goal fixated on learning all about Warren Payne's adamant urgency to squash his future with the firm. It seemed almost personal to the outraged partner, especially when the other one was willing to negotiate. Matt vowed to force the ludicrous man to change his mind, no matter how far he had to push the issue. Protecting his family and his own future was paramount. He'd already embarrassed himself so deeply, he feared he could never regain their respect and trust.

Matt punched a hole in a bag the gardener had left on a nearby table, watching clumps of soil rain to the floor in a steady stream. He flung piles around the garage in a fury, hoping to alleviate the tension rising inside his body like volcanic ash. *I will not be intimidated by this man. All I wanted to do was take care of my family. Please help me fix this!*

Chapter 5 – 2:00 to 3:00 PM (Teddy)

The bouquet of calla lilies and gladiolas hadn't decorated Ben's grave the prior afternoon. Teddy knew because he'd visited the cemetery every day over the last few weeks, eager to make sense of all the tragedy in his life. His mother must've been there earlier that morning. According to her text messages, ones he'd intentionally unanswered, Olivia had arrived in Brandywine to celebrate her birthday with the entire family. Teddy had little interest in attending the event, but his silence and absence would pay an unfortunate price in the long run.

As he gently nudged a wilting, rogue lily in the opposite direction—everything must always be in proper order, a trait Teddy inherited from his mother—white petals fell from its bloom. They glided through the air and landed on a pile of dirt where the grass had shriveled up and died from lack of attention and winter's harsh retaliation for an extended summer. While pressing one between his gloveless fingers, the petal cracked, slipped from his fingers, and took flight from a startling gust.

"Nothing good ever comes of change. Hope is an intelligent man's downfall and a fool's retribution." Teddy staunchly tore the now flowerless stem from the metal bucket sitting near his father's gravestone, impervious to the drops of water spraying his cheek. He crunched it in half, tossed it to the ground near the broken petals, and cracked his knuckles. "Old habits die hard, eh, Dad?"

Teddy's salt and pepper hair had retreated into a proper widow's peak, even though he'd barely entered his early thirties. Wide set, sparkling green eyes drew attention to his pale and pasty skin, and his thin, flat lips often made him look angrier than he intended. He was not an attractive man, but looks weren't of much use to him. Intelligence, determination, and creativity drove his passions.

During the months since his mother had taken off for Italy, his life traced the hairpin curve of a road less traveled, leading him into an existential stupor of the highest caliber. He wound up exactly where he'd started, before his mother had interfered in his decisions and set him up for failure.

Sarah had cheated on him. Though she supposedly had the best intentions in mind when she slept with Zach, it was a harsh betrayal. Teddy initially lashed out at those around him, slinging readied fists and vile words at his wife and brother. After several days of pondering the impact of their actions, Teddy eventually accepted their drunken encounter as a one-time occurrence, undertaken to impregnate her because he suffered from low sperm count. Zach's sperm were livelier. Better equipped. Previously proven. Sarah had focused only on achieving their goal of becoming parents.

In the end, Zach's baby-making expertise wasn't needed. Teddy and Sarah had attained success on their own, preparing to have their first child just days after Matt and Margaret. Two new infants in the family, three if you counted Caleb's adopted son. Teddy never did. Blood mattered to him. Though he was happy for his brother, Caleb's new child wasn't really a Glass. Had Sarah's baby been Zach's, he never would've given the woman a chance at repairing their marriage. Blood, his blood, not the blood of a sibling who shared DNA, was all that mattered. Fidelity and honor, love and truth, were all that mattered.

Then something shifted inside him, rooted out by Olivia's unwelcome guidance and ill-timed pressure to change his ways. She'd begged him to acknowledge the past was in the past. His mother never truly accepted Sarah, once calling her a tramp. Olivia had been the one to discover the truth about Sarah and Zach's one-night stand, then forced the secret from seclusion. Unfortunately, it leaked out the same day the family combusted over the news of Ethan's terminal illness. Sarah had won over Olivia's affections, or perhaps Olivia had blindly pushed through the negativity to conjure a source of happiness for the family. Either way, when the two women bonded and committed to fixing Teddy as they often told him must happen for the marriage to succeed, everything changed.

Teddy believed he'd made too many adjustments to his life in the previous year. After his father died in the car accident, he'd found the voice and courage to reject anticipated leadership of Ben's law firm. Obliged to assume control of the practice, Teddy had never been passionate about his career. He understood it, respected it, followed it without hesitation. He breathed the law every morning, afternoon, and night because it was what he'd been groomed to do since early childhood. As long as he kept his emotions at bay, veiled by an iron gate he refused to unlock, he could proceed each day in his murky and ignorant haze. But Olivia and Sarah had tempted him with a life that promised an alternative reality and happiness. Would they soon learn their actions had caused things to disintegrate so grievously?

The one constant in his life, the law firm, was gone, sold to Wittleton and Davis. Matt's careless financial machinations had sullied the comfortableness of the place. Now they had Warren Payne's lawsuit to unravel. Teddy pushed himself to accept the loss of not only his father but the firm his father had assembled for thirty years. In all honesty, at first, he was thankful to move forward, focusing on his love of painting and building his new art career. But that single event, his father's untimely and devastating death, had led to this string of horrid decisions. Granted, in the subsequent weeks after his brother's death, Teddy had learned how to grow and expand his mind. Sadly, with growth came the knowledge of things never meant to see daylight.

Teddy's eyelids pressed down tightly, willing the pain to disappear. After saying goodbye to his father, he navigated a few rows away to his brother's grave. More flowers, bursts of vibrant orange this time, for Ethan. He bent to his knees and rested a palm on the headstone. "You are the luckiest of us all. All your pain is gone now, brother."

Death had never emotionally crushed Teddy in the past. He'd buried grandparents, but they'd never developed an intimate relationship. Losing his father and brother within six months of one another had compensated for the heartbreaking pain he'd never experienced in his thirty-two years. His core, shaken beyond recognition, had been ripe for the challenge of interpreting unfamiliar feelings. Could he recover from so much tragedy thrown at him in such a brief period?

Diane had always told him death comes in threes, like the ghost of a Charles Dickens novel. Teddy's father, Ben, represented the past. His brother, Ethan, represented the present. Who would claim the future? Teddy had dismissed his aunt's eccentric beliefs until the unthinkable happened.

Days after Teddy and Sarah reconciled, they'd gone to the obstetrician for a seven-month checkup on the baby. Their doctor discovered an abnormality in the fetus's heartbeat. "He may grow out of it," the physician suggested, accidentally revealing the baby's gender. "Bed rest for now." A couple of weeks later, Sarah went into early labor. "He might be okay. We've saved premature babies before." The doctor staved off the delivery, confident he could sustain the child inside Sarah's womb for another month. "Let's hold off as long as possible." Teddy and Sarah told no one, suffering through a future parent's worst nightmare in solitude. On New Year's Eve, Sarah and Teddy solemnly rode in an ambulance to the hospital. Ten minutes before midnight, their premature son was born. He lived for ten minutes before his tiny, underdeveloped heart abandoned any hope of survival. Dead, newborn son, Theodore Junior, at 12:00 AM on New Year's Day. The perfect way to begin a new year—facing the reality of his empty world.

Sarah refused to speak to anyone that first week, even Teddy, especially after what he'd done behind her back. He had no choice but to follow his instinct and deal with the situation as any reputable attorney would—follow the process, address the urgent tasks, and put the case to rest. He told his family that they planned to attend an art conference in New York City, so no one would bother them during their misery and mourning. A week later, Sarah shocked Teddy by announcing that she wanted a divorce. "This is a sign we don't belong together anymore."

Teddy informed his family that Sarah was confined to bed rest, too sick to see anyone. Margaret couldn't come by because she was too close to her own delivery date. Zach was busy launching his music career in Brooklyn. Caleb returned to Maine to play parent to his adopted son. No one ever visited Teddy in his home. If they had, they would've encountered a broken man holed up in his bedroom, alone and losing his last echo of faith that goodness could win out. Staring at the blank wall was the only thing that kept him from collapsing into a puddle of sad history.

Sarah eventually retreated to Savannah. She and Teddy fought by text message, email, and voicemail for weeks. Never once would either pick up the phone to speak with the other. Sarah blamed Teddy for arguing with her about her indiscretion with Zach. Teddy insisted the culpability belonged to Sarah for lying to him during the initial stages of the pregnancy. "This is justice for the mess we've made of our lives."

Several weeks ago, Sarah filed the paperwork for an official separation. She decided to seek money from the Glass family. As a result of the damages sustained during the baby's delivery, Sarah could no longer bear children again. "I'm taking every penny you inherited. You left me with nothing after ten years of marriage. Only ten minutes of happiness later ripped from my soul. My only reason for living is gone because of your carelessness and anger." She hadn't responded to Teddy in weeks, and he hadn't once summoned the urge to reach out to her. The loss of a precious infant, one with no future happiness to offset their bitterness, was all that lingered in the stifling air between them, miles and miles apart.

Teddy shuffled a few more rows across the cemetery to the corner plot where all the infants, including his own, were buried. "Bad things do come in threes. I never should've doubted it." Teddy ignored the steady stream of tears that riddled his cheeks. It'd become his routine for the last few weeks… visit his father, visit his brother, visit his son. Everything in his life was ruined, tarnished beyond belief. He knew that was his last chance at ever having a child. No woman would ever want him now, in his current condition and with his decaying attitude toward life.

Teddy brushed the stray leaves from his son's grave before returning to his car and snapping from his distractions. Since enrolling in an art program the previous semester, Teddy had grown closer with one of his professors. At first, they bonded over similar life experiences. Teddy had always meant to tell Gina Appel about his wife and baby, but he had never learned to socialize properly. Their discussions were kept to the art world and future creative paths, not their personal lives. Teddy didn't even know whether the woman was married or had children.

He'd only scheduled their coffee meeting today to withdraw from art school and leave the country for an undetermined period of time. If pressed for a reason, he'd cite family obligations, but in his heart, he knew abandoning his family was the only obligation left for him to fulfill. Attending Olivia's birthday party this evening would be his last goodbye before he disappeared into his own world, updating no one else in the Glass family about his future isolation. If it had worked for Caleb during the last decade, why couldn't it work for him? The irony of the anger Teddy once dispensed at his brother for sneaking away to Maine failed to reach the surface of his mind at this time.

A few miles past the cemetery, Teddy pulled into a corner café. He'd selected a place in a slightly seedier part of town, where no one in his family would ever go, except possibly Zach, who was stuck in Brooklyn that afternoon, based on the latest family text message confirming everyone's arrival time for the evening's festivities. The location also happened to be in the more creative and artistic section of the town, not too far from the university where his courses were held, which comforted him from time to time. Upon exiting his car and scampering through the parking lot to avoid being late, he unintentionally dropped his keys. When he bent over to pick them up, a nearby conversation caught his attention.

Teddy looked near the row of dumpsters and spotted a guy in his late teens communicating with the driver of a car idling in an adjacent spot. The slim and wiry stranger barked, "This is all I have right now. I'm picking up my shipment later today. Are you sure it's safe for us to meet later? You're not busy with something else, dude?"

"Yep, I gotta find a way to make this work," replied the driver, hidden from Teddy's view. "Same place as last week. Text me when you're close so I can sneak out."

Teddy shook his head, deeming the conversation another drug deal in progress. Before rounding the corner, he thought he recognized the voice coming from the man in the running car. He stopped and focused as the driver rolled up the window and backed out of the parking spot. If he hadn't known better, he would've thought it was Matt. Even the car was the same color as his brother's.

The young guy approached Teddy, dark and empty pupils concentrating as he confidently strutted down the sidewalk. "You looking for something, bro? Maybe I got what you need."

"That all depends. Who were you just with?" Teddy crossed his arms and clicked his jaw, not threatened by the guy's intimidating and deliberate stare. He had little to lose these days. Why ever be afraid of something when you had nothing left to give up but your life?

"A client. If you'd like to become one, step into my office," the obnoxious dealer muttered, pointing an extended arm toward a blue Toyota Camry with rust on the front fender.

"Never mind." Teddy stomped up the steps into the café and convinced himself to ignore what he'd seen. The guy was only eighteen or nineteen, too young for his brother to know. Matt had sought therapy and stopped risking his life by taking drugs. There was no reason to believe that was him in the parking lot a minute earlier.

Gina waved to Teddy from a high-top near the display of pastries. He caught a waiter's attention before arriving at the table and ordered a medium coffee, black, no sugar. "And fill it to the top please. I'll be checking."

Gina patiently waited for Teddy to remove his coat and sit before addressing him. Long curly blonde hair, parted down the middle, fell against the sides of her contoured cheeks. When she smiled, two dimples formed, and hazel-green eyes lit up the room. "I'm excited to talk with you today. I have some news."

Teddy nodded his head once. "I have some news too. You go first." Although he wanted to thrust the decision to exit the art program off his chest, it'd be easier to listen to her news, then drop his bombshell and quickly end the conversation, claiming he had another engagement to attend. Gina knew he despised being tardy, so she wouldn't detain him any longer.

The professor pulled a sheet of paper from a glossy folder and handed it to him, just as the waiter dropped off a hot coffee and the pastry Gina had selected before Teddy's arrival. Teddy snatched the paper from her but first opened the lid to his coffee, then proffered the man a ten-dollar bill. "Thanks. This should cover both items." As he perused Gina's letter, a disgruntled expression crossed his face, highlighting the angular features he despised. "I don't understand."

Gina explained that she'd shown one of his paintings to a friend who owned a gallery. Though it was only an opportunity to discuss her students' work and not one to request any special favors, the balance of light and dark elements in the piece intrigued her friend. The gallery owner was in the market for young, up-and-coming artists to display their work in an exciting summer collection. "The owner wants to meet with you. The letter is a formal invitation to her second gallery's opening next week, so you can negotiate possibilities for the future. Isn't this fantastic?"

Teddy carefully allowed himself to convert his frown into the makings of an ear-to-ear grin. He'd only been painting again for a few months, and even though Gina had planned to include him in the school's spring art show, he still lacked the confidence to consider displaying his work in a legitimate gallery. "Are you sure this is a serious offer?"

Gina leaned back in her chair and expelled a heavy breath. "I've known her for decades. The woman's a genius, and if she invited someone to visit her next big opening, it's the real deal."

Teddy was certain Destiny had guided him to move on, to escape the imbalanced ecosphere currently occupying his stifling existence, to put space between him and his family. He planned to negotiate a fair settlement with Sarah's attorney, guaranteeing she had enough money to start a new life on her own. With his remaining inheritance and the sale of their sizable house, he'd vanish to Europe and decide what to do next with his currently pitiful but potentially fulfilling life.

Maybe he'd paint the beaches of Crete or bazaars of Turkey, something exotic and unfamiliar. Teddy had suffered so much from his inability to embrace change that he now insisted it was time to explore the future's limitless boundaries. Europe and the Middle East represented the cradle of civilization; it offered him the opportunity to center himself and release the abstract grief, broken promises, and rampant anger that'd comprised his body over the years. When he was painting, Teddy felt as if the doors to an alternate universe were being opened. He suddenly found a source of water that rejuvenated his thirsty body with the anticipation of a rewarding life.

Was Gina presenting a new opportunity for him to consider? Did it mean he should try to contact Sarah one more time to discern the proper way to say goodbye to a life he wasn't entirely convinced had to disappear?

"Earth to Teddy," Gina called out, gently nudging his shoulder. "Most students would jump at the chance. Are you sure you heard me properly?"

"Yes, sorry. I... I have a lot going on right now. Do I need to give you an answer today? It's a generous offer, but—"

Gina reached for Teddy's clenched fist, tenderly rubbing her thumb across his palm to relax him. "I seem to have shocked you, not necessarily in the way I expected to. Sure... not a problem. I didn't tell my friend we were meeting today. I told her I'd discuss it with you in class next week. Then you suggested we meet for coffee. What's going on?"

"I'm grateful, truly. It's just that... my family is going through a lot right now, and I guess it's weighing heavily on my mind." Teddy knew he couldn't confess the truth to Gina. He'd have to wait a day or two to contact Sarah and process the news before deciding whether to leave Connecticut.

"You're a mysterious man, Teddy Glass. Something about you assures me you're worth waiting for, but don't take too long. Opportunities like these don't come along every day." Gina tore a piece off her pastry and patiently waited for Teddy to volunteer why he'd asked her to coffee. "I can only stay another fifteen minutes. Isn't there something you wanted to talk about?"

"Yes," he hesitated before summoning a proper excuse. "I'm interested in switching my project for the spring show. I didn't want to surprise you in class in front of everyone else next week." Teddy scrolled through his phone to locate the partially finished painting of the nightmare he'd endured the prior week, when his body had been consumed by an agony of fire and his thoughts melted into a sea of faceless infants at the hospital's neonatal intensive care unit.

"It's magnificent, Teddy. I can see the raw pain in your work as if your suffering is leaping off the pages and begging the critic to console you. Tell me, do you have children of your own?" Gina brushed some curls away from her pinkish cheek and tilted her head to the side to focus on her student.

He'd told no one about the baby's death. He'd never even talked about his father's or brother's deaths either. Building new friendships and trusting others wasn't an option for him. Teddy closed the app on his phone and shoved his chair away from the table, cringing as the metal legs scraped the concrete floor. "I'm so sorry, but I need to go too. Family obligation. I'll be in touch." He gathered his coat and briskly walked out the café's front door. When he settled in his car, he thumbed through his recent call list to find Sarah's number. Having contacted few people in the last three weeks, hers was still near the top. The phone rang endlessly, convincing Teddy that Sarah would never acknowledge his presence again.

Then she answered, her Southern accent bringing a slight smile to Teddy's face. "I should know better, but maybe this time you're ready to listen."

Teddy nearly dropped the phone when she accepted his olive branch. "Sarah, I… I'm not really sure why I phoned, but something made me want to talk to you today."

Sarah made a gurgling sound before summoning the words to respond. When she did, a static-filled announcement blasted in the background, almost blocking her voice. "I'm not sure there's anything we have to discuss. My attorney says you haven't formally responded to the latest request."

Teddy scratched at a cuticle on his left index finger. He'd begun tearing them out, picking until they bled profusely the last several days. "We are going to send our comments back on Monday. My mother returned this week, and I'm on my way to her party this evening."

"I'm aware, Teddy. Your family still includes me on the group messages. I guess that means you haven't told them about the divorce." Her voice was cold, distant as if she spoke in a tunnel. "This ends today, Teddy. If you don't agree to my demands, I'll be forced to take very deliberate action, which includes informing your family myself that they need to stop contacting me." Sarah disconnected the phone, nicking Teddy's chance at any sort of reply.

Unrestrained fury and angst erupted like hot lava from his stomach, lining the path upward through his chest. It settled at the base of his throat, churning and wallowing until he recognized his old habits refusing to disappear. A dollop of confusion suddenly emerged in the residual anger, clawing its way through the acidic simmering of his emotions. Had he heard the distant message properly? Teddy dialed Sarah again, but the phone immediately went to voicemail.

Before they had hung up, an announcement in the background confirmed the arrival of a train. For a fleeting moment, Teddy believed the voice indicated Hartford as the name of the station. Was Sarah back in Connecticut?

Chapter 6 – 3:00 to 4:00 PM (Zach)

"Awesome set, ladies. I've got enough vocals for today. Lemme play with the tracks for a few hours, then I'll reach out next week on a new schedule." Zach hugged all three women in the new band he'd recently heard in an underground Brooklyn club and invited to the studio to record a demo that week. They had a unique vibe he was searching for, but propelling them into the sweet spot of success had been tricky. A few more rounds in the recording booth and he would accomplish his goal.

Zach, donning acid-wash jeans, a black V-neck, and ratty hoodie, was the most attractive of all the brothers. He maintained a constant five o'clock shadow, balancing his puppy dog eyes and a suggestive desire to cross over to the dark side. His clothes clung to a well-sculpted body and hid many tattoos and a new piercing he'd yet to show anyone given where it wound up. After losing a bet to someone, Zach had tossed caution to the wind and let her choose the body part. Despite a week of pleading, she wouldn't relent, and Zach now worried what sex would be like in the future after he fully recovered. The things he did for pleasure… or pain… never seemed to be enough to overcome his pride.

Once they slipped out the side door, Zach tugged on his hungry and sensitive crotch. It'd been way too long since he got any action, and the three ladies who'd just departed each left him semi-erect throughout the afternoon's mix of beats. Not one to blend business and pleasure or ever make them feel uncomfortable, he redirected his impatient dick to keep its presence unknown. Mostly, it'd worked, but any longer and he might've slipped off to the men's room to take care of a primal urge.

Other than a few hours relieving some tension on Halloween with his sorta bestie-occasional lover who more frequently dug the ladies lately, he hadn't gotten any action in months. He and Tressa had been hooking up for most of the early half of last year, but when she decided to give the lesbian side of her longings a fighting chance, he searched elsewhere for his indulgences. That's truly why he'd found himself in his sister-in-law's bed one drunken night. Thank God he hadn't actually gotten her pregnant. Sarah had been insistent Zach's sperm were no different than his brother's and since Teddy couldn't get his wife pregnant, the runner-up was good enough for her uterus.

Unfortunately, shortly after that encounter, things took a turn south and caused his libido to put itself on a confusing hiatus. The death of his father and brother Ethan knocked the wind from Zach's sails, pushing him to think about the true purpose of his life. During the interim, he'd focused on comforting his brother's wife, Emma. As Ethan slowly succumbed to his brain tumor, Zach fell for the magical, attractive girl who made everyone smile. They shared a tender moment one night, but after cuckolding his brother Teddy, Zach had learned his lesson. No more bedding sisters-in-law, at least not until an appropriate length of time had passed after death or divorce. Thankfully, Matt's wife was too prissy, and Caleb was gay. Even if forced to choose, he'd sleep with Caleb's husband before bumping uglies with Matt's wife. The obnoxious woman annoyed the crap out

Zach, but as a loyal and kind brother, he kept his opinion of Margaret to himself.

When Tressa sashayed into the recording studio, he grunted. "One, I need a cigarette break. Two, am I an asshole for sleeping with one brother's wife and longing for another? Three, is a totally random handy out of the question, babe? Let's test drive the new hardware you picked out!"

Tressa laughed so raucously she snorted like a pig in a trough. After she crossed the room to reach Zach, she jostled his body toward hers, so he could feel her lusty breath waft across his lips. One hand clutched his firm ass, and the other crawled the length of his well-defined chest and eight-pack abs. Tressa popped the button on his slim-cut jeans and seductively zipped open the fly. When Zach moaned, Tressa grasped a hand tightly around his growing parts and squeezed as hard as she could, to the point he yelped like a newborn puppy. "If you ever ask me that again, papi, the only handy you'll get again is a vengeful nurse swabbing the cauterized wound where your manhood used to be." Once Zach silently nodded at her, she kissed his cheek, zipped up his jeans, and refastened the button. "Te amo, papi."

"Thanks, babe. Glad to know where we stand," Zach choked out, shaking his body to release the increased adrenaline and oddly erotic shock. "At least I'm no longer horny as fuck."

"Mama's good to you, isn't she?" Tressa playfully slapped Zach's forehead and shoved him down the hall so they could grab a smoke in the alley. She wouldn't participate but understood Zach couldn't relinquish all his vices. He'd stopped snorting coke and crystal years ago, even limited his alcohol intake in the last few months. All to ensure he would be a better parent for his daughter, Anastasia. "Besides, I know you're a good catch. You're a prince among men. You just like to mouth off every once in a while. The right woman will be able to tame you."

"You're the best. Thanks for putting me in my place." Zach rolled his eyes, retrieved the cigarette pack from his pocket, and lit up. "I can only be a good and loyal boy so long, you know that, right?"

Tressa had suffered through this conversation with him too many times to count. "Listen to me for the last of all last times, pendejo. Emma was your brother's wife. It's hardly been three months since his death. She told you to wait until she was ready. There's nothing else you can do."

"We have this amazing connection. I know it's too soon, but the girl creeps inside my skin like no other woman has before. She's better than perfection. She…" Zach paused to conjure the best word. "She makes me want to do the right thing, like all the time."

"And propositioning me is on the list of acceptable things?" Tressa shivered when a breeze whipped through the alley and caused her to curse the weather in four distinct types of Spanish.

Zach stripped off his hoodie and tossed it at her. "None. I've been celibate for months. That's never happened before. Emma's turning me into an angel."

"Now there's two images I've never associated together. Zachary Glass and an angel. You got wings hidden beneath your slippery, tattooed skin?"

"Whose side are you on?" Zach finished puffing on his cigarette and flicked it to the ground. "That's my third today. I'm only allowed one more. Shit!"

"Your side, papi. Always. Amor will do that to you. But really, you have to be patient." Tressa slipped into Zach's hoodie and moaned. "God, I can smell you all over my body now." She breathed in his powerful scent, smiled coyly, and purred. "So, I shouldn't tell you all about my naughty sex life with the bartender? The girl is super flexible, like way more than me that time we—"

"You're pure evil. Even Lucifer would think twice before inviting you into his den of iniquity."

Zach hoped Emma would eventually be ready to spend time with him on a more-than-friendship level. They kept in touch via text messages and the occasional call, even met up for two days in Boston around the holidays. Zach had headed north to pack Ethan's belongings and help Emma move into a new place. Always friends, never anything more, but she told him they might have a future, once she dealt with her grief over losing Ethan just days after their marriage. Since the day they discussed a future relationship, Emma had returned to work and subsequently grown surprisingly distant. Something big must've happened on the phone call she'd taken during their dinner at *Le Joliet* right before Christmas. Zach had wanted to ask but respected her privacy too.

"You and your brother are nothing alike, at least from the two times I met him. You don't even resemble one another," Tressa quipped, urging Zach to head back inside. Neither Zach nor Tressa knew Ethan had been adopted, which accounted for why the brothers looked so dissimilar.

"That actually makes me feel better. I know she's not longing for Ethan and settling for his more studly badass lookalike." Zach smirked and wrapped a muscular arm around Tressa's shoulder. "Listen, we're throwing a birthday party for my mom. I gotta head back to get there in time. Wanna be my plus-one?"

"That's such a gringo thing to ask." Tressa bopped her head back and forth. "Hmmm… you returning to the city tomorrow? I got dinner plans and a game involving handcuffs with the fetish-loving bartender."

"Bruja! Nah, I promised my mother I'd stick around for a few days. Anastasia and I need some quality time together." Zach shut down his laptop and packed his backpack. "And my Aunt Diane is back. She's my rock. I kinda wanna hear all about their trip."

"Lemme think about it. I can't go with you right now, but I'm down with the extended drive. It's only a couple of hours."

Tressa shimmied out of his hoodie, intentionally revealing the deep cleavage between her breasts, and hurled it at him.

"Haven't you messed with me enough? I'll give you the entire bed. I can bunk with Anastasia tonight." Zach pecked Tressa's cheek before strutting toward the exit, the crack of his bubble butt peeking from the top of his jeans.

"Damn right, papi. I always come first."

"I remember. Too bad you're not interested in my rock-hard body anymore." Zach winked, turned the doorknob while licking his lips, and left Tressa standing with her mouth hanging open.

Zach had landed her a part-time job at the studio doing administrative tasks for one of the owners, so she stayed behind to lock up before heading out. He loved their banter, and even though she'd practically castrated him thirty minutes earlier, she was the second-best part of his life, after his daughter, of course. By the time Zach reached the parking lot, he texted Emma about attending Olivia's party.

Zach: *You coming? Last train to get you there on time leaves in an hour.*
Emma: *Probably not. Got lots going on. But I'll find time for you soon, okay?*
Zach: *Ugh! Don't make me deal with them on my own. I need your strength and beautiful smile.*
Emma: *You need a savage beating and a reminder not to pressure me. Gotta go. Hugs.*

Zach slipped the phone into his backpack and scrounged for his keys. He had to swing by his Brooklyn apartment and pick up a few essentials, then he could drive to Connecticut for the upcoming week. As he pulled onto the main boulevard, his phone rang. He pushed a button on the steering wheel to answer the call, uncertain who it was. "Yo, what's up?"

"Zach? It's Aunt Diane. Are you on the road yet, honey? Anastasia's here with me and wanted to talk to you."

Zach missed his aunt's cheerful presence in his life. Three months of separation had been difficult. Although Olivia was his mother, Diane had always been the one to praise him and believe in him. "In about twenty minutes, I just need to grab Mom's birthday gift and some clothes. How's my little penguin doing?" Anastasia was so enamored with the adorable black-and-white seabirds when he'd taken her to the local zoo, it became his treasured nickname for her. Everyone in the Glass family had one; it was a ritual. While some loved their monikers, others, like his brothers Teddy and Caleb, hated theirs.

"She's great. All done with her bath and picking out an outfit. One that will hopefully make your mother proud and prevent you from losing your mind."

"Let her wear whatever she wants. It's called creativity!" Zach turned onto his street, double-parked near a fire hydrant, and switched on his flashers. He only lived a few blocks away, but he usually parked in the studio's gated lot where he didn't have to worry about vandalism on the streets.

"I'm sure she'll impress everyone. Currently, she's planning to wear her flannel pajama pants and a fuzzy pink sweater that Caleb and Jake gave her at Christmas."

"God, she loves that sweater. I'm afraid to let Pilar wash it."

"Listen, honey," Diane hesitated during a brief silence. "Katerina rang earlier to talk to Anastasia. I told her to call back tonight when you got here."

Zach mumbled a few expletives under his breath. "Did she say anything important?"

"I'm not entirely sure. Something about a message for your mother. She joked about stopping by to drop off a gift." Diane noted that Katerina spoke very deliberately and became irrational when denied the chance to talk to her daughter.

Zach checked his mail in the lobby before sitting on the dilapidated stone steps to the second floor. He lived in a four-story walk-up, refusing to spend a dime of his inheritance on himself. It all went to the lawyers to stop his ex-girlfriend's fight for joint custody and was squirreled away in an account for Anastasia's education. "I'll deal with her, thanks. She's itching for trouble. I can feel it."

"Don't do anything rash now." Diane asked Zach to hold while she passed the phone to his daughter.

Anastasia giggled when Diane tickled her belly. "You're silly! Is Daddy on the phone?"

"Yes, he is. Talk to him for a minute while I go downstairs. I think I heard someone at the door. Maybe another birthday gift has arrived," Diane suggested.

Anastasia said, "That was earlier. Some man delivered an envelope. I put it on the table."

Suddenly calmer, Zach bellowed into the phone, "I'm gonna get you tonight, baby girl. You're in trouble… an entire week of me torturing you for hours with tasting new vegetables and watching boring black and white television shows. No internet."

"Nooo," Anastasia screeched in jest.

Zach heard Diane update Anastasia that she already found the envelope on the floor. "It was at the top of the stairs. I put it in the living room. Someone will read it later. Don't know whose it is."

Zach and Anastasia spoke for a few minutes before he told his daughter that he had to hang up and drive to Connecticut. "Put Aunt Diane on for a sec, honey."

"What's up, Zach? I've got to return a phone call." Aunt Diane separately instructed Anastasia to find her cousins and finish getting ready.

"You okay? You seem a little off today." Zach knew his aunt well enough to recognize when she worried about something excessively. "Is this about Ira Rattenbury? I talked to him earlier today regarding a recording contract he was helping me out with. He mentioned that you uninvited him to tonight's party. Seemed a bit sad. I told him to come anyway."

"I'd rather not talk about it right now. Uncle George is being difficult, and I have to get that settled before I see Ira." Diane cleared her throat, then directed Zach to withdraw Ira's invitation again.

The last time Zach had talked with his aunt, they'd agreed to support one another through their dating woes. Being in her sixties, Diane had little memory of what it was like to start dating someone again. Ira had asked her out before she left for Italy, and she initially turned him down. Zach eventually talked her into giving him a chance, even though the man was two decades younger than his aunt. Zach thought the date had gone well. Then Diane mentioned something about a mysterious man she'd met on her vacation but wouldn't give her nephew any details. "Is this about the European guy you had cocktails with? Has that started up again?"

"No. Really, I'm just not ready. Whether it's him or Ira, until I fix the mess Uncle George has caused, I just can't let myself think about dating."

Zach hated his uncle, but he was a good mechanic. Killing two birds with one stone was always something that made Zach feel accomplished. "Do you want me to talk to Uncle George? I need to have a little work done on my bike. I could tell him to back off, even—"

"Please drop the subject, honey. I'm not going to ask again, okay?" Diane informed Zach that she had to get going and disconnected without saying goodbye.

Certain his aunt was hiding something, Zach decided to hold off on confronting her until after the party. He sprinted up the stairs to his apartment, where an unpleasant surprise teasing her curly burgundy and black-streaked hair hovered outside his door. "Sometimes life just sucks ass! Then you show up and I realize how much worse I had it when your lips were glued to my anus."

"Don't be a crude bastard! I've been waiting for an hour. You're usually home by now on a Saturday." Dressed in a pair of heavy black boots, skinny jeans, a low-cut halter top, and a leather coat, the irritated woman threw her hands to her hips and glared. "We need to talk."

Katerina and Zach had never married. She'd gotten pregnant while Zach was in college and threatened to abort the baby. Zach eventually convinced her to keep their child, promising that he'd raise their daughter. Katerina agreed only because he'd given her money to stay sober for nine months. Regrettably, as soon as she gave birth, Katerina reverted to old habits. For a while, she and Zach had grown closer again, but he knew she would never be a fit mother. He'd fought her for custody while she completed a treatment program, and won, but he could never be sure she'd truly clean up her act. Her callous treatment of their daughter's safety infuriated him even more than her betrayal of their once intense love. He'd find a way to repair his own broken heart, but he'd never forgive her for abandoning their daughter. Katerina's selfishness had sent Zach spiraling out of control for a brief period, but he pushed through the pain and found inspiration and support in his family.

Zach rumbled loudly. "What are you doing here? I made myself clear last week. The court granted full custody of Anastasia to me. You can see her once each month for a few hours with supervision. Go home. Now."

"Are you sure you want to keep playing this game? Things are different than they were months ago. I've got a job. I've got a boyfriend. I've got money coming my way soon too." Katerina implored Zach to give her another chance.

"I don't have time for your delusions. Let it go for another six months. If you can prove that you stayed drug free for an entire year and you can keep this supposed new job, maybe I'll reconsider more time with our daughter." He didn't really mean it, but the only way to dispense with Katerina was to let her think she had a fighting chance. Zach hated what he had to do to keep Anastasia from her train wreck of a mother.

Children should be with their parents, but his ex-girlfriend was an abomination. Zach had to protect his daughter, even if it meant getting his family involved in supporting his efforts. Without Olivia's help last fall, the judge might not have sided with Zach. The judge wasn't thrilled about Zach raising Anastasia by himself in a studio apartment in a rough part of Brooklyn. Olivia and Diane testified that Zach would spend a majority of his time in Connecticut with them, where Anastasia would attend a private school with her cousins and live in the Glass family home. The judge relented, keen to ensure the child's best interest.

For Zach, he'd have signed a deal with the devil to protect his daughter. Some days, he thought he did too. After Olivia departed for Italy, Zach had to ask Matt and Margaret to look out for Anastasia two days a week, when he had to be in Brooklyn for work. Margaret's control-freak nature often caused several family disagreements that Matt ultimately had to mediate.

"You don't seem to understand, Zach. I said… things are different. I know better now, and I've learned stuff. I can stop you from turning Anastasia against me." Katerina stepped forward, so she was in full view under the light. She'd trimmed her hair, applied subdued makeup, and appeared less like a drugged-out whore. Even the dark circles lurking below her eyes had disappeared.

"Are you off the crack finally?" Zach approached his door and inserted the key into the lock.

"Four months, not even a drop of liquor, babykins. Maybe we can be a family again." Katerina buttonholed him against the wall and lifted a hand to caress his cheek. "Don't you miss the good times we used to have?"

Zach paused, recollecting all the intense, memorable moments of their past. When they hit the bars and clubs every weekend and celebrated like it was their last night on Earth. When they spent the day at Coney Island, devouring hot dogs and pretzels until they were so stuffed and exhausted, they fell asleep on the beach overnight. When they promised to always care for one another, no matter how hard life got. Katerina had once been a beautiful soul, but the drugs destroyed all her potential.

For a second, he softened his attitude and let her pull him close to her lips. He wanted to feel intimacy again, love from someone who reciprocated on an equal level and treated him like there was no one else in the world. Then he remembered the times Katerina had left Anastasia home alone for hours while she disappeared in a desperate search for a hit to get her through a deep depression. When she dropped off the baby at her dealer's apartment as collateral, begging him to front her a fix while she went to the bank to withdraw money from Zach's account to pay for the drugs. When Zach finally found Katerina passed out in the gutter outside their former apartment and Anastasia was nowhere to be found, he'd gone ballistic.

"I'm not a fool, Katerina. As much as we had an amazing run, you broke us. You put your own greedy needs first and endangered our daughter." Zach recoiled from her touch and entered his apartment. As he collected his clothes and the birthday gift, Zach remembered that he too had compromised Anastasia's safety. But Zach had recognized the error of his ways, with his father's persistence, and enrolled in therapy. He'd been clean for years and made his daughter the number one priority each and every day of their lives.

Katerina followed him into the apartment. "This is your last chance to listen to me. I told you... I know things. Secrets that people might want buried. Don't underestimate a woman scorned."

Zach ignored Katerina and finished gathering his stuff. He grabbed her by the wrist and dragged her outside the apartment, locked the door, and tossed the bag over his shoulder.

"I don't care what you know. There's nothing you can do to hurt me anymore. I have custody. We're no longer together. Keep your promise to be a better mother, and we'll talk about it again in six months." Zach pushed past her and descended the unstable stairs, nearly cracking one in half.

Katerina rushed after him. "Off to your mother's birthday party, right? Maybe Olivia Glass would like to catch up tonight. It's been a while since she and I chatted. I've got a few things to discuss with the Queen Bitch. You know, about one of her sons' pasts… maybe not so recent past. I'm not talking about you either."

Zach stopped and narrowed a venomous gaze at her. A cockroach skidded across the steps in front of him. He crushed the bug with the heel of his chunky boot, then turned to Katerina. "I'm warning you. Leave us alone. I'll stop anyone who tries to interfere in my life again."

"We'll just see about that. What would you do if I showed up tonight?" Katerina loitered at the top of the stairs, arms crossed, seething with a deeper hatred and desire for revenge.

"You don't want to test me. You lost last time. I'll bury you next time."

"And you have no idea what I'm capable of finding out about your family. There are secrets even you don't know about, you prick. You'll regret this conversation, Zach. I promise you that much." Katerina pulled out her phone, made a call, and wandered further away from him on the second floor. "Our plan's a go. Meet me in fifteen minutes. We've got someone to crush, babe."

Zach had no desire to confront Katerina, only to get as far away as possible. What secrets could she have been referring to? Her juvenile nonsense would have to wait because he had other priorities. Zach would deal with his ex-girlfriend another time, another place, another life.

Chapter 7 – 4:00 to 5:00 PM (Emma)

Blessed with a classic hourglass figure and exquisite ivory skin, Emma kept her auburn hair trimmed short and swept to the side of her head with a jeweled butterfly clip. To adorn her barely five-foot-tall frame, she selected a body-hugging navy-blue dress Ethan had purchased for her days after their engagement. It now lent Emma the confidence and strength to pursue her complicated but critical evening plans. Though certain she'd attended to every task before leaving the apartment, Emma checked her appearance one final time. It was important for everything to function like clockwork that night. While Emma held a compact mirror as her guide to reapply eyeliner, a foul-smelling man unexpectedly elbowed her arm. She rubbed the resultant black smudge from her cheek when he offered a drunken apology for their collision and inquired about sitting next to her.

Emma slid across the cushioned leather bench in the loud, crowded, and tiny space, permitting him to commandeer more than half of the seat. She mumbled something about the obnoxious roars and chants surrounding them in support of an upcoming sporting event. The unfortunate raucous and the forced hot air pouring from a noisy and vibrating vent above them stifled any hope for relaxation on the rest of the journey. Emma sank further into the seat and her own percolating depression, noticing a forlorn bulk of apprehension rising inside her body.

The substantial heaviness chose to congregate in her chest, forcing Emma to blink away a smattering of tears and concentrate on a handful of difficult but precious memories. Poignant memoirs Ethan had repeatedly shared with her throughout the course of their relationship, one that had barely lasted two years before a vindictive and aggressive brain tumor stole their well-earned chance at happiness. Now a widow for just over three months, Emma habitually mourned the treasured lifetime she and Ethan had lost the opportunity to experience.

Today, Ethan's admiration and love for his father was most prevalent on Emma's mind. According to her late husband, unless none were in the picture or the individual was a cruel and indifferent human being, a boy loved and admired his father from the instant he was first cradled in the man's arms. Society regularly spoke of the connection between a mother and her daughter, but the one that blossomed between a father and his son offered equal power and fortitude. Ethan often regaled Emma with tales of the inscrutable bond he shared with Benjamin Glass.

After Ethan had returned to Boston from Ben's funeral, he'd crawled into a dark corner of the bedroom and crumbled into a devastated little boy craving the comforting touch of his recently departed father. Emma held Ethan's hand for hours as he conveyed memories of every childhood and teenage moment that had proven Ben was the single best father ever created. Ethan had talked until he was hoarse that afternoon, about all the ideas and plans he'd dreamed up to fix the country's most significant problems. It had been a passion project for Ethan after he'd learned so much about his father's ancestors who were unsung heroes and accomplished veterans throughout the previous centuries. Ben had been the one descendant to choose a different life, a professional career that enabled him to amass a sizable fortune and bequeath an enormous sum of money to each of his sons. Ethan often told Emma that Ben's one regret was never doing anything to honor his ancestors' war service and dedication to protecting the country. Ethan's last regret was never having fulfilled his father's wishes to honor them too.

Emma and Ethan hadn't discussed specific numbers that day, and once everything exploded over the summer with news of his shortened lifespan, Ethan's priorities changed. Between planning his wedding to Emma and his imminent funeral, Ethan neglected to revisit the subject of the inheritance with her. Emma assumed he'd forgotten to write a will and chose not to raise any immediate inquiries. When the appropriate time came, Emma believed Olivia would initiate the conversation with her. She trusted her mother-in-law implicitly, especially because until that time Emma had only known the version of Olivia who'd eliminated or controlled most of her negative and domineering behaviors.

An older couple, the wife balancing on a less than sturdy cane and the husband carefully latching on to his beloved, hobbled down the aisle beside Emma and the drunken man who'd sat next to her. Comparing herself to the two of them, octogenarians who'd probably shared a perfect lifetime together, Emma swallowed thoughts of her unluckiness. A widow at twenty-two years old was unfathomable to most people, at least in modern times. To Emma, it was more familiar than she preferred. Her older sister's husband had been killed in combat while fighting in Afghanistan, and her high school best friend's husband had been fatally injured on a construction site one week after their hurried wedding to avoid the scandal of an unwed pregnancy. Always one to intrinsically feel emotions on every possible level, any human's pain or death would crush Emma like a weight of infinite size.

Part of Emma knew her harrowing history justified why she'd rushed into marrying Ethan when he revealed his terminal diagnosis at their favorite Boston restaurant, *Le Joliet.* Although they'd only begun dating during her sophomore year of college, they'd lived together long enough to commit their futures to one another. When faced with looming tragedy, losing the person you loved most above all others, there was little time to analyze the pros and cons of a traditionally complex decision. Accepting Ethan's proposal was as much about his needs as it was about hers. Ethan deserved to die knowing he'd found the love of his life and experienced as many of the blessings that humanity offered given the little time he had remaining.

When Ethan expelled his last breath, Emma's heart burst into jagged shards as though Cupid's arrow had permanently destroyed its union. Each portion persistently refused to recognize the other or mend the fiery incision, even if the repair would leave only the slightest of visible scars.

The good half, the half that understood life was unfair and often excruciating but clung tightly to a hope for a positive outcome, allowed her to remain in contact with Ethan's family. Olivia Glass was devastated by her son's death, and if Emma could provide an interim connection while the grieving woman found her footing, it was the proper thing to do. Etiquette was essential in all situations: no matter the private agony, you must always subdue the public pain—Olivia's advice at her son's funeral.

Emma had stayed in Brandywine for a few weeks after Ethan's burial, waking early to stroll the family estate with Olivia and observe the sunrise each morning. They gazed at the brilliant oranges and reds of the fading foliage, the blinding yellow rays of the sun as they pierced clouds and shimmered in the stream that snaked along the property. Sometimes huddled together, hand in hand, seated on a bench in silence. At others, chatting about Ethan's boyhood imagination and unparalleled innocence—the things they'd never see again but were equally determined to never forget. Emma shared with Olivia Ethan's desire to fulfill his father's wishes and memorialize their ancestors who'd fought to secure so many freedoms. Ethan had planned to build a clinic that would offer free services to veterans coming back from war, especially those who'd been injured or suffered grave losses. Though Olivia deemed it a nice idea, she hadn't been in a place to process anything other than Ethan's death. Emma recognized Olivia was holding back from her, as if there was something important to convey between the two women who'd shared many common losses that year, but it never happened.

The battered part of Emma's heart, the half that rejected the harshness of reality and an indelicate paralyzing sorrow, hid beneath a well-concealed surface. Not even Emma knew that anger and darkness lurked below, at least not until it exploded from within her inadequately contained walls. All it had taken was that single incident where Emma became privy to something she'd never been meant to discover. Shortly after learning the shocking and confusing secret, around the time Olivia announced her three-month trip to Italy, Emma expressed an urgency to vacate the Glass home. The conversation she overhead between Diane and Olivia, now deemed *the incident* whenever it dared invade her mind, initially made little sense. Over time, Emma convinced herself she'd misunderstood the revelation and attempted to move on. Ignoring and burying any curiosity was the best solution. Besides, she had more important tasks at hand—to reassemble her life and devise a plan with incremental steps toward reaching her new normal. But deep inside, the news chafed and incited Emma not to let it go.

Though claiming a return to Boston after Ethan's funeral, Emma booked a flight to visit her family in Cleveland for Thanksgiving. They'd understood when she asked them not to attend her impromptu wedding as the occasion was about

Ethan's final weeks with her and his family, not about celebrating one of the biggest milestones in a girl's life. When Emma arrived in her hometown, she expected her family to comfort her, but she'd forgotten how much had changed. They instead pressured her to move on, focusing on decisions Emma wasn't yet ready to make.

Emma had been close with her parents as a young child. When her sister's husband died, Emma stood on the sidelines as they focused solely on their eldest daughter, prompting Emma to fend for herself as a teenager. She'd grown stronger during that awkward and difficult period, deciding to leave Cleveland and attend Boston University, where she ultimately met Ethan and learned how to support herself. Always interested in singing and teaching children, she quickly settled on majoring in music education and becoming a choral director. A passion for social media and journalism developed as a hobby, and she found herself blogging and influencing other young women who needed guidance. Whenever Ethan had been stuck late at the hospital during rounds, she built a network of followers around the world. Generosity and compassion leaped to the top of Emma's most favored ideals in others, courtesy of Ethan's benevolent ways. He had always been supportive of her goals and dreams, but upon his death, no one stood by Emma's side any longer. Emma was a lone star shining in a sky destined to serve millions.

Although Emma's parents half-heartedly soothed her trauma the first night, the following morning they demanded she return to Cleveland and help raise her sister's fatherless kids. *"You're all alone now, Emma. Your family needs you. You have bigger responsibilities than teaching music at that silly school. Forget your old life. Nothing worked out there, did it?"* Somehow, Emma's parents had forgotten how to properly console a daughter who'd lost a spouse, as they'd done when Emma's older sister suffered a similar loss. Emma was subsequently left to process her own grief and allotted minimal sympathy, at least nowhere near the level her sibling had received. According to her family, it wasn't the same because Emma and Ethan had no children. *"No money, no kids, not even your own house. Ethan might've been a good husband, but he's gone and left you with practically nothing."*

Despite the sudden shared tragic circumstances between the pair of widowed sisters, they couldn't regenerate an intimate connection. A wedge had been driven between them years ago, one too impactful and unwieldy to be repaired. *"Try living with this grief for years, baby sis. You barely knew the man. Don't you dare think you deserve more than me!"* Emma's sister offered no advice on how to handle the devastating grief—punishment for abandoning her years ago when moving to Boston—and when Emma attempted to open the doors to commiserate about their experiences, it was slammed shut. *"Get on with your life. Don't sulk when you've got people around you who need real help."*

To excavate her brittle heart from the razor-sharp ice newly enclosing and protecting it, Emma promptly left her parents' home and returned to Boston. She'd mistakenly assumed that Ethan's family would provide her with the intimacy she'd lost in her own, that she could trust the Glass clan to do right by her no matter how difficult. Emma wanted them to wrap her in their newly close-knit bonds and make her one of them. But given what she'd heard, it would never be possible. Lost and confused without any direction after Ethan's death, the *incident* with Olivia and Diane, and the lack of parental and sisterly support, Emma decided to post a memorial page on her blog so others could recognize the inexplicable loss of an amazing man named Ethan Glass. She merely wanted to ensure the world knew what was gone forever—a doctor who might find a cure for disease, a humanitarian who'd donated money to every needy cause, a genuine person whose soul shined brighter than all others.

Responding to the condolences and comments on her site motivated Emma to trudge through the pain and improve her outlook on the future. During that time, she accepted the possibility of a limited but forthcoming capacity to love again. Emma considered her previous conversations with Ethan's brother. Zach had made his intentions known; he was eager to fill the freshly open spot in her life, down the line when she was ready. Emma eventually invited him to visit her in Boston and help her move apartments before the end of the year. They developed a stronger friendship in the subsequent weeks, but she kept him at arm's length, uncertain whether he knew about Olivia's secret. Zach never pressed her for more, but occasionally, the temptation to take the risk of trusting in the universe's plan overwhelmed Emma. Ultimately, it was too soon, and she needed to allow herself a year to recover before opening her heart to another man.

Although Olivia had called from Italy a handful of times, Emma wasn't ready to reveal what she'd overheard in the conversation with Diane weeks earlier. At first, Emma harbored no intent to question her mother-in-law about the specific details. All she'd really caught was the tail end of their conversation when Olivia declared she had no intention of relinquishing control of Ethan's inheritance to Emma. Olivia had mentioned something about taking care of Emma's short-term expenses, but the full amount Ben had left his son belonged in the Glass family. Emma knew she'd only married Ethan so soon because he was about to die, and she had little interest in the money for herself. It was the other more shocking part of what she'd learned that day that fueled Emma's apprehensions and rising angst about the situation. Lingering doubt at the back of Emma's mind continued to pressure her about the exact words Olivia had uttered to Diane, forcing an uncontainable resentment to emerge after everything Emma had already suffered through that month.

They can't know Ethan was never blood related to us. The decision has been made. Diane and Olivia had been debating whether it was a mistake to hide the truth from everyone else, stunning Emma as she inadvertently eavesdropped outside the room. She wondered whether Ethan knew he had been adopted, and she developed a growing obligation to ascertain the answer on his behalf. Keen to discover whether she'd misunderstood the conversation, Emma employed her journalism skills to research Ethan's birth records, ultimately finding a record stating that he was undoubtedly their son. Had she misconstrued Olivia and Diane's peculiar chat?

The week after Thanksgiving, Emma had unintentionally confirmed what she'd overheard. Thousands of people around the country had commented on her blog memorial to Ethan, including someone who reached out to Emma and asked if they could have a private conversation. Emma agreed, curious to know what the individual wanted to discuss. Once they exchanged contact information, Emma learned the heartbreaking story of Ethan's true entry into the world—how Olivia Glass gave birth to a child who died quickly, and another woman had given up her son, hopeful he would have a better life with a man like Benjamin Glass.

Despite it having little direct bearing on Emma, the news was difficult to accept. Not only had Ethan been adopted, but he'd probably died without ever discovering the truth. Surely, he would've told his wife something so huge. Emma pondered the information, uncertain whether to confront Olivia or ignore what she'd learned. Ben had brokered an agreement with someone to adopt Ethan, and Emma had no right to insert herself in the situation. Ethan was never a blood member of the family; therefore, Emma wasn't truly a member of the Glass family. Although Emma had been Ethan's wife, it was only for a brief period, and Emma had little power to intervene. The news ultimately explained why Olivia wanted to keep the money. Emma vowed to trust the universe would fix things in time.

For weeks, she waffled between asking Olivia to tell her the truth and moving on as if it never happened. She even kept silent about everything when Zach visited her to help with the apartment move. Disillusioned by the actions of everyone around her, Emma chose to forget the entire situation, to ignore her own relatives and the rest of the Glass family, to start her life over from scratch. Soon after learning the truth from the person who'd contacted her on the blog, Emma began feeling increasingly depressed in her new apartment. One morning after waking up with jabbing pains in her stomach, Emma remembered that Ethan had actually mumbled more details about the inheritance on his deathbed. He'd referenced the specific two-million-dollar amount several times. Initially, she'd thought the pain medication had made him delusional, but he must've wanted her to inherit the money. Ethan had also said something about his brothers and his mother already being taken care of, and that he wanted his gift to go to Emma. He'd encouraged her to use some on herself but to also continue his philanthropic dream of helping others around the world. To honor his father's relatives.

Between the anger and the depression over Ethan's death, her family's selfishness, and Olivia's secrets, Emma found herself vomiting regularly in the period leading up to the holidays and growing further exhausted. She feared everyone had abandoned her, and in her slow descent into darkness, Emma developed a need to lash out at those around her. Emma had given up hope that Olivia would call her and relinquish the money, especially after remembering the conversation she'd eavesdropped on with Diane. All Olivia cared about was keeping her secrets hidden and preventing the money from leaving the family. Emma stopped returning Zach's phone calls, ignored Olivia's voicemails, and focused solely on befriending the person she'd met through the blog. Unfortunately, every little thing began to fester inside her like a mosquito that needed to be squashed.

Eager to quell the burgeoning frustrations before they exploded into something worse, Emma inquired directly with the Glass family attorney, Ira Rattenbury, if there were any tasks she needed to complete concerning Ethan's estate. Initiating the conversation directly with Olivia was no longer an option, at least not until Emma had gathered enough facts to properly prepare to face off with her mother-in-law. Emma assumed she might learn something important from Ethan's will, if he'd prepared one. Ira promised to investigate the situation, claiming he hadn't written a will for Ethan and wasn't aware of any other attorney who might've done so either. A week went by before Ira returned Emma's call, a period which left her progressively irritated and cynical. Emma soon lacked any faith in Ira's ability to be fair and honest despite the kindness he'd showered her with on the call and during Ethan's funeral. He'd been a trusted advisor to the Glass family for almost a decade, and Emma had only been around for a few months. Naturally, his loyalty would remain with the blood members of the Glass family.

While the inebriated man lounging next to her snored and jostled around, Emma recalled her conversation with Ira...

"As his wife, you're entitled to a portion of Ethan's inheritance. He died intestate, that means without a written will. Given Ethan had no children, but his mother is still alive, Connecticut law allows for a split between you both." Ira noted a small number to her, then mumbled several other words amounting to nothing other than legal jargon, and Emma had little understanding of inheritance law.

"I'm not quibbling over the ten thousand dollars in his bank account, but I was under the impression Ethan received a substantial inheritance earlier this year. Can you share the terms of it?" Emma stood her ground, eager to clarify the confusion and confirm the truth.

"Ah, yes, that is true. Ethan inherited the same amount as his brothers, but this money was specifically placed in an account for his future. He also designated his mother as the beneficiary. It is not included in anything that would be open for discussion on an inheritance."

At that point, Emma thanked Ira for his assistance and terminated the call. Ira's news began to rankle inside Emma. Both he and Olivia had lied to her, or, at the very least, withheld key information about Ethan's estate. Ethan wanted her to have the money; Emma had been certain he'd told her as much on his deathbed. What if Ira had been helping Olivia hide the money because Ethan wasn't Ben's biological son? Part of Emma considered provoking her mother-in-law, yet part of her hoped Olivia would confess everything and release Ethan's inheritance. Olivia never did. Emma even hinted about the money in a brief email just before the holidays, noting that she had plans to fulfill a dream of Ethan's. Olivia's reply indicated Ira was handling everything and that Emma should focus on healing.

Emma's cell phone suddenly vibrated, pulling her from the memory of the conversation with Ira. Caller ID indicated it was Ethan's aunt. Emma wouldn't have answered if it'd been Olivia or Zach as she wasn't prepared to talk to them. Diane had always been kind to her. They'd exchanged emails while Emma was in Boston and Diane visited Italy. She pressed accept and held the phone to her ears. "Welcome back. How was your trip?"

"Oh, Emma, I'm so glad to hear your voice. I'd love to tell you all about it, but I'm hoping I can do so in person. Please tell me you're planning to attend tonight." Diane's calm but enthusiastic voice carried through the phone comfortingly.

Emma hesitated, awkwardly smiling at the people sitting across from her when the man beside her snored again. After responding to Zach's earlier messages, she'd finished packing her luggage, waved down a taxi, and headed to the train station. Of course, she would attend Olivia's birthday party, but she preferred that no one else knew. The element of surprise needed to work in her favor. The truth needed to come out tonight. Ethan deserved as much, but he was gone and unable to speak for himself. Emma had to ensure that his brothers were aware of Ethan's true parentage, to connect everyone involved in the foolish attempt to keep the inheritance from her and prevent her from honoring his last wishes.

Emma swiftly refocused on the call. "I cannot lie to you, Diane. But I need a huge favor." Emma explained that she was planning to visit but wouldn't arrive at the beginning of the event. Between the train schedule and arranging a taxi to the house, she'd show up sometime later on. "Keep this a secret for me, please. I want it to be a big shock for Olivia."

Diane laughed like an innocent child being asked to keep a surprise. "Absolutely. I won't tell a soul. Olivia and I miss you. I hope you know that."

Emma kept her true thoughts to herself. "I'm sure you do, Diane. I look forward to seeing you." As much as Diane's role in concealing the truth frustrated Emma, she assumed Olivia had forced her sister to remain quiet.

Diane asked Emma to call when she knew her arrival time. "Maybe I can ensure everyone sticks around long enough tonight to see you."

"I'll let you know. It all depends on whether I catch my transfer in time." Emma hung up the phone and held back the tears. Her stomach had been off all day, but the smell of the man next to her and the uncomfortable phone call put her over the edge.

Confident her frequent colds, nausea, and exhaustion were simply distractions meant to play tricks on her and to push her into misguided sympathy for her mother-in-law, Emma refused to bury any doubts. It was important to confront Olivia, and what could be better than her birthday party when the entire family would be around to see it happen? Everyone deserved to know the truth. It's how Olivia had handled the situation last time, and it was how Emma would handle it this time. Challenging Olivia about the inheritance and Ethan's true origins would not be easy, but it was unavoidable. She was on a quest to fulfill a legacy, and much had changed in the previous days.

Ethan would understand, especially after everything Emma had recently learned, including the one remaining fact she was waiting to be proven. When the final unexpected secrets had become known not long ago, they were the straws that broke the camel's back. Had this merely been a small misunderstanding about Ethan's wishes and had Olivia agreed to transfer the money, Emma might've found a way to ignore the confusion or original hesitancy. Now there was too much at stake. Tonight, everyone would find out the truth, and things would be set back on the right course.

Emma leaned forward, resting her elbows on her knees and clasping her hands beneath her chin. "That wasn't easy. I can't believe how everything's ending up."

The person seated directly across the train from her replied, "You're certain they don't know I'm traveling with you tonight?"

Emma shook her head. "Most of them will be quite shocked. Seriously, what are the odds?"

"Of you showing up after ignoring them for weeks?"

"No, of the billions of people in this world, you and I somehow connected and joined forces to remedy what's imploding among the Glass family."

Chapter 8 – 5:00 to 6:30 PM (Everyone)

Olivia lingered outside the living room's entrance, massaging her temples and battling an exasperating migraine. No matter how much she pretended the blackmail letter hadn't arrived, it wouldn't stop torturing her. And now, not only was Ben's original letter missing, but this new extortionist's infernal letter had disappeared after her accidental and alarming collision in the hallway with Matt. Olivia interrupted herself from calling out her sister's name when she heard Diane talking to someone. Thirty seconds later, the caterer nonchalantly strolled by Olivia. "Oh, your sister is on the phone, ma'am. Just received the call."

Olivia thanked the girl donning a cherubic face and cocked her head toward the living room to determine whom Diane spoke with. Barging in to unleash her frustrations and fears wouldn't go over well. Diane was organizing various tapas dishes on a table in the far corner, her neck cradling the phone as she grunted. Though Diane couldn't see Olivia, she gritted her teeth and shouted, "I have nothing further to say on the topic. I cannot believe what you've done, George."

While waiting for Diane to finish the conversation, Olivia pondered the context of their argument and adjusted her treasured pendant containing a picture of all her boys.

With exasperation, Diane replied, "I don't know. I haven't seen Olivia all afternoon. What exactly did you send my sister for her birthday?"

Olivia gasped. Could George have sent the blackmail letter to her? She quietly slipped into the room and approached her sibling. Diane finished answering George's litany of questions, hung up the phone, and turned around to find Olivia staring at her.

"Ah, the birthday girl is finally awake," Diane bellowed as Olivia bit her lip and attempted a smile. "We've just set out all the food. Folks are still arriving, but you're welcome to grab a snack before we toast your special occasion." She clenched her fists, then slowly released them.

Dressed in a stunning black A-line dress, elegant turquoise shawl, and silver accessories, Olivia guardedly reached for Diane's hand. "What was that about a birthday gift?"

Diane shrugged angrily. "I'm not sure. George was being his usual aggravating self. He apparently sent you a birthday present. A photograph of something he thought you'd be very interested in seeing. He wouldn't tell me what it was, some piece of art, I gather. I assume you haven't opened it yet?"

Diane's response puzzled Olivia. The blackmail note was merely a few words on paper. Nothing that included pictures or imagery. It couldn't have come from George. "Did he specifically say photograph or a letter? Think, Diane. This is important." She clung to her sister's sweaty hand, both trembling noticeably enough for them to lock eyes, startle, and focus elsewhere.

"Liv, what's wrong? I…" she stammered before finishing. "I… yes, he said a photograph he thought would be perfect in our new home. It must be one of those packages over there." Diane released her white-knuckle grip on Olivia and pointed to an unopened stack on the table.

"Oh, that was oddly kind of him. I'm fine. I'll be fine, I mean. Thank you. I think the jet lag has knocked me out of whack."

Olivia wasn't ready to share the details of the mysterious and missing letter. Brushing her clammy palms against her hips, she recognized the caustic heat rising within her body. The pounding inside her heart reached the most sensitive part of her ears, where she swore it might explode with the wrath of an angry soul desperate for answers.

When Diane had tapped on Olivia's bedroom door earlier that afternoon, she received no response. Upon asking Pilar, the maid indicated Olivia had mentioned the need for an afternoon nap. Diane spent the next few hours setting up the living room for the much-anticipated event, changing into her party dress, and gathering everyone's presents and tokens as they arrived. "You'll need all your energy for that pile of cards and gifts on Ben's favorite console table."

Olivia scanned the shiny, sturdy piece of furniture and smiled. "Thank you. It means so much to be with everyone today." She stepped toward the family antique and studied the brilliant colors and mouthwatering scents emanating from the various tapas dishes. "The fig and prosciutto wraps look divine. I could use a relaxing drink. Is the bottle of champagne open, or should I fix myself a cocktail first?"

"We'll uncork the bubbles in thirty minutes. What'll you have in the meantime?" Diane stopped rearranging the plates and fixated on her sister's uncanny ability to appear bold and deferential at the same time.

"I'll get it. I'm in the mood for a martini, I believe. Something strong and classic." Olivia strode to the sideboard and prepared her drink. "Where is everyone else?"

"Teddy just arrived; he's on the phone in the study. Caleb and Jake are settling in upstairs. Zach took Anastasia for a walk outside. Matt and Margaret are changing clothes for your party. They'll be down shortly."

"I suppose Emma hasn't confirmed her attendance. I'm worried something terrible is going on with her. She's been distant, and Ira mentioned she contacted him a few times about Ethan's estate or will." Olivia dropped an olive in her drink and nervously swigged from the glass.

Diane turned in the other direction. "I'm not sure about Emma's arrival, to be honest. I guess we'll have to wait and see. What did she expect Ira to tell her?"

"He wouldn't say. Or rather, he couldn't say. Emma posed a few legal questions." Olivia separated two lace curtains and peered out the frosty window. "Are you planning to see him tonight? Ira's quite the splendid younger catch. I suppose that would make you a cougar. I've always liked that man," she replied, a hint of affection and admiration in her tone.

"No. Bite your tongue, sister. Now… tell me, does this table setting look off to you?" Diane had a fastidious nature above all else. Clearly, it was perfectly configured for the equivalent of High Tea.

"But you two seem to have a lot in common." Olivia glided past a leather sofa, gently tracing her palm across its arched spine. The table setting was immaculate, and Olivia knew Diane was intentionally changing the topic. "I invited him. It's my party, after all, right?"

"Yes, but I asked him not to attend. Please do not badger me about it. I told you earlier, I'm not ready to discuss my dating life. I need more time." Diane shifted her body so that Olivia couldn't see how flustered she'd become or the extent of her anxiety's rise to the surface, in particular the rash developing on her neck and upper shoulder.

"Fine. Tell me, does the sun always set this early?" asked Olivia, accepting Diane's intent to remain vigilant. "The evening seems rather dark and disturbing already."

Diane cautiously nodded. "Usually. It is February, still winter. No different from when we were in Italy." She paused and concentrated on her sister's diverted attention. "Expecting anyone else besides the boys to arrive?"

"No." Olivia closed the curtains and grasped her glass with both hands. A noise in the hallway redirected her interest.

"Happy Birthday, Mother," Teddy greeted as he entered the living room, firmly clutching a small package and a card. "Would you like to open your gift now or later?"

"Later," Diane insisted, grabbing both items from his hand and squeezing his shoulder. "I'll put them on the table with the others. We'll open them after drinks and appetizers."

"You both look well. How was the trip?" Teddy beelined it to the sideboard and fixed himself a Manhattan. "I trust the Italian lifestyle suited you well?" As he turned to await their response, the muscles around his jaw twitched twice, ultimately settling in a withering scowl.

Olivia noticed his dour facial expression. "Italy was fine. You seem… unsettled, possibly annoyed. Anything wrong, Theodore?"

"Of course not. He's worried about becoming a father any day now. Tell us, how is Sarah doing?" Diane joined him at the makeshift bar and poured herself half a glass of chardonnay.

Teddy was about to answer when Zach and Anastasia sauntered into the living room. He stole an extended gander at his brother and sighed, choosing to ignore his aunt's question. He downed a third of his cocktail, placed the glass on the sideboard, and shoved both hands in his pockets. "It's been a while, Zach. How's your little music career taking off?"

Although Teddy and Zach had begun to repair their relationship, Sarah losing the baby had eliminated any chance of immediate recovery. Teddy hadn't seen his brother since the holidays, associating much of his grief and anger to Zach's careless actions.

"Always good to see you too, Teddy," Zach muttered as he embraced his aunt. He whispered in her ear, "What crawled up his bum today? One day he's tolerable, the next he's a giant piece of—"

"Be nice. I haven't seen you in three months. I don't need to hear that language, Mister." Diane squeezed him with all her might and lightheartedly smacked his cheek. "You're no bucket of sunshine yourself." She hoisted Anastasia to her waist and nuzzled her neck. "I love your pink sweater. Is this your favorite outfit?"

Anastasia cocked her head, appearing to think about her response. "Ummm... second favorite. I like the blue overalls you gave me even better."

"She wears them all the time!" Zach poured himself a glass of seltzer. "You're gonna have to buy stock in that company at this rate."

Olivia cupped Zach's reddened cheeks in her hands. "I'm so proud of you. No drinking. No cursing. On time for the party. It's like you're a changed man, my son."

"Happy Birthday. It's like you never even left, Mom." He rolled his eyes at Diane and held his fingers and a thumb to the side of his head like he intended to shoot himself.

During the next ten minutes, Caleb, Jake, Matt, and Margaret wandered into the living room. Everyone scooped various tapas onto their plates, poured cocktails, and caught up with pleasantries. They hadn't been together since Christmas, and so much had happened in the last five weeks.

Margaret had initially brought the new baby downstairs to meet everyone. When Madison fussed, Margaret announced she was carrying her back upstairs to the nanny.

"No, I'll do it," Matt interjected, dropping a mini quiche into his mouth and snatching Madison from his wife. "I left something upstairs and need to get it. Besides, I'm craving some daddy and Maddy time!" Although the room was fairly comfortable, almost cool, his brow had begun to sweat, and his eyes darted around suspiciously.

When Matt disappeared, Margaret approached Caleb and Jake, who were speaking with Teddy. "So, you two have the same look of death warmed over as I do. Does your son like to wake you up every two hours to be amused and coddled?"

Jake palmed his forehead. "It's like clockwork. Just when I settle into a deep sleep, his screams start up again. I wonder if he was a tortured prisoner in a past life! Poor kid. I've taken to striking Caleb with my pillow to wake him up. He ignores it every time."

"That's how it always is," Margaret snickered, resting a hand on his forearm. "One of you is the crazy-nonstop-hears-every-sound parent, and the other is a lazy oaf! Guess which one I am?"

Caleb snorted. "I've known my brother for almost thirty years. Matt can sleep through a hurricane."

Jake enthusiastically added, "It must run in the family." He turned to Teddy. "What say you, soon-to-be-papa? Are you gonna be like the rest of your brothers or surprise us all?"

Margaret stood erect, both hands on her hips. "Based on Sarah's recent actions, I think Teddy might be the one to notice every single noise. Why doesn't your wife return my calls anymore? It's been over a month since we've seen her."

Teddy gritted his teeth. "Honestly, these are my last few days of freedom. Maybe we could talk about something other than babies?"

Margaret, Jake, and Caleb remained speechless at first. Jake was the first to cut the increasingly obvious tension. "Sure, no problem. I get ya. So… I understand you enrolled in art school. How's that going?"

Before Teddy could answer the question, Pilar and the caterer entered the living room with several bottles of champagne and a non-alcoholic sparkling cider. Pilar declared, "It's time to toast to the special birthday girl."

Matt snuck in behind them with his daughters, wiping his sleeve against his nose. "Glad I got back in time, birthday *girl*."

Olivia stared at her son, her brow wrinkling. "At sixty-eight, I don't think I'm a birthday *girl* anymore." She called her two oldest granddaughters to her side and hugged them both. "These are my girls, and I'm so glad to be home with them."

While Pilar and the caterer poured champagne and cider for everyone, Diane gathered all the birthday cards into a single pile. "First, we toast, then Olivia opens her presents. I'm glad you decided not to do a formal sit-down dinner."

"If there's one thing we learned in Italy, you eat all day long. Who can maintain a svelte figure with such an enormous meal?" Olivia smiled at her daughter-in-law. "Isn't that dress lovely, Margaret? Looks like you're doing a great job at getting back in shape! Don't give up hope. It'll happen soon."

Margaret wrinkled her nose, then dug her nails into Matt's forearm. "You've been such an inspiration."

Olivia turned and accepted a flute from Pilar, frowning at the woman's low-cut blouse. "And I thought décolletage was considered a faux pas of the past. You must be awfully chilly, Pilar."

Zach rolled his eyes and tossed out the first toast, allowing Pilar a chance to avoid responding. "To my dearest mother, a woman who's suffered one of the roughest years of her life. Losing a husband and a son may have taken its toll on you, but I'm impressed at how much you've grown these last few months. Cheers."

Olivia narrowed her gaze at Zach. "I could say the same to you, son."

Diane noted, "We've all lost people we loved this year, but it's brought us closer together. For that, I'm grateful to each of you, but mostly to my getting my sister back again. For years, we let too much history overwhelm us. I won't let anyone take it away from me again." She held her glass up again and wiped away a smattering of tears. "To all that the future brings."

Once everyone else added a toast, Margaret sent her daughters upstairs to check on their younger sister. Anastasia followed closely behind.

When the phone rang, Olivia jumped forward and knocked Margaret's glass from her hand. Some spilled on her dress, the rest to the floor. "Pardon, I guess it spooked me."

Pilar exited the room and answered the phone in the study across the hall.

Diane brought the bottle of champagne to her sister. "Need a refill, Liv?"

"That might not be such a good idea. I have plenty to say tonight. It is my birthday, and I should be as alert as possible." Olivia shrugged, then nervously chuckled while fetching a napkin.

Pilar returned to the room. "Ira Rattenbury is on the phone. He said it's urgent that he speak with—"

"Tell him I'll be right there. I'll take the call upstairs in my bedroom." Olivia handed her champagne flute to Diane and strode toward the entrance, where Pilar timidly shifted her body weight.

"Ummm... no, ma'am. The call isn't for you." Pilar stepped into the hallway and clasped her hands together.

"I don't understand. Who else would he need to speak with?" Olivia glared at the maid, disgruntled over her inability to properly address the room when someone had a phone call.

Pilar glanced at Diane. "It's for you. If you'll come with me, you can take it in the study."

Diane handed hers and Olivia's flutes to her sister. "I haven't a clue, but I'll be right back." Diane followed Pilar through the hallway. After Pilar shut the sliding door, everyone continued their conversations. Stunned over what just happened, Olivia wiped up Margaret's spilled drink.

"You okay, Mom?" Caleb asked as he walked toward her, resting his head against her shoulder. "I missed you while you were away. I'm glad we've started rebuilding things between us."

Olivia cradled a hand against his cheek. "So am I. Jake is a lucky man. I am a lucky mother. So much in our lives to be grateful for, Caleb. Don't ever take your family for granted." Her eyes appeared watery, but she retained control of the floodgates.

"Don't cry! I understand what you're saying. Sometimes things can be difficult, but we have to push through them. We all do foolish things, right?" Caleb looked across the room at Jake, who was engaged in an animated conversation with Zach involving inappropriate hand gestures.

"Everyone makes mistakes. It's important not to let them impinge upon the best of you. When you've done something wrong, you can't hide it. You have to be honest with the people closest to you." Olivia fussed with a few bangs that had fallen out of place. "Marriage is difficult. Parents make tough decisions to protect their children."

Caleb's chest puffed out as he inhaled a deep breath of air. "Don't you think things need to stay hidden sometimes? What if the mistake will hurt the person you love, and it will never happen again?" He swallowed the rest of his champagne and set the glass on the nearest table.

"I've asked myself that question many times in the last year, Caleb." As Olivia pondered his inquiry, her finger circled the rim of her flute. "The past is never fully gone and forgotten. It lives on through other people. Sometimes our mistakes stay buried until we think they'll no longer be a problem. Life has a funny way of surprising us with the truth."

Caleb dragged his mother closer, placing his hand on the back of her shoulder. "Are you saying it's better to admit what you've done wrong rather than conceal it?"

Olivia wobbled her head in slow motion. "I'm not the best person to ask that question anymore. Living with the burden of something you should confess will take years off your life."

The sliding pocket doors opened again, interrupting Caleb and Olivia's conversation. Diane grimaced as she approached them.

"Everything okay?" Olivia inquired casually, offering her a champagne flute.

"It's not okay, but it's not a problem we have to deal with this evening." Diane reached for her glass and chugged the remaining sparkling wine.

A loud guffaw erupted across the room. Bent over and laughing hysterically, Zach pointed at his brother and then stuck his middle finger up in the air. Noticing his brother's mischievous nature boiling over, Caleb excused himself to check on Zach's discussion with Jake. "Sorry, Zach needs to be put on a leash soon. If he's telling Jake the story about how he found out I was gay, I'll kill him."

"It's got to be easier than how I found out," Olivia replied as her face flushed, recalling Jake's tumble down the steps wearing nothing but a towel. "Be kind to your brother, Caleb." When he wandered away, Olivia crossed her arms and studied Diane's body language. "What's going on? You're looking a bit haggard, sister."

"George changed his mind about the divorce settlement." Diane and her husband had been separated for over a year, and shortly before she'd left for Italy, they had a final discussion to agree on splitting any money and proceeds from the sale of their home.

"I'm confused. He does or doesn't want a divorce anymore?" Olivia watched as Zach, successfully controlled by Caleb and Teddy, collected and sorted through all the birthday cards.

"George still wants a divorce, but apparently he found out about the money Ben left me last summer. He's requested fifty percent of the inheritance, claiming it's part of our marital assets." Diane rested a free hand against her chest. "George doesn't deserve a penny of that money."

"He wants one-hundred-thousand dollars from you? That's ridiculous!" Olivia's body stiffened.

Zach approached his mother and his aunt. "This is supposed to be a birthday celebration. Why do you both look so glum? Are you upset because of how many candles we've crammed onto your birthday cake, Mother? Don't fret, you're not that close to a century yet!"

Diane regained her composure, even laughed at his witty remark. "No, no. It's okay. We were just discussing something that can wait until tomorrow. George is stopping by in the morning." She noticed the cards in Zach's hand. "Let's open presents. Cards first, save the big items for the end."

Olivia smiled and frowned, tension marring her forehead. To alleviate her discomfort about Diane's phone call and the blackmail note hiding within the recesses of her mind, she exhaled loudly and shook her head slightly as if to nudge the painful worries away. "That's a good suggestion. Hand me one, Zachary. I could use some pleasant news."

Everyone gathered around Olivia as she opened the first item. All the ladies from the charity organizations Olivia previously ran had signed a card and given it to Margaret to deliver to Olivia for her birthday. "Oh, how lovely. They chipped in and purchased me a spa getaway next month. I can't wait." Olivia thanked Margaret for bringing the card to the party and promised to call her friends the following day.

"I'll read the next one," Zach said, selecting an envelope from the pile. "Isn't that our tradition? We read the cards aloud to the birthday *woman*?"

Olivia was focused on a discarded napkin that had fallen on the floor when Zach yanked something out of an envelope. "This one appears to have been opened already. And it's a little sticky. Yikes! Who did what to this envelope?" he announced before turning to his brother. "Were you thinking about Ryan Phillippe's ass again, Cabbie?"

Caleb flushed a wicked shade of red, recalling the time Zach and his other brothers had walked in on him jerking off to the naked swimming pool scene in *Cruel Intentions*. "Drop it before I tell Mom about your new *hardware*!"

"Lord, I can't deal with the likes of you terrible boys right now," Diane interjected, covering her eyes and forehead. "I found that near the stairs earlier. I think someone dropped it."

Zach snorted and unfolded the paper. "It's not exactly a card, but a letter. Here goes—"

Olivia looked up at the precise moment Zach began to read, nearly hyperventilating. "No, that's not a birthday card. It doesn't belong in the pile."

Zach uttered a discouraging, judgmental noise. "Oh, is this from a secret admirer you met in Italy? Guess what, everyone… Mom doesn't want us to read her naughty sex letter. I guess we know where Cabbie gets his dirty mind from!"

Olivia jumped up and tried to snatch it from Zach's hands, but he was too quick for her. He read…

You took something from me. I'll be back after sunset tonight to collect my payment for silence. If you don't come through with $100K, it'll be an honor to shatter the House of Glass into dozens of broken shards. Time's up!

The room remained still except for a sudden burst of scorching air from a ceiling vent. Zach gripped the letter and rotated from face to face like a warped carousel ride. When he landed on Olivia, she cast her eyes to the floor and winced. "My news wasn't supposed to come out like this."

"I don't understand. What's this all about?" Zach inquired, his eyes widening.

Diane gasped. "That's the same amount of money George just asked for."

Fire soared through Olivia's veins, eager to blast through every pore of her skin and singe the world around her. She clenched her teeth, channeling Teddy's uncontrollable habits. When she reopened her eyes, the pounding in her chest grew more intense. Olivia lifted her head, willing herself not to lose control in front of her granddaughter who'd returned to the room. "I will tell everyone shortly, but first, I need a few minutes to myself."

"What kind of a joke is this? Not another stupid letter again." Teddy grabbed the envelope from Zach's hands as Anastasia wiped a milk stain coating her upper lip.

Matt joined his brother in perusing the envelope. "The letters on the front are smudged. I can barely make out the name *Glass*."

"Then how do we know whom it's for? It's not a birthday card, maybe it belongs to someone else," Margaret suggested, clinging to Matt's arm.

Caleb studied Jake, then cocked his head to the side. "It can't be for you, Aunt Diane. Your last name isn't Glass. If George asked for the same amount of money, it's merely a coincidence."

"Who left it on the stairs, where Aunt Diane found it?" Zach queried.

"I must've dropped it after reading it earlier today. Just give me a chance to think. Please stop all this chattering. I can't stand it!" Olivia pulled her shoulders back and stood tall, compelling herself to deal with the change in circumstances. She bobbed her head to regain her focus on preventing an outburst, keenly aware of the sweat pooling at the back of her neck.

"Did you wipe your name off the front? This looks like a food stain of some sort." Jake sniffed the envelope in Teddy's hands. "It's sugary sweet, but it also smells like the bottle of Ben's cologne that Caleb brought home last fall."

Anastasia pawed at her father's arms. "It's my fault, Daddy."

Zach picked her up. "What do you mean, penguin?"

"Somebody delivered it this morning. I used it as a coaster because Grandma said not to put glasses on the table." When Anastasia wept, she buried her head in her father's chest. "I'm sorry."

Realizing she needed to set a better example, Olivia rushed over to hug her granddaughter. "It's okay, honey. You did the right thing."

"Did you answer the door all by yourself, baby girl?" Zach nudged his daughter's head away so he could look into her eyes and comfort her.

She shook her head. "He gave the note to Melanie and said to give it to an adult. I forgot."

"I found it on the table after the juice spilled on it," Olivia noted, then instructed everyone to remain silent. "I'm certain it's for me. I'll explain the reasons in a little while. Can we take a thirty-minute break, so I can prepare for a difficult conversation?" If she didn't escape the room, Olivia couldn't be held accountable for her actions. It was imperative to isolate herself, to ground her anger and terror, to carefully address yet another family drama in the best possible manner.

Diane was the first to respond. "Of course. Margaret, Matt, why don't you check on the kids? Teddy, I could use some help in the kitchen."

Caleb and Jake volunteered to clean up the dirty plates in the living room while Zach consoled Anastasia, who thought she was in trouble for answering the door and losing the envelope. Teddy handed the letter to Zach and stomped away.

After everyone left, Olivia bolted up to her bedroom, mumbling to herself about the true severity of the predicament. She'd tried to contain her unbridled rage all afternoon, hopeful the note was only a foolish attempt to scare her. But now that everyone had heard the blackmailer's words, the situation grew all too real. Secrets had defined her entire last year, and nothing permitted her to move forward. Clawing at her hair and scratching her fingernails on her scalp helped unleash the fury building inside her. The pitch black and eerie calm of the bedroom prompted her to wail like a woman on the verge of a nervous breakdown.

Olivia kicked the door shut with the force of a dozen horses, grasped the doorknob with tenacity, and arched her back against the solid wood barrier that kept everything and everyone temporarily distant. "All right, whoever you are... the sun has finished setting. My patience has worn thin. Just when do you plan to arrive this evening? And what the hell is this nonsense all about?"

Chapter 9 – 6:30 to 7:00 PM (Olivia)

As Olivia paced the floor of the guestroom, the soles of her shoes created a scratchy, raspy sound. It bounced and echoed around the insides of her head, unnerving her further. Devastation clogged every pore in her body, stifling her ability to think clearly or navigate a path away from the disaster unfolding downstairs. She'd already worked out a solution earlier in the day, one where her family would never know about the extortion attempt. Ravaged by the accidental revelation of the extortionist's note in front of the entire family, Olivia recalled what she'd accomplished since finding the envelope on the table and mistakenly assuming it was a birthday card six hours earlier after brunch…

Upon reading the blackmail letter, scaling the stairs, crashing into Matthew, and locking herself in the guestroom, Olivia threw herself on the bed and pounded her fists into both pillows. While sobbing and nearly hyperventilating, she experienced an unusual and alarming reaction. Her body and mind separated into two distinct versions of herself. One was eight months younger, blissfully unaware of a charging veracity about to change her life, standing only a few feet away in the study moments before opening the last letter she would ever read from Ben. The other version hovered behind her, one hand supportively placed on her shoulder, another thumbing the new blackmail note and willing her to set it aflame in a roaring fire in the same study a mere twenty feet away from the table where it'd been found.

Olivia cursed herself for not destroying Ben's original letter upon its arrival, when he confessed that one of their sons had been secretly adopted. She'd previously stood in the corner of the kitchen with a match burning in her quivering hand. In the end, she hadn't been able to relieve herself of the letter's burden and locked it in her bedroom safe. Once she calmed down, Olivia accepted Destiny's gift to her. If given the choice, Olivia would still have wanted to know Ben's secret last spring. While Ethan's true parentage impacted every aspect of her life, it also oddly altered much of it for the better.

During each of the visits with her sons the prior summer, when she allowed herself to witness their pain and brutally relive the mistakes of failed motherhood, Olivia had learned that being a mother wasn't about giving birth to an infant. Nor was it about creating a precious new life to design an idyllic, more perfect image of yourself. Had she bore a daughter, Olivia might've been tempted to raise a clone, one that was stronger and more admirable. But she bore only sons, and instead of coddling, adoring, and prioritizing them, she delegated to *the help* to address those necessities.

Eager to appear stronger than she was, Olivia often bragged about her children's successes to the ladies in her society organizations. As her sons grew older, she pushed them to do more whenever they failed to meet her expectations. When they made decisions she disagreed with or refused to support, Olivia privately rolled out the red carpet for her passive-aggressive personality to intercede, thus ensuring her sons would shift their actions and plans. It'd worked almost every time, frequently with little pressure. Olivia hadn't been a mother to them when they were children; she functioned as the driving force that propelled each toward a path of failure. Ben's letter had thankfully redirected a future destined for unfettered disaster, by forcing Olivia to evaluate her life and its associated blunders.

Everything she'd gone through the previous summer had taught her a lesson—never run from the truth. Despite all the grief it had caused, Olivia gathered the entire family together last fall to thrust every issue into the open. The family needed to know about Theodore's desire to become a painter, Matthew's addiction to pills, Caleb's secret husband, Zachary's cheating with Sarah, and Ethan's death sentence. Though certain things required a delicate hand and to be shared with a limited group of people—only Theodore should be privy to what'd happened between his brother and his wife—all the facts tumbled out, except the most critical one.

Olivia had labored over the decision for months, but Ethan deserved to know the truth. He'd been weeks away from dying, and he had an opportunity to meet his biological mother, Rowena Hector. Simultaneously, she feared the devastation upon learning his father had traded infants with another woman, and that he belonged to a different set of parents, might've pushed Ethan closer to the grave. Ethan had already lost his adopted father. His biological father, a journalist, had been declared dead during an explosion in the war in Bosnia. Olivia knew the only way to allow herself to blossom into a genuine and selfless mother was to let Rowena decide whether to meet her son after all the years. Rowena ultimately preferred not to disrupt her son's life, and Olivia respected the woman's choice. Ethan died without knowing the truth. His two mothers had reached the verdict together, thinking only of his best interests.

Olivia contemplated the things that might not have happened if she'd never confronted her sons with their secrets. Theodore would never have unearthed the courage to sell Ben's law firm, ultimately a significant impetus to force the entire family to heal. Matthew would have overdosed or risked the lives of his children one too many times such that it conjured irreversible tragedy. Caleb would have remained secluded in Maine, Olivia none the wiser to his husband and adopted son. Zachary would have yielded to Katerina and consented to raise Anastasia in an unhealthy environment. Despite every prayer, Ethan still would've succumbed to his terminal illness. The only difference might have been how Olivia responded to the utterly dreadful defeat.

When a loud knock had startled her earlier that day, Olivia ignored Diane's tap on the bedroom door, too weak to raise such an accusatory question at that point. She disregarded Diane's persistent voice and forced herself to recognize the new challenge facing her. Olivia quickly combed through her purse and realized the blackmailer's note was missing. Hopeful it had fallen somewhere in the hallway, Olivia waited until Diane closed the door to her bedroom further down the hall—she'd been watching through a small crack in the frame to be certain—and raced outside the room to scour the entire space. It wasn't anywhere, including the staircase. She was about to check if it'd plunged to the first floor when she heard another door open on the opposite side of the hallway. Olivia wasn't ready to talk to her sister or anyone else in the family, so she rushed back to the bedroom and locked the door again. After freaking out that someone else would find the note, she convinced herself to focus on the immediate priority. How should she handle the blackmailer's request for money?

First, it was important to consider who had sent it. Olivia listed people she believed knew the secret. Only Diane, Rowena, Ira, and Olivia were cognizant of Ethan's true parentage. Diane would tell no one. Ira had been a trusted family advisor for years. Olivia conjured no other explanation than assuming Rowena must've changed her mind upon learning how much money Ben had left the family when he died. Olivia dialed Rowena's number, but she received no response and left a voicemail asking her to call back as soon as possible. Olivia mentioned nothing about the blackmail note, wanting to hold the upper hand for now. Rowena harbored all the evidence she needed to prove that Ethan had been switched at birth; Olivia had delivered Ben's second letter, the one originally meant for Ethan, to the woman. But if Rowena had that letter, why would she need the one Ben had written to Olivia? Olivia was still unable to locate the letter Ben had written to her too; someone other than Rowena must've stolen it and used it to blackmail her.

A wide realm of new explanations navigated through Olivia's overburdened mind. Had Ben been mistaken all those years ago? Could their baby have survived? No, it wasn't possible. Ben had clearly explained the child died. Had some nurse reappeared to cash in on the secret? In today's developing panic, wild possibilities plagued Olivia with an intensity so grand, her brain was willing to accept any ridiculous notion. Maybe the nurse had lied to Ben, or he was so distraught that he couldn't tell her the whole story. If her real child were still alive, could this be the blackmailer who wanted their fair share of the inheritance? No, too far-fetched. Was one of her son's involved? Could Ira be trusted? All the potential theories made increasingly less sense. Her boys would just ask for the money. Ben was an intelligent man who never would've let a stranger or the nurse take advantage of him. Ira had earned a significant amount of money from the Glass family throughout the years. Rowena was a kindhearted and generous woman. Olivia couldn't believe the blackmail note stemmed from the woman's loss and pain at never meeting her son. Although they hadn't spoken in person since their final conversation in the park, and only once via a brief telephone conversation when Rowena promised not to reveal the truth, Olivia trusted the woman.

Olivia scrounged through her luggage and purse one final time, but Ben's letter had assuredly vanished. In her anxious state, she couldn't recall the full history of its presence in her life. Olivia decided to step through everything she'd done with Ben's letter since deciding not to burn it, including placing it in her bedroom safe, to which no one else had the combination. It was her personal safe, not the one she shared with Ben. She used a special number from her childhood that not even Ben had guessed, though she ultimately told him what it was one day.

Olivia had removed the letter several times last summer and fall, rereading it to find a clue that'd reveal which son Ben had spoken of. When Ira located Rowena, and Ethan's two mothers met in the park, Olivia decided to keep Ben's letter as a reminder. One that would ensure she'd always do the right thing in the future. The week before her trip to Italy, Olivia removed the letter from the safe and stashed it on her bed with the rest of her clothes, intending to transport it with her. She left to run several errands, and when she returned to instruct the maid to pack her luggage, Olivia noticed the letter was in a different spot. She tossed it in her purse, thinking little of it at the time; it had probably just blown over from the air vent or a pile of clothes had fallen into it. No one in the family was a snoop, and the servants had all been properly vetted. Olivia again read the letter in Italy, eager to hear Ben's voice or visualize his words, even if it continued to deliver traumatic news. She last remembered seeing it the morning before she and Diane had departed for the Rome airport to return home.

Had the letter been lost between Italy and Connecticut, no one would've known it belonged to her. It had her and Ben's names in it, but no addresses—nothing truly traceable to them. The blackmailer had to be someone close to the family. Olivia planned to confront Diane despite implicitly trusting her sister. Diane would never do anything to hurt her, but she had been acting peculiar in the last two days since their arrival home.

Rather than believe Diane was involved, Olivia considered what to do about the money.

She processed the blackmailer's request, deliberating on the meaning behind each individual word, ultimately deciding one-hundred-thousand dollars, while an enormous amount of money, was easily accessible to her and wouldn't hurt her future ability to survive financially. Once certain no one was looking for her, Olivia snuck out of the house and borrowed Diane's car to drive to the bank. She obtained a certified check made out to cash, waffling on whether she'd later go through with paying the blackmailer. Olivia simply knew she had to have the money available in case she decided to keep the secret hidden. Ben's reputation was at stake. Her privacy was incredibly important. When she returned, she debated the best approach to question Diane and to prepare for the blackmailer's arrival. Though she searched in a few places for Ben's original letter and the black-mailer's new threat, neither turned up. She finished dressing for the party and prayed everything would turn out for the best.

Now, after Olivia escaped to her room a second time, once the letter was read aloud to everyone, a more fervid confusion materialized. When Ira had called the house during the party, Olivia thought he wanted to further discuss the unresolved issue resulting from Ben's accident the previous spring. During Ben's car collision with the overpass, Destiny snatched not only his life but that of his chauffeur too. Ira ensured Olivia that Ben's insurance would cover any potential costs when the driver's family requested a small settlement to cover their losses. Olivia had agreed to an amount and was waiting for Ira to confirm everything was finalized. But Ira hadn't called for Olivia; he wanted to speak with Diane.

Olivia eventually assumed that if Diane had taken Ben's original letter for safekeeping, George must've found it in Diane's possession; that was the only potential explanation. She'd heard her sister mention something about the dollar amount shortly after Zach read the extortion note downstairs. George had foolishly requested half of the inheritance Ben left Diane, the exact amount indicated in the blackmailer's missive. George had to be the one extracting money from Olivia, and that's why Diane was acting strangely the past few days. What was she hiding?

Was he trying to dupe them both out of money? Had George simply navigated two separate avenues to collect what he felt belonged to him? If the blackmailer were George, reasoning with the man would amount to nothing but aggravation. He'd always hated the Glass family, insistent that Diane ignore her relatives and spend every waking moment catering to his needs. George would never walk away. Olivia decided she would convince Diane that they should pay George for his silence. If they were aligned, the entire family would assume the threat had come from him and was connected to Diane's divorce.

Olivia peeked at her watch. She'd been gone almost fifteen minutes. As she walked toward the bathroom to rinse her face, someone knocked on her door. "Yes?"

"Liv, open up. It's Diane."

Olivia scrambled to the door and dragged her sister inside the room. It was finally time to discuss the situation. At the same second, they both said, "It's George."

Diane hugged her sister. "I'm so sorry. I don't know how he found out."

"The letter. Did you take Ben's letter?"

Diane stepped backward. "No. I... you mean the one he left you last year revealing your baby died?"

Olivia's body begged to scream loudly, but it emitted only a low grumble. "Yes, George must've found it at your house."

"That's not possible." Diane informed Olivia that she hadn't seen the letter since last fall. "Did you open his birthday gift? Did you find the photograph he was talking about?"

Olivia shook her head. "It's probably downstairs in the pile. We should check as soon as we go back to the living room. I don't know what that has to do with this blackmail request. Do you?"

"Liv, I need to tell you something—"

Olivia interrupted her sister. "Unless George somehow sneaked over here, how else could he have gotten Ben's letter?" Olivia explained to Diane that she'd taken it to Italy and had last seen it at the airport in Rome. "It went missing in the last forty-eight hours. I thought it fell out of my purse and you picked it up."

"No, I'm sorry, Liv. I never took the letter. I don't understand how George found out. Maybe the two amounts are just a coincidence." Diane insisted they ransack the bedroom even though Olivia had already rummaged in every nook and cranny. "Are you talking about the envelope in your purse? A white one, if I recall correctly."

Olivia began to fear the blackmail note wasn't from George. If Diane had never taken Ben's letter, then it meant someone else was behind the shenanigans. But who would do such a risky thing? Olivia collapsed on the bed and cradled her head to her knees. "Yes. When did you last see it?"

Diane paused, reflecting on the flight home. "I remember wondering what it was on the plane, but I'd fallen asleep and forgot to ask you. I believe I saw it in the car on the way home from the airport."

"You saw it here, when we pulled up to the house?"

Diane nodded.

"The driver carried our bags to the front door. Matthew was home and brought our bags upstairs." Olivia paced the room, worry lines furrowing deeper on her forehead.

"What did you do with your purse?"

"Tossed it on the bed. Then I went downstairs to see my grandchildren." Olivia rubbed her hands together, squeezing them into fists.

"Maybe it fell out. Did you check in between the mattress and the frame?" Diane rushed over to the bed and tossed all the pillows aside.

"I slept there last night. Pilar made the bed this morning, then I took a nap. Could she have found it? I don't trust that woman." Olivia dropped to her knees to search underneath the bed. "Could the envelope have tumbled to the floor?"

Diane joined her sister on the carpet and peered between the bed frame and nightstand. "I found it!" She sat back against the side, handed the envelope to Olivia, and inhaled deeply. "Maybe no one noticed it."

Olivia tore the envelope open only to find it empty. They feverishly wrenched apart the bed, moved the nightstand, and delved high and low. "It's not here."

Diane shook her head. "Then either the blackmailer found it and left behind the envelope or you are mistaken about when you last had it in your possession."

Olivia growled. "I'm going to confront Pilar. I bet she took it."

"Stop, Liv. You can't blame that poor girl until you know she's responsible. Let me ask her. I'll be a little more rational in my approach." Diane grabbed her sister's arm and rubbed her shaky hand. "Even if she did, that doesn't solve our problem."

"What do you mean?"

"Blackmailers don't give up. I've watched too many television dramas to know better. You can't give in to the request."

"Then what are you suggesting?" Olivia yanked back her hand and leaned on the mattress to lift herself off the carpet. "I tell everyone the truth?"

"Yes." Diane gripped the nightstand to support herself as she stood.

"I know I should, but I don't think I can." Olivia had wavered throughout the day. Nothing would change if the rest of the family learned the truth. Ethan was gone. Ben had insisted his money be divided equally regardless of one child being adopted. It might even bring everyone closer. "What if my sons are furious that I kept this secret from them for the last few months? We've only just begun to grow closer again."

Diane sighed. "I spent a few moments watching everyone earlier. I'm not so sure everything is truly fixed."

"What do you mean?"

"Teddy seems angry. I caught him gritting his teeth and cracking his knuckles several times. Matt's eyes are distant and unable to focus. Could he be using drugs again?" Diane paused, waiting for her news to sink in.

"I saw it too. Do you really think it's a good idea if I tell them what was in Ben's letters? They finally stopped asking about it while I was away." Olivia slanted her head toward the door when she heard a noise.

Diane rushed over and twisted the door handle. When it opened, Pilar loitered in the hallway.

"Everyone's waiting for you both to return, ma'am. Shall I tell them you're on your way?" Pilar folded her hands together and smiled. Diane moved to the side when Olivia called her name.

"Pilar, I seem to have lost a piece of paper. A letter, perhaps yesterday when I arrived. Do you know anything about it?" Olivia stood tall and gently dabbed a tissue under her eyes.

Pilar shook her head. "No, ma'am. I left your things alone, exactly as requested. I saw an envelope under the bed, but I didn't touch it. Is that what you're looking for?"

Diane replied, "It was. Unfortunately, the letter that was once inside it is no longer present."

"I can help search, if you'd like." Pilar's offer appeared genuine to Olivia.

"No, thank you. We'll be down momentarily. You may leave." Olivia waited for the maid to head downstairs, then turned to Diane. "I can usually tell when someone is lying."

"Was she?"

"No, I don't think so. She's hiding something, but I doubt it has anything to do with Ben's letter." Olivia entered the bathroom to fix her hair and makeup.

"So now what do we do, Liv?"

"We're going to face the rest of the family. The blackmailer's note said he or she would show up sometime this evening. I will meet with this scoundrel, and once I know what he or she intends to do after tonight, I'll remedy the situation." Olivia applied replacement mascara to her lashes and a fresh coat of lipstick, then stared inquisitively at her reflection in the mirror.

"Meaning you will tell everyone the truth." Diane joined her sister's side and met her gaze in the mirror. After holding it tight for several seconds, she flinched and looked away.

"Meaning I will collect all the facts, inform the blackmailer I won't play his or her game, and then I'll confess my sins. If my family is still hurting or hasn't learned to change their ways, they need another dose of reality." Olivia sealed her makeup bag and seized her sister's hand. "Let's get back downstairs while I still have the courage to do the proper thing. Wait... didn't you have something you wanted to tell me?"

Diane shrugged and stopped her sister from leaving the room. "I... yes, I guess maybe I'm concerned about—" she vacillated before Olivia's interruption.

"Is this why you've been acting so strange lately? You're not yourself. You haven't been since Italy." Olivia worried that Diane was considering returning to George, which was something she intended to prevent if necessary.

Diane took a deep breath and patted her chest. "Never mind. I'll be fine, but I thought of something else, Liv."

"What's that?"

"The first name on the envelope was illegible."

"So?" Olivia gaped at Diane in confusion.

"We keep wondering who sent the blackmail note, but…."

Olivia grunted. "Out with it, Diane. We don't have all day. I need to tell the boys the truth."

"Liv, what if the letter wasn't meant for you? Maybe someone else is being blackmailed."

Chapter 10 – 6:30 to 7:00 PM (Caleb)

"You people need your own television show. A soap opera has less drama than the Glass family." Jake dragged Caleb upstairs to check on their son. "Seriously, who blackmails someone with a letter in the twenty-first century? It's so 1980s. Like Alexis Carrington a la Dynasty and Angela Channing a la Falcon Crest."

"Once again, I have no idea what you're talking about. You've kinda got an obsession with these Grand Dames, Jake. Maybe I should start coaching you on famous architects or landscapers." Caleb followed his husband into their assigned bedroom and watched as Jake peeked in on their kid.

"He's conked out. Must be the Connecticut air." Jake excused himself to use the bathroom.

Caleb recalled the blackmailer's message. His mother had assumed it was meant for her. Caleb worried she was incorrect, especially after receiving an unexpected phone call hours earlier.

While Jake had been settling into their room that afternoon, Caleb ran to the store to buy a few toiletries. In the morning rush to leave Maine on time, he'd accidentally forgotten a bag at home. When he pulled into the parking lot to buy the replacement items, Chester from the adoption agency called to notify Caleb and Jake about an incident that'd recently occurred. Their adopted son's birth mother, Caitlyn, had incorrectly identified the baby's biological father on the official paperwork. The man who signed a legal document terminating his parental rights was not the child's father. The child's father was a parolee Caitlyn had dated and never wanted to see again. He'd been picked up by the police and reincarcerated for the last six months. Upon release, he tracked down Caitlyn and learned she'd given birth to his child.

The man had contacted the adoption agency to find out his son's location, but the agency wouldn't provide him any details without proof of paternity, and even then, it would be too late to do anything. The supposed biological father hung up, promising to sue the agency. Chester intended to call Caleb and Jake the following week to keep them informed of the situation, but someone had broken into the place last night. Although the agency stored a majority of the paperwork electronically, because they'd just had a discussion with the potential father, a few printouts remained on Chester's desk. He'd planned to go through them again on Monday. While Chester had no proof the biological father stole the paperwork, it was currently still missing.

Chester confirmed the files listed Caleb's and Jake's names and address. It was possible that the biological father would show up and try to see his child. Chester didn't think the baby was in any danger. The man hinted at receiving payment and seemed disinterested in raising a kid. Caleb initially freaked out but realized it was the agency's responsibility to remedy the situation. He directed Chester to apprise him of any further developments, then left a voicemail for his neighbors to ask them to look out for anyone hanging around their house in Maine while they were gone. He didn't tell them why, only that he thought someone might show up without warning. Caleb intended to tell Jake later that night, after the birthday party, so he didn't ruin the evening for his mother. A few hours wouldn't cause any harm.

But now, the blackmailer's note suspiciously reminded Caleb of his discussion with Chester. There was no way the black-mailer had his family's address in Connecticut, though. How would he have tracked him down? Caleb ignored his develop-ing wild theory about the guy showing up to ask for money for his son. Even if he had, Caleb and Jake would refuse to give in to the guy. It made him nervous that the man had been in prison several times, but there were enough people in the Glass family to keep everyone safe. Caleb need not make the situation any worse.

Jake returned from the bathroom with his cell phone in hand. "Did you leave the neighbors a voicemail earlier? They've been trying to reach you, but you didn't answer."

"Oh, crap. Ummm, give me a minute." Caleb checked his pocket and realized he'd left his phone on the dresser. He rushed over and scrolled through the device.

"No worries. They said some guy was knocking at our door when they were dropping off the mail. Maria told him we were visiting your family in Connecticut this weekend." Jake yawned and stretched his back.

"She what?" Caleb's heart pounded as he braced himself against the dresser. "Why would she do that? Don't people know how to keep their mouth shut!"

"Whoa! You having a moment, S*ybil*?" Jake leaned into the crib to monitor their son. "Don't wake him up. We've got some craziness to deal with downstairs."

Caleb read the text messages from Maria, who hadn't given out the Brandywine address but confirmed he was at his family's place. She had communicated with the guy prior to receiving Caleb's message. Caleb had also noticed a message from Warren indicating he was eager to get together again. He turned to Jake and said, "There's something I need to tell you. It's important."

"Would this have anything to do with that new text on your phone from Airport Guy? You left the phone here while you were showering. I happened to be standing nearby and caught his message pop up on the screen." Jake crossed his arms and leaned against the wall. "What did he mean about having fun hanging out at the bar with you *that night*?"

"It's silly. Really. He's nothing important right now. But we need to talk, Jake. I should've told you sooner. I thought it could wait." Caleb approached Jake, a nervous grimace occupying the lower portion of his face, and reached for his hand with a tenuous grip.

Jake scowled, pulling further away. "Is something going on between you and this guy?"

"Please. Don't worry about him right now. Listen to me." Caleb jerked his husband closer. "I think that note we just found might've been meant for me."

"The blackmailer? What's going on Caleb? I was only teasing you earlier about your family being as cray cray as a daytime drama. Are you playing games with me?" Jake gently shoved Caleb away and snatched the phone from him. He searched for the main messaging app.

Caleb tried to steal the phone but failed. "Chester called. Something happened today. I need to tell you about it."

Jake ignored Caleb's recent call list and perused the last few lines of his and Airport Guy's exchange. His cheeks flushed as he internalized the words. Jake's trembling jaw dropped before he read aloud from the messages. "Airport Guy asked you '*Does Jake know we've been meeting?*' You responded, '*Not yet. I hope he'll forgive me. I feel horrible for lying to him.*' Do you want to explain what this means, or should I keep on scrolling further back? I kinda get the picture already. Maybe you know your 1980s drama queens better than you've led on, you stupid, callous ass. What the hell is wrong with you?" He clasped his hands together and shook them furiously at Caleb, then collapsed against the nearest wall and sucked in every ounce of air around him before roaring so loudly he scared himself. "Can you feel my heart pounding, Caleb? You did this to us! It's gonna bust out of my chest and crash onto the floor. You've made my skin crawl. It's sickening to think what you've done."

Caleb finally reached the phone and hurled it across the room. It rammed into the lamp and awakened their son. "Please, it's not as bad as you think. Don't worry about that right now. We've got other priorities, Jake. The blackmailer might've tracked us down here, and he wants money—"

Jake gripped the corner of the nightstand and considered flipping it over. At the last second, he thought of his son and released the immediate need to retaliate against Caleb. "Seriously? What kind of guy did you get involved with? If you're gonna cheat on me, at least choose someone who doesn't fuck you over once he's done screwing you the first time. First because you lust after him and then to make you pay for the pleasure of it." Jake collected their son from the crib and threw up his palm at Caleb. "I need some time to process this. I deserve a full explanation, but right now, I want to be alone. With our son. Does that even mean anything to you? Or has everything been a lie?" Jake didn't offer Caleb an opportunity to answer. After storming out of the room with disappointment and fury emanating off his entire body, Jake trudged down the hallway toward the front staircase.

Caleb remained in the doorway, wallowing in his embarrassment and panic. He'd explain everything to Jake later. He'd fix their problems and make everything right again. His priority was figuring out if the blackmail note had come from their son's biological father. He tried to use his phone, but it had cracked and would no longer turn on. He removed his laptop from its case and booted up the device. Once it connected to Wi-Fi, he looked up two phone numbers, then commandeered the phone extension on the nightstand.

His first call was to Chester, where he explained that he might've gotten a note from the baby's father. "I'm not sure the guy knows where my family lives, but if he knew my name and that I was in Connecticut, he probably could've found this address."

Chester stuttered before replying uneasily, "I can't tell you how sorry I am this has happened. When he and I spoke, he only seemed to desire money. Do you want me to update the police? They're here now, finishing the report on the burglary."

"No. Not yet. I need to talk to my mother to see how certain she is that the note was meant for her. I'll get back to you when I know more, but please, keep trying to find this guy and call me if you learn anything." Caleb hung up and kicked the laptop case across the floor.

Chester had said the alarms went off at the agency between three and four in the middle of the night. Maria had seen someone outside Caleb's house around eight o'clock that morning. Even if the guy had figured out where Caleb would be tonight, was there enough time to arrange for the note to be delivered that quickly? He'd need to find out from Aunt Diane when she'd found it near the stairwell and Anastasia when it had originally arrived. The timing was close, but it could've happened.

Caleb dialed the second number and waited for Warren to answer.

"Hello, who's this?"

"Warren, it's Caleb. I'm calling from my family's house in Brandywine."

"Hey, Caleb. So, you're actually at your family's place?" Warren noted, slight agitation accompanying his voice.

"Yeah, long story. You seem upset."

"I thought you said you weren't gonna go," Warren added, his voice growing more distant and thinner. "Anyway, ummm… how's the visit going?"

Caleb recalled telling Warren that he might skip the family event, but he'd only said it because he changed his mind about trying to see him while at home. "Not well. Jake found out about you. Well, sort of... he saw your message and knows you by the name Airport Guy. Things have spun out of control." Caleb explained about the adoption agency too.

"That's awful. How's Jake taking the news about me?"

"He's angry, of course, but he wouldn't discuss it. I didn't have time to explain what happened. He took off, and now, well—"

"You're in Brandywine, right? Caleb Glass. Glass is your last name. I didn't get that wrong, did I?" Warren queried.

"Yes. Is there a reason you're asking?" Caleb cocked his head, confused about whether they'd shared surnames. He was pretty sure it'd come up before, but the way Warren just spoke made the tiny hairs on his neck rise. Although he didn't know Warren all that well, his voice and responses were currently unrecognizable.

"Are you related to the people who run the law firm Glass, Wittleton, and Davis?" As Warren finished speaking, a clicking noise appeared in the background.

Caleb pulled the phone away from his ears, suddenly alarmed. Had someone else picked up the line? "Yes. My father owned the firm, but he passed away. We sold it a few months ago."

Warren cleared his throat. "I'm actually not too far away from you right now. I drove in for an upcoming meeting. If you need any help, I could come by. I have a commitment this evening but would be happy to connect tomorrow."

Caleb suddenly wondered whether Warren could have sent the note demanding money. He decided not to mention anything about the blackmailer's request. What exactly would Warren gain by blackmailing him? The only leverage Warren had was that he and Caleb had met up several times, and that wouldn't be worth one-hundred-thousand dollars. Something felt odd, and Caleb couldn't relinquish his concern. "I should probably go,

Warren. I only called to tell you that Jake found out about you. Depending on how upset he is, he might contact you. I'm sure he has your number from my phone."

Warren replied, "I'll let you know if I hear from him. Maybe it's a good thing if he and I talk. Would fix a bunch of problems between us all, wouldn't it? Anyway, if you need anything, you can count on the new and improved Warren. Hopefully, I'll see you soon."

Caleb prepared to hang up when he heard breathing on the phone. "Is someone else on the line?" The call dropped, and Caleb hung up the receiver. What was going on? He needed to find Jake and get everything sorted out. Caleb rushed out of the bedroom and bumped into Matt in the hallway.

"Why were you just talking to *Warren Payne* on the phone?" Matt whispered, aggressively pushing his brother against the wall. "Are you in cahoots with him?"

Caleb shoved Matt with a burst of anger that'd built up inside him. Puzzling lines stained his forehead. "How did you find out about Warren?"

Matt reached into his pocket and squeezed a crumpled napkin, feverishly looking through it for the pills he'd bought earlier from the dealer in the parking lot. "Where are they? This is so fucked up. I need one to calm down."

Caleb slanted his head forward and grunted. "I thought you were done with that stuff. Have you relapsed, Matty?"

"Is this why Wittleton and Davis won't give me my job back? Are you helping Warren Payne with his lawsuit against the firm? Are you trying to get me fired?" Matt seized his brother's neck and slammed him against the wall multiple times. A blind rage had overcome him, and he couldn't prevent himself from assaulting Caleb.

Surprised by the attack and frustrated with everything going on around him, Caleb elbowed Matt in the ribs and punched his jaw—not viciously, just enough to keep him from retaliating while he escaped. When Matt pulled away and cradled his abdominal area, Caleb tore off down the steps. "What the heck has gotten into you?" Caleb wondered what Matt had meant about the lawsuit, but he had other priorities to solve. How did he know anything about Warren Payne? That made no sense; he'd never said the guy's last name on the phone. Upon running into Pilar, he asked if she'd seen where Jake and the baby had gone.

"They're in the kitchen with your brother Teddy," she responded, scanning his torn shirt and shortness of breath. "Is everything okay?"

"No. Yes, sorry, family issues. I don't know what's going on. But we're all going to find out very soon." Caleb shuffled down the hallway and entered the kitchen. "Teddy, will you excuse us for a minute? I need to speak to Jake alone."

Jake hovered near the stove, watching over a bottle he was warming up. Teddy sat at the breakfast nook, holding Caleb's son in his arms. "Sure," he replied, with an unusual melancholy in his voice. "It's been so long since I've held a baby." Teddy pulled the infant more securely against his chest as he stood. "Do you want me to look out for him while you guys chat?"

"No, thanks." Amongst all the chaos, Caleb couldn't help but notice how comfortable Teddy looked with the baby in his arms. "You might be a natural, brother. Even better than my first time holding him."

Jake nodded, accepting the baby from Teddy. "He looks like a real father, doesn't he?"

Teddy exited the kitchen and walked toward the dining room, leaving Jake and Caleb alone. Jake noted that the caterer had stepped outside to make a phone call but would be back shortly. "What happened to your shirt? You better keep these anger issues away from our son. It's like you've been replaced by someone I no longer recognize, Caleb."

"I'm sorry, Jake. I promise you; I will explain what happened. You shouldn't have found out from a text message. It was stupid, and I will make it up to you." Caleb remained near the breakfast nook, unwilling to make Jake any more uncomfortable. He knew Jake was nervous about being in the Glass family home, especially with all the drama unfolding around them. It would be foolish to add embarrassment and a deeper concern.

"I just don't understand it. After everything we've been through together. Everything I endured in the past, how much I've been hurt and abused. I thought I could trust you, Caleb." Not usually prone to freaking out in front of others, Jake struggled to stop the angst from building up.

"We'll talk about it more soon. You need to know what happened back in Maine before I tell the rest of the family." Caleb explained the news from Chester, including his panic that the blackmailer's note could be about money in exchange for their son. He decided to wait on exploring his suspicion that Warren could be involved, as it seemed too far-fetched to be possible.

Jake rushed over, then paused and hesitantly embraced Caleb, still upset about Airport Guy but needing to focus on protecting their son. "We have to do something. No one will take Ethan away. He belongs to us."

"I know, babe. We have to safeguard him. I think the best way is to tell everyone that the blackmail note is for us. When the fool shows up to collect his or her money, if it is our kid's biological father, we'll have safety in numbers."

"I'm so angry with you right now, but I can't let that stand in the way," Jake tentatively snuggled closer to Caleb's chest. "Don't we have enough money from your Dad's inheritance? We can use that to get the guy off our back."

"I don't think it's a good idea to give him the money tonight, though. We need to fix this legally, okay? Believe me, you don't want extortionists following you around forever." Caleb pulled Jake away to look him directly in the eyes.

"Are you asking me to trust you with this decision?"

"Yeah. I know I screwed up earlier, but we can't let someone else step in the way of our happiness. We should also talk about my relationship with—" Caleb stopped just as the caterer returned to the kitchen.

A short blonde with pigtails apologized and quickly turned the opposite way to walk toward the stove, avoiding direct contact with them. "Oh, I'm sorry. Should I come back?"

"No, it's okay. You have a knack for showing up at just the right moments today, huh?" Jake replied to her back as she still hadn't turned around to interact with them. He took a minute to acknowledge her kindness, then said, "Well… yeah, I should get our son back to his crib." He offered Caleb a strange look over the caterer's weird reaction, then exited the kitchen saying, "We also need to finish talking with your family in the living room."

"Yep, but I hope we don't have bigger problems than we realize." Caleb needed to fix everything, to make his father proud. His and Jake's son came first, above anything else, and if it meant ignoring his innate desire to keep the connection with Warren, he'd have to let the man go.

The caterer finally turned around when Caleb cleared his throat, noting, "I'm sorry if I interrupted anything. This place is a little crazy today. Makes me nervous."

Caleb shrugged. "Me too. Something bad is gonna happen tonight. I just can't shake the feeling."

Chapter 11 – 6:30 to 7:00 PM (Matt)

Once Zach read the blackmail note aloud to everyone in the family, Matt had flattened his hand against one of his jean pockets and cringed. He'd waited for Olivia to run up the stairs, then grabbed his wife's hand to hold anything tangible that might calm him down, rather than the contents lurking beneath the denim. They were the next two to exit the living room. During the break, he planned to check on the children, but as soon as they reached the second-floor landing, Margaret pulled her husband into their bedroom. "What was that all about?"

"I don't know," Matt sheepishly responded, shoving one hand in his pocket to ensure both pills he'd earlier wrapped in a tissue were still present. Only one was, though, at least it seemed to be the case. He began freaking out about where he'd lost the other one. "My mom was stunned, huh?"

Margaret threw up both hands and groaned. "She's back for a day and a half and inciting drama here already. Seriously, why is everything always so complicated with the Glass family?"

Matt had been tempted to tell his wife earlier that Wittleton and Davis refused to bring him back into the firm. In the end, he decided it could wait until tomorrow, after his mother's birthday party. Matt hated lying to his wife, but too much was orbiting around him and gravity was failing at a remarkable rate. She'd done so much for him, and he hated to continually disappoint her. But he recalled his sponsor's constant reminder, *one day at a time.*

"Give her a break. She's back home after two months away, and it's her first birthday without my dad around. She'll be fine tomorrow." Matt wrapped one arm around Margaret and kissed her cheek, his other hand digging into the deep hole of his jeans. He found nothing but lint and a few wood shavings. "Love you to pieces, babe. Why don't you check on the kids? I'll see if Mom's okay and find out what this crazy note's about."

"Okay. I love you very much too. You know that, right?"

Matt nodded, then detached from his wife's comforting embrace. "Of course."

Margaret began to leave their bedroom, then turned back around with an inquisitive glint in her eyes. "Nothing from Wittleton and Davis yet?"

"Nothing."

Once Margaret departed, Matt tore apart his pockets and searched for the missing pill. Upon coming up empty-handed, he slumped on their bed and recalled everything that had transpired in the last several weeks between him and his drug dealer…

Matt had fruitfully avoided all non-prescription, prescription, and recreational drugs since entering rehab. He was committed to staying clean and sober, and he owed it to himself and his family to correct his past slip-ups. During one of his outpatient counseling sessions, Maude introduced Matt to a friend who'd been drug free for over a decade, attributing his success to the practice of keeping a bottle of pills as a reminder. Many recovering addicts thought this was a stupid idea. Although meetings and friends could help him ignore the cravings, maintaining a bottle in his medicine cabinet was too risky. To Maude's friend, it was a safety net. Knowing he had access to them but committed never to taking them helped him stay on the straight and narrow.

Around the same time Matt found himself tempted to overdose on a variety of over-the-counter medications, he'd received a text message that he interpreted as a sign. Quinn, Matt's former drug dealer, had been sprung from jail and contacted him. Matt decided to take Maude's friend's philosophy to heart and tested out the theory. He met Quinn two weeks ago and purchased a bunch of pills, something he could carry around as his own reminder. Afraid to share his real address, Matt didn't want to meet him at the house. However, Margaret was due any minute with their impending child, and Matt preferred to stay home all the time to be available for her and the kids. He had no other choice but to arrange a meeting a few blocks away, claiming he needed a bit of exercise and was just taking a jog through the neighborhood.

For an entire week, knowing he had the pills available killed his desire to use any drugs at all. Then Margaret found them in his coat pocket. Rather than confess the truth, Matt explained that he'd discovered them in an old jacket he hadn't worn in months and was planning to give them to his sponsor to dispose of. Keen to remove any impulsive reactions from her husband, Margaret insisted she throw them out. "It's for your own good, honey," she promised, cupping Matt's cheek and making him feel even worse.

Days later, Matt's cravings stirred again. He fought them off until the day his mother arrived home and upended the balance of their family's temporary status quo. All night long, he'd dreamed about the magic of the pills. When he woke up this morning, he tried everything to keep himself busy and prevent himself from organizing another deal with Quinn. After Matt hung up with Wittleton upon learning he couldn't return to the law office, he'd caved and convinced himself to take the plunge.

Matt lied to Margaret and claimed he'd forgotten about a coffee meeting with his sponsor. Margaret never questioned when he went to see Maude, citing that she understood the bond between the two of them and the importance of seeking guidance whenever it was needed.

Given Maude had just denied him the possibility of joining her company, Matt had no desire to meet her. He instead arranged to meet Quinn in the parking lot of a café just outside town. Quinn only had a handful in his possession at the time, but Matt purchased them just to get through the weekend while he conjured the best way to change Davis and Wittleton's response. Quinn was expecting another drop that afternoon, and he offered to meet Matt later that night in the same place they'd convened a couple of weeks ago. When Matt noticed his brother Teddy in the parking lot, he quickly agreed to meet Quinn on the same corner a few blocks from his house. He instructed Quinn to contact him later when he was close to the spot. Matt planned to sneak out of the party and buy the balance of the pills.

After rushing out, he returned home and focused on his wife and kids, totally forgetting to check the special app he'd installed to communicate with Quinn. He'd gone to extra lengths to ensure Margaret would never stumble upon his exchange with the drug dealer in the regular texting app on his phone. After working on the dollhouse in the garage a second time, where he kept removing and replacing the pills in his pocket like a machine stuck on repeat, he'd persuaded himself not to take the pills that evening, even though he kept them in his pocket as his beloved safety net reminder.

Forgetting about the earlier part of his day, Matt now concentrated on the blackmail note as he shifted positions on his bed. Currently, Matt was the only Glass who lived in the Glass family home. Teddy and Sarah lived several towns away. Zach only slept at the house occasionally when he wasn't traveling for work or stuck in Brooklyn at the studio. Caleb lived in Maine, and their mother had only just returned to the country that weekend. Margaret would never get herself caught up in something so scandalous as blackmail. Matt convinced himself the note couldn't belong to anyone else but him. Might it all be a joke? No, he assured himself... it was too blunt. Someone had gotten access to his home and delivered the note directly to him.

Matt considered all the possible suspects, people who'd possibly have a grudge against him. The first person that came to mind was his drug dealer. Matt recalled a bit more of their past together when he'd stolen from Quinn before the guy had gone to jail. He never fully paid Quinn back, and despite his youth, the delinquent was wily and cunning. He could be holding proof of Matt's previous mistakes and illegal activities. Had Matt's decision to maintain a bottle of pills purely as a crutch blown up in his face? Or had he gotten away with it? Until this point, they'd only exchanged first names and phone numbers. What if Quinn figured out Matt's identity and planned to extort money out of him? The guy was shady, but it'd be quite a leap to go from buying several thousand dollars in drugs to asking for one-hundred-thousand dollars to keep silent about some mysterious secret. Besides, Quinn didn't know his address. Matt was safe.

Matt checked the clock on the nightstand and verified their proposed exchange was at least an hour away, so he switched over to read his texts in the special app, in case Quinn had changed the eight o'clock time. Somehow, Matt had missed the guy's response minutes after he'd pulled out of the café's parking lot earlier.

Quinn: *Rumor is you've come into a bunch of money. Maybe the price of my special products needs to increase, especially if you want to keep this our little secret, buddy. I suspect you had something to do with my arrest. Let's meet at your place this time. If I understand correctly, your address is...*

Matt gasped when he read his address in Quinn's text message. He debated how to respond, ultimately choosing not to do so at all. How had Quinn figured out the exact location of the Glass estate? If Quinn had learned Matt inherited two million dollars, and he presumed Matt had caused his stint in jail—even though Matt had nothing to do with it—maybe Quinn was plotting to score off his client. Matt curled into a ball on the bed, wondering whether he should consider Quinn a legitimate suspect. Although it'd be a longshot, Matt worried it was entirely possible Quinn had delivered the blackmail note. He had only one other option, and it was even more flimsy.

Matt originally thought he'd only stolen about ten grand from Warren Payne, but it could've been more than he remembered. And since Warren was adamant about Matt being terminated from the firm, there was something larger going on with the situation. Matt decided to search for Warren on social media. Matt only had a *Facebook* account, so he started there. No one remotely seemed like a match, so he googled him. Matt learned Warren had grown up in the Midwest, launched a business with a college buddy, but after the two had a falling out, they sued one another over rights to the patents for their innovative technology software. That's when the Glass firm had been hired to solve the issue, which ultimately led to Matt stealing money from them to cover his own financial woes.

Unable to discover much else on Warren, Matt decided to call Wittleton and Davis to see if they heard anything else from him. If they couldn't offer anything new, maybe it was a sign that Warren had nothing to do with the blackmail note. Despite speaking to them several hours ago, he had to try every option, to ensure the note had nothing to do with him or his past foolishness at the firm.

Matt picked up the extension in his bedroom and heard Caleb talking to someone. After listening for thirty seconds, Matt realized his brother and Warren Payne knew one another. The Warren on the phone had an identical voice to the Warren Payne whom Matt had previously spoken with on many conference calls. When the discussion ended, Matt rushed out of his bedroom and down the hall, catching Caleb just as he exited his room. He confronted him in the hallway, and during the struggle, Caleb elbowed and punched Matt before running off. "You coward!" Matt groused before checking his pockets again. The two pills were supposed to be wrapped tightly in the napkin in his pocket. But one was missing. What had happened to it? It must've fallen out somewhere, he convinced himself.

Matt sat against the wall in the hallway, contemplating his next move. What exactly was going on between Caleb and Warren? Were they having an affair? Was Caleb helping Warren to sue the Glass family firm to collect more money? Hadn't Caleb gotten enough from their father's inheritance? As Matt considered the conversation and his brother's personality, he struggled to believe Cabbie, his brother's dreaded childhood nickname, would intentionally hurt anyone. Although they'd grown apart for a number of years, Caleb was the kind, generous brother. Maybe not as much as Ethan, but Caleb was a close runner-up.

Matt winched himself up and walked down the hall. His body trembled with angst and disappointment at the thought of his brother's betrayal. When he poked his head into the nursery, Margaret held a finger to her lips and mentioned Madison was sleeping. His little angel was nestled against her mother's chest, a picture-perfect memory he'd hold on to for years. Their serenity immediately comforted Matt despite the storm brewing inside his mind. Matt told her he'd meet her downstairs in a few minutes and returned to their bedroom. He slipped into the master bath to check if he'd suffered any damage from the tumble with his brother. Staring into the mirror, Matt recognized the dichotomy of his personality and conscience battling for control. The rational husband desperate to heal for the sake of his family versus the monster compelling all the drama and fear to disperse once he consumed a magic pill.

How could my brother be so foolish!? Matt questioned how Caleb had gotten himself into such a convoluted and dire situation with Warren Payne. It seemed bizarre to accept Caleb was being dishonest or making cavalier mistakes; he was too smart and careful. Maybe Warren was blackmailing someone else in the Glass family. If Warren knew Caleb was in Brandywine, and he also had discovered the address of the Glass family home, Warren could've sent the blackmail note. What if the guy was somehow trying to extort money from several people in the family? Any idea was a possibility, at least in his paranoid delusion.

No matter how hard he tried to stop it from happening, Matt's world was crumbling around him again. He only had one pill in his pocket. The other was lost, probably gone forever. One pill would calm him down for the evening, just enough to deal with all the drama. When they discovered the blackmailer's identity that night, everything would end. If the note had been meant for him, he'd willingly tell his family about his role in Warren Payne's lawsuit. If it was Caleb who'd gotten himself into trouble, Matt would support his brother. If Caleb were scheming with Warren, then maybe he and Jake could talk Caleb out of whatever he planned to do.

When he extracted the tissue from his pocket, Matt knew he harbored little conviction to stop himself from swallowing the pill. He turned on the faucet, let the chilly stream pool in the palm of his hand, then eagerly brought it to his lips. After he popped the pill in his mouth and slurped the water, Matt turned off the faucet and exited the bathroom. Relaxation would be moments away.

As he strutted down the hall, he crossed paths with Jake, who carried the baby with him. "Some party, huh?"

Jake shook his head. "Yeah, I never expected all this drama tonight. I need a stronger drink. Your brother can be an ass sometimes."

"Is everything okay with Caleb?" Matt grew curious about Jake's words.

"Minor squabble. Well, maybe not so minor, but I shouldn't have said anything." Jake shrugged and shuffled down the hall. "Gotta put our son to bed."

Matt waited for Jake to walk away before he descended the stairs. Had Jake learned about Caleb's affair or whatever was going on with Warren Payne? Maybe he should talk to Jake about it during the party. It might identify the blackmailer more easily. He checked his watch and realized he'd been gone for almost twenty minutes. While heading down the stairs, Anastasia asked Matt a question then rushed to her bedroom. He could barely understand her and kept on walking.

Just as he arrived in the foyer, the front door opened, and Diane brusquely trundled inside. "Hey, honey. Have you seen your mother? I went outside to check on her, but she's not there. I can't find her anywhere. Maybe I'll check her room again." Diane removed her coat and hung it in the closet.

"No. I was with Margaret, then Jake and Caleb. I haven't seen her since we took a break." Matt reached out to hug his aunt. "You look like you could use one."

Diane squeezed him back. When they separated, she gently patted his cheek. "Thank you. I have something important to tell your mother, but I'm not sure how to do it."

"Is this about that blackmail note?" Matt inquired.

Diane shook her head. "No, I don't think so. At least, well, I doubt it."

"Oh, okay… you think it was meant for her, though, right?" Matt pinched the bridge of his nose and gulped. "It's super warm in here, isn't it?"

"Not really. You okay, Matt? Your eyes look a little glazed over."

"Yep. Just thrown off by that note. Can you tell me what you think it's about?"

Diane looked in the opposite direction, then bit her upper lip. "No, not really. That's something I should first discuss with your mother. Let me check upstairs again."

As Diane bounded the steps, Matt had the distinct impression his aunt was hiding something from him. Was she aware of the blackmailer's identity? He thought back to the events in the living room earlier, when Pilar interrupted to tell Diane she had a call from Ira Rattenbury. Was it really possible that Diane's husband, George, was the culprit? Matt admitted he could've read far too much into the situation with Warren and Quinn. It could be a coincidence that he was also hiding something from his family. People's minds often played tricks on them, worrying they'd be caught for the littlest things. Criminals usually gave themselves up with the smallest details. *Just keep your mouth shut, Matt.*

Matt felt the pill kick in and begin to calm his nerves. It wouldn't be enough, though. He jogged into the living room and directly to the sideboard. No one else had returned to the party yet. He poured himself a glass of merlot and swallowed a large gulp. He'd have preferred a beer, but there was none in the room. He finished the first glass of wine quickly, then poured another, just as he heard his name being called from the hallway.

Once Matt approached, Pilar said, "The caterer would like to know if we should hold the next set of dishes or if you'd like us to set them out? She's eager to get back into the living room for some reason, something about the timing being off. Maybe one of the appetizers is ready, I suppose."

Matt rolled his eyes. Margaret had planned the party. She should make the decision. "Hold off ten minutes, then bring them back in. We have important business to attend to tonight." As Pilar slunk away, Matt noticed his aunt returning downstairs.

Diane met him in the hallway as she was texting someone on her phone. "I found her upstairs. Your mother should be here any second."

Matt returned to the makeshift bar and soon heard his voice called when Olivia slipped into the room. "Would you please fix me a drink? I am gathering everyone together to address the note Zach read earlier. I have something to confess."

Matt watched as his mother rotated one-hundred-and-eighty degrees and vacated the room to locate Pilar again, wondering why everything seemed to swirl around him. He fixed her favorite cocktail, then swallowed the contents of his second glass. "This ought to be quite the night. Someone's got us all stirred up, and I'm beginning to feel quite relaxed finally. This party needs to liven up a bit!"

Chapter 12 – 6:30 to 7:00 PM (Teddy)

"Hand me a dishrag, Teddy," Diane said as she rinsed her sticky fingers under the faucet and caught it midair. "Thanks, honey. I must've spilled the wine after your brother read that note aloud." Her voice trembled, a side effect of her history of subservience to George. While her husband had never physically abused her, it was made clear on multiple occasions that she often ran off her mouth more than he'd like.

Teddy clasped his hands together, pensive and moody over the turn of events. "Of course. Do you really believe Uncle George would've sent that to you?"

Diane shook her head and shrugged. "Possibly."

"I'm afraid I must agree with Caleb. The letter was meant for someone with the surname Glass." Teddy's gaze drifted from his aunt to the caterer who appeared to be eavesdropping on the conversation. He politely directed the woman to leave the room for a few minutes.

"I've got to watch the mini quiches. They'll burn if I don't remove them soon." She smiled and bent in front of the oven to check on them. "I think I'll just stay inside. Pretend I'm not here. Happens all the time at big parties."

"You work for us. Now get out of the kitchen before I'm no longer civil about it, you foolish girl." He crossed his arms and shot lasers into her exterior, eager to solve the blackmail riddle before his family imploded once again. "I've had enough of this lunacy today."

The caterer, offering an astonished and annoyed glare, focused on Diane, waiting for confirmation that she should skedaddle. "Would you mind taking them—"

"Of course, I'm so sorry. My nephew's a little out of sorts." When the caterer stepped outside, Diane turned to Teddy. "That was uncalled for. You need to apologize for being so rude."

Teddy's jaw clenched. As his eyes bulged, he thought better of releasing an outburst and relaxed his posture. "Sure, I'll do that later. The letter has me quite frustrated. What did Ira specifically say about Uncle George's rejection of the divorce settlement? How did your husband find out about the inheritance?"

"Some mail arrived at the house while I was in Italy. George sneaked over and rifled through my mailbox. I suspect he opened a few pieces of it." Diane wrapped her arms around her shoulders and sighed heavily. "I thought I'd be rid of that man by now. But he's done something far worse now." As Diane's sentiments barraged her body, she reached for a paper towel and blotted her cheeks.

"Crying won't help. I never understood why people can't control their emotions." Teddy took a seat at the breakfast nook and waited for his aunt to compose herself. "Did you want me to discuss it with Uncle George? Perhaps man to man, he'll back away."

"No, don't you dare do anything to make it worse." Diane closed her eyes and turned away from Teddy. "I don't know what happened to you while I was in Italy, but you have regressed back into an angry, detached man again." She finally crept toward him, resting a hand on his shoulder. "Is there something you'd like to talk about, sweetheart?"

Teddy paused, contemplating his reaction. He never intended to hurt his aunt, but she meddled too often in other people's business. While her words rang a bit of truth, he was in no place mentally or physically to reveal the facts of his recent weeks. "Of course not. Why don't you take a break? We can chat about Uncle George afterward. I need to think about what we've just found out."

Diane sniffled and dried her cheeks. "I'm always here for you. Don't ever forget it." She bent forward and kissed the top of his head, then bolted from the kitchen to retrieve her coat and search the grounds of the estate for Olivia.

Teddy banged his fist on the table and growled aloud to himself. As easy as it would make the entire fiasco, the letter couldn't have been from Diane's husband. When they solved the identity of the crook and put the fool in prison, Teddy would reengage with his aunt to offer assistance by convincing George to back away from the inheritance.

The day had been full of surprises. Gina's revelation about Teddy's artwork being displayed in a professional gallery had impacted him in a way he couldn't have expected. Four hours earlier, he was ready to hop a plane out of the Northeast and start his life over again. Without his family. Without a job. Without his wife. Without his son. A moment of regret or confusion had left him eager to try one final time with Sarah, but when he'd reached out to her, she was cold and merciless on the phone.

Could Sarah have anything to do with the blackmail note? She'd adamantly informed him that she deserved half of the marital property too, just like George. In Teddy's case, he refused to give in to her demands. They'd fought for weeks about the division of assets. Had she become so angry that she'd taken a train back to Connecticut to confront him in person? Teddy was certain the announcement in the background shortly before Sarah hung up had indicated she was in a nearby station.

They'd married quickly, perhaps too quickly, all those years ago. Teddy thought he knew his wife well, but if someone could sleep with a man's brother and consider passing off his child as her husband's, he realized he hadn't known her all that well. Wasn't blackmail a mere step up the ladder from adultery and prevarication? Could Sarah have hired someone to send the letter earlier that morning, knowing it would arrive in time for Teddy to read the note before Olivia's birthday party? Was she inciting him to react in front of his family?

Teddy had only gotten a brief look at the handwriting. He would need to see it again to decide if it were Sarah's penmanship. Even if it weren't, she could've dictated the message to someone on the phone. There must've been a receipt or something else included when the envelope had been delivered. Brandywine wasn't that vast of a town. He could call the local shipping companies, FedEx, and UPS to extract more information about the delivery.

As Teddy reached for his phone, he realized it was a foolish task. For one, none of the companies would release information about the sender, particularly if it had been handled confidentially. Even if he found the right one and forced them to furnish any facts, like whether any instructions had been mailed or dropped off at the delivery company, or from what original source location, Teddy would never figure it out in the thirty-minute break everyone had just taken.

Teddy had little other options but to assume Sarah had authored the note. She'd been pressuring him to agree to something he refused to consider. He'd made his decision, and nothing she could do would alter his judgment. Because of what he'd done, Sarah never wanted to see Teddy again, and she never planned to return to Connecticut. Teddy had agreed to give Sarah enough money to buy herself a small place wherever she wanted to move. The settlement was more than enough for a cheater, in his opinion. She hadn't backed down from requesting an additional one-hundred-thousand dollars, and if she intended to make a huge scene at the party tonight, there was even less chance he'd give in to her demands.

Teddy analyzed his options. If Sarah were behind the blackmail, she'd crossed a line by sending the letter to his family's home. She could've mailed the threat to him privately, told him on the phone, even texted him to reconsider his decision not to increase the divorce settlement. Sarah had obviously taken the wrong approach to resolving their differences.

If Sarah showed up tonight, his family would learn that their baby had died. They'd comfort him, but Teddy assumed they'd also see it as a punishment for his detached behavior in the past. Sometimes, he believed the theory himself. At this point, why would he remain in the Glass family home? If Sarah crashed the party, it would be awful, even if she pretended to be a happy wife until cornering him to allow him one last chance. No matter what played out, Teddy would lose tonight. He revisited his earlier decision to leave town. If he sneaked out right now, no one would know where he'd gone or what was going on. If Sarah revealed the truth about the baby and their marriage, Teddy wouldn't be present to deal with the consequences. But was he really a deserter?

Teddy approached the rear window and observed the caterer chatting on the phone under the nearby portico. She appeared to be arguing with someone judging by the expressions on her face. He decided to make a clean break. He'd apologize to the girl once she ended her call and ask her to give his family a message, indicating that he had to leave and not to worry about him. Simple. Short. It'd do the trick and clear a path for him to follow through with his plan. If one gallery owner wanted to meet, Teddy was certain another would approach him in the future again. As things settled down in the coming weeks, Teddy could arrange a visit with Gina and the gallery owner outside

Connecticut and use a pseudonym or alias, so no one could ever find him again.

As Teddy convinced himself of his plan, the kitchen door swung open. Jake entered the room carrying his and Caleb's son in his arms. Jake's distracted gaze reminded him of the pity in Sarah's voice and hopelessness in her expression minutes after losing the baby.

"I'm sorry, Teddy. I didn't think anyone would be in here." Jake scanned the room in search of something.

"I was just leaving. I need to get a bag from my car," he lied, quick to invent an excuse that wouldn't seem unusual.

"Would you mind holding the baby? Just for a minute? I need to get his bottle ready." Jake passed his son to Teddy and coached him on how to best support his neck.

"I'm really not good at this."

"Not yet, Mr. Mom," replied Jake as he rifled through the baby bag and withdrew the formula. "Neither was Joan Crawford in Mommie Dearest, but she supplied a few solid moments of sanity. Just help me for a sec, please?"

Teddy rolled his eyes while holding his nephew close against his chest, yielding to the serene and sweet baby scent. As his chest heaved in anger and pain, the baby's head rose and fell with innocence. Teddy couldn't help but remember watching as Sarah held their newborn son against her chest, when she cried out that her baby wasn't breathing. Caleb and Jake's precious little boy looped his tiny fingers against the collar on Teddy's shirt and murmured a slight noise.

"Maybe you should take him. He's restless," Teddy muttered while approaching Jake.

"You need the practice. From what Caleb tells me, children have never been a part of your life. I am the youngest in my family. I hadn't been around infants much either. I only learned in the last few years." Jake told Teddy that he'd been through the process with a few girlfriends who had babies in the past, which is when he'd discovered how much he wanted his own child.

Teddy stared into the baby's eager and alert eyes. He saw hope and beauty, a zest for everything. One that he had hardly ever experienced in his life before. Occasionally with Sarah, they'd reached the blissful state in their marriage, especially when they were in the final stages of her pregnancy. Before it had been viciously ripped from him in the most unexpected of ways.

"They're so dependent. Weak. Aren't you scared you'll do something wrong?" Teddy pressed his lips against the baby's cheek. "All they have is you."

Jake finished pouring water into the pot to warm the bottle and scrutinized Teddy. "We all are like that sometimes, Teddy. You'll figure it out quickly. New fathers always do. And as much as babies are weak and dependent, they're also cherished miracles who force us to smile and enjoy the wonders of life."

Teddy's heart twanged at Jake's last comment. "Don't you ever worry that he's not... I mean... biologically, he's not your son."

Jake again examined Teddy, appearing to take in his question and ponder the appropriate answer. "What does biology have to do with being a parent?"

Teddy had spent little time with Jake since he joined the family. Although they'd shared Thanksgiving together in Maine and Christmas in Connecticut, they hadn't been left alone for any length of time to get to know one another. Teddy had never really thought about Caleb's sexuality in the past. He assumed Caleb was a novel kind of guy, one who had the audacity to escape the clutches of his family. When he'd learned Caleb had married Jake, Teddy opened his eyes more to the world around him. He had no issues with two men sleeping together or raising a child together. While he was the kind of guy to pass judgment on others, and he accepted that fact about himself, it was always about a person's actions and treatment of other people, not about their personal interests or relationships.

"Isn't it every father's or mother's dream to create a stronger, better version of themselves? To start with similar DNA and do everything properly the second time around?" Teddy was careful not to thoroughly distance himself from Jake. Jake had never done anything to annoy him. In fact, of all the people in their family, by blood or by marriage, Jake seemed to be the one who genuinely cared about everyone else.

"Maybe at first that's what crosses an expectant parent's mind. But the moment you see your child for the first time, everything changes." Jake explained what it was like when he and Caleb first held their son, how everything they did suddenly became about what was best for the child's future. "Children aren't an opportunity to fix your past. They're a chance to improve the world's future."

Teddy had never thought of it that way before. "But don't you worry that someone might try to take him away from you. I've never studied adoption law, but it's risky. Aren't you afraid of what could happen?"

Jake smiled. "Every single day. But truthfully, it's rare, and we did everything we could to protect ourselves from the child's birth parents wanting him back. More than paperwork. We took care of the mother in our home. We met the father, and he convinced us it was in the child's best interest for him not to be involved."

"What about health issues? Or looking different? Or—"

"Or aliens invading the planet and kidnapping him." Jake cooed at the baby, waiting until Teddy followed suit. "A parent will always worry. That's what makes you a parent. Not DNA, Teddy. Is there something going on that's concerning you about Sarah's baby?"

As Teddy opened his mouth to respond, Pilar poked her head in the kitchen. "Pardon. Have you seen the caterer? We need to get more food prepared soon, and she keeps disappearing with her phone."

Teddy told Pilar the caterer had stepped outside. "I'll convey your message when she returns."

"Okay, I'll find your mother and Diane." Pilar thanked him and backed out of the kitchen.

"Whatever you do, remember to trust your wife and always be good to her." Jake bit his upper lip and lowered his head. "Trust is the only way to maintain a successful marriage. I know first-hand."

Teddy wanted to respond but couldn't find the words. He sat at the breakfast nook again, cradling little Ethan and rubbing his warm back. The precious boy's tiny fingers curiously reached out to Teddy's nose, forcing Teddy to grin widely. "Aren't you so smart? Who's gonna give his daddies so much grief!" Teddy surprised himself by developing an immediate connection with his nephew. Each time he remembered the boy wasn't truly blood-related, a wave of emotions encouraged him to recognize the instant bond he'd already felt. "Such an innocent, amazing blessing in life. Maybe I've been looking at things the wrong way."

A sniffle suddenly appeared in Teddy's nose, then a lump in his throat that he couldn't hold back. With the infant's heartbeat reverberating against his chest, Teddy imagined what life could've been like had things worked out for him and Sarah. Although he'd been obnoxious and distant with everyone in the past, he'd made progress in the prior months. He had dreams of teaching his son all the things he'd never opened his mind to. Teddy wanted to be the kind of father Ben was. He pictured his son graduating from high school and saving the world in the future. Could he ever return to the person he'd temporarily become before his son died?

The eldest Glass brother decided at that moment he couldn't leave the house. If Sarah showed up, he'd pull her to the side and apologize for everything. He'd convince her to stay in Connecticut and rebuild their marriage. If Jake could love his child, his adopted child, then maybe Teddy could love an adopted child just as much as if he or she were his biological child. It'd been difficult for Sarah to conceive a child for so many years, but they'd gotten lucky once. It could never happen again. Teddy would explain that adoption was a real possibility this time.

Feeling the gentle breath of the baby across his cheek, listening to the adorable sound of him nestling against his neck, compelled Teddy to realize family wasn't about blood. Family was about tangible connections. Honesty. Communication.

The kitchen door burst open again. This time Caleb interrupted and asked to speak to his husband alone. Teddy sensed something awkward or difficult had occurred between his brother and Jake. Perhaps they'd disagreed about the baby, or maybe the letter had worried them both. After offering to watch their son and Caleb declining the help, Teddy exited the kitchen and stepped into the dining room. No one else was in there. He'd use the moment alone to reach Sarah again, before locating the caterer and dealing with the blackmailer.

Unfortunately, his call went to voicemail. He almost hung up, but at the last minute he left a message. His heart was too full to give up hope forever, and this might've been his last opportunity to repair everything. "Sarah… it's Teddy. I think we need to talk…."

Chapter 13 – 6:30 to 7:00 PM (Zach)

After everyone took a break during the party, Zach escorted Anastasia outside despite the chilly temperature. Reading the mysterious letter had caused an eruption the size of Vesuvius, and although Zach normally loved to watch his family implode, he worried the situation had gone too far this time.

"Where are we going?" Anastasia asked as she walked hand-in-hand with her father around the side of the house. As she skipped down the slate pathway, pointing at various flowers beginning to awaken from their winter's nap, the moon lit the darkening sky.

"To the garage. We need to get away from everyone for a little while." Zach considered heading upstairs, but he would've run into his brother Matt and all of Anastasia's cousins. He preferred to chat with his daughter alone, to find out what else she could remember from earlier that morning when the deliveryman had knocked on the door.

"Uncle Matt said I wasn't allowed in here." Her little legs struggled to keep up with her father, and she let him know by dragging her feet and nearly slumping to the ground. "Slow down, please."

"Sorry, honey. It's freezing outside and I don't want you to get sick." Zach nudged open the garage door and directed his daughter to sit in a folding chair near the side window.

"How come you can bring me here?" Anastasia's inquisitive eyes scanned the room, half in alarm, half in delight.

"I'm your dad. I can do anything I want. Like tell you how much I love you, penguin," Zach responded, kissing the top of her head.

Anastasia giggled and pointed to the ground. "What's that?"

"Sawdust. Uncle Matt must've been working on a project recently." Zach tossed a blanket around his daughter. Even though the space was warmer than the outside air, he wanted to keep her safe and healthy. "So, tell me if you remember anything about the name on the envelope."

Anastasia shook her head. "No. We were playing hide and seek. I wasn't paying attention."

"Did the deliveryman say a name?" Zach kneeled before her and smiled, hoping to assure his daughter that he wasn't angry.

"Nah. Just to find an adult."

Zach pretended to grab his daughter's nose between two fingers and made a popping sound. "I thought you knew better than to open the door on your own. Someone might try to steal your nose from you. We wouldn't want to lose that pretty little beak, now would we?" Although he'd raised his daughter to be independent and not just do something because someone told her to, he also spent many hours explaining the reasons he settled on certain decisions.

"Melissa did. I might've told her to." Anastasia stretched a fist to the middle of her face.

"How silly! A penguin without its nose," quipped Zach.

"I like my nose. It reminds me of Mommy's."

And there it was. The invisible presence always lurking nearby. Anastasia enjoyed spending time with her mother, and Zach had done a decent job of never bad-mouthing his ex in front of her, but it was always worrisome. If Katerina pushed hard enough and had truly cleaned up her life, the judge would increase the visitation schedule. A supporter of families first, he'd been on the fence about Zach retaining sole custody in the beginning. Could Katerina be up to something with the blackmail note? When he asked Anastasia if her mother had been around lately, Anastasia admitted she'd dropped by the playground at school several times.

"Did she say anything specific?" Zach ruffled her hair.

Anastasia smiled. "That I'd get to spend more time with her soon. She was gonna make it happen. Mommy promised it."

Zach considered his daughter's words, then pulled the blackmail note from his pocket and reread it. He had no secrets. If it were Katerina stealing the money to force him to fund her lawyer to fight for custody, what did she suspect she could hold over his head? Before he navigated the dusty arches of his memory to itemize the various possibilities, Zach handed his phone to Anastasia so she could play a game. "Ten minutes. Try to beat your last score. Then we'll go back inside."

In every past scheme together, Katerina had been part of the situation. When they'd been so high that they broke into a liquor store and screwed on the counter amidst all the tiny bottles of booze. Upon knocking over a dozen of them, Katerina had noticed the camera in the ceiling and searched for the tape storage. They found it under the register and left with the only evidence of their crime tucked away in her purse. Zach had forgotten about that incident until just now, but even if she attempted to use it to get the cash, Katerina would never risk going back to jail. It would only be a bluff. Unless he was forgetting something important.

While Zach engaged in his trip down memory lane, Anastasia laughed boisterously. "I beat it. I beat it!" She jumped off the chair to show him the fireworks on the screen, declaring her a champion.

"That's fantastic. Let's head back inside." Zach pointed to the door and followed his daughter through the garage.

"What's that, Daddy?" Anastasia studied something small on the cement near the base of the wood saw.

Zach bent down, collected, and examined the round white object. When he turned it over, he saw a distinct mark that convinced him it was one of the pills Matt had previously taken. His brother had never lived in the house until after he completed his stint at the rehabilitation center. If there were drugs on the floor of the garage, among the fresh sawdust, it meant the pill was recently dropped, possibly while someone had been working on the wood project. Zach picked up the broken doll house roof and groaned. He'd overheard Matt talking to someone earlier about working in the garage on a surprise for his daughters. Was Matt addicted to drugs again?

"It's just some medicine. I'm glad you found it. Remember, never take medicine unless I tell you it's okay. Right?" Zach stooped before his daughter and inserted the pill in his jean pocket.

"What about Mommy? Or Grandma? Or Uncle Matt? Can I take medicine if they tell me it's okay?" Anastasia's astute eyes sparkled as she grinned widely.

Zach contemplated his response. "No, you shouldn't. Only if I tell you it's okay, or if you're very, very sick and the doctor or nurse says it's okay."

As they strolled back to the house, Zach debated whether to confront Matt about the pill. He wanted to give his brother the benefit of the doubt, but given Matt was responsible for watching Anastasia a few times each week, Zach needed assurance that his daughter was in a safe and drug free environment.

When they reached the house, Zach instructed his daughter to enter through the back door and go directly to her bedroom. "Pick out a video and I'll set it up for you and the other girls to watch. I've got to talk with Uncle Matt and see everyone else at Grandma's birthday celebration."

Zach decided to address his problems one at a time. First, he called Katerina's cell phone. It appeared to be turned off. Then he dialed the landline in her apartment. Katerina's roommate picked up the phone. "Nah, she came home earlier but left with her boyfriend. Said something about going on a trip tonight."

"To where?" When Zach had left her outside his apartment earlier that day, she was angry and promised not to let up about knowing something. Was she on her way to his house?

"Connecticut. And the bitch took something from me too." Anger punctuated the roommate's voice, a staccato delivery of heated words accompanying the awkward conversation. "If it wasn't something I might've illegally obtained, I'd call the cops on her."

Zach cared little about the squabble between Katerina and her roommate unless it might help him keep her away from Anastasia for a longer period. Or permanently. If this were about Katerina's chronic drug addictions, he'd use it to his advantage and prevent any future custody arrangements. "Did she say where in Connecticut? Specifically? I need to track her down."

"How the hell should I know? Ain't that place full of stuffy old white assholes? She probably went to steal something or find a new connection with that dope dealer of hers." The insufferable roommate hung up, leaving a moment of silence for Zach to decide his next steps.

After checking the time, Zach knew he had to update his mother. She should know there was a possibility the letter had come from Katerina. He waved at the caterer, who chatted away on a call. Before heading inside, he contacted Tressa to confirm her impending arrival. She answered on the third ring. "Sup? I'm halfway to your house."

"Cool. Listen, something strange happened. Lemme forewarn you." He explained what'd transpired with the blackmail letter, the pill in the garage, and the earlier run-in in with Katerina.

"Do you think your ex is supplying your brother with drugs?" Tressa honked and swore at someone who swerved into her lane.

"It could be a coincidence, but what if Katerina is trying to set up Matt? She knows he watches Anastasia during the week for me." Zach was concerned that Katerina had intentionally gotten Matt hooked on drugs again and was planning to show up tonight to steal money from them, then fight for custody of her daughter. If she could prove drugs were in the Glass household, Zach's chances of retaining sole custody would grow much slimmer.

"I don't know, papi. That'd be some sneaky shit, and that bitch is bad, but not that bad. You really think she'd rip Anastasia from a home she finally loves?"

Zach no longer knew what to believe. Rarely would his life stabilize long enough for him to make these types of decisions. He wondered what Emma would do in a situation like this. "Listen, Tressa. I need to make another call. Do me a favor. Ring the house later when you're close. I'm worried who might show up. I'd rather know when you arrive, okay?"

Tressa confirmed the instructions before hanging up. Zach tried to reach Emma, thrilled when she picked up the phone.

"Hey. I'm still on my way. Everything okay?" asked Emma.

"Huh? On your way where?" Zach pulled the phone from his ear, wondering if he dialed the wrong person. When he checked, it definitely showed Emma's name and cell number.

"Zach?"

"Yeah, who did you think it was?"

Emma gasped. "Oh, I'm sorry. I thought you were someone else. I… I guess I didn't look to see who was calling and wrongly assumed it was… never mind. Apologies."

"No worries. I'm glad I reached you. Are you sure you can't make it tonight?" Zach had high hopes she would secretly show up. Given the way his night had progressed so far, it was unlikely things would turn around anytime soon.

Emma hesitated. "No, it's not a good time. I gotta go."

"Wait, I need to talk—" When Emma abruptly disconnected, Zach's heart skipped a beat. It was too late for him to stop her. He also knew calling back wouldn't help the situation.

Instead, Zach reached in his pocket for a cigarette. He'd already smoked an extra one today, and again he was digging into tomorrow's stash. He had no other options and felt his body acquiesce to the nicotine. When he finished the last drag, he tossed the cigarette butt behind a nearby bush and returned to the house. Since Caleb, Teddy, and Jake were chatting in the kitchen, he passed through the hallway without interrupting them and ascended the back staircase.

At the top, he made a left into his bedroom and set up a video for Anastasia. She'd chosen a modern retelling of Cinderella where a boy was tortured by his stepbrothers and the princess set out to find him again. "Where are your cousins?"

"Uncle Matt said they were going to sleep early." She curled up in her bed and pulled the covers to her chin. "He sounded funny too."

Zach asked Anastasia what she meant, but all she could explain was that he talked slower than usual. Zach assumed it meant Matt had been slurring his words. If that were the case, then he'd likely swallowed several pills and had dropped one in the garage. After kissing his daughter's cheek and securing a promise that she wouldn't leave the bedroom, Zach exited. She wanted to sleep in his bed that night, and Zach didn't have the heart to move her. Tressa wouldn't mind sharing the bed, and Zach had planned to crash on the couch in his room, anyway.

When he entered the hall, his phone lit up. Katerina was calling. Maybe she hadn't taken the trip to Connecticut after all. "I've been trying to reach you. Where are you right now?"

"I'm in the same place I was when you called fifteen minutes ago." It wasn't Katerina. It was her roommate again. "I want you to give her a message if you see her."

"What's that?" Zach had no interest in relaying words between Katerina and her roommate, but the faster he agreed to it, the faster he could end the call and figure out where his ex could be hiding.

"Tell her if she doesn't return to the apartment before midnight with my gun, I'm tossing all her stuff on the street and changing the locks." The roommate swiftly hung up.

Zach panicked. If Katerina headed to Connecticut with a gun, her intentions were far sketchier than he'd considered. His exgirlfriend exhibited classic signs of a bipolar personality, yet she'd never gone to a shrink for confirmation. Given some of her unseemly actions in the past, Katerina was capable of devising a deranged plan that could have horrible implications. Was she going to kidnap Anastasia? Hold them at gunpoint until Zach handed over the one-hundred-thousand-dollar blackmail demand? What had she meant about lording a secret over one of his brothers? The girl was certifiable, and he was missing something that would clarify her hidden intent.

At the same time, Zach also struggled to accept she was solely a bad person. Katerina had a softer side and once wanted to be a better person for their daughter. She just couldn't find the proper balance. Should he give her another chance? Maybe the roommate was lying about the gun.

He had no sense of direction at that point. All he knew was that he had to protect his family from Katerina if she descended upon the family home in the next few hours. Zach had never been a fan of firearms, nor had he ever owned one. He knew

Matt was an avid hunter who visited the range to target practice all the time. Had Matt kept anything besides rifles in the house?

Before returning to the living room, Zach stopped in the nearest restroom for a private moment to think. What was his best next step? Tell everyone else what he suspected Katerina might be up to? Confidentially discuss the situation with Matt and ask him about the guns and the pills? Loop in his mother and aunt together to protect their family?

All he knew was that he'd do whatever he could to gain control of the situation that night, but a gnawing pain in his gut reminded him that things had a funny way of shattering into pieces in the Glass family home.

Chapter 14 – 6:30 to 7:00 PM (Emma)

Emma opened her eyes from a brief catnap and checked her watch. "Only a few minutes left. We're almost there. Are you doing okay?"

"I've traveled much farther before, dear." Rowena Hector smiled at her daughter-in-law and lovingly squeezed her knee. "You look a little pale, honey. Are you feeling alright?"

"I haven't eaten much all day. Just a little lightheaded." Emma settled her palm on her stomach, then looked at the empty seat next to the woman and scrunched her brow.

"Restroom. Then getting our bags. We'll meet up when the train arrives."

When the train stopped unexpectedly, throwing its passengers forward with impressive force, the drunk sitting next to Emma woke up, belched, and shuffled down the aisle. "Off to see my team win! Have a pleasant journey, ladies."

The oaf's stench had become intolerable to Emma. "Phew. I'm glad he's gone. I thought I was gonna get sick. Come on, let's sort out the bags, then we can make our transfer. It's about a forty-five-minute drive to the final destination, don't forget."

Rowena nodded. "Okay, you should grab a snack at the station. I still can't believe what we're doing. You sure you're not coming down with something? We can wait another day before taking the next step."

"Of course, everything will be fine, Rowena. I promise." While waiting for the line of people to disembark the train, Emma closed her eyes and willed herself not to back down from her hasty decision. Meeting Rowena had changed her life, and everything needed to be put back in order again.

Months earlier, after Emma had overheard Olivia and Diane talking about the letter Ben left for his son, Emma's last remaining tenuous grip on her belief in people's goodness dissipated into the sky like smoke from an extinguished candle. That's when Rowena had found her. Out of the blue. Almost like an angel had descended from Heaven and offered to remedy all that was wrong.

At first, Emma struggled to believe the truth. Rowena was kind, gentle in their initial phone chat. "Your blog post was so beautiful, thank you for taking my call." She'd introduced herself as a friend of the Glass family, someone who had stayed her distance in the last few months when Ethan succumbed to his illness. Rowena mentioned that Olivia had told her all about Emma and Ethan's marriage, and how Emma had returned home to start her life over again.

Emma agreed to visit with Rowena in Boston for lunch, under the auspices that Rowena simply wanted to meet the girl Ethan had fallen in love with. Emma only consented because the woman claimed to be in town for a few days. She also missed talking to others about her late husband, and if Rowena was willing to listen, Emma was eager to talk. During their brunch, Emma found herself immediately impressed and comforted by Rowena. Strangely, she saw traces of Ethan's mannerisms in the woman and reasoned out they must've spent a lot of time together when he was a child.

Then Rowena confessed the truth, that she was Ethan's birth mother. Emma had sensed the news before it was spoken but wasn't ready to acknowledge it. Rowena was the one to explain the letters Ben had left behind, the precipice for Olivia's lies. She even tried to rationalize why Olivia had made it difficult for Emma to inherit Ethan's estate. "She's shaken up and not thinking properly. Olivia is a good woman. I'm sure when she returns from Italy, she'll fix everything. Don't let this cloud your perception of her, Emma. You're both grieving, as am I."

Rowena confessed to Emma that she'd never planned to interrupt the Glass family's lives again. When she and Olivia had departed the park the previous fall, their unusual connection layers deep and filled with tepid trust, Rowena recognized that it was best for everyone involved if she pretended Ethan wasn't her son at all. She returned home and slipped back into her serene life in Michigan. A week after she arrived, her much older and sickly husband had suffered another heart attack. He died two days later, leaving Rowena on her own. She had her stepchildren for comfort, but they'd all grown up and moved on with their lives in the days afterward. Emma was the only person she could think of reaching out to.

At first, Emma understood why Olivia had never told Ethan. He'd been too ill. But as she got to know Rowena, Emma felt pity and sorrow for the woman who'd lost everything in the last few months. Over the early winter season, they bonded as if they'd been mother-and-daughter-in-law for decades, not minutes. Emma deemed Rowena the mother she'd always wished for but never really had, especially in recent years. She wanted Rowena to experience her rightful place as Ethan's mother too. Olivia and Rowena could share the privilege, especially now that he was gone. But Rowena eventually persisted in convincing Emma to stand down. "Don't tell her. We have each other now." Once Emma decided to give Olivia a chance to explain before agreeing to bury the truth, Rowena called with another startling discovery. One Emma couldn't ignore. One that changed her decision to remain quiet and persuaded her to go after Olivia Glass with all her might.

After gathering her bags from the top shelf, Emma strolled through the center of the train and waited for Rowena to finish deboarding. "Shall we catch that taxi? I think we need a bigger one given everything here. I'll sit up front, and you two can take the backseat. Okay?"

Rowena grabbed the pale hand of the third guest in their trio and smiled. "Yes, that sounds wonderful. I'm so glad we're finally together."

While Emma instructed the taxi driver where to go, and the third member of their group loaded the bags into the trunk, Rowena reflected on how the three of them had come together that winter.

Soon after their brunch in Boston, Rowena had departed for Scotland to visit her family. They'd only become reacquainted recently. She knew they would never fill the missing hole inside her heart but wanted to spend time with them, having just lost her husband and said goodbye to the son she'd given up years ago. While Emma was a welcome addition to her small circle of intimate friends, her roots compelled her to connect again with her long-lost relatives.

Rowena and her sister met up at a bar several towns away, sharing a pint and talking about their younger days as carefree girls and hopeful dreamers. Two rowdy men huddled together at a nearby table. When Rowena heard their voices, something startled inside her body. One of the voices sounded so familiar. She stood from her table and drifted closer. When the man looked up at her, she fainted.

A few minutes later, as she laid supine on the floor, she stared into the brightest green eyes she'd ever seen in her life. Except she'd seen them many times before when she was a young girl living in Scotland. They belonged to Ethan Flynn, her former boyfriend. Ethan, who'd been called Flynn most of his life, was a journalist who'd been shipped off to Bosnia to cover the war. Around the same time Rowena found out Flynn was killed in a surprise bombing, she'd also discovered she was pregnant with his child.

But in the bar, twenty-four years later, as a dozen strangers flitted about her and a kindhearted one handed her a glass of water, Rowena assumed she was witnessing a mirage. "Is it really you, my amazing hero?"

"Yes, Rowie, it's really me," Flynn said while embracing the woman he'd loved his entire lifetime. He was real. Flynn had never died in the bombing. He'd been kidnapped and held hostage for three years. When he was finally released and returned to Scotland, he searched for Rowena, but the unwed and pregnant teenager had already been kicked out by her family. Rowena had moved to America, secretly given birth to their son, and let him be adopted by Benjamin Glass. Ben had even agreed to name the boy Ethan, in honor of his biological father.

Rowena spent the next few days catching up with her long-lost love in Scotland, debating whether to tell Flynn about their son. She wanted to spare him the pain of learning he had a child only to realize the boy had recently died. One night, she'd been close to revealing the truth when she convinced herself to check on Emma, who'd been busy packing up Ethan's apartment with Zach. Rowena decided to tell Emma about her discovery, and moments later, Emma hastily exited her dinner so she could chat with Rowena in private. They discussed the situation for hours, then Rowena shared the entire story with Flynn before her scheduled departure from Scotland.

Flynn wanted to meet Emma, to see where his son had grown up. He and Rowena flew to Boston, met with Emma shortly after New Year's, and conversed at length about Ethan. Emma saw her late husband's resemblance when she sat before his two biological parents in their hotel's lobby. Rowena suggested showing Flynn where his son was buried but didn't want to introduce him to Olivia Glass. She sensed something was different about her former lover, worrying he hadn't truly recovered from his experiences decades earlier in Bosnia. Baby steps, she suggested to Emma and Flynn.

Over time, Emma convinced Rowena that it was crucial Flynn have an opportunity to meet the family who raised his son. Emma wanted to confront Olivia about the money Ethan had left behind, and she pressured Rowena into accepting that the only way for them to heal and move forward was if they forced Olivia Glass to realize the truth needed to come out. "Flynn will recover if we do this. Help him bridge his past and future."

Today, in the back of the taxi, Rowena sat next to Flynn and rubbed his hand, confident she could help him recuperate from his nightmares. As much as she loved her husband, Rowena had never forgotten about her first love. She and Emma were ready to show him where Ethan had grown up, maybe even drive by the Glass house when no one was home. After Olivia's peculiar message earlier that day, Rowena became more hesitant. There had been a weak cellular connection when she was commuting, and the call had gone directly to voicemail. Olivia's inquiry came out of the blue. Rowena sensed something was off with the tone of the woman's voice. Had she discovered Rowena and Emma were on their way? Surely no one in the Glass family knew that Flynn was still alive, could they?

An average-sized, ordinary woman, Rowena preferred darker colors and simple fabrics. She'd earned little money and rarely spent any of it on herself. Splurging on a variety of hats was her only creative outlet. Today, she donned a delicate black bolero with a wide brim and low, flat crown, adorned with a tiny red bow. She wore little makeup but had attempted to shine a little brighter knowing she'd introduce Olivia to Flynn shortly. Rowena turned to him and said, "I really think you should go directly to the hotel when we arrive in Brandywine. I would like to talk to Olivia first. The woman was exceedingly kind to me, and she let me decide whether or not I would tell our son the truth."

Emma turned around from the front passenger seat and beamed at her in-laws. "I know this is difficult, but Ethan wanted me to use his inheritance to do something good for other people. We need to move forward with our plan as soon as possible. There's a lot at stake, things I haven't shared with you yet."

Rowena nodded. "But we don't have to confront them tonight. I doubt Olivia told the rest of the Glass family the truth because she didn't want to hurt them anymore. We need to be cautious unless you think Olivia has more selfish reasons for burying everything."

Emma turned back to the front window. "I've made my decision. We need to do this."

Flynn leaned closer to the love of his life, sloping his head against her shoulder. His strong cheekbones and rosy cheeks were dotted with a smattering of freckles, his body frame tall, thin, and wiry. "I only want to see where my son grew up. What harm can come of me appearing tonight at a birthday party? Didn't you say they hoped Emma would show up? Maybe they're expecting extra visitors tonight."

Emma turned the heat down, claiming she was feeling a little faint. "I promised Diane that I'd be there. She doesn't know about the two of you coming with me, but she'll understand why when I explain everything. Diane is the sensible one in the family."

"What about your relationship with Zach?" Rowena wrinkled her brow.

"Zach is a friend. Maybe more one day. But for now, I need to do what's best for my late husband. And once that business is settled, we can see where everything stands." Emma checked the time on the dashboard clock when the taxi stopped at a red light. "Right on time. We'll be there in thirty minutes."

Rowena grabbed Flynn's hands and squeezed tightly. "Are you sure you're ready to take the next steps? We can always see what things look like in the morning, after a good night's sleep."

Flynn shook his head. "No. It has to be tonight, Rowie. I've prepared for this in all the right ways. Everything just feels like it's coming together. Come on… let's do this as a family, okay?"

"Sure. As a family." Rowena closed her eyes and rested her head on Flynn's shoulder for the last leg of the drive. Everyone was quiet for the remainder of the trip. When the taxi driver announced that they were just a handful of minutes from their destination, she prayed that everything would turn out for the best.

In the front seat, Emma rifled through her purse in search of something to settle her stomach. She'd been queasy all afternoon from pondering what might happen that night. Before finding the medicine, she noticed a new voicemail that she'd missed earlier when the connection was spotty. It was the call she'd assumed would confirm something she'd only recently begun to suspect. Emma attentively listened to the message, then dropped the phone into her lap with a heavy thud. "I knew it! This changes everything."

Chapter 15 – 7:00 to 7:30 PM (Everyone)

Olivia scanned all the presents but found nothing from George. She wondered whether Diane had misunderstood him about the photograph. Maybe he was being intentionally confusing to throw her off the track about sending the blackmail letter. Something critical was missing from this puzzle, and the only way to figure it out would be to tell the truth in front of everyone. After she'd revealed everyone's secrets at the last big event, the family embraced their healing process. Could lightning strike twice?

Once the remaining family congregated in the living room, Olivia addressed everyone in a strong, determined tone. "Being together on my birthday is something to celebrate. If your father were still alive, he'd be the first one to share another toast." She willed herself to do the right thing while scanning the full breadth of the room and scrutinizing everyone's wild expressions. It was time to tell the truth. "Before we can relax and indulge ourselves in dinner and more drinks, we must address the elephant in the room."

Teddy aggressively cleared his throat. "I, for one, think we owe it to ourselves to agree on the best approach to handle the individual blackmailing us. I suspect it's someone who's suffered a substantial loss recently, and we should be careful not to reproach them."

"Of course, that's the only thing we can do," Matt added, wiping his sweaty brow and clinging to Margaret's arm. "We can't be certain who the letter was intended for, but I suspect it will become rather obvious in the next few minutes. Let's not be too judgmental or believe them right away."

To release the tension building up over Katerina's impending visit, Zach cracked a joke that only Caleb and Jake could hear. Jake seemed to fake his laugh while Caleb rolled his eyes and stepped closer to the fireplace. Diane had already taken a firm stance beside Olivia, shoulder to shoulder, a resolute support system that refused to weaken despite the heavy load being placed upon it that afternoon.

"I'm so sorry George assumes he can try to hurt the family this way," Diane apologized, her voice wavering high to low at different points. "I'll talk to him tomorrow morning when he comes by."

Olivia interjected. "Obviously, we don't know with any certainty to whom the letter belongs until the person confesses, but I can tell a few of us believe it was meant for them."

Zach noted, "Perhaps we should each be given a turn to express our feelings about the situation. God, I can't believe I'm suggesting such a ridiculous approach, but… well, that's it, I guess. Let's just hash it out like other families do."

Teddy eyed his brother acutely. "Too bad you didn't hash something out with me before crossing a line with my wife, huh?" He turned his back to everyone and fixed himself another drink.

"Yep, that's right, Pickles," Zach blasted, addressing Teddy with his dreaded childhood nickname. "Make it all about you and your anger. Teddy's the oldest. Teddy's had the most pressure. Well… screw Teddy. You don't make the decisions in this family. We all do."

Diane shook her head at Zach. "Don't instigate more trouble. You're only making things worse."

Matt guffawed upon noticing his mother's sullen and worried expression. "What's with this family? Mom's trying to talk, and we keep interrupting her."

"Thank you. Please, let me say a few things, and then we'll take a vote on how to handle the state of affairs." Olivia separated from Diane and leaned against the back of the sofa, eager to relax her body and focus her mind on the situation at hand. "Someone mistakenly thinks they can blackmail a member of this family for one-hundred-thousand dollars." She suggested that everyone receive time to speak their concerns. "I'll go first. I have something shocking to tell everyone."

During the next ten minutes, Olivia shared all the details about Ethan's adoption, including how she'd never learned the truth until the previous spring. Silence initially pervaded the awkward space as everyone processed the news and considered all the implications. Each of the brothers individually recollected his relationship with Ethan, determining how it correlated with the blackmail note and their own fears about the villain's identity. Olivia first watched the wheels turning inside Theodore's crafty and analytical brain. Blood was the only thing that mattered to her eldest son. Was he going to be accepting or angry over the news?

Teddy's skin took on a yellow pallor, almost as though he'd been physically assaulted by his mother's news. He reflected on his strange rapport with Ethan as the oldest and youngest brothers in the family. They'd been too far apart in age to properly bond, yet Ethan's death had shaken and woken him up. Life was too short to dawdle and remain angry about everything. Teddy wished Sarah would return his call, but she had turned the phone off the last time he'd rung her again. Though he left her a voicemail asking for a chance to work things out between them one final time, he retained little hope of it happening.

Teddy was certain she'd boarded the train back to Connecticut and planned to confront him in front of the entire family that evening.

Caleb immediately recognized the similarity in fate between his son and his brother. He turned to Jake, who grabbed his husband's hand and squeezed it several times. Despite the rift that'd opened between them just forty-five minutes earlier, Jake's only concerns at the moment were in supporting Caleb. If the letter was an intent to blackmail Olivia about Ethan's true parentage, maybe their son's birth father would not be the biggest obstacle to overcome that weekend.

Zach struggled with understanding the news, possibly managing residual anger or disappointment in his father's actions. While his emotions were highly tweaked and it forced him to realize how much he still missed Ethan, what did this mean in terms of his relationship with Emma? Had she known all along? Was that part of her reluctance to grow closer to him? Did her distance have anything to do with these letters? The message from Katerina's roommate about her gun suddenly popped into his mind. Zach still hadn't found a minute to talk with Matt about it or the pill he'd found, but he would decide later whether to tell everyone else. Would she really show up and try to take Anastasia away, just because he didn't give her more money?

Matt stepped to the side near Margaret, engaging in a private conversation with his wife. He was dealing with the chemical changes inside his body from the pill he'd swallowed and found it harder and harder to concentrate. "How much more can this family take, Margaret? There's so much drama." He fought the desire to laugh out loud, not because the news amused him but because it changed so much and nothing all at the same time. He cared little whether Ethan was his biological or adopted brother. To him, this meant Ben hadn't been perfect. His father had made mistakes too. If Ben could screw up and still be so beloved, then Matt could one day attain the same goal.

"I know this was tough to find out, but it doesn't change anything. Ethan will always be your brother, and we must cherish our memories of him forever." Olivia nibbled on her lower lip to keep herself from losing control. "You must spend more time together. Love one another. Forget the past."

Teddy and Zach eyed one another with lessening doubt. They had attempted to but unsuccessfully patched their relationship. Knowing that Ethan had died without ever learning the truth impacted them both immensely. They embraced an eagerness to fix the past, even shook hands and awkwardly hugged one another. "We'll try harder, brother."

Diane decided to regain control of the room and redirect the conversation back to the blackmail note. "Boys, your mother was heartbroken, but she's pulled herself together and become a stronger woman because of it all." Diane squeezed her sister's hand and asked the most important question. "Liv, are you certain the letter is about this secret?"

"As of right now, I am. Somehow, I lost Ben's letter in the last few days. I had it with me at the airport, but it wasn't in my bag when I went to retrieve it in the car or upstairs." Olivia drew a heavy, exasperated breath.

Margaret said, "Maybe we should ask Pilar if she found it. She could've moved it somewhere accidentally and not have realized it was yours."

Olivia nodded. "I've already done that. She claimed to know nothing, but I don't think it matters much. Whoever found the letter will show up tonight to collect their money. My bet's on George."

"But what exactly does Uncle George think you stole from him?" Matt asked his mother, recalling the specific language in the blackmail note.

Olivia shrugged. "I'm really not certain until I speak with him."

Teddy said, "I'm not convinced he sent the note. Anyone could've found Dad's letter."

A pool of sweat puddled on Diane's brow as she prepared to confess her own secret. She'd been attempting to convince herself to reveal everything to Olivia earlier, but she was too stunned to say the words aloud. Finally summoning the courage, Diane shouted, "Oh, enough! I know what George wants. He wants money to keep silent about something he's holding over my head. I've been trying to fight him, but it hasn't helped. This is all my fault."

Olivia said, "What does this have to do with me? You said he never knew about Ethan."

"I'm not sure it has anything to do with you. George has something on me. He knows I value my privacy, my reputation. That you would do anything to protect me. I was a fool, Liv. That's why he's holding up the divorce." Diane swallowed heavily and confessed what she'd been hiding for months. "Before we left for Europe, I slept with Ira. He'd comforted me one night, and one thing led to another." Diane explained that she'd succumbed to his affections and wanted to let herself be loved for the first time in a very long time. Unfortunately, George discovered she'd slept with Ira, and because they were technically still married, he was using her actions to demand more money in the divorce. He wanted fifty percent of her inheritance from Ben, plus more to remain silent. "George is trying to prove that I slept with Ira before we separated, which would mean he has a stronger claim on all the marital assets. I don't understand how it all works, but he's intent to steal as much as he can."

"How does he know?"

Diane shrugged. "I haven't figured it out."

Olivia shook her head, then smiled supportively at her sister. "Is that why you told Ira not to come tonight? Are you afraid he'll get mixed up in everything, and someone will get hurt?"

Diane sniffled and began trembling. "Yes, I asked him to stay away until we sorted out this divorce. But then George muttered something else a little while ago. Something that could change everything. I'm scared of what it might mean."

Caleb and Jake helped Diane sit in a nearby chair. "We're here for you. We'll protect you. Just tell us what Uncle George is trying to do to you."

Diane rested a hand on her chest. "George said something about Ben's accident being quite a lucky windfall for everyone in the family. That we all inherited a lot of money from his death." She closed her eyes and whimpered like a small child.

"That man is such a louse. I lost a husband. The boys lost a father. And he cares only about the money!" Olivia gripped the back of the chair with one hand and pounded on it with the other.

"There's more, Liv. I'm so sorry I didn't tell you earlier. I was scared. George reminded me that he did some maintenance on Ben's car that morning. The chauffeur had brought it to his garage for an inspection and oil change." Diane looked around the room at everyone, wishing she could disappear into the paint on the walls and never return again. "George hinted that we all owed him a favor after everything he did for us that day."

Olivia gasped. "Is George saying he purposely caused Ben's car to have an accident?"

The room erupted in a series of denials and arguments. No one knew what to believe. To think the accident was anything more than an accident was as catastrophic as reliving the man's death. Olivia defiantly shook her head, clinging to Diane's arm and leaving imprint marks. "It can't be true. The police would've found something."

Diane countered, "I said the same thing to Ira. He's going to look into it further, but he explained that very little was left of the car after it collided with the overpass. Given the torrential weather, everyone assumed it was just an accident. It's unlikely they will be able to find anything at this point."

"Don't let this news get to you, brother!" Caleb seized Teddy's arm and prevented him from throwing his glass against the wall, then responded to their aunt. "But wait…if Uncle George told you he'd come by tomorrow morning, why does the note indicate the blackmailer will be here tonight. This doesn't make any sense."

Zach rested his cocktail glass on the sideboard and approached the rest of the group. "You're absolutely right. We won't know until the person shows up. Let's not make any rash judgments yet."

Teddy growled at his brother. "So, you want us to forget what Uncle George might have done? That's insane. He needs to be held accountable. I'll kill that son-of-a-bitch if he purposely—"

"Calm down. We need to approach this logically. Let's talk about the alternatives and figure out all the options before we do anything hasty. Who else could be behind the blackmail scheme? I'm concerned the note is actually from Katerina." Zach explained his theory and rationalization, including what the roommate had revealed on the phone earlier about Katerina's trip to Connecticut. He held back on sharing the news about her carrying a gun as it was too early to scare everyone. He wanted to assimilate everyone's input into a reasonable explanation before revealing the information. "She was quite sober this morning. If she's truly been off the drugs, I could see her writing a note and hoping to steal from our family without telling me a thing about it. I just don't know what secret she's holding, if it's her." Zach explained that his ex-girlfriend was usually impatient and demanded results quickly. He internally worried that she'd only partially planned out the scheme, and now that she had a gun, she'd act irrational and reactionary.

"Surely, if it's Katerina, we can stop her again," Olivia offered, hoping to appease and relax Zach. "If she has any evidence of something you did in the past, we'll figure out how to stop her. Anastasia does not belong with that horrific woman."

Matt slapped his brother's back in support. "Absolutely. I'll do whatever I can to prevent her from doing any damage. After seeing how amazing you are with your daughter, there's no doubt in my mind how good a father you are."

"What if she's planning to use you to hurt me?" Zach asked Matt, pulling the sawdust-covered pill from his pocket and deftly placing it in Matt's palm.

Matt clenched his hand when he felt his brother drop something into it. He angled his face downward and whispered, "You found it."

"Found what?" asked Margaret, a flurry of concern washing over her face.

Olivia crossed the room and reached for Matt's hand. "What's going on?" She struggled to pry his fingers from a fist, then yanked harder on his arm. Mother and son stared at one another, recalling when Matt had accidentally hit Olivia after she forced him to tell her about his problem with addiction. "Don't do this again, Matthew."

When he relented and unfolded his hand for everyone to see the lone pill in his palm, Margaret gulped. "You promised." She pounded against his chest with fury. "The girls. What about the girls?"

Zach took back the pill from Matt. "Maybe he hasn't taken any yet. Let my brother explain and stop overreacting."

Matt grabbed his wife's hands and pressed them to his lips. "Babe, everything will be okay. I promise. I only took one pill today, and it was just because of that stupid letter and the…" he paused, realizing he'd truly swallowed the pill after learning Wittleton and Davis wouldn't allow him back into the firm. "Well, I took it for a lot of reasons. The point is… it won't happen again. But I think the guy I bought the pills from might be the person who sent the letter."

Olivia closed her eyes, then exhaled loudly. "I don't understand. Did this guy find out the truth about your brother being adopted? How would he even know to blackmail us over something like that? Is this about ruining Ben's reputation?" Olivia explained that she was more apt to pay someone to protect her husband's honor, and she'd rather keep secrets within the family at this point. "People gossip too much. We've dealt with enough in the last year. I just need this to go away."

"I don't have all the answers, but while he and I met up earlier this afternoon," responded Matt, shaking his head in Teddy's direction when his brother acknowledged their incident in the café's parking lot, "he told me that he'd stop by tonight to sell more pills. He somehow knows this address and about the inheritance from Dad. I might owe this creep money from before he went to prison when I was buying drugs from him. I'm missing a few details, but too many odd things are happening around here." Matt also explained the situation with the firm's client, including how he'd stolen money and caused the two partners to sue Wittleton and Davis. Initially, Matt didn't mention Warren Payne's name as he preferred to discuss the situation with Caleb privately. Now he considered revealing what he knew.

Teddy crossed the room, thumping his finger against his brother's chest. "You caused a hell of a problem, Matt. Davis and Wittleton told me about the incident with Warren. I hoped they were mistaken, but I guess that's not possible, huh?"

Matt's temper had begun to overheat, and he couldn't hold back the brewing rage. "Wait! I'm not the only one around here involved with Warren," Matt barked, staring down Caleb like a pack of wolves. Now that Teddy had let the cat out of the bag, he had to keep the pressure on.

Caleb grunted and joined the conversation. "Exactly how do you know Warren? I met him at an airport over a month ago. I don't understand what's going on."

While stepping forward, Jake's face turned white. "I'd like to know the answer to that too. I'm confused how you know—"

Caleb turned to Jake. "I'm sorry. I didn't want everything to come out like this. When I met him at the airport and his hotel room, I thought it was just a random coincidence. Now, I'm concerned he's the one who—"

Olivia huffed. "Caleb, how could you? Is that what you were trying to tell me earlier?"

Matt insisted everyone remain quiet, then clarified that the money he'd stolen from the firm had been part of Warren's dispute with his business partner. "I need to understand what's going on with this guy. He is suing Dad's firm because of me."

"We sold the firm," Teddy interjected in a nasty tone. "No thanks to you."

Diane yelled, "Stop it! Stop it, everyone. We can fight amongst ourselves another time. We need to figure out what's going on with the blackmail request and determine whether George did anything to hurt Ben. Maybe he was just lying to pressure me into giving him more money. George thinks I'm still weak and that I don't know how to defend myself. He's banking on me agreeing to give in so that no one ever digs into the truth. If we don't have any evidence, how can the cops put him in prison?"

"I'm sure he left something behind that might implicate him. But let's keep looking at all the options. We're in this together, all as one family." Matt explained that he thought either the drug dealer was trying to blackmail him, or possibly Warren had discovered their address and was going to show up that night to confront him. "I owe him way less than one-hundred-thousand dollars, but maybe he's being greedy. Caleb, could this guy be responsible for all the drama? You apparently know him fairly well. How unstable is he?"

"Really, this is a lot to handle right now." Caleb collapsed into the nearest sofa, then turned to comfort Jake. "I promise you, everything will be fine between us, but we need to tell them about the baby's biological father."

Jake and Caleb explained what they'd learned from the adoption agency. The birth father could've called the delivery company and dictated the contents of the blackmail letter. Caleb even went as far as suggesting the creep had claimed it was a joke, anything to convince the company to deliver his message until he could get down to Connecticut that evening. "The guy could be the person who wants money from us in exchange for his son. It's a little extreme, but I suppose it's plausible."

Olivia summarized everything she'd heard. "Zachary thinks it's Katerina. Matthew thinks it's his drug dealer or a former client of Ben's law firm. Caleb thinks it's his son's biological father. Diane thinks it's George, who possibly admitted to doing something to Ben's car. I don't know what the right answer is, but we're gonna find out soon enough." Olivia had waffled on the culprit's identity. Based on everything she'd heard, facts and details that were putting her too close to the edge, she again rationalized that George was the person trying to get money from them. But the thought of him intentionally damaging Ben's car to cause an accident would change everything. How could she have been so blind to everything in the past?

Teddy quietly stated from the corner in a haunting voice, "It could be Sarah. My wife filed for divorce a few weeks ago. I've been keeping it from everyone because… because the truth was too hard to share."

Olivia hesitantly approached her eldest son. "Theodore, I'm so sorry. What about the baby? Doesn't she want to find a way to make it work for your future family?"

Teddy stared into his mother's eyes, then focused on a nondescript section of the floor. Anything to avoid his emotions from bursting out in front of everyone. But it was too late. "There is… no baby. Sarah hasn't been on bed rest for the last month." He wiped the first tear from the corner of his eyes and swallowed several times to prevent the rest. "On New Year's Eve, she went into early labor," Teddy mumbled a few more words that no one understood, ultimately breaking down in front of everyone. He was unable to finish telling his family what'd happened and quietly knelt in front of Olivia, "Momma, I need you desperately. It's all gone. I have… nothing." Teddy's distressed, muffled voice and gentle weeping brought many in the room to tears.

Olivia dropped to the floor and comforted her oldest child, slowly eliciting the entire story from him as best as she could, as only a mother could. As a mother who'd neglected so many duties in the past, she could think of only protecting him right now. "Oh, my baby, I'm so sorry. I knew something was wrong, but I never expected this to happen."

When the room began to spin around her, Olivia accepted it was time to muster hearty strength for her boys. Crumbling now would do nothing but hurt them. It crushed her to learn that her eldest son had suffered through the same paralyzing grief of losing a child before ever having the chance to watch him find his way in life.

Teddy regained partial composure a few minutes later, clutching his mother's hand for support. "He's buried a few rows away from Dad. I go every morning to see my son. I don't know what else to do with myself." Teddy wept against his mother's shoulders, allowing her to temporarily soothe his pain. In reality, the agony would always skulk under the surface of his skin whenever he let down his guard. "Sarah blames me. I think she sent the letter because she knows I haven't told everyone about our loss. She's intent to punish me for everything."

The Glass family spent the next ten minutes discussing the various options and approaches to address their alarming predicament. When Pilar opened the sliding pocket doors and entered the room, Olivia looked up with the beginnings of an aggravated snarl. While Pilar wasn't to blame, Olivia needed someone outside the family to lash out at. "What do you need? We're having a private discussion right now."

"My apologies, ma'am. There's someone at the back door who says you're expecting them. Something about sending a note earlier today." Pilar retreated into the hallway, awaiting the response. "What should I do?"

"Whom did they ask for?" Olivia inquired, a wild streak of panic dancing on her face.

"You, ma'am. Specifically, a private meeting with Olivia Glass." Pilar clasped her hands together and slowly exhaled.

"Bring our guest to the living room. There will be no one-on-one discussion. It's time we dealt with all this drama as a family," replied Olivia, directing Diane to pour her another drink. Though her confidence was rising, no matter how much she attempted to trust her decision to confront the blackmailer in person, the outcome was bound to have casualties. She'd known all along that the extortionist was after her. Just not the exact reason. Now it was time to find out.

Chapter 16 – Flashback (Olivia)

Olivia and Diane spent the last month wandering around Italy, traveling from the northern cities to the southern ones, ultimately enjoying the last few weeks of their trip on the Amalfi Coast. Although the weather had been moderately cool, it was nowhere near the wintry blizzards back home in Connecticut. After eight weeks of constant companionship, Olivia suggested they do their own thing the morning after their arrival in Ravello.

Diane chose to read a novel on a secluded beach at the base of the cliffs below their hotel. As she slipped away, Olivia smiled at the vibrant aquamarine water, tempted to dip her toes in its gently rippling waves. But she knew better. It would be too cold to accomplish anything other than shock her system. She elegantly dangled her strappy sandals from her fingertips and climbed two hundred steps to reach their hotel's reception lobby at the top of the cliff. At the end of the driveway, she leaned against a polished stone wall and slipped into her footwear. A local bus pulled up in front of the hotel, and Olivia jumped aboard and validated her ticket with the driver. He shrugged, indifferent to his tourist passenger, and jolted away from the hotel, barely making the narrow turn around the cliff.

Olivia clutched the fronts of a few seats as she navigated her way toward the middle section to claim the first open space. The trip to the nearest town took fifteen minutes, and apart from a brief nod at a young woman feverishly pounding keys on her mobile phone, Olivia communicated with no one else. She needed a day to herself, one where she could reflect on all the changes in her life. Once the bus stopped, and the driver called out the name of her destination, she exited her seat.

As Olivia descended the steps, a kind gentleman with soulful eyes and caterpillar brows held out his hand and helped her off the bus. He tenderly kissed the top of her hand and nodded briefly. She smiled and replied, "Grazie. Buona giornata." After he wished her a good day too, Olivia retrieved a map that the hotel concierge had lent her and oriented herself to her surroundings. It was lunchtime, and she had only eaten a few pieces of fruit and prosciutto for breakfast in the hotel. Upon debating between a sit-down lunch at the closest restaurant versus ordering a panini to go, Olivia took off on foot to the conservatory attached to another hotel and rested on an ornate, rustic bench to enjoy her meal.

It reminded her of the day Ben had arranged a private afternoon lunch in the southern nursery of Connecticut's finest botanical gardens. The chiffon dress and its violet straps around her neck. The voluminous twenty-foot cherry trees and colorful sky. The perfectly manicured grasses, shrubs, and flowers. The four-piece string orchestra playing romantic melodies. And the stunning engagement ring. Although no cherry tree cascaded above her this time, she could almost smell their sweet scent when she closed her eyes and lost herself in the memory. "You would have loved this trip, my darling Ben."

For hours, Olivia explored the tiny villages near the sea, hopping on and off the bus, snapping photographs of mesmerizing views, each one better than the last. When she stumbled upon a quaint and charming pottery shop, the enormous size of the lemons on the tree's branches became an instant obsession. She hunted and searched for larger ones in every shop, shocked to see they could grow to the size of the pumpkins her boys had carved as children.

Midafternoon, Olivia stumbled upon a hidden gelataria, uncertain whether to stick with her favorite flavor, Italian Stracciatella, or sample a tart lemon. She treated herself to a scoop of both, enjoying each as an individual flavor, not fully thrilled by the combination. Nonetheless, she intimately understood the passion Italians imbued in their foods, particularly desserts. As she tossed the spoon and cup into a nearby trash bin, her mobile rang. Ira Rattenbury was calling, and it was still early back home. Would he have updated news about the impending lawsuit that had come up the day she left for Italy?

"Good morning, Ira. I cannot tell you how beautiful this country is. You really ought to visit it sometime this year." Olivia had gotten to know her husband's lawyer better the previous summer and fall when he'd searched for Rowena Hector and probated Ben's estate. Although he was at least two decades younger, she often wondered whether he'd make a suitable match for her sister, Diane.

"Olivia, I hope so myself. Between your descriptions and the photos Diane emailed me, it's marvelous." Ira paused, allowing a moment for Olivia to respond, but she did not. "I am so sorry for bothering you again, but there's been some movement with our unfortunate situation."

"The people suing Ben's estate over his car accident?" Olivia meandered toward a small patio and leaned against the stone wall overlooking a valley between two of the cliffs. She couldn't help but recognize how far of a fall it would be had she dropped anything, including herself.

Shortly after she'd arrived in Italy, Ira had contacted Olivia to inform her that Ben's insurance company cut a check to the family of Ben's driver who'd also been killed when the car careened into the steel overpass. There were numerous depositions and revisions with the insurance adjuster before they could reach the final settlement. Ben's driver had been employed by another company, and they'd closed shop shortly after the accident. The driver's family tried to collect from them when he'd been killed, but it'd amounted to extraordinarily little. By the fall, they'd set their sights on the wealthy Glass family in the hopes of a larger payout for their loss. Olivia had never met them as Ira handled all the interaction. He'd convinced Olivia to authorize an amount he thought fairly reflected their loss, given what the insurance company had already paid out. Olivia had hoped to avoid a lawsuit and was eager to learn if they'd accepted her offer. Everyone seemed to want her family's money these days.

"Yes. I've extended the proposal to them, but they are unwilling to decide until they meet with you face-to-face. Apparently, they feel you share a mutual loss and want to talk with you before closing the deal." Ira prattled on longer but was mostly ignored in favor of the architecture surrounding Olivia.

Olivia's instinct was to decline the request. She'd suffered enough heartbreak and desperately wanted to move on from the accident. Any memories of Ben were strictly focused on their life together with the boys, not about the secret he'd kept from her, his law firm, or what happened to others because of his accident. She wasn't closed-minded or unsympathetic, but she had to concentrate on her own needs. After waffling on the decision, Olivia interrupted Ira. "Let them know I'll give it some thought. I'm away for a few more weeks, then I need to find a new place to live. We can decide when I return."

Ira accepted her decision and ended the conversation. An hour later, as Olivia departed the bus and meandered back into her hotel, Ira called again with the results of his discussion with the driver's family. "They've asked to set a meeting for the end of February. That gives you a few weeks once you return home. We can delay if you need more time. I'll take care of the situation.

Please give my regards to Diane. I haven't been able to reach her this week." He promised to email Olivia the date and time, offering to pick her up and drive with her to the conference.

"Thank you. I know you worry about me, but I realized these people are hurting too. We share a common loss, death of a loved one, and if talking to them can alleviate even the smallest inkling of grief, it is my duty to do so." Olivia strolled through the lobby and returned the map to the concierge. She hated to waste things, and since her trip to the nearby towns had finished, she wanted others to have the opportunity to experience the same beauty.

Olivia had learned so much from the devastating and unexpected death of her husband. She knew nothing of the driver's family, whether he had a wife or children, or elderly parents who needed care and attention. As a woman of wealth and privilege, giving them some money was the logical decision. Assuming they accepted her offer at the face-to-face meeting in February, Olivia could permanently close the door on Ben's accident and move on to the next phase of her life, sans any unraveled threads.

Ira replied, "You're a kind and generous woman. I'm sure they will be pleased. I believe they simply want closure too." He paused and confirmed the details of her return flight, then asked about Diane again. "Is she around? Perhaps I could say a quick hello. Has she said anything to you about our—"

"No, she's not here. I'm hoping she's having fun with the gentleman she met yesterday. My sister needs to have a little fling to get over her failed marriage and to embrace her new future." Olivia noted that Diane was somewhere in the hotel, but she wasn't sure of her exact location.

"Fling? Is she seeing someone else already?" Ira asked, hints of coldness apparent in the strain of his faltering voice.

"Seeing? No, I don't think she's ready to engage in anything serious, but I'm planning to set her up with someone she met last night, if she hasn't initiated it herself. By the way, is her divorce from George final?"

"Almost. I'm meeting with him and his attorney tomorrow to review the final paperwork. Everything's been agreed to, so it will happen any day now, I'm certain." Ira excused himself for another meeting, a darkening of his mood clearly obvious from his tone.

Olivia reflected on her solitary excursion, confidently acknowledging her strength was returning. The first few weeks had been difficult, but with Diane by her side, traveling to Italy without Ben progressed better than she'd expected. Once their trip was finished, she would return to Connecticut and search for a new home to share with Diane. Although they'd been close as sisters when they were children, their lives had taken different paths and needed to weave back together again. After six months of being a widow, Olivia knew she needed to take the trip to Italy to finish her and Ben's dream. She'd also been certain there wouldn't ever be another man in her life. No one else could compare to Ben, and she'd been privileged to spend nearly forty years with the love of her life.

Although they were only in their late sixties and had plenty of life left to live, both women sought friendship and platonic love. Unnecessary romance was not on their bucket lists. Diane had even remarked that she could now afford to pay for someone to occasionally show her an enjoyable time. Olivia knew her sister had only been joking, and they often laughed uncontrollably at the thought of hiring an escort at their ages.

Olivia wandered to the outdoor bar on the patio overlooking the hotel's Mediterranean inlet. It was late enough to enjoy a cocktail before she found her sister and arranged their dinner plans. As she sauntered across the lobby's shiny tiled floor, Diane's voice wandered in from the hotel's restaurant. Olivia began walking toward her sister, then noticed Diane chatting with the same distinguished gentleman as the previous day. She listened to their conversation before deciding whether to interrupt them. Perhaps Diane had grown the courage to proposition him.

Diane sat in a high-back stool, her long pastel-blue skirt billowing from the swaying twist of the seat as she nervously listened to the man next to her. "You're quite charming. I appreciate the first drink you bought for me. I really shouldn't have another."

The distinguished gentleman's head towered several inches above Diane's. He lifted his hand and wiggled two fingers. When the bartender nodded, he lowered his hand and draped it across Diane's shoulders. "You're a beautiful woman. I'm honor-bound to offer you a drink if I want to spend more time in your company."

Diane's back arched when he caressed her softly. Olivia knew her sister was too shy to relax in the man's presence. Diane had only ever dated George before their marriage. Between work and other responsibilities, romance was never a priority. Although his actions worried Olivia, as Italian men could be quite a handful, she wanted her sister's trip to be memorable. Maybe she should sneak upstairs to change for dinner and let them finish their drink together.

Olivia continued listening, waiting to find out whether her sister even remembered how to flirt anymore. Olivia had nearly forgotten herself, but she could coach others if needed. A mini fling might do Diane some good. Olivia stepped away and approached the elevator. There was only one in the entire hotel, and she'd walked enough throughout the day already. It took two minutes to ascend, and just as the doors opened, someone sang out for her to hold them.

Olivia turned around, pressing the third-floor button with one hand and holding the doors open with the other. "Of course, what floor are you heading to?" When she looked up, it was Nate, the distinguished gentleman who'd just been with her sister.

"Grazie. I see we're going to the same place." He stepped into the opposite corner, although there were barely a few feet between them in the tiny space. "It's such a beautiful night. Are you dining anywhere special this evening?"

The man's piercing blue eyes penetrated Olivia's skin. His hair, beginning to turn an exquisite salt and pepper combination, was thick and luxurious. His skin, smooth and tanned, offered the hint of someone familiar with replenishing sunrays and rejuvenating waters. He removed his sports coat, hung it debonairly over his right shoulder, and opened the first two buttons on his collared mint-green shirt. He had an authentic nineteen-sixties movie-star look but had successfully transitioned it to the twenty-first century. No wonder the man had rattled and charmed Diane.

"I'm about to conduct a little research. My sister and I arrived in Ravello this week. Any suggestions?" Olivia smiled as his eyes sparkled, curious where he was from. The longer she studied his features, he looked less Italian and more British.

"Ah, if only we were back home, I'd offer to cook for you. Alas, I am a newcomer to this region myself. Perhaps the concierge could help us both." When the elevator doors opened, he stretched his arm and indicated Olivia should exit first. "I met the loveliest of women and considered asking her to join me. I'm sure we could all eat together, your sister and you, and the two of us."

Olivia paused, curious to see the location of his room. He pointed at the opposite hallway and shrugged. "That's a kind offer. Are you in the market for meeting the loveliest of ladies? Is the one you've just met someone you find yourself interested in?"

The man inhaled deeply. "The night is young. We shall see." As he navigated the hallway to his room, Olivia waited for him to swipe his card in front of the reader, then turned to walk away.

Something about him felt familiar, perhaps comforting given she was vacationing in a foreign place without Ben. She couldn't determine why, or who he'd reminded her of, but she was happy for her sister. Olivia selected appropriate evening wear, then texted Diane that she would arrive in the hotel lobby in a few minutes to decide on dinner. She also noted that she was fine staying in on her own if Diane was otherwise occupied or gallivanting about Ravello. While eager to discuss their mutual days, Olivia needed to give Diane the chance to schedule dinner plans with Nate.

Diane replied a moment later that she was also in the hotel lobby and hungry for dinner whenever Olivia was ready. Upon dressing, Olivia wandered downstairs and joined her sister at the corner bar.

"Before you share all about your day, I have a suspicion something intriguing happened to you while I was out. Care to tell me all about it?" Olivia reclined on a petite sofa across from Diane, staring out a gigantic picture window at a dark, glimmering sky full of radiant stars. It was clear and endless, reminiscent of Olivia's trip to Yellowstone with Ben and the boys twenty years earlier.

"Oh, you know, nothing big. An ordinary outing. Tell me all about yours," replied Diane, unwilling to look her sister in the eyes.

"No conversations with handsome men you might want to get to know better? What about Ira, for instance?"

Diane scowled. "Ira and I cannot be together. It's just not a good idea. Don't bring him up again. I need to focus on my divorce first."

Olivia knew it was too soon to reference the banter with Nate that she'd just overheard. She would wait a few more days to see if the gentleman appeared again, or if Diane mentioned him at all. "We're in the most romantic of all the possible places, dear sister. Perhaps you'll meet a gorgeous stranger on this trip. One who will change your life in the future."

"No, I doubt it. My future is not destined for good things. Every time I hope for something positive in my life, things fall apart far worse. I'm unlucky, Liv. I'm only meant for misery and pain."

Chapter 17 – Flashback (Caleb)

"I'm surprised you called at all. It's been several weeks since we met at the airport." Caleb twisted the cap off a local bottle of pale ale and generously swigged from it.

"Happy New Year to you too, Caleb." Warren traced both hands through his wavy brown hair and exhaled. "I had a lot on my mind. I wasn't sure it was a smart idea to call you again."

Caleb and Warren relaxed at a dive bar near Boston's Logan International. Warren had called a few days earlier and informed Caleb he'd be staying in Boston for another client trip. He inquired as to whether Caleb would be able to meet him anytime that week. Caleb had a client in the city and decided he could kill two birds with one stone. He needed to present an alternative design to his difficult homeowner, and he wanted to halt anything further from happening with Warren. Their original conversation had been an unexpected distraction, but Caleb had luckily stopped himself before getting physical with Warren. He loved Jake, and at the time, he'd felt exceedingly disappointed in himself for even thinking about what it would be like to kiss another man. Today was the perfect opportunity to end the conversation and temptation with Warren.

"That makes two of us. I need to tell you something." Caleb tapped his feet against the wooden floor, considering whether to blurt out he was married and run off, or kindly tell Warren he wasn't interested in anything more than friendship and stay for another beer. The problem was that he genuinely liked Warren on a visceral and connected level. Caleb could see them hanging out and watching movies together, grabbing brunch with friends, and complaining about politics and the economy.

"You're married. I figured out that much already." Warren signaled to the bartender to order another round. "We might be here a little while. I have something to tell you too."

"You go first. My kitty's already out of the bag. I should've mentioned it the first time, not that I ever thought about something happening between us." Caleb had promised the little fantasy he'd permitted himself to entertain for a few hours was just that—a fantasy that could disappear as quickly as it had appeared.

Warren leaned back in his rickety chair and tossed his hands behind his head. "I've already met your husband. We knew each other a long time ago."

Caleb failed to swallow a mouthful of beer before it sprayed from his lips all over the table and Warren. "You know Jake?"

Warren's head bobbed awkwardly as he wiped up the mess. "I knew him before he was Jake Glass. When he was Jake Payne. My name is Warren Payne. We never exchanged those details."

Caleb's usually safe and secret world came to an immediate and paralyzing crash. "Did you say Warren *Payne*?"

"Jake's my younger brother. One of the eight siblings I told you about last time." Warren pulled out his wallet and showed a picture of him and Jake playing together in their house back in Iowa. "I'm a few years older than him. I escaped as soon as I could, but I never should've left him behind."

Caleb processed Warren's news and studied his facial features. He'd completely missed it the first time around. Jake and

Warren shared the same high cheekbones, dimples, and hairline. As he continued noting all the similarities, Caleb realized why he'd found himself attracted to Warren in the first place. Warren had so much in common with Jake, and it was a momentary but hidden recognition in the back of Caleb's mind. He wasn't truly attracted to Warren; his head was just messing with him.

"I don't understand. You knew this whole time?" Caleb pushed back his chair, unsure whether to walk away or question what was going on.

"Not at first. I should probably tell you a little more about myself." Warren suggested they head back to his hotel room to chat in private. He had a complicated story that would reveal what'd happened to him the last few years. They paid the check, walked across the street, and rode the elevator together in silence. Once seated on a loveseat across from the bed, Warren shared his story.

When he'd turned eighteen and left for college, Warren forgot about his siblings and pretended he didn't have a family. He began dating a girl at his school, even considered proposing to her in their senior year. Once she asked to meet his family, Warren realized it was time to return home and verify if his secret desires had disappeared. After he arrived, he discovered things had gotten even worse.

Warren's brother, Jake, had recently come out of the closet to their parents at thirteen and was beaten within inches of his death one night. Warren wanted to defend his younger sibling, but the uncanny predicament hit too close to home. Warren was also struggling with his attraction to other men, and he'd only proposed to his girlfriend to continue to cover up the truth. Luckily, their older sister stepped in and brought Jake to a clinic to address his wounds.

Warren had taken off after the beating, unable to safely get anywhere near his brother. He went to a local bar and flirted with a guy he'd always suspected was gay, except the guy wasn't. The guy pummeled Warren in the parking lot. Mercifully, friends convinced him to walk away before he killed Warren. Warren wasn't hurt too severely, but the experience forced him to realize that he'd abandoned his brother when he was most needed. Warren returned home and informed his parents he was also gay, and if they laid another finger on Jake, Warren would turn them into the cops. Unfortunately, Warren's parents threw him out and demanded he never return home again. Warren searched for his brother at their sister's neighboring farm, but when he arrived the next morning, Chloe informed him that Jake had run away.

"I haven't seen Jake since that night in Iowa. I spent weeks looking for him, but I had no idea where he disappeared to." Warren quietly wept but wouldn't let Caleb do anything to comfort him.

"It's okay. You made a mistake. He'll forgive you." Caleb thought about the similarities that had occurred between the two brothers in the last decade. Both had been disowned by their family and run away to start a new life. If they'd only been able to help each other, so much pain would never have seen the light of day. When Warren used the restroom, Caleb attempted to call Jake to tell him what was going on. He couldn't reach Jake and didn't want to leave a voicemail with the news, so he waited until the following day.

Once Warren returned, Caleb inquired, "When did you figure out who I was?"

"While we were having drinks at the airport last time, you went to the gate agent to ask for a status on your flight. You left your phone, and Jake called. I saw his face on the screen and recognized him."

Caleb remembered that Warren had quickly ended their conversation at that point and suggested his flight was leaving shortly, so he had to move along. "You could've said something then."

"I know. I wasn't sure, and I didn't want to do that whole weird 'we have a connection' thing at the airport." Warren indicated that he continued researching Caleb and Jake, using the little information Caleb had provided about his home and work locations. "You never gave me your last name, but I looked up weddings from the last decade in Maine. I found an article in your hometown's local newspaper, and it confirmed your last name and his last name. That's when I was sure."

"And you never told me until now?"

"I thought my brother would reject me for not helping him. But then my life turned to shit this month." Warren explained that he'd been involved in a lawsuit with his former business partner who'd stolen the software programs that ran their technology products. "I might lose everything if this lawsuit doesn't work in my favor. I realized it was time to reconnect with Jake again. So, I called you."

"And here we are," Caleb whispered, uncertain how to handle the entire situation.

"Would you be willing to talk to him for me?" Warren explained that he had no way of contacting his brother, nor did he want to shock him with the past. "I know how much he hated our parents. Probably as much as I did too."

Caleb nodded. "He's told me bits and pieces, but not everything. I knew there was physical and mental abuse. He's blocked most of that period in his life. Doesn't want to talk about it now."

"Does that mean you'll help?" Warren leaned closer and grabbed Caleb's hands. "Please, I feel like this is why you and I ran into one another at the airport."

Caleb promised Warren that he would give it some thought. "Look, maybe we can arrange a dinner back in Maine in the coming weeks. I need a little time, okay?"

"I understand. I know where you guys live. I saw it in the news article, so I can come by whenever you want. This will be great."

Warren thanked Caleb for considering the entire scenario and saw him to the door.

Caleb returned to his hotel room, messaged Jake that he loved him, and fell asleep. Caleb knew how much he missed his own family when he'd kept his distance throughout the last decade. He only realized what he'd thrown away when his father died. What if Jake's family were more open-minded now? Maybe some of them would even grow to accept their son or brother and his new life. Caleb had to converse with Warren more as he wasn't sure whether the Payne family were back in his life or if they'd been permanently rejected.

Caleb met with his client the next morning to resolve the concerns with the house drawings. Upon finishing, he called Jake to check in. "How're my two favorite guys?"

"One's cranky and sitting in a diaper in his swing. The other's clutching an empty bottle of Jack Daniels. I know it's only eleven in the morning, but our son looked thirsty."

"Ummm… does that mean you're in the diaper and our child's drinking whiskey?" Caleb knew Jake was kidding but loved to push the jokes as far as possible.

"Does the thought of me in a diaper turn you on?" Jake snorted after asking the question.

"Not really. But you should know how much I miss you."

"Ditto." Jake covered the details of his prior day with their son. Playgrounds. Turning himself over. New foods. Tantrums. Earsplitting screams. "The fun stuff!"

Caleb summarized his meeting with the difficult client. Then he tested the waters by asking about Jake's family. "Losing my father and brother in the same year made me think about your family a lot more. Do you ever see yourself attempting to reconcile with them?"

Jake wasted no time responding. "Hell no! When I left Iowa ten years ago, I buried those people so deep, it'd take an earthquake to jolt that tragedy back into my life." Jake confessed that he'd never explained the complete story about his reason for leaving Iowa. "I told you I came out to my parents when I graduated college, and that's when they disowned me, but I didn't want to face the truth. I'm sorry I left a big piece out."

"Aren't any of your siblings open-minded? You said your sister protected you the night your father hit you, right?" Caleb finished packing his luggage and prepared to check out of the hotel.

"Yep, Chloe was a big help. She drove me to the free clinic a few towns away. Told me she couldn't risk being seen in her hometown with a dirty fag. She thought someone would assume my pimp had beaten me up. Real good sister. She cared more about becoming a caterer and growing organic foods on her farm than caring about what happened to me." As Jake spoke, pots and pans repeatedly clanged in the background, drowning out part of his voice.

"I thought you said she helped." Caleb didn't understand what Jake had meant.

"Chloe loved me, and she wanted to protect me, but she also agreed with my parents that homosexuality is a sin. We spent the entire car ride talking about how to fix my deviant behavior. She's not a good person underneath it all." Jake explained that his sister sought medical help so he would be strong enough to repent and move on, not because she loved him. "She always wanted to move to the New York area. When we're in Connecticut, I worry I'll run into her sometimes."

"I'm so sorry. I didn't realize things were that bad. Even your brothers?" Caleb didn't want to mention Warren as Jake had never revealed the names of all his siblings.

"They all knew what happened. Even the one brother I thought might've stood up for me. Warren watched our father drag me by my hair across the backyard to the henhouse. He heard me screaming for help and did nothing."

Jake's father had tied his thirteen-year-old son to the wall, his hands bound together with coarse rope. At first, Jake thought his old man planned to hang him. His ruthless father made him stand on a chair while he tied a knot and looped it over a hook on the dilapidated shack. When he placed it around Jake's hands and secured them together, the jerk lifted his son higher to ensure the hook caught the rope, then kicked the chair out from under him. Ultra-thin and weak compared to his brutish father or other boys his age, Jake was too scared to retaliate. He dangled against a bug-infested wall among the dirty chickens, tears streaming down his cheeks, begging his father not to hurt him anymore.

"He wouldn't listen to me. My father whipped me for ten minutes, reciting Bible verses like they were the specials of the day at the local diner. My skin cracked open and bled like a leaky garden hose to the ground. Never enough to kill me. Just enough to teach me a lesson."

Jake's sister eventually ran out and begged their father to stop before he killed his son. Jake's mother had immediately taken the rest of the children to church to pray for their brother, the sinner. Jake's father spit on his son and insisted he change his ways or that whipping would be his new daily punishment. That's when Chloe released her brother from the wall and drove him to the clinic.

"I don't know how you ever survived all of this, babe." Caleb's body shivered at learning what his husband had truly suffered through years ago.

"That night, I left Iowa on a crowded bus. Stole money from Chloe's purse while she was working in the field, and I never went back." Jake had no desire to see or hear from his brother, and he told Caleb he never wanted to discuss the past again.

"I am so sorry. I will never bring it up." Caleb comforted his husband for a few more minutes, then hung up the phone. Enormous amounts of guilt weighed him down.

Caleb understood why Jake didn't want to see his family, particularly Warren, who'd done nothing to stop their father. But Jake didn't know Warren felt guilty and harbored the same secret. They were both teenagers, burdened with parents who should've known better. Who should've been in prison for every nasty punishment they'd delivered. In that moment, Caleb was torn between helping his husband heal from a horrific past and finding a way to mend the future. Would meeting Warren now make things easier to accept? Would it bring back the trauma of the past?

Days passed before Caleb returned Warren's call. When he did, Caleb decided not to reveal anything he and Jake had spoken about. Caleb had already gotten too involved in something that wasn't his decision to make, and he wanted to respect his husband's wishes. Warren claimed to understand, but he checked in a few times during the next couple of weeks, even begged Caleb to reconsider his decision. They argued about it too, especially when Warren threatened to show up at Jake's and Caleb's house in Maine and declare he'd located his brother on his own.

Caleb believed Warren had nothing but good intentions, but his priority was to protect Jake. As the days passed, Caleb wavered on his decision, wondering whether Jake would regret it in the future. Their son might want to know more about both of his fathers' families and childhoods. The conversation would undoubtedly resurrect itself again when Ethan was older. If Jake wouldn't confront his past now, it could be much harder when their son began asking questions in the coming years.

Caleb decided it would be best if he secretly engineered a casual run-in where Jake and Warren would be in the same place. He informed Warren about his mother's upcoming birthday party and considered giving him the exact address. Caleb instead directed Warren to meet him in Connecticut that weekend, and they'd pick a coffee shop nearby to chat. At the last minute, Caleb decided not to give him the address until the day they met. Caleb planned to ask his aunt or his mother to watch the baby so he could take Jake on an afternoon date. They'd stop for a snack and Warren would surprisingly be in the café. Caleb knew it was wrong to deceive his husband, but if he told him the truth, if he asked Jake to give his brother a chance again, without having run into him, Jake wouldn't agree.

To Caleb, one slight lie or hidden truth was worth reuniting two brothers who clearly needed each other again. Caleb would give anything to have another chance with his brother Ethan, to not throw away a decade of their time together when they could've bonded and shared hundreds of more memories with one another.

Caleb and Warren chatted a few times in the weeks before Olivia's party. Caleb sensed Jake knew something was going on, but he was careful never to say too much or be caught chatting on the phone with Warren. Jake had gotten a mite suspicious, even asked if things were okay between them. Caleb assumed Jake was just nervous about returning to Connecticut to see Olivia again. As much as they'd gotten along the last few times, Caleb's mother could be a handful to digest all in one sitting.

Even Warren seemed inordinately nervous to meet his brother. He mentioned several issues with his job and business partner. He appeared excessively interested in Caleb's family. Caleb assumed it was because he'd likely have to meet them at some point, and maybe Warren was reluctant to trust others after the experience in his own family.

A few days before the trip from Maine to Connecticut, Caleb confirmed the plans with Warren. He picked the time and location to meet—the day after Olivia's birthday party. When he packed the car and they drove off, Caleb promised Jake that he felt a positive vibe concerning their trip. Things were going to change, that their family would grow closer. In his heart and mind, he meant Jake's family, but Jake thought Caleb's comment referenced the Glass family. Sometimes you had to tell a white lie, make the tough decisions, do what someone wouldn't initially like… simply to protect them in the long run. At the last minute, he left a message for Warren indicating the trip was canceled. Caleb kept changing his mind, unwilling to hurt his husband any further. Warren seemed upset about the news too.

Chapter 18 – Flashback (Matt)

Matt answered the front door, eager to meet the third and final candidate for the role of housekeeper in the Glass family home. His mother had already left for Italy, and the previous maid and cook both resigned after many years of service to Matt's parents. It was up to him and Margaret to choose their additional help, and for Matt, it remained one of the only things occupying his time these days.

Margaret had already interviewed several nannies and selected the best candidate, in her opinion as she fiercely reminded him on multiple occasions. One who had thirty years of experience, followed the same child-rearing methods, and responded to Margaret's questions with the most direct and clear answers, never any wavering or excessive chatting. Margaret had truly raved about her, convincing Matt that he didn't need to meet any of the potential nannies. He accepted her decision, and the woman showed up at the house the Monday after Thanksgiving. She was not the kind of person he wanted looking after his new baby, nor his three older daughters, but Margaret wouldn't let him do anything once he'd returned from the rehabilitation center.

"You need to rest. I'll take care of the household for now. You get better," she often repeated, pinching his cheeks and patting his head like a spoiled puppy.

At first, Matt went along with her mandates. Then, when he happened to be home during the interviews for the second open position, he vehemently put his foot down. There would be no more old, stubborn, ornery women running his life. Matt had insisted the agency send someone younger and cheerier. Someone who would bring levity and happiness to a house that had been grieving too many months since Ben and Ethan died.

When he opened the door, a mid-twenties Sicilian woman named Pilar introduced herself to him. "The agency sent me over this morning. I hope it's still a good time."

Matt smiled at her, inwardly excited that someone had finally listened to him. His father's law partners, Wittleton and Davis, hadn't returned his calls about the possibility of returning to the office sooner than originally planned. His brothers were all busy with their own lives and couldn't meet him for long lunches, golf games, or fishing trips. Margaret was engulfed in her new role assuming control of Olivia's charities. She barely spent any time at home other than to monitor his every move with a fine-tooth comb. The girls had a nanny to keep them occupied, and she was extremely strict about her schedule.

"It's perfect timing. I'm so glad to see the agency understood what I was looking for." Matt felt odd stating his thoughts in such a way as he meant no disrespect. While Pilar was a gorgeous woman, he was committed to Margaret and had no inclination or desire to cheat on her. Having a minor temptation in the house was his reward for behaving at the rehab center for over a month. Eye candy was just that… eye candy.

"But we haven't even talked about the job yet, sir," she replied. Pilar stepped inside the hall when Matt ushered her through the threshold. "What a beautiful home! I could definitely see myself living here and keeping everything in impeccable shape."

"Yes, that would be ideal, wouldn't it?" Matt led Pilar into his late father's study and suggested she sit on the sofa. He dragged a single chair closer to her. "I've read your resume, and I met with all the other candidates, so... let's have our interview, and then I hope to decide very soon."

Margaret returned home during the interview, apologizing for running late. She took over the questioning and politely escorted Pilar to the door at the end. Once Pilar left, Margaret ripped the woman's resume in half and tossed it in the wastepaper basket. "No, no, she's not the type of woman we're looking for."

Matt had no energy to argue with his wife. If he pushed back, she'd yell at him for stressing out. If he put his foot down, she'd worry he was hooked on drugs again. Whether he spent the entire day surfing the internet, binging his favorite television shows, or wandering around the property, he felt tired and useless. Matt needed to get back to work, where he could focus his attention on projects, accounts, and financial planning.

Maude, the sponsor he'd only just begun to connect with, had suggested he wait until after the holidays before considering a return to his old job. She insisted it would be beneficial if he completed the outpatient portion of his recovery process and learned all the tricks and skills to manage his anxiety and addictions. Matt ultimately caved, not because he believed Margaret and Maude were right, but because his late father's partners still hadn't committed to his return date to the office.

After another quiet afternoon, Matt called the agency himself to inquire if there were any other candidates. Upon learning no others existed, he requested that they send Pilar back the following morning for a final interview. The agency agreed, and that night, Matt convinced his wife to give herself twenty-four hours before deciding between the first two women they'd met with earlier that week. He needed to buy himself some time to verify if Pilar was qualified and ready to handle the entire Glass family household.

The next morning, Matt waited for Margaret to leave for her appointment with her fellow board members. Matt kissed each of his daughters goodbye, told the newly hired nanny that he had his own meetings to attend to, and briskly left the house for his two-mile walk. He could've driven to the café where he decided to meet Pilar, but the drive would take less than ten minutes and a walk would keep him busy for at least thirty, possibly more if he strolled casually and peeked in on all the neighbor's yards and renovations. It was still warm for early December, and if there were anything Matt had on his hands these days, it was time to explore the world around him.

During their discussion, Pilar told Matt that she'd immigrated to the country with her parents two decades earlier and had gotten her Green Card recently. She wasn't currently married and had no children, which would make moving into the Glass family home much easier. Pilar's parents had passed on several years ago, and she desperately needed a new job, something to throw herself into. She'd fallen into a rut in the last few months. "Perhaps taking care of another family will help me feel better."

"I've experienced that rut too. Things haven't gone so smoothly for me, but you don't care to hear all those details." Matt held himself back from saying too much, fearing if he unloaded about all his personal problems, Pilar would run from their interview and never look back.

By lunchtime, they decided there was nothing else to cover. Matt thanked Pilar for her time, certain she was the ideal person to hire. He would find a way to persuade his wife to listen to him for just this once. That night, during dinner, after the children were fed and retired to their rooms for bed, Margaret and Matt discussed the candidates. "So, have you decided, babe?"

"I really can't choose. They're both qualified and got along well with our new nanny. I think either will be an excellent fit."

Margaret pushed food around her plate and reclined against the back of the chair in the dining room, waiting for Matt to finish his meal.

Matt had been taking his time, thinking about how to best convince Margaret that Pilar should get the job. When Margaret stood to clear the table, Matt blurted out his opinion. He explained to his wife that he couldn't have two clones running around the house, reminding him of what it was like when he was a child. "Pilar will bring life to this place. She will keep our children energized and happy. I have asked you for nothing in the last two months. I've done everything that's been requested of me at the rehab center. I see my sponsor several times a week. I'm waiting until the new year to go back to work. Please, just this once, can you trust me to make a decision?"

Matt apologized for screwing up so many things in their life in the previous months, when he'd almost lost the house because the mortgage fell behind, when he'd endangered their daughter because he'd gotten high on pills, when he'd stolen money from his father's firm to support his habits. Matt knew he had little chance of winning this battle with Margaret, but he had to give it his all and hope for the best.

Margaret leaned in and kissed her husband's forehead. "You've been an amazing husband and father for so many years. I know all the stress got to you, and your light just burned out this summer." She paused, staring at him for at least another minute without saying anything. "You've also done an incredible job at turning things around in a very short time period."

"I'm not sure what you're saying," Matt mumbled, confused by her statements.

"If it's that important to you… if you need to have some control or say on this decision, I can go along with hiring Pilar. I don't want to be a nagging wife who treats you poorly." Margaret told her husband that she hadn't forgiven him for everything that happened in the last year, but she trusted him enough to let him choose their new housekeeper. "Let's hire her. But if she screws up in the first week too many times, you better send her back to the agency immediately. Deal?"

"You're the best, babe. I've got this one, I promise."

"Ugh! Your mother is gonna think I've lost my mind for choosing Pilar. You must tell her this was your choice. Olivia already throws too much shade at me, hon."

Matt pressed his lips against his wife's, then led her to the bedroom. They made love and cuddled with one another for hours. Something about being seven months pregnant had ignited Margaret's sensual side, and they fell against the sheets, sweaty and exhausted. Margaret had never even gotten up to pee the entire night, and when Matt saw the nanny in the morning, he smiled for the first time in weeks.

By the afternoon, the agency called to confirm that Pilar could start working the following week, and she'd swing by later on to see her bedroom and determine what she would need to buy or bring with her. Matt and Margaret discussed how to manage their new life together, and for once since everything had fallen apart in his life, Matt had positive hope for the future.

After reviewing instructions and touring the house with Pilar the next day, Matt called his mother to check in on her trip. Diane answered the phone, explaining that Olivia had gone to the spa for a few hours.

"What are you two doing for Christmas? We're going to miss you. It was very different at Thanksgiving without Mom and Dad around this year." Matt plopped himself into the easy chair in his bedroom and got comfortable under a blanket.

"I think it was by design, Matty. Your mother needed to be somewhere else for the first major holiday without her husband. It was hard enough handling his birthday earlier this year." Diane also noted that Olivia had told her it was important to give her sons a chance to make the Glass estate a new home for their families too.

"Maybe Mom will actually become a stronger woman. She's done so much to change her ways." Matt had always loved his mother, but he was determined not to grow up like her. When he married Margaret, he knew that he'd found someone with similar tendencies as his mother, but Margaret had also possessed a distinct energy, a modern outlook on life. With each child they had, she had grown more weary and antsy, but she had still retained much of her beauty and charm.

"You all have. I'm proud of your recovery." Diane explained that she had met someone new recently too. "It's the first time a man has flirted with me in years."

"But you've been married for almost thirty of them."

"Exactly. Your Uncle George is a tiresome cad, and if this divorce doesn't go through soon, I might just hire a hitman!"

Matt and Diane finished their conversation, leaving him with stronger hope for his future. He decided to call Wittleton and Davis one more time, and if they didn't respond, he'd abandon it until the new year. It was his only option.

When Davis answered the phone, she told Matt that he'd begun to make a nuisance of himself. "You must listen to me. Things are not going well here at the firm. Several clients have terminated their contracts with us."

"But why? What's happened?"

Davis replied, "I am not sure yet. They all seem to prefer working with your father. He's no longer around, and they have to understand it's necessary to move forward. I am not being harsh, but we have a business to run."

"Maybe I could help. I've got time on my hands." Matt wanted to do something useful, and this seemed like an ideal opportunity.

"No. We will discuss this again in February when your six-month leave of absence is over. Besides, I'm still trying to sort out all the financial problems you caused. Warren Payne will be the death of me!" Davis hung up the phone.

Matt knew he'd made a mess of things, but this was all in the past. He scrolled through his phone, searching for contacts who might help him get a new job. When he stumbled upon the name Quinn, his stomach plummeted. Matt hadn't thought about his former drug dealer in months. Shortly after Matt had entered the rehab center, the guy had been locked up in prison. Matt checked the date on the calendar, realizing Quinn was scheduled for parole soon. Would he reach back out to Matt? Quinn hadn't even known Matt quit using drugs. It had been around the time Matt bought his last bottle of uppers when his family confronted him, insisting he attend rehab. Quinn was then sent to prison for three months.

Matt almost deleted the contact from his phone, hoping if the name didn't pop up, he could ignore the call. He was tempted to block the number, but something convinced him to keep the lines open. His life was on an upward trend, and he was strong enough to fight off the temptations. There was no reason for him to go back to drugs again. All he had to do was get a job and focus on his wife and daughters.

Chapter 19 – Flashback (Teddy)

Chilly air poured from the air conditioning vents in their hospital room, the rattle of its noisy mechanics ending the awkward silence that lingered among all three inhabitants. Sarah rested in the bed, the covers pulled above her head, ignoring the doctor's questions. Teddy sat across the room in an uncomfortable chair containing a hole separating the pleather fabric from the scratched and splintered wooden frame. He picked at the tiny void until his index finger penetrated enough of the weakened surface and clawed at the yellow foam layer underneath. No one had uttered a word in the last two minutes.

"It's useless. She hasn't spoken to me since it happened," Teddy barked at the on-call physician who'd stopped by to conduct a final exam before releasing Sarah from the hospital. They lost their baby two days earlier and she had crept into a pit, unwilling to express any grief or comfort her husband who'd lost a child too.

The doctor nodded as though he understood the intense pain they were experiencing and signaled to Teddy to join him in the outside hallway. Teddy hesitantly rose from his chair, a few drops of blood dripping from his finger to the floor. He called out to his wife, "I'll be right outside if you need anything." When the door lock snicked against the metal clasp, a series of chills cascaded down Teddy's spine and aggravated the nerves in several sensitive teeth. He'd forgotten how often he clenched his jaw when anger or bitterness got the best of him.

"The nurses tell me she's refused any food, has been awake for over forty-eight hours, and declines to utter a single word." The doctor rested a hand on Teddy's shoulder, jumping when Teddy flinched and stepped backward to avoid the man's grip. "In tragic times such as these, patients react differently. It's not uncommon for one spouse or partner to avoid the other. When you take her home, she'll make significant progress. Open up about the loss. You need to be there for her."

Teddy angrily scanned the physician from head to toe. Old enough to be retired, the man had lost any sense of genuine bedside manner. Once Sarah had chosen to go mute, unwilling to share the inexplicable loss with her husband, Teddy knew he would need to find his own path to accepting the death of their baby. The floor staff wanted the room back to care for other patients, citing that insurance wouldn't cover unnecessary, lengthy hospital stays. Had this man ever lost a child before? One of his own? Not a patient's sickly, underdeveloped infant who'd never been given a fighting chance to survive. But a child of his own flesh and blood?

"I know how to take care of my wife." Teddy shoved both hands in his pockets and crossed to the opposite side of the hall. "Perhaps you can give her something to jolt her system, force her to deal with our new reality?"

The doctor shook his head, and a scratchy tsk tsk sound reverberated in the hallway. "It's too soon. I don't like to overmedicate my patients. I've already authorized something to address any physical pain, but we need to focus on stabilizing her mental faculties. Getting her mind well again, I mean."

"Well? How can she ever be well again?" Teddy reflected on the conversation from earlier that morning, when another specialist had told them both it would be impossible for Sarah to give birth to a child in the future. He understood little about women's physical anatomy, but if her uterus had been damaged that severely, Sarah wouldn't be able to carry another child to term.

"It's still very early. There are injuries from this pregnancy. Once the swelling goes down, we'll run another battery of tests before we conclude our final analysis." The doctor marked something on his clipboard and handed it to a nurse as she walked by. She waited at his side and smiled at Teddy.

"You shouldn't have told us this soon. We just lost the baby. Can't we grieve for one loss before thinking about another?" Teddy scrunched his fists together inside his pocket, tensing his leg muscles and back until he became so jittery, he forced himself to stop.

"We told you there was a strong likelihood she couldn't conceive another child. Not one hundred percent. It's better to address everything at once, then take steps to determine our potential solution." The doctor turned to the nurse. "Is the bereavement counselor stopping by soon?"

"Yes, she's waiting at the station for you." The nurse stepped away when the doctor dismissed her, noting she'd escort the woman to Sarah's room momentarily.

"If Sarah's not speaking to anyone, what good is a damned counselor?" Teddy growled at the physician, no longer willing to sugarcoat his feelings.

The doctor explained that it was often helpful for a new parent who'd lost a child to listen to the counselor's soothing voice and helpful advice, to hear various options about next steps. "We also need to discuss how you'd like to handle the burial or cremation, whatever you decide to do. The counselor can recommend several funeral homes that specialize in the loss of an infant."

Teddy had been focused on dealing with the future, helping his wife adjust to their son's death. He hadn't thought about a funeral service or final resting place for a newborn.

When the doctor excused himself to see another patient, Teddy returned to the hospital room. In the five minutes he'd been outside in the hallway, Sarah had risen from the bed, washed her face, combed her hair, and put on the clothes she'd been wearing when he'd first brought her to the hospital. She sat in the chair he'd previously occupied and slipped her feet into a pair of shoes. Sarah winced as she bent over, swallowed loudly, and stood tall.

Teddy rushed over to help balance her as she had almost teetered to the side. "What are you doing? I'll help you. Don't move too fast yet."

Sarah batted at his hands. "Go away." She grabbed her coat from the hook on the far wall and shuffled toward the door. "I'm leaving you. For good. We're done, Teddy."

"You don't mean that. We need to support each other, Sarah." He watched as she flicked the door handle and exited the room.

Sarah turned to him, grasping the door frame for support, and shouted, "Don't follow me!"

"We need to talk about this. We're scheduled to see the bereavement counselor any minute. The baby needs a proper burial." Teddy stepped forward to prevent his wife from leaving the room, but his body flooded with all the emotions he'd buried in the last forty-eight hours.

Sarah left the room and wandered down the hallway. Teddy couldn't bring himself to stop her. He tumbled to the floor, wanting to weep for the loss of his child. His future. Potentially his wife. No tears would come. Five minutes passed before he could lift himself off the ground and regain his composure. When he entered the hallway, the grief counselor approached him to discuss next steps.

Teddy listened to the woman's words, explaining that Sarah had just left the hospital and needed more time before she could discuss their loss. The counselor urged Teddy to follow his wife, which he quickly did, stumbling upon her arguing with the security guard who demanded to see her paperwork before she could depart the hospital.

"I'll take it from here," Teddy advised the guard. "There's been a misunderstanding."

But there hadn't been. Sarah reluctantly agreed to wait for the doctor to officially release her from the hospital. She declined to chat with the grief counselor, and once she arrived home, Sarah went directly to bed. For three days, she refused to speak with Teddy about anything. He attempted to talk to Sarah about the decisions they needed to make regarding their son's burial, but she snubbed engaging with him in the conversation. Teddy told her that he'd delay the process as long as he could until she was ready to discuss it.

Sarah was never ready. After she recovered physically in that first week, while Teddy was out meeting with the doctor, grief counselor, and the funeral parlors, Sarah packed several bags and holed up in an unknown hotel room. Teddy was unable to track her down, and she wouldn't return his phone calls. After two weeks, Sarah left him a message that she'd hired an attorney and was filing for a divorce. She demanded fifty percent of their marital assets and instructed Teddy to let the lawyers work everything out.

During that time, Teddy processed his grief in his own way. He met with someone from the funeral home where he selected and reviewed all his options for burying their dead infant. When asked if he wanted to provide a name for the child, or list his son's death by stating Boy Glass, Teddy took a minute to decide. If Sarah couldn't have any more children, and he was dead set against adoption, it meant they would be a childless couple. He knew then that he had to bestow a piece of himself on the child, and so he advised them to call the child Teddy Junior.

Having lost his father and his brother in the last year, Teddy buried his son in the same cemetery. He told no one else about his son's death, and he had no service other than a brief reflection in one of the rooms at the funeral parlor where he offered a teary goodbye. After forty-eight hours, the cemetery staff interred his son. Teddy visited the grave every day in the last month, stopping to grieve for his father, brother, and son—the trio of losses he'd suffered that year.

When Sarah learned he'd buried their son without her input, she verbally assaulted him on the phone. Although he'd given her several opportunities to participate, Sarah couldn't accept his decision. After nearly a month had passed since her baby's death, she found a way to cope with the loss, but she also insisted he be buried back home with her in the South so she could visit her son whenever she wanted to. Teddy tried to reason with his wife, but it always failed and exploded into smithereens.

Instead, Sarah returned home to Savannah and requested a larger settlement, including a demand that Teddy authorize an exhumation of her son's remains. Teddy refused to disturb his son's final resting place. For once in his life, he'd made the proper decision. He also knew the value of moving on and accepting everything that had transpired in the last year. His life was never meant for anything but tragedy and pain.

Chapter 20 – Flashback (Zach)

"Are you sure this is where you want to eat dinner?" Zach halted in front of *Le Joliet's* picturesque window displays and scrunched his face at the ornate and gilded exterior of the building. Modern yet designed with authentic French furniture, art, and music as if you'd stepped into the Montmartre arrondissement in Paris.

It was the type of place where men usually wore ties and women dressed to the nines. Not his kind of establishment. Also, he no longer owned any ties. Tie. He used to have one tie. For weddings and funerals. And even then, only if he cared about the person. He'd worn it three times last year. His father's wake. His brother's wedding. His brother's funeral. By Thanksgiving, he'd been so tired of wearing the tie that year that he tossed it in a campfire on Caleb's property in Maine. Watching the burning fabric turn to ash was cathartic.

"*Le Joliet* feels like the proper way to say goodbye. Don't you think?" Emma grabbed hold of Zach's arm and rested her head on his broad shoulders.

Zach considered his response. After driving to Boston the previous day, he and Emma had successfully gone through all of Ethan's belongings. Emma had asked him to help her sort everything into keep, throw-away, and maybe piles. Even then, the keep pile would be further subdivided into items Emma herself wanted to preserve and those Zach would bring back with him to Connecticut for the rest of the family to retain mementos.

"I don't believe in saying goodbye." Zach turned to the side and cupped Emma's cheeks in his hands. "Nor should you. Ethan lives on in our memories. With all those things we packed in boxes today." He stared into her eyes, falling for her beauty even more than he thought possible when he'd first arrived.

The trip to Boston had come up unexpectedly. He'd just spent Thanksgiving with the family at Caleb's house in Maine. Emma called while he was driving home with Matt, Margaret, and all the kids in their minivan. Anastasia had insisted the cousins all travel together, so Zach had been forced to ride along. Margaret was six-months pregnant and claimed that lengthy car rides made her nauseous, so she had to sit in the front passenger seat. Zach was relegated to the furthest row in the back with Matt's one-year-old daughter in her car seat. The other girls commandeered the middle row, and each watched a different loud movie on their various devices.

Emma invited Zach to sort through Ethan's items with her. She'd found a new apartment on her own and needed to be out of the one she'd shared with his brother by the end of the month. Zach knew Matt and Margaret could watch his daughter, so he arranged a date to meet Emma in Boston in December. He'd been thinking a lot about Emma since his brother died and she'd run off quickly one morning, declaring it was important to return to Boston. He knew she was torn between forcing herself to move beyond her husband's sudden death and wallowing in the comfort of his childhood home. But something had happened in the days before she left Connecticut, and Zach was determined to find out what it was. Of course, he needed to be the one to pack up Ethan's apartment and do something to help his sister-in-law when she begged for his help.

Emma's eyes sparkled, but she glanced away in discomfort with their growing intimacy. "Come, I've asked for the table where he proposed. You should see the view everyone had of us."

A few minutes later, Zach and Emma settled at the tall table in the center of the room. The maître d' recognized Emma and immediately smiled. "The beautiful newlywed. But this… this man is not your husband. I don't understand." His English was clear, but with the French accent and his intended humorous jest, it appeared comical.

Zach laughed, uncertain how Emma would react. The man had no idea Ethan had died shortly after their marriage. To cover, Zach replied in his own faulty and abominable French accent, "But of course. I am her husband's brother. You must not tell him we were here. It is a dark family secret."

Emma dropped her head to the table. Zach wasn't sure if she were crying or laughing.

The maître d's face reddened quickly. "Ah, yes. You Americans become like us French romantics more every day. I know nothing of your dinner tonight." He offered to bring two glasses of champagne for them before retreating from the table.

"Make that two shots of whiskey and a couple of lagers. Whatever you've got on tap will be fine." Zach lifted his eyebrows and winked at the maître d' as he skulked away. "This is where you got engaged? No wonder I'm not getting married in this lifetime."

Emma's head rose from the table. She had been giggling, not sobbing at all. "Never?"

"I wouldn't say never, I guess. I just mean… if I get married, it will not be a fancy affair with crystal goblets, food that you need a half dozen forks for, the ones where no one but people like my mother know which one is used for which course." Zach described his perfect wedding to Emma. It took place on a beach beneath the setting sun, with waves crashing behind them, and only the necessary people—two witnesses and a justice of the peace—in attendance. "Or an ordained Voodoo priestess. Now that's the way to do it."

Emma cocked her head, startled by his retort. "Thank you for making me laugh. I needed it. There just wasn't an uncomplicated way for me to tell the poor maître d' what happened to Ethan."

Zach reached across the table for her hand, which gently brushed the cloth napkin she still hadn't unfolded. "Put your bib on, girl. We're gonna get sloppy tonight, and I don't want to stain Ethan's favorite sweater. I'm taking that gift home tonight."

They'd argued all afternoon about who got to keep Ethan's prized wool sweater. All five brothers had previously admired the one Ben had custom-made for them when he and their mother traveled to some Scandinavian country decades earlier. For years, they took turns getting chances to wear Dad's sweater until it deteriorated from all the use. That's when Ben surprised them with one for each son last Christmas, including a new sweater for himself too.

Somehow, Zach had lost his sweater back in Brooklyn that spring. He suspected Katerina had broken in and stolen it as Ben had paid a lot of money to have them custom-made for his five boys. It was one of the only expensive things Zach ever felt attached to in his life. They were the softest fabric he had ever touched, and when he wore it, something made Zach feel secure and loved. Olivia had kept Ben's sweater for herself, and Zach would never ask his mother for it. When Ben died, Zach mourned the loss of his father and his sweater, because to him, the two went hand-in-hand.

"I'll make you a deal," Emma bartered, raising the shot of whiskey a waiter had dropped off while they were talking. "You can have the sweater, but I get to keep Ethan's framed picture of the two of you and Michelle Obama."

Zach's heart crumbled into pieces. The Obamas had visited Ethan's college several years ago, and five students were permitted to attend a cocktail party with them. Zach had been visiting Ethan that weekend, missing his brother for some reason at the time. It was before Ethan and Emma had met. After all the background checks, Zach was approved as Ethan's guest, and they were permitted a single picture that night. They agreed on one with the president's wife as she represented everything good in the world to them, based on all she'd accomplished in her role. Ethan had kept the photograph with him, and Zach had lobbied hard for years to convince his brother why he should have it. In the days before he died, Ethan had finally gifted it to his brother, and Emma knew it was important to Zach.

"You, Emma Glass, are evil. That's so unfair." He withdrew his hand and downed his shot of whiskey. The waiter dropped by to share the specials and take their orders.

When he left, Emma rolled her eyes at Zach. "I'm only kidding. You can have the picture and the sweater. I've already kept so much of Ethan's stuff." She stood, unbuttoned the sweater, and draped it around Zach's shoulders. Before returning to her chair, she kissed his cheek. "Thank you for being here today. I couldn't have done this without you."

Zach's instincts declined any diversion from watching Emma move. The curve of her hip as she sashayed back to her chair. The heart stopping cleavage she accidentally revealed when she bent down. The smell of her innocent, sweet body when she approached him. The girl was a perfect ten, and if he didn't control himself, he'd do something regrettable in the middle of the restaurant. Kiss her. Lift her onto his lap. Take her on the table. All the things he'd permitted to roam the perimeter of his brain but would never act on in person until she was ready. Until she gave him permission.

"Eh, I'm a good guy. Someday, you'll realize it." Zach knew he was pushing too hard, yet he refused to stop himself.

"Ah, yes. We should talk about what's going on, shouldn't we?" Emma swallowed a heavy gulp of beer, then slumped against the back of her chair. Before she could speak, her phone buzzed. Emma pulled it from her purse and squinted curiously while reading it.

"Everything okay?" Zach held his hand up as the waiter walked by, requesting two more beers.

Emma's face scrunched like a wrinkled pug. "It's a friend. I need to take the call. Do you mind?"

Zach shrugged. "No problem. Go ahead." As Emma walked away, Zach read the name on the face of the phone, but he had no idea to whom it belonged.

While Emma stepped into the lobby, Zach pulled out his own phone and ignored several messages from Katerina requesting to speak with him about custody of their daughter. He dialed Tressa and inquired about her day.

"It's fantastic. The bartender and I just went on our first official date. I think she likes me," replied Tressa, teasing Zach because she knew she could easily get to him.

"Don't. I can't handle it today, princess. I've got more issues with the women in my life than I know how to handle." Zach watched Emma pace the lobby carpet, her expressions growing more animated as the conversation unfolded. He had no idea who Rowena Hector was, but the woman had obviously shocked or upset Emma.

"You're with Emma again, aren't you? Papi, nunca eschuchas, tonto estupido." Tressa continued to berate him in the background.

"I'm not a stupid fool. And I do listen to you, but she asked me to help. I didn't push her this time." Zach caught Tressa up to speed on their dinner at *Le Joliet*. "I think she's warming up to me more. Should I stick around another night? Or head home after dinner?"

"Home."

"You sure?" he whined, unable to accept her first immediate response. "That was too quick."

"Loco. All the men en mi vida son locos." Tressa yelled at someone else in the room with her, then returned to Zach. "Take her lead. Stop being a pussy. When I met you, you were too much to handle all at once because of how masculine and wicked you were. This girl has reduced you to a boy again."

"Have you ever been in love?" Zach ignored her insults and comments.

"If this is love, then I hope it never finds me. I gotta go. Boss wants answers on something. Te amo, pussy boy."

Zach laughed when Tressa hung up on him. She'd truly been his equal when it came to how they approached life, from drinking to cussing and fighting and fucking. Unless it came to love. Zach had a soft spot for love. He'd been hurt too many times, and even though he never thought he'd get married, he wanted to feel that all-powerful, consuming love. The kind he'd kill to experience just once in his life. Some days, he suspected that girl might be Emma.

As he sighed, Emma approached the table, her skin almost translucent. "I'm so sorry, but I must go. Something came up. Can we head back to the apartment? I need to deal with an issue, and you should probably go."

Zach tried to coax more out of her, but Emma wasn't interested in chatting on the walk back to her and Ethan's apartment. When they arrived, he loaded the remaining boxes into his car and offered to stick around to help her with whatever had come up.

"No, really. I need to do this by myself," Emma noted. When she went to kiss his cheek to say goodbye, Zach turned his head in the nick of time.

As their lips briefly met, Zach felt every breath inside his body yearn for more. He pulled her closer to him, wrapped his free hand around her waist, and passionately kissed her more deeply.

Emma appeared to encourage his affections at first, but then she pulled away. "No, we can't. Really, I just… you should go." Emma tossed the last bag at him, then pushed him into the hallway.

Zach winced as she closed the door. He waited for her to open it up again and invite him back inside, but she never did. Had he pushed her too far? Had Rowena called her and said something horrible about him? If Katerina was involved, he'd kill the woman. Zach wanted to break down the door and ask Emma to listen to him, to give him a chance to be something more than a friend. But he remembered Tressa's words and let Emma take the lead.

As Zach wandered to his car, he wondered whether he would ever see Emma again. She'd become someone so important to him, so vital to his future, that he couldn't visualize one without her. Zach closed the car door and started the engine. "Emma, I will find a way to make this work between us. I think we were intended to find one another, and my brother was the guide bringing us together."

Chapter 21 – Flashback (Emma)

On the day Zach helped Emma pack all of Ethan's belongings, she decided to give him a chance to prove himself to her. While she wasn't interested in pursuing a relationship with him in the immediate future, something about the man made her feel special and loved. Ethan had always made her feel that way, but he was gone forever. It was too soon to let her heart open up again. In time, she would be willing to explore the options.

During their dinner at *Le Joliet*, Emma received Rowena's phone call informing her Ethan's biological father was alive. Emma wanted to meet him. She invited Rowena and Flynn to visit her once she moved into a smaller one bedroom on the other side of Boston and before she began her new job as a choral director. After Rowena and Flynn celebrated the Christmas holiday in Scotland, they flew to the United States and arrived at Emma's apartment early one morning after New Year's Day. They spent several hours discussing the past, cooking a traditional Scottish lunch, and getting to know one another.

"I can't imagine what it was like for you in Bosnia," Emma said, her heart full of love, admiration, and anger. "But you're alive, and you found Rowena again after all these years."

Rowena and Flynn turned to one another, holding hands and lovingly staring into each other's souls. "When I lost my husband two months ago, I had no idea what life would hold for me in the future. I guess God always has a plan in place, even when we don't realize it."

"Being a prisoner of war is something that will live with me forever," Flynn stated matter-of-factly, stretching his limbs and stepping away from the couch. "I used to wake up every night, screaming and sweating. It's taken years to accept everything."

"I've read a lot about your experiences. When Rowena shared what happened to you, I couldn't help but research the war more." Emma had never realized the atrocities that'd been committed in the recent past. She assumed that soldiers had been captured and tortured only in the previous wars, stopping by the late twentieth century, after Vietnam and Korea. "You never hear about the details of Bosnia, and even the Persian Gulf and Afghanistan wars seem different." This was why Ethan had wanted her to do something special for his father's ancestors who'd been war heroes.

Flynn shook his head, grasping the frame of a dining room chair while arching his back. "No, the general population never understands what POWs go through in modern times."

"Are you still having nightmares? Is it... is it dangerous to others around you?" Emma didn't intend to insult him, but she'd never met someone who'd been imprisoned by another government or rogue militia before. "I don't want to ask anything if you're uncomfortable answering."

Rowena joined Flynn at the table. "He can talk about it sometimes. Not always."

"I've been safe, back home now for two decades. The biggest truth I can tell you is that it's not the same for everyone who's been captured." Flynn explained what happened when he first went to Bosnia to cover the war.

Once combat began, he'd been pressured by his newspaper to report on the conflict. Flynn was assigned to cover a story on ethnic cleansing, a common goal among some insurgents. There were so many views on how Yugoslavia was broken into smaller territories and countries, and Flynn thought his best angle would be to address them all. During an interview, a chain bomb exploded. Several people died around him, but he survived. In the first hour, he was dragged to a nearby building and shackled to a wall. The group who'd bombed the building where the interview was being held did not understand who he was, but once they learned he was a reporter, they forced him to tell their story to the public.

"I interviewed them for days, using a translator, pen, and paper. At some point, tensions escalated even further inside the area where I was detained." Suddenly, he was kidnapped by another group of nationalists and taken miles away to an underground facility. The kidnappers tortured Flynn for days as they believed he knew secrets about their opponents. "After two years, things began to calm down. A kind guard took pity on a few of us, and he helped me escape."

When Flynn excused himself to use the bathroom, Rowena finished the story. "That's when the effects of his imprisonment struck Flynn the most. He struggled with suddenly being free and having no idea how to get home. He roamed Eastern Europe in a daze for two years, accepting odd jobs to survive." Rowena explained that Flynn hardly ever spoke about what happened in those two years, but one day, he'd found the strength to return to Scotland.

Flynn rejoined them in the living room. "Could I make a cup of tea, please?"

Emma rose from the couch and put the kettle on. "Of course. How silly of me. I should've suggested it earlier." She offered him a selection of teas, and when he picked one, she placed it in his mug. "You're a brave man, Flynn."

"I don't know about brave. I know I'm a changed man. I know things will never be the same for me again. The concepts of trust and comfort mean so much less to me now." Flynn cupped Emma's cheek in his hand. "But maybe in time I'll accept everything that has been lost."

Rowena revealed that Flynn would be moving to the United States in the subsequent weeks. "We're going to spend more time together. Maybe we can find our way back to one another again." Rowena had been a teenager when she'd gotten pregnant with their child in the early nineties and Flynn had been presumed dead. They were currently both in their forties and still had plenty of life left to live.

"I've never been here before. I'm looking forward to what America has to offer." Flynn watched as Emma poured hot water into his mug. "Your country is obsessed with guns, though. I'm not sure I'll ever be okay around them again."

Although Flynn laughed, Emma could see the fear percolating on his face. "It's a difficult issue to understand. We're so divided right now about our identity in the United States. I write about it a lot on my blog. Hearing people's stories has become a passion of mine."

"Until you've had a gun pointed at you numerous times, no one truly understands the fear that polarizes your mind and body." Flynn warmed his hands on the mug and shuffled back into the living room.

"You should stay away from them as much as possible then. It must be a trigger for you?"

Rowena accepted her mug from Emma. "Yes. We've talked about it. My husband was an avid hunter. I've asked my stepchildren to take all the guns away."

After Rowena's husband passed away, she and her stepchildren had discussed how to handle his estate. He'd been married before Rowena, and while she'd been a mother to his children in small ways, they'd all been older when she entered the picture.

They insisted on collecting from their father's insurance policy and retaining any family heirlooms. Rowena agreed to give up most everything else, but she kept the house and a portion of his pension so she could live affordably.

"We'll make it work, somehow," Flynn added, an affectionate sparkle in his gaze.

"What will you do for work?" Emma joined them in the living room, sitting in a recliner she and her late husband had purchased the previous year.

"I went back to the newspaper once I returned to Scotland. I couldn't write or report anymore, but I learned how to repair the press machinery and manage some of the offices where we kept equipment." Flynn explained that he'd always been a hard-working mechanic and enjoyed using his hands. "I volunteered at the veteran's association too."

"What did you do there?" Emma admired Rowena and Flynn. They reminded her of solid, strong people who were the backbone of her country hundreds of years ago.

"I met with guys returning from overseas. Some women too. Helped them process reentry back into a normal life. Mostly just offered them advice and talked about my experiences." Flynn grew quiet, reflecting on his last twenty years since returning from Bosnia.

"Don't be modest." Rowena smiled at him. "He's considered a hero to everyone that comes back home after being on the frontline. He might not have military training, but he has life experience as a POW. Sometimes that's all you need to know how to survive."

Emma processed everything Flynn and Rowena shared with her. An idea began to formulate inside her cluttered brain. "Maybe you could do the same thing here in the US. We don't treat our veterans as well as we should. They need help, especially from someone who's been through it before."

"What are you suggesting?" Flynn asked, leaning forward to attentively listen to Emma's suggestions.

"Your son left money behind when he died. Money that the Glass family seems to be holding up." Emma explained that her husband had inherited two million dollars when his father passed away. Some had been spent to care for Ethan in his last few months, but the rest was in a trust somewhere. "Olivia, his adopted mother, controls it, at least based on what their attorney has informed me. But Ethan told me about it the week he…" Emma paused, still unable to say the words.

Rowena comforted her daughter-in-law. "It's okay, child. We understand what you're going through."

Emma brushed away a few tears. "You've lost your husband of twenty years. Flynn lost years of his life during his captivity. I have so much to learn from you both."

Flynn joined Rowena and kneeled next to Emma. "Maybe the three of us can be a little family. Help each other through the rough times."

Emma nodded. "That's why I think my idea is such an amazing one. If we can convince Olivia to release the money that Ethan meant for me to have, we can build an organization to help people like you who've suffered through so much pain."

Emma, Rowena, and Flynn discussed her idea for several hours that afternoon. They could create a charity to counsel people returning home from war or assignments where they were placed in tragic locations. People who suffered from military abuse, insurgence, and trauma. By dinnertime, they agreed on various approaches to building out their dream. Ethan's dream. Ben's dream.

"We need to talk to Olivia Glass," Flynn announced, his excitement feverishly brewing.

"I haven't confessed that I know the truth. I've been so angry that she hasn't told me about the money herself. Why would she hide this from me?" Emma fidgeted in the chair, the teacup bouncing on the saucer against her knee.

Rowena paced the room behind her. "Perhaps Olivia hasn't thought about it all that much. She could've thrown away the letter Ben left behind. She wasn't obligated to search for me. But she did. There is goodness in the woman."

Flynn replied, "So, you think she's processing through her grief and has forgotten about the money. You don't think Olivia's intentionally hiding it?" His agitation became more apparent as his speech grew rapid and flustered.

Emma leaped from the chair, confused and uncertain about what to do next. "I don't know. I just can't believe she departed for Italy and left me behind without answers." The teacup flew out of Emma's hands and fell on the floor, shattering into dozens of pieces.

Flynn had been looking out the window when the crash occurred. His body tensed, reminding him of all the incidents he suffered during his imprisonment. He screamed and dove behind the couch, momentarily unable to differentiate between the past and the present.

Rowena rushed to his side. "It's okay, Flynn. It's just a broken teacup. You're safe," she repeated many times in a soothing voice.

Emma watched as Rowena attended to Flynn, remembering how she'd taken care of her own husband in final weeks of his life. When he died, she lost part of her identity. While moving on was an option in the future, she needed something now to focus her attention on. She wasn't ready to give Zach a chance, and even though her new job offered possibilities, her passion was in helping people.

Emma decided she must get access to the money Ethan had left with Olivia. She would build a place to help people like Flynn recover from their trauma. It was the only thing that might help her process her own grief. And she owed it to Ethan and Ben.

While clinging to her husband's picture, Emma suddenly experienced a sharp flash, envisioning Ethan calling out her name as she disappeared into a strange tunnel with a blinding light. Every path she took was empty and quiet, and her heart thumped uncontrollably. "What was that about?" Emma whispered, observing her in-laws comforting one another.

Emma wanted to approach Rowena and Flynn, but her feet wouldn't listen to her heart. She yearned to feel the kind of love they had, and she'd lost the one man who'd given it to her. Instead, she steadied herself against a nearby wall and remembered the look in Ethan's eyes moments before he passed away. It was the only thing holding her together these days. "What are you trying to tell me, Ethan?"

Chapter 22 – 7:30 to 8:00 PM (Everyone)

"Are you sure the study won't be more private, ma'am?" queried Pilar, pausing to let Olivia consider the suggestion.

"No. Follow my instructions, exactly as I indicated. Bring the guest to the living room," demanded Olivia as she walked into the hallway with the maid. As Pilar hesitantly stepped toward the back of the house, the front doorbell rang. She glanced toward Olivia, who shrugged. "I thought you said our guest was at the back door?"

"Correct. I left the guest in the mudroom. Maybe someone else has arrived?" Pilar looked toward the back of the house, then again to the front. She appeared as perplexed as Olivia, uncertain what to do next. "I guess you'll want me to check on the doorbell first?"

Olivia grumbled. "No, I've waited long enough to see who sent this nasty note. You fetch our mysterious guest. I'll address whoever rang the doorbell. I have no patience for neighbors or salespeople right now."

As Pilar sprinted down the hallway, Diane informed everyone she would check on the children. "I need a minute before we see whom Pilar brings in. If it's George, I might just kill him tonight."

Diane dashed up the front staircase as everyone else murmured and whispered to one another.

Olivia strode toward the foyer and approached the front door. She peeped through the small hole and grinned widely. "Oh, it's Emma. She finally made it." She swung open the door and greeted her daughter-in-law. "Thank you, my darling. You're the best possible surprise."

Emma slowly withdrew from the embrace. "I couldn't miss your birthday, especially not when I have a few surprises to share with you." From the shadows, Rowena and Flynn moved into the amber light radiating from the outside porch lantern. When Emma's stomach fluttered, she flinched just long enough to remember the details of the life-changing voicemail she'd listened to in the taxi. "Happy Birthday, Olivia. I brought some friends of yours with me."

Given all the drama going on that afternoon, Olivia initially failed to recognize the man standing next to Rowena. Once she studied his face and glanced back and forth from him to Rowena, everything became clear in an instant. Her heart skipped several beats as the truth swam to the surface. They had the same virtuous eyes, what she used to call Ethan's window to his soul. But it confused her. Ethan was innocent. His biological father couldn't be the jerk behind everything. "This just can't be. Rowena told me you were dead. What kind of scam are you trying to pull?" The shock caused Olivia to almost faint. She reached out to find something to prevent her from falling.

Emma surged forward and caught Olivia's arm. "Let's go inside. We have a lot to discuss."

"No! These two sent the note. You're behind the blackmail," cried Olivia, pointing a shaky finger at Rowena. She wasn't sure what was swirling around her but knew she'd been intentionally misled. "And to think I respected you for the sacrifice of giving up a final moment with your son!"

"You've misunderstood, please," Rowena begged as she and Flynn followed Emma and Olivia into the main hallway. Others from the living room had begun assembling there too. "We mean no harm, Olivia."

Emma said curiously, "I'm not sure what you're referring to. Who's blackmailing you?"

Olivia shook her head and huffed loudly. "How could you do this to us? We welcomed you into our home, Emma."

Rowena helped stabilize Olivia when she yanked herself away from Emma. "Olivia, please. Let us explain. So much has happened in the last few weeks. It's not what you think."

With Zach following quickly behind, Teddy approached the unplanned guests. "I don't know who you are, but you've given my mother one hell of a shock. I think she needs a drink." Teddy led his mother into the living room. Rowena and Flynn followed them.

Zach reached for Emma's hand, but she held up an arm. "Please, don't be angry with me. I… I have important news to share with everyone."

"What have you done?" Zach inquired, marching to the opposite side of the foyer and motioning for Emma to come closer.

"Shall we move inside. We all need to hear this together." Emma nodded at Zach and shuffled into the living room, where everyone was silent. She slipped out of her coat and draped it across one of the armchairs.

Just outside the living room, Zach looked up and noticed Pilar escorting a tall, older man down the hallway, a man he did not recognize. "Who's this?"

Diane descended the staircase and turned into the main hallway, catching Pilar's entrance with the stranger. When she reached the bottom step, she grabbed hold of Zach's arm for support and gasped. "What is he doing here?"

Zach looked at his aunt. "You know this man?"

"His name is Nate. I met him in Italy with your mother. I… I… don't understand. I never gave him this address." Diane leaned closer against her nephew's shoulder, contemplating her and Nate's history in Italy. They'd said a permanent goodbye at the airport two days prior.

Nate pulled a handkerchief from his pocket and dried nervous sweat from his brow. "I'm so sorry, Diane. Perhaps we should join everyone else to address the letter Olivia received earlier this morning."

"You sent the blackmail note asking for one-hundred-thousand dollars? You son-of-a-bitch," Zach barked and rushed toward the man.

Matt had already entered the hallway and held his brother back from attacking Nate. "Let's all calm down and discuss this like reasonable people."

Matt directed Nate to go into the living room, then followed him inside. Zach pulled Pilar to the side. "Call the police and have them get here as soon as possible. I don't have a good feeling about this situation. I'd rather be safe than sorry."

"Yes, sir. I will call them right away. What shall I say… is the…" she paused, searching for the words, "is the reason for their visit?"

"I don't give a flying fuck what you say. Tell them they need to prevent a murder." Zach crumpled his hands into a fist, wrapped his other arm around his aunt, and led her inside with the rest of the family.

"Zach, please, don't say such a thing. Nate was kind to me in Italy. This must be a misunderstanding." Diane looked back at Pilar and noted, "Just tell them we have a domestic quarrel and might need some backup."

"I'll do my best, ma'am." Once everyone assembled inside the living room, Pilar closed the sliding doors and dashed down the hallway.

Rowena and Flynn sat on the main sofa taking in the room's ambiance and confused faces of the Glass family. They quickly removed their outer garments and smiled awkwardly at the remaining group. Other than Emma, Olivia was the only person who knew their identities. Some might notice their resemblance to Ethan as he looked very much like the combination of both his biological parents. But Olivia wasn't concerned about the rest of her family's thoughts. She was intent to find out why Rowena had suddenly shown back up. She lifted her head to observe Diane and Nate enter the room and sneak quick glances at one another, unable to determine why the stranger they'd met in Italy had descended upon their house. Did he have something to do with the blackmail note? Had Olivia misinterpreted Emma's arrival with Rowena and Flynn?

Caleb and Jake waited in the far corner near the potted palm tree, engaged in small talk, trying to ascertain the identities of the three new strangers in the room. They were predominantly focused on confronting their baby's biological father, curious if either of the two men who'd just shown up was the former parolee. They reasoned out that Diane seemed to know one of them, and Olivia recognized the other pair. Caleb let his guard down, determining that neither was likely the guy who'd been trying to contact them. If that were true, and one of these new strangers was behind the blackmail note, maybe things would turn out okay for them.

Matt and Margaret joined Teddy near the sideboard and poured drinks for everyone. Matt wondered when his dealer would call, or would he just show up? He was supposed to be there by now. Had he been delayed or was one of these worrisome guests sent as his replacement or lackey to get the money? Margaret asked Matt if he knew what was going on, but he indicated he was just as confused.

Teddy checked his phone but saw no messages from Sarah. If she'd been at the train station a few hours ago, she would've had enough time to arrive at the Glass family home to collect on the threats in her blackmail note. Perhaps she had nothing to do with the extortion. Was either of these new people her lawyers? He'd never met them, only spoken to them on the phone in the past.

Pilar opened the sliding doors and peered into the room. Margaret said, "Yes, did you need something?"

Zach inquired, "Did you call the police like I asked?"

Pilar nodded. "Shall I wait for them in the front hall?"

Nate stood and placed both hands inside his coat pocket. "No, I think everyone needs to remain inside this room until I finish explaining why I've interrupted Olivia's birthday party."

Everyone began shouting over one another. Pilar stepped inside and closed the sliding doors, appearing nervous and unsteady. Matt noticed and asked if the children were all upstairs with the nanny.

"Yes, they're either in the nursery watching a children's show or sleeping in their bedrooms." Pilar sat on a small ottoman near the entrance.

"Nate, please tell us what's going on," Diane insisted.

Olivia focused her attention on Rowena and Flynn, uncertain how everything fit together. Why had they shown up at the exact same time as Nate? Was there a connection between them? Had either of them stolen Ben's letter from her purse? She thought back to her trip to the airport in Rome before she and Diane flew home. Diane had been watching their bags when Olivia took a walk around the airport to get some exercise before the flight. Had Nate shown up, seen the letter, and taken it for his personal gain? Diane had never mentioned seeing him there, but her sister was behaving strangely this week.

If Flynn and Rowena were previously in Scotland, they could've flown through Rome and possibly noticed Olivia there. Rowena had her opportunity to tell her son the truth, but she chose not to do it in the end. The entire evening was wearing her down. Olivia wanted to confess to her family who they were, but until she found out what was going on with Nate, she intended to keep quiet about their identities.

Nate strutted around the room, studying everyone as he passed by them. One by one, he addressed each person by name as if he knew them or had met them at some point in the past. When he stopped in front of Rowena and Flynn, his eyes squinted in confusion. "I'm not sure who you two are. Introduce yourselves, please."

Teddy interrupted in a rage. "This is nonsense. Forget all this drama. Just tell us who *you* are and what *you* want from us. No one here will freely give you one-hundred-thousand dollars because you say you have a secret over someone in this room."

"That's just the thing. I've gathered several secrets, but that's no longer the reason I'm here today." Nate pulled an envelope from his left pocket and read aloud from its contents.

Olivia stopped him as soon as she heard the first words of Ben's letter from the prior year. "You stole my letter. You know the truth about my son's birth parents. Well, it's too late. I've already told everyone that Ethan was adopted. I beat you at this little game."

Emma collapsed against the back of the sofa upon hearing her husband's name. She cradled her stomach and whispered softly, so no one else could hear her. "What am I going to do now?"

Flynn stood, ready to disrupt their argument, but Rowena held him back. "We'll have our time. Let's hear what this man has to say first."

"Of course you did, Olivia. You try to control everything, all the time. Don't you?" Nate wiped another drop of sweat from his brow, continuing his march around the room.

"What does that mean?" Diane questioned, scanning him with a deeper curiosity.

"Did you think our meeting in Ravello was a chance en-counter?" Nate explained that he'd intentionally followed Olivia to Italy. He'd been watching her for weeks, hoping to learn more about the woman. "It wasn't fate intervening in your affairs. I needed to know what kind of a woman would ignore the aftermath of everything her family had done to mine."

Olivia leaned back against the couch, eager to stop the man from harassing her any further. "I don't even know who you are. What is this about? Have we met in the past, and I don't remember you?"

"Yes, in a way, we've met in the past. We've had many conversations and negotiations, just never face to face." Nate scanned the full breadth of the room, finally settling on Pilar. "You've just met the woman recently, haven't you? What do you think of Olivia Glass?"

Matt interjected, "Leave her out of this. She works for my family, and she has nothing to do with this crazy vendetta you have against my mother."

"Nate, please stop playing games. What is it my sister has done to you?" Diane approached Olivia on the couch and motioned for her to stand. "Let's take this into a private room to discuss why you stole her husband's letter and are trying to blackmail us. Did George put you up to this?"

Nate shook his head. "You're innocent in all of this, Diane. Believe it or not, I genuinely like you. I may have initially set my sights on you in Italy to get closer to your family, but through it all, I discovered that you are a wonderful woman."

"I don't even know your last name, Nate. This is getting more bizarre by the moment," Diane responded, taking Olivia's hand and leading her toward the sliding doors. "Let's go chat elsewhere."

Pilar stood to open the doors for the two women.

"No one calls me Nate, except for you, Diane. I thought you'd prefer a more casual, common name when we met in Italy. Perhaps my full name, Nathaniel Sheffield, rings a bell for a few people in this room," he noted gruffly.

Teddy made a gurgling noise, then looked at his mother. "I know that name. It came up last year at the firm. Let me think a minute."

Olivia gulped. "You don't have to do that. I know who he is." Olivia approached Nathaniel and looked him squarely in the eyes. "You're the man suing me because of Ben's car accident."

Nathaniel nodded, ignoring a series of erratic twitches in his eye. "My son was Ben's driver. The one who died with him in the collision. My only son, dead before his own father. And you refuse to settle the lawsuit for his death."

Everything flooded Olivia at once. Ira had been handling the details with the insurance company. He'd been trying to protect the Glass family by settling outside court. She was supposed to meet this man soon, at his request, before they finalized the lawsuit and moved on.

"And this is why you followed me to Italy? Stole Ben's letter?"

Nathaniel explained that he initially only wanted to confront the family who'd employed his son and failed to attend the man's funeral. "None of you showed up. You were all so distraught over Ben's death that you ignored the second victim in the accident."

After a wave of silence filled the room, Olivia was the first to speak. "I'm so sorry we neglected to properly behave and provide our condolences. After Ben's death, he left behind the letter you stole, and I was consumed with anger and pain."

"You were all being selfish. I attended Ben's funeral. I stood in the back and watched you grieve. Hundreds of guests, friends, family, and colleagues. An outpouring of support for the esteemed Benjamin Glass."

"He was a well-respected and loved man, Nathaniel," Caleb noted.

"And so was my son. At his funeral, there were only two of us present. Me, and his wife. We were a small family, and now we're even smaller."

"What if George really did engineer the car accident? He's guilty of murdering Nate's son too!" Diane collapsed against a nearby table, unable to accept what her husband might've done.

"What did you just say? It wasn't an accident?" Rage boiled inside Nathaniel, blinding him with such fury that he retrieved a gun from his right coat pocket. "I no longer have my son. The least you could do is settle this lawsuit, let us have something for all the pain and grief we're suffering. And now, to learn that you monsters might've intentionally caused his death!"

Everyone froze when he pulled out the gun. Diane regained her strength and slowly approached him. "Nathaniel, there is no need for you to wave that around. It's dangerous. We can work this out. None of us ever meant to hurt your family. If it wasn't an accident and George engineered this, we only just found out now. We can put him in prison."

Olivia ambled a few steps further and stood next to her sister. "Careful."

Nathaniel cocked the gun. "Do not go anywhere until this is settled."

Everyone stepped away from him. The Glass brothers studied each other, determining how to stop this man. But they had little time.

Flynn jumped up wildly. He'd spent years in a prison being tortured during the war. His tormentors had forced him to run around a noisy field as they took potshots at him. When they'd captured him, they blindfolded him in a brightly lit room, then fired at each light one by one until he was in utter darkness. They'd put the gun to his temple and clicked many times, all when there were no bullets left inside its chamber. Flynn had been traumatized by his imprisonment, and when he finally escaped, he found it difficult to adjust to living as a free man. He now suffered from post-traumatic stress syndrome, and when Nathaniel cocked the gun, it sent a flurry of nightmares and fear throughout this body.

Flynn sprinted toward Nathaniel, flailing his arms and screaming about revenge against his capturer. Rowena had tried to hold him back, but she wasn't strong enough. Emma grabbed his other arm as she stepped around the couch and rushed toward them. "Please, don't... I have something to tell you. It changes everything."

Determined to protect everyone, Flynn unknowingly dragged Emma in his wake. He was enraged by adrenaline and had developed a hypnotic focus on attacking Nathaniel Sheffield.

Nathaniel had never used a gun in his life before. He'd only pulled it out of his pocket at the last minute because no one seemed to listen or understand the turmoil wreaking havoc on his body over the loss of his only son. His hands shook crazily as an unbalanced Flynn dove across the room with Emma in hot pursuit. Worrying about Flynn's next steps, Nathaniel freaked out and unsuccessfully tried to back away. Flynn grabbed hold of Nathaniel's arm and twisted it until they were stuck in a battle neither man wanted to lose.

Although Emma hoped to intervene and de-escalate the tension, Destiny had other plans in mind. The struggle between the two men forcefully knocked her to the ground. Emma rolled across the floor, stopping before she collided with a bulky armoire. She stood in a daze and watched them fight.

Flynn eventually overpowered Nathaniel, but in their scuffle a shot rang out, and the bullet whizzed through the chilled and tense air. Everyone feverishly glanced around the room to determine where it struck. Amidst a dozen shrieks, Pilar stumbled and bumped into the light switch, causing the ceiling fixture's bulbs to flicker off and on as though lightning pounded the roof and delivered an impressive electrical surge to an already highly charged environment.

During the commotion and darkness, the two men inadvertently pressed the trigger a second time. Everyone's ears experienced an unimaginable ringing from the blast's reverberation and the victim's piercing scream. Someone had definitely been hit the second time, but no one knew whom. No one except the stunned victim who gasped for air and fell backward onto the plush carpet.

Chapter 23 – Flashback (Nathaniel)

After months of getting nowhere with his lawsuit, Nathaniel grew frustrated with Olivia Glass. He considered multiple options for how to make the entire family pay for ignoring his son's death. His son had been driving Benjamin Glass around for a long time, and the insurance payment wasn't large enough to offset the devastating loss of his only child. Though money wouldn't bring him back, it could provide Nathaniel with a better future. Eventually, Nathaniel's lawyer indicated that Ira Rattenbury wouldn't go above a certain number, and Nathaniel believed his son's life was worth more than that amount.

Nathaniel decided to further investigate the Glass family. He brought his car to George's garage for minor repairs and struck up a conversation. He'd previously met George a handful of times when accompanying his son, Ben's chauffeur, to George's service station. All it took was a couple of questions for Nathaniel to learn from George that the Glass family sought a new housekeeper and Olivia and Diane would be leaving the country. That's when he'd come up with his brilliant idea for his daughter-in-law to apply for the job once Olivia departed for Italy.

If Pilar used her maiden name, it wouldn't draw any attention to her late husband's surname, Sheffield. Once Pilar secured a job at the Glass estate, she poked around in every room to find something useful. Unfortunately, she failed to discover anything in the first few days, which meant he had to step up his plan. Nathaniel decided to follow the two sisters around Italy.

Nathaniel befriended Diane on the trip to Ravello, eager to understand whether Olivia had any remorse for his son's death. He got lucky when Diane wandered into the hotel bar one evening. He casually mentioned topics that might push Diane into talking about the accident. They chatted for several hours, and though he didn't learn anything significant, he could tell Diane was ripe for the picking. All he needed were a couple more drunken conversations and she'd reveal family secrets that he could use to his advantage. Things progressed for a couple of weeks but then time ran out. Diane and Olivia were returning to Connecticut. Since she believed Nathaniel lived in Europe, he suggested they could get to know one another remotely. Diane indicated she was open to the opportunity and requested some time to think about it.

Nathaniel booked his flight home from the Rome airport at the same time as Diane's but via a different airline. He needed to say goodbye and convince her to keep in touch. Nathaniel waited for Olivia to step away, then approached Diane at the gate. They spoke for a few minutes until she received a strange call and argued with her soon-to-be ex-husband about his refusal to sign their divorce papers. When the call ended poorly, Diane admitted that her husband had done something awful. He'd threatened her about a man she'd been involved with after their separation. Diane excused herself to use the restroom, and Nathaniel agreed to watch their luggage.

As soon as she disappeared, Nathaniel rifled through her and Olivia's bags and found Ben's letter in Olivia's purse. Based on its contents and a few tidbits from his conversations with

Diane, he realized that Olivia had been keeping a huge secret from her family. Nathaniel photographed the letter on his phone and stuffed it back inside Olivia's purse before Diane returned. Something had changed in Diane during her phone call with George. Although they'd connected a few times on her trip to Italy, Diane suddenly claimed she wasn't interested in communicating any further with Nathaniel. She told him things had to end between them in Italy. Nathaniel suddenly lost his opportunity to gain any additional information out of the woman.

Nathaniel noticed Olivia approaching from the opposite side of the terminal and claimed his flight was leaving soon. After sneaking away, Nathaniel updated Pilar about Ben's letter, urging her to be on the lookout for it when Olivia returned. Pilar and Nathaniel debated what to do with the shocking news. Wait to see how Olivia would react when they finally met in the coming weeks with the lawyer? Try to get money from her now to hopefully help make their loss easier to handle? As if Destiny herself was on their side, a gift landed in their laps the morning of Olivia's birthday party.

While Pilar had been doing the laundry in the basement earlier that morning, she heard someone knocking at the door. When she returned to the foyer, no one was there, and she chased after the girls on the second floor. After playing for fifteen minutes, the nanny took over watching the kids, and Pilar returned to the first floor to prepare for Olivia's event. That's when she found the blackmail note on the table in the foyer. Pilar opened the envelope and read its contents. Inside were three photographs of Diane in a compromising position with a younger man. Pilar sent a picture of the photos to her father-in-law, who'd returned from Italy the previous day. Nathaniel recognized the younger man as Ira Rattenbury, the lawyer he'd been talking to about the car accident.

At that moment, Nathaniel and Pilar decided to substitute the real letter with a new one. The original letter had been meant for Olivia, and the sender indicated that he or she would show up the following morning to discuss the pictures and to demand money for silence. Pilar and Nathaniel moved up the time to tonight, so they could get the money, and if for any reason Olivia wouldn't give in, they had a secondary blackmail option—Olivia would want to protect Diane from any scandal or issue with her divorce from George. Neither sister would want those photos shared with anyone else. By then Pilar had already stolen Ben's original letter from Olivia's purse. She placed the envelope in between the bed and the nightstand in the guest room. Although Nathaniel had a photocopy of Ben's letter revealing Ethan wasn't his son, they wanted Olivia to worry that the original letter had been stolen, so she would believe the blackmailer had something to do with Ben's secret, thus keeping the suspicion off any other possible theories.

After carefully debating their options, Nathaniel planned to show up at the Glass household shortly after seven o'clock. Pilar would arrange for him to meet alone with Olivia in the study, while the Glass family continued their party in the living room. Olivia would likely be anxious to complete the transaction quickly so she could eliminate any further suspicions. When they met, Nathaniel would indicate that he'd learned about Ben's secret through someone who knew them well. Olivia might recognize him from Italy, but it had only been one casual encounter in an elevator. It didn't really matter anyway. He'd show her Ben's letter, demand the money, then walk away. And if she wouldn't play ball, he'd use the shocking pictures of Diane that the real blackmailer had sent.

Either way, Nathaniel would collect his payoff, then leave. He never intended to reveal Pilar's identity. Once he had the money, Pilar would quit several days later, and the two of them would continue with their lives, mourning the loss of a son and husband. Olivia would never know Pilar was one of her blackmailers, and she wouldn't dare alert the police in fear her secret would be revealed. When the real blackmailer showed up the following morning to collect on the pictures he or she had sent, the entire situation would explode. The Glass family would suddenly crack into dozens of pieces, possibly even turn on one another. Between the insurance money, the amount Olivia had agreed to for the lawsuit, and the blackmail, they would be set for life. Nathaniel would decline the meeting with Olivia so his identity as the blackmailer wouldn't be compromised. He felt little guilt over his role in tricking them. Had Olivia agreed to meet sooner or provide him with the full amount he requested in the lawsuit, things would be very different.

Earlier that day, when Pilar realized the blackmail note had gone missing, she updated her father-in-law that their plan was in jeopardy. All afternoon, she kept close tabs on Olivia to figure out what she was going to do about the missing note. She attempted to notify Nathaniel but couldn't reach him without anyone listening in on her conversations.

Nathaniel arrived at the Glass estate at seven o'clock, the time he and Pilar had agreed to earlier that day. Pilar had assumed the caterer would leave around then, which meant there would be one less person in the house during his confrontation with Olivia Glass. He had been careful to park his car several blocks away and walk to the estate. It was dark out, which meant it would be harder to notice him wandering around the property. Pilar had provided specific instructions on which pathway to use, so no one would catch him walking through the backyard. Nathaniel sent his daughter-in-law a text message confirming that he was near a garden at the back of the property. Pilar instructed him to hide near the garage until she could tell him that the blackmail note had been read in front of everyone and Olivia had confessed about Ethan's adoption. Pilar had been eavesdropping outside the living room the whole time, so she was ready to rearchitect their plans.

While Nathaniel waited there, he heard a commotion near the bushes. He investigated it, and as he approached a giant evergreen in the corner, he noticed a man and woman having sex. They'd been calling one another's names aloud, Quinn and Katerina. He had no idea who they were, but as he watched them, it became clear they were on some type of drugs. The young couple had been talking about the strangest things, seeing fairies floating in the air and people throwing money at them. He had to get rid of them before they caused any impacts to his and Pilar's plan to confront Olivia.

Nathaniel ran at them, pretending to be a cop. The young couple were mostly naked, except for the socks he wore and the bra she barely had on. They sobered up just enough to grab all their clothes and run toward the garage. Afterward, Nathaniel noticed the gun on the lawn, near where they'd been screwing around. He quickly placed it in his pocket. He had no intent to use the weapon, since he knew there were several young kids living in the house. As horrible as he felt for lying and blackmailing Olivia, he had a soft spot for protecting children, especially now that he'd never gave any grandkids of his own. Nathaniel planned to toss the gun later that night, after he collected the money from Olivia. He'd also inform her of the young couple who'd run into her garage, a freebie to offset his cunning actions.

Nathaniel was about to check on them when Pilar called back. "Come to the back entrance. We need a new plan." Minutes later, Pilar opened the door and dragged her father-in-law into the kitchen. "Things have changed a little bit." She explained everything that'd happened that afternoon, including how everyone knew about Olivia's secret and Ethan's adoption.

Nathaniel knew he had little choice but to wing it. Confronting Olivia in front of everyone would be fruitless. He had to find a way to get her alone. Once Pilar brought him inside the room where everyone else attended the party, Diane would recognize him. Perhaps Olivia would agree to meet privately, and then he could show her the pictures that had come in the original envelope. If push came to shove, and she wouldn't yield, Nathaniel would ask if she recognized him, but he was certain she wouldn't even connect his name to the lawsuit. The Glass family was too focused on money, secrets, and their own reputation. It would be different than Nathaniel and Pilar's original strategy, but they'd improvise as best as possible. They were due for a win, especially after all the setbacks they'd suffered.

Nathaniel said, "Tell Olivia that I requested a private discussion. Find somewhere for me to meet with her alone." When Pilar left the mudroom alcove to announce his arrival, Nathaniel wandered around the kitchen, curious what it was like for the rich people of the world to live in such luxury.

A few minutes later, Pilar returned to update him. "Okay, Olivia's distracted by someone at the front door. I think I can sneak you into the study while she's dealing with it. Everyone else is in the living room. We'll have to be quick."

Nathaniel said a small prayer that their plan would be successful. As he adjusted his jacket, he remembered the gun he'd placed in his pocket. He thought about leaving it somewhere in the house but worried one of the kids would find it. He never had a chance to wipe his fingerprints from it either, so he'd have to clean the gun off before dropping it somewhere in the neighborhood.

Pilar and Nathaniel hugged one another, then exited the kitchen and sauntered down the hallway to implement their plan. Unfortunately, as soon as they made it halfway down the hallway, everything fell apart.

Chapter 24 – 8:00 to 8:30 PM (Everyone)

Once Pilar caught her balance and stepped away from the switch, the lights burst back on and the living room began to spin around her. Loud gasps and frightened moans scattered the guests, generating an inordinate amount of anxiety and restlessness. Several people in the room had feverishly dove to the floor, screaming and crying out for their loved ones.

Nathaniel and Flynn tumbled around for control of the gun, ramming into furniture and other people in their way. The recently fired weapon suddenly flew out of Nathaniel's grip and crashed into the back of the couch. Olivia and Diane dropped to their knees, crawling and clinging to one another like they'd done as small girls during the Fourth of July fireworks shows. Rowena began praying, calling out for God to have mercy on everyone around her. Matt grabbed Margaret and pulled her away from the center of the room, eager to protect his wife above anything else.

Shocked at the turn of events, Caleb and Jake initially froze in place. Neither had ever been around gunshots before, other than a few hunting excursions when they were both children. When Caleb saw the gun fly into the couch, he immediately chased after it to ensure no one else picked it up and continued shooting. Jake lunged forward and grabbed Nathaniel, who'd been so astounded that his initial reaction was to try to escape from the room.

Flynn scuttled on the floor and looked for a spot under the desk to hide from the traumatic event. As soon as the gunshots had rung out, instinct cut in and he could only think of protecting himself. His mind had no other alternative option but to revisit those awful experiences when he'd been forced to disappear inside himself to escape the pain and horrors surrounding him.

"You shot her!" Zach shouted as he raced across the room once the lights stabilized. He'd only grown close to Emma in the last few months, but part of his body erupted into flames when she became an unintended consequence of the duo's intense struggle.

Emma cried out while falling to the floor, "No, it's all I have left of Ethan." After both bullets struck, she clutched her abdomen, blood pooling through a hole in her favorite blue dress like a slowly erupting volcano. "I don't feel so well, Zach." She closed her eyes and silently prayed for the child growing inside her. For Ethan's child. The child they'd conceived days after their wedding the previous fall on the last night Ethan had the strength to make love to his wife.

Ever since Ethan's death, Emma felt sickly and depressed when conjuring all the things she'd lost in addition to the love of her life. Her body reacted to his passing just as her emotions had. She'd presumed her menstrual cycle was out of sorts because of his tragic demise and the shocking secret about his adoption. Finally, after three months of constant pain, weariness and dejection, Emma had gone to the doctor for blood work. It'd never crossed her mind that Ethan could've gotten her pregnant in the remaining days before he passed away. Emma falsely assumed all the drugs in his body would prevent conception from happening. But a miracle had occurred, and she'd gotten pregnant during their last tender moment together when he was alert enough to treasure her mind, body, and soul. Hours earlier on the train, the doctor had left a voicemail congratulating her on the news he'd discovered in her blood work. Emma was going to be a mother. Ethan was going to be a father.

Teddy bent down to help his brother with Emma and noticed the blood-stained blackmail envelope on the ground. Zach must've dropped it, and someone had accidentally kicked it toward Emma in the darkness. Teddy's wife, Sarah, a nurse, had taught him what to do in emergency situations. "Cover the wound. Don't let any more blood escape. We have to check for two bullet holes." Both slugs had torpedoed through her chest at a downward angle. They either remained lodged somewhere inside her body or had exited and struck something else in the living room.

"Call 9-1-1," Zach demanded, glaring through Pilar. "Now."

Pilar rushed out of the room to the phone in the study across the hall. She wanted to comfort her father-in-law, but she had no chance with Jake and Caleb holding him back. She'd also never called the police earlier when Zach had asked her to. She did now as guilt tore at her conscience.

Rowena and Diane attempted to coax Flynn out from underneath the desk where he was mumbling to himself and speaking incoherently.

Olivia knelt next to Zach, Teddy, and Emma. She directed Matt to take Margaret upstairs to check on all the children. Matt wanted to stay close to do whatever he could to help Emma, but Olivia insisted he focus on managing the rest of the house.

"Emma, my darling girl. You're going to be okay." Olivia nodded at Zach, who partnered with Teddy to see if the bullets had exited Emma's body.

When they tried to move her, Emma screeched and sniffled. "Please, don't let it happen. We can't lose Ethan again."

Zach and Olivia looked at one another. "She's delirious. We've got to get her to the hospital."

Teddy briefly studied her back. "There's blood there too, possibly one hole." He stood and crossed to the other side of the room in search of the bullet. It was wedged in the armoire.

Everyone heard the ambulance sirens grow closer outside.

"I'm so sorry. It was an accident," Nathaniel muttered repeatedly, clinging to Pilar's arm when she returned to the room.

"Of course. I don't think you intended to fire the gun. Just to warn everyone. This was all an accident," Diane noted with tremors in her voice. She glanced from Rowena and Flynn to Emma and Zach. "A horrible, horrible accident."

Olivia suddenly recalled something Nathaniel had said earlier. "You mentioned your son had a wife. Was she involved in your plan for revenge?"

"I'm right here," Pilar revealed in the most demonstrative voice she'd ever used inside the Glass family home. "I've been here all along, not that any of you ever took the time to notice me."

Matt and Margaret, who'd just returned from verifying everything was okay upstairs, overheard Pilar's confession. "You were near my children, you monster. Did you do anything to them?"

"Never! I'd never hurt a child. We only wanted to get what we deserve." Pilar crossed her arms and turned away, crying against her father-in-law's shoulder.

Margaret looked to Matt and shook her head disapprovingly. "You made me hire her. This is all your fault. How could you choose this woman?"

Before Matt could respond, the emergency technicians rushed into the house and prepared Emma for transport to the hospital. Once the cops showed up, Teddy took charge of the situation. Olivia was too distraught, and Diane wandered from small group to small group, checking on everyone. Teddy told them what'd happened, leaving out the specifics of the letter's contents or the blackmail request. "I have no idea who those two are," he said, pointing at Rowena and Flynn, "but the guy flipped out when he saw Nathaniel with a gun."

Rowena had calmed Flynn down enough that he sat in silence in a nearby chair, shivering and staring at a blank spot on the wall. "He fought in the Bosnian war. Suffers from PTSD after being kidnapped and tortured." She told everyone that he only wanted to prevent Nathaniel from using the gun on anyone, but during the struggle, it accidentally went off.

"And who owns the gun?" asked the lead cop.

Nathaniel replied, "I found it outside. With the naked couple who's probably still hiding in the garage. A girl with a bunch of tattoos and too much makeup. A younger guy with blond hair, an eyebrow piercing, and a skull cap."

Zach mumbled under his breath. "Katerina."

By the time Emma was transferred to the stretcher and loaded into the ambulance, she was unconscious. No one knew she was pregnant with Ethan's baby, and it would be up to the doctors to save her and the unborn child. The paramedic indicated one person could ride with Emma to the hospital. No one had Emma's family's contact information, but Zach grabbed her purse from the couch. "It's probably in here. I'll call them from the ER. I'll go with her and keep everyone updated."

Olivia hugged her son, then whispered in her ear. "Take care of her, Zachary. She's all I have left of Ethan. I can't say goodbye to him again."

Rowena nodded at Zach. "Emma is a good girl. All she wanted to do was let Flynn see where his son grew up. Watch over her, please. I need to take care of Flynn."

Zach realized what her words meant. Emma had found Ethan's biological parents and brought them to the Glass family home that evening. That's why she'd been so distant in the last few weeks; she'd discovered the secret too, just like Nathaniel

Sheffield had. Before Zach exited the house with the paramedics, his cell phone rang.

After he answered, Tressa said, "Hey. I'm pulling onto your street. What's going on? There are cop cars and an ambulance out here."

Zach explained everything to Tressa as he jumped into the ambulance. "Please check the garage. Katerina might be hiding in there. Tell the police about her for me. I think she brought the gun here. I want her worthless ass to go to prison forever for doing this to Emma."

Tressa agreed to check. As she walked around the side yard, the ambulance siren grew louder, and the vehicle rushed Emma to the hospital.

Inside the Glass house, Matt, Margaret, Jake, and Caleb met with one of the police officers to convey what had transpired that evening, including confirming Jake and Warren were indeed brothers. After the police took notes from their explanations, Margaret and Caleb went upstairs to grant the nanny a few days off. They needed less outsiders around right now. Matt and Jake stayed behind in the downstairs foyer.

"Warren Payne is really your brother?" Matt inquired hesitantly.

"Yes. We lost touch years ago."

"Do you know much about the company he owns with his business partner?" Matt pulled Jake into Ben's study.

Jake shook his head. "Nothing. I just found out he and Caleb have been talking for the last few weeks. Your brother was trying to repair the broken relationship I have with mine."

Matt explained how he had stolen money from Warren's company to cover his drug habit and that Warren was potentially seeking revenge. "Maybe we should all sit down together and work this out."

Jake agreed to think about it. "I need time to understand what Caleb's found out about him. I thought he was cheating on me until I discovered it was my brother earlier. Eventually, we can discuss where to go next."

Caleb returned downstairs and assured Jake that their son was doing okay. His cell rang as he wrapped his arm around his husband. "It's Chester. Maybe he has news."

Jake and Caleb excused themselves to talk to the adoption agency about their son's birth father.

Matt ran upstairs to check on Margaret and call Quinn. After six rings, the guy picked up his phone. "Yeah, I'm here but there's some crazy shit going down right now, man."

"Where exactly are you?" Matt whispered into the phone.

Quinn snorted. "The garage. I came here with my girlfriend and we kinda dropped some ecstasy. The shit kicked in and well, we started messing around. Then some guy chased us away, and we were about to leave but, dude, there are cops on your property."

A door squeaked in the garage. Katerina hid behind Quinn. "Who's that?"

Tressa closed the door and tiptoed away slowly. She went back to the house and found a police officer standing guard near the driveway, then shared with him what Zach had told her. "They're hiding in the garage."

Matt asked Quinn, "What is happening? Slip out of there now, man. You won't have time to get away for much longer." Matt had no idea that Quinn's girlfriend was Zach's ex, Katerina. Nor did he know Tressa had just led the cops to them.

While the cops searched Quinn and Katerina and found enough drugs in their backpacks to hold them for the night and possibly send them to prison for years, Matt hung up the phone and paced the hallway. He worried whether they'd turn him in for buying drugs again, but he quickly pushed it out of his mind. His priority was to contact Maude and inform his sponsor that he'd taken a pill and needed help.

As Matt dialed the phone, Margaret prepared to leave the nursery and kissed her husband's cheek. "I'm sorry I yelled at you about hiring Pilar. This isn't your fault, babe." She advised him to talk out his concerns with Maude while she gathered snacks for all the kids who'd woken up from the shots and the blaring sirens.

Margaret wandered down the stairs and bumped into Diane. "Is Emma going to be okay?"

Diane closed her eyes and hugged Margaret. "I don't know, sweetheart. I really don't know what will happen to her."

Teddy approached his sister-in-law and his aunt. "The cops are planning to take Nathaniel to the precinct for further questioning. Pilar is going with him. I hope you don't mind, Margaret… I just fired your maid. She may not work for me, but I felt like it was a necessary action."

"Good job, Teddy. I'm proud of how you took charge tonight." Diane patted his shoulder.

"Well, the cops have my statement. They said I could take off for the night. Mom doesn't want to talk about anything right now." Teddy told Diane that he was trying to reach Sarah, who'd left him a message that she was back in Connecticut to settle the terms of their divorce.

Margaret excused herself and approached the kitchen. "I'll let you two discuss this alone."

Once she left, Diane noted, "I should probably contact George soon too, huh? It can wait until we find out how Emma is tomorrow. I'm in no mood to talk to that man tonight."

"Why don't you leave it to me? It's about time I started acting like the eldest son in this family. It's not that I don't think you can deal with him, but he's after my father's money. And he might have intentionally killed Dad too. I should be the one to stop Uncle George." Teddy began walking away, then paused to embrace his aunt. "I love you."

Diane told him she loved him too, then returned to the living room and joined Olivia, who was discussing the shooting with Flynn and Rowena. Nathaniel had admitted to being the one to fire the gun during the struggle. It had been an accident, but he wanted to do the honorable thing by confessing his role, just as he'd expected of the Glass family from the beginning.

"Do they all know who Flynn is?" asked Rowena.

Olivia wrinkled her nose. "I'm really not sure. Some of my sons are perceptive and probably noticed the resemblance. But right now, all I care about is Emma's recovery and putting this entire mess behind us."

"What happens next?" asked Diane, pouring herself a glass of chardonnay, then drinking a large gulp from the bottle itself.

Before anyone could answer, two police officers escorted Quinn and Katerina into the living room. "Pardon the intrusion, but we caught these two sneaking around your property, ma'am. They have enough drugs in their possession to put them away for a long time. It'd help if you confirm they were trespassing or had any other information to provide about their presence here tonight."

Katerina sobered up enough to recognize Olivia. "You know I was only here to see my daughter, right, Olivia?"

Tressa leaned over to whisper to Olivia. "I'm Zach's friend, Tressa. We've never met, but he told me the gun used to shoot Emma belongs to Katerina's roommate. Katerina stole it and brought it here tonight. We don't know why."

Olivia's phone rang, and she handed it to Diane. Diane pressed accept and spoke to Zach. "What's happening, honey? Is Emma at the hospital yet?"

Zach could barely speak. His voice was weak and hollow, but he had devastating news to deliver. "Emma... didn't... make it. They couldn't... revive her."

Diane pressed the phone to her chest and stumbled into the couch. Zach's penetrating wail echoed inside her head. "No, she can't be gone…."

Olivia focused on her sister, desperate not to hear the news she feared would come anyway. "Please don't say it aloud." Tears sprang from her eyes as she turned to the cop who asked her about Katerina's unlawful entry on the property.

When Olivia began to choke, Tressa comforted her. "I'm so sorry. Lean on me, Mrs. Glass."

"I'll be okay." Olivia assured her, then stomped over to Katerina. She slapped the girl hard across her cheek, then a second time, watching Katerina's face seesaw from left to right. "This awful excuse for a mother has caused nothing but trouble for my family. I'll do whatever it takes to keep her in prison for the rest of her life."

Olivia wiped the drops from her eyes, begged the cops for a moment alone, and exited the living room. As she climbed the staircase, she faltered once again on the thirteenth step but caught herself from sliding further down. She had only enough energy to push herself to reach the guest room in the house she'd built with Ben from the ground up. In the house where she'd cared for her son Ethan in his last seconds before he died in the very room they'd just been standing in. In the house where her son's wife was shot and killed, all because Olivia hadn't told everyone the truth during the reading of Ben's will.

When she entered the guest room, her temporary home and only personal space, she closed the door and flipped the lock. Olivia perched on the bed and pulled the letter from her pocket, the one that Pilar and Nathaniel had stolen from her, the one she'd found on the floor in the living room after Emma had been shot. Nathaniel had dropped it during his struggle with Flynn.

"So many secrets. No matter what happens, I can't stop this family from imploding. What do I do, Ben? What do I do? Give me a sign. Did George really cause your accident?" Olivia wept into her pillow, blatantly ignoring the persistent knocks outside the room. She couldn't face her family anymore that night. It was time for her to be alone and process another senseless death.

And then Olivia remembered Ben's favorite morsel of advice: *It's never too late to do the right thing.* She grabbed a matchbook from a nearby drawer and the metal garbage pail from the bathroom. She flicked a match against the scratchy section of the matchbook and brought the flame toward the letter. "This time, I have the strength to do what I should've done the first time, Ben."

Chapter 25 – The Following Day (Caleb)

Caleb tried to visit his mother the previous night, but she'd locked herself in one of the guest rooms. Before bed, he texted her an important question—where could he and Jake find a discreet place to have a lengthy discussion? Despite all the drama unfolding in the Glass home with Ben's letter and Emma's death, Caleb couldn't ignore the priorities before him and needed to address his marriage and his son's safety. Olivia responded at some point in the middle of the night while Caleb was sleeping. He'd barely gotten much shuteye at all, especially after all the police interviews and caring for his son, who'd caught a minor cold during the drive down from Maine.

When Caleb awoke that morning around ten, his mother was gone, and Jake had already fed and changed their son. Caleb showered, dressed, and shuffled to the kitchen in a daze. Jake was nervously speaking on the phone again with Chester at the adoption agency, asking for the final status on the location of their adopted baby's birth father.

While Jake nodded and responded to Chester's questions, bouncing baby Ethan on his right hip and tapping the countertop with brutal force, Caleb poured himself a cup of coffee. He rested his chin on his husband's shoulder and kissed his son's cheek.

During part of the night, when his heavy eyes were unwilling to grant him any sleep, Caleb perused the internet from his laptop to review adoption laws. He and Jake had already completed all their research the previous year when they'd partnered with an adoption agency to find a child. Although it made sense now, they hadn't initially focused on the fact that it was illegal to buy a baby. Most states in the country had specific laws about what could and couldn't happen during an adoption proceeding, ranging from open to independent adoptions, but their agency had been incorporated in Connecticut and ran a satellite office in Maine. By abiding by the various laws in both states and paying for all the medical expenses, they'd found the ideal way to become fathers to their son. Now that the birth father had never officially surrendered his rights to the child, the situation had grown more complicated. Regardless of his many research hours, Caleb hadn't found an easy solution other than somehow paying the guy to go away.

Jake hung up the phone and transferred the baby to Caleb. "I've got news. Are you ready to chat about it?" Although comforted to know Caleb had never cheated on him with another man, Jake was still crushed and disappointed in his husband for hiding the friendship he'd built with his brother. He couldn't yet bring himself to forgive Caleb, which he'd made clear the night before when Caleb tried to engage with Jake before retiring to bed. They hardly ever disagreed in the past; their relationship was based on open-communication, total honesty, and mutual respect. Jake recognized Caleb was struggling with his own brother's death, and he was merely trying to be proactive about the future, but it still opened a sensitive wound in their usually steadfast and safe connection. They'd have to work more diligently to repair the issue, which wouldn't be easy. Jake's good-natured adoration for Caleb would win out in the end, but time and patience were necessary.

"I'm ready, but let's take a ride. It's warmer out today. The storm must've passed by and dropped off some extra sun. Let's go." Caleb strolled out the back door without looking behind him, carrying his son and the baby bag he'd brought from the upstairs bedroom.

"Where are we going?" Jake ran after Caleb, grabbing his keys from the breakfast nook where he'd previously been sitting before Chester had called with an update.

"Willoughby Park. I asked my mother where we could have a private conversation and talk about the future." Caleb had remembered the hidden gem as soon as his mother had replied to his text message. When she also confessed that it was where she'd met Rowena Hector to learn the identity of which son had been adopted, Caleb immediately felt a stronger bond with his mother. He knew that's where he and Jake needed to have their own important discussion about their adoption issues.

Jake agreed to wait until they got settled in the park. It was only a few minutes of a drive to reach the secluded sanctuary, and when Caleb led Jake and their son to the far corner, an enclosed area where eager bulbs pushed their way through the newly loosened soil, they relaxed on a cozy bench and faced one another. Given a series of trees covered one side and the back of a stone building protected the other, it offered shelter from the breeze and the slight chill in the air.

"You're so impetuous. It's one of the things I love most about you."

"Isn't that a good thing?" Caleb stuck a pacifier in the baby's mouth and covered most of his body with a light blanket. The temperature was a balmy fifty degrees, but he didn't want his son's cold to worsen.

"And it's also what drives me nuts." Jake leaned into the back of the bench and crossed his arms. "When an idea attaches itself to your brain, there's no stopping Caleb Glass from seizing what he wants."

"I don't understand what this has to do with Chester's call."

Caleb's least favorite thing about Jake was how vague and random he could become on the flip of a dime. All couples had small issues or concerns with each other's personality and behavior. For the most part, Caleb knew he and Jake retained the bare minimum of differences in how they approached life. It had been one of the reasons they'd fallen in love so quickly, including why Caleb had no concerns about immediately gifting Jake half of the house he'd built before they got married. There was an implicit trust and connection between them and never had they thought about the other one breaking his vows. How had Jake convinced himself that Caleb was sleeping with another man?

"I took a page from your book this morning." Jake explained that he also hadn't slept well the previous night. He'd checked on their son several times, pacing the hallway and rocking him until he fell back asleep. "I was staring out the window, watching the sun rise. It was piercing through two trees with little green buds. All I could think about was how far we've come together."

Caleb rested his free hand on Jake's knee. "We'll find a solution to protect our son."

A grin formed on Jake's lips, slow and steady, but eager to present itself. "A little birdie sent me a suggestion via email this morning. I followed up on it and contacted the adoption agency. Chester verified that our son's biological father just wants money."

When Caleb asked who Jake's birdie was, he declined to provide a name. Caleb sighed. "We talked about this yesterday. We can't just pay the guy off. Cut a check to purchase our son. It's illegal."

"I know. That's not how it needs to work." Jake explained that they had a fifty-fifty chance of winning a court battle to retain custody. Although their adoption had been fully legal at the time, the fact that Caitlyn had misrepresented the true father's name could invalidate the agreement. While a court would most likely side with Caleb and Jake, the country's current stance on homosexuality and adoption laws was at risk with the new administration.

"So, what did you and Chester discuss?" Caleb squeezed Jake's hand as a bluebird landed on the stone wall behind them. The baby's carrier had been facing in that direction, and their son's eyes brightened as the little bird hopped around in search of something to eat.

"They found the guy last night. He had an unbreakable alibi. Meeting with his parole officer, then cleaning a warehouse where he worked. They had a camera recording of him there." Jake revealed that the burglary at the adoption agency was random. The paperwork hadn't disappeared. The cops found it later that evening, buried under an overturned water cooler. Their son's biological father had taken a photo of the paperwork earlier that day when Chester was looking elsewhere in the room.

"So, what does that mean? He still went to our house and tried to track us down. How do we get him to go away?" Caleb grew impatient with his husband. Jake liked to take his time telling a story, and he'd probably been proud of whatever idea he'd come up with that morning. "What's your solution?"

"If we can avoid court or reviewing the terms of the adoption, the whole thing might just go away. Chester is talking to the guy about signing away his rights this morning." Jake bit his tongue, waiting for Caleb's response.

"In return for what exactly?" When the bird took off, Caleb stood and faced the wall. He scanned the cracks between several of the stones and redesigned the space in his mind. Nature and architecture grounded him, made him feel safe and relaxed. If he could keep himself from overreacting to the situation they faced with the adoption, he could eventually find a solution. He appreciated how much his husband had been trying to do the same, but Jake was often too emotional to see through all the obstacles.

"The guy just got out of jail. He has a part-time job and is living at a halfway house in a bad section of Bangor. We could find him a better apartment and prepay the rent for a few years." Jake confirmed that Chester thought it was risky as it could easily be considered a bribe and fall under the category of buying a baby.

"Do you think he'd go for it?" Caleb's voice grew higher and louder from his excitement. "Could we get in trouble?"

Jake informed Caleb that someone had put him in touch that morning with an adoption lawyer who confirmed there were ways they could handle it, assuming they didn't pay the guy directly and there was nothing connecting the man's signature on the document relinquishing his rights to the baby. "It's probably not the ideal way we'd want to fix the situation, but if the man signs away his rights, and all he wanted was money, he might go for it."

Caleb and Jake continued chatting about the potential solution. Chester was going to let them know whether the baby's father would agree to this type of an arrangement. Jake had hoped if the dollar amount on the apartment's lease was close enough to the dollar amount that the man requested, it would even out. They'd cover the costs of the apartment lease with an anonymous cashier's check once the adoption paperwork was signed, and then everything would revert to how it was before Chester's call the previous day.

"It's not a guarantee, and it might be unethical, but we haven't done anything wrong. We actually did everything right, and someone else lied to us." Caleb rationalized that the biological father never wanted the baby, so it was the best solution to making everything legal again.

"But it doesn't fix what happened between us." Jake watched as their son's eyes closed and he fell asleep. "We still need to talk about my brother."

Caleb and Jake discussed everything that happened in the last month. Caleb explained how he and Warren had met at the airport, including that Caleb had no idea the man was Jake's brother that first time. "I did call you when I met him the second time in Boston. I should've told you that I chatted with some strange guy at the airport, but I assumed it was just a way to pass the time."

"You found him attractive." Jake cupped his chin and absent-mindedly scratched at his cheek. "I guess if he still looks like me, I should consider it a compliment, huh?"

"Because I find myself attracted to men who look like you?"

Jake squished his face and squirmed on the bench. "Really, I can't think about you and my brother. This is worse than an episode of the gayest Jerry Springer show."

"Can I be the newest addition to the cast? Maybe Sharon Needles or Hedda Lettuce if I wear a dress and heels? Or should I behave as poorly as the Kardashians do?" Caleb winked, highlighting two famous drag queens he'd come to know from watching RuPaul's Drag Race, not to mention the trashy pop culture icons Jake loved to watch.

"Oh my God! Did you finally come up with an appropriate modern-day quip on your own?" Jake's mouth hung open.

"I did. Deal with it. You've got competition now, baby." Caleb approached Jake and tenderly caressed his cheek. "I never meant to hurt you. If I knew what happened all those years ago, I wouldn't have let him into our lives now."

Jake sighed and embraced his husband. "Do you really think he's gay too? I always suspected, but that night he let our father beat me, I gave up on him forever."

"People change. Look at my mother. Or Teddy… he used to say adoption didn't count."

Jake stepped away and peeked on their son. "Teddy's matured. I could see it in him yesterday. To lose a child must be the worst pain in the world."

"We need to spend more time with him. Maybe we can focus on Teddy if you'd rather not get to know your own brother, Jake."

Jake took a moment to consider Caleb's words. "I think it's time I gave Warren another chance. Why don't we set up brunch with him before we head back to Maine tomorrow afternoon?"

Caleb pulled out his broken phone. During his inability to sleep the night before, he'd successfully gotten the device to turn on, but it wouldn't make outgoing calls. He read Warren's number to Jake and insisted he make the call right now. "He'd love to hear from you."

Jake dialed the number while Caleb monitored their son. When Warren accepted the call, Jake said, "It's Jake. Caleb's told me everything you've been through. Maybe it's time we forgot about the past. I'm willing to give this a try if you are, Warren."

Once Caleb noticed Jake's smile, he knew the brothers were on the right path again. Caleb's unforeseen meeting with Warren at the airport two months earlier had been something engineered by Destiny. Brothers were supposed to be as close as they possibly could be. Caleb wasn't sure what would turn out between Matt and Warren, especially if Matt had stolen money from Warren's company, but they'd figure out how to deal with that problem next time. One issue at a time.

As Caleb relaxed into the bench, listening to his husband's excited voice on the phone, the birds chirping in trees above them, and their son's mellow breathing, he thought about his own brothers. Just as his brother Ethan had been adopted, his own son Ethan was adopted. His brother Ethan had passed away too soon, and now Ethan's wife, Emma, had been killed because of the secrets kept among the Glass family. The circle had to stop with his generation, if they ever had a hope for becoming a happy family in the future.

Since his phone was still broken, Caleb borrowed Jake's and sent his three remaining brothers a text message.

It's Caleb. Listen, there are only four of us left. Mom needs our support. Why don't we forget the past and focus on rebuilding our connections? Fishing trip. Two weekends from now. Just the four of us, okay?

Within thirty seconds, Caleb had three confirmations. They chatted for several minutes about establishing a regular monthly brothers-only outing, where they each chose a location and theme that reminded them of their late father and brother. No matter what, they would learn how to trust one another again. Although they'd made similar promises in the past, this time Caleb felt certain it would stick. By the responses alone, he was willing to place a bet that things were looking stronger.

Matt: *Sounds awesome. I woke up thinking the same thing. Let's make it a competition, players. Loser has to clean the winner's car for a month. Every single day!*

Zach: *Fuck yeah! I'll bring the beer. It'll be like old times. We need this. We gotta honor Dad and Ethan, the best part of this family. But you're all gonna lose your asses.*

Teddy: *I can make that work. Thanks for inviting me. Getting away has been on my mind lately. And it's about time I taught my younger brothers to look up to me for a change. Pickles is in charge now, boys.*

Chapter 26 – The Following Day (Matt)

While Margaret pulled the car to the front of the house, Matt asked for a minute to talk to his aunt before he and his wife met his sponsor. "Are you sure you can handle all four of the kids?"

Diane sucked in an enormous gasp of air. "It'll be good for me. Besides, it's no different than helping raise all five Glass boys. Girls are much easier. They don't hold so many secrets as the men in this family." Diane winked at her nephew to convey her attempt at humor.

Matt nodded, then leaned in to peck his aunt's cheek. "Any idea where Mom went this morning?" He'd already exchanged a few text messages with Caleb and knew his brother, Jake, and the baby had gone out for a drive. Pilar was downtown at the local precinct with her father-in-law, Nathaniel, talking to the cops about how he'd come across the gun in the backyard and whether he'd be charged with the accidental shooting. Since Emma had died from her injuries, the entire tragedy didn't bode well for Flynn and Nathaniel.

"Not with any certainty. She won't return my calls, and I can't decide whether she went to the cemetery to visit Ethan's grave or if she's taken off on a flight to Cleveland to tell Emma's family what happened." Diane's eyes welled up, but she tried to control them from turning on the waterworks.

"I still can't believe what happened. Ethan only died last fall, now his wife is gone too. How can two people so young die in such devastating ways?" Matt leaned against the hallway wall, unable to process the prior day's events.

"It's an atrocity. An absolute abomination, and I am so angry right now." Diane shared with Matt that she felt guilty for allowing Nathaniel to enter their lives.

"You didn't know who he was when he approached you in Italy, Aunt Diane."

"True, but I could've asked more questions. All I know is that he's grieving too. His son died, and no one in our family reached out to him." Diane wrapped her arms around her body and sucked in a deep breath. "Tragic. Sad. Unfortunate. Maybe in retrospect, it will awaken all of us to what we let happen."

"This isn't the universe trying to tell us we did something wrong. Accidents happen. If this were a game, we're the team who's down. We lost Dad, Ethan, Teddy's baby, and now Emma. Nathaniel only lost his son." Matt felt remorse for comparing the deaths and not recognizing the common pain they all shared. Had anyone in the Glass family known of Emma's pregnancy, it would've been another hit for their team.

"I know what you mean. Unfortunately, Nathaniel was an honorable man who made a stupid decision. He was greedy, and he schemed to get money to compensate for his loss."

The world was unfair. They both agreed on that count. "Except, now he might go to prison for what he did."

Diane covered her mouth, unable to respond. As Matt stroked her arm gently, she said, "When you get back, I'm planning to visit him in jail. I don't know what will happen, but it's important to find out what he and Pilar are up against. He never intended to shoot the gun. Everything just happened all at once."

Matt agreed. "I understand, but a woman's life was lost last night. I can't imagine what Mom's going through or even this Rowena Hector woman and Flynn dude. The man needs help."

"I know very little about him. I think Emma wanted to tell me on the phone yesterday, but she was caught up in her own shock and confusion." Diane told Matt that she'd be fine with the kids, encouraging him to introduce his wife to his sponsor. "You've got your own demons to battle today, Matt. Let Margaret help you with this one. Don't try to do it all on your own."

During the drive to Maude's house, Margaret and Matt discussed everything that'd happened at Olivia's birthday party. "How are you handling the news about Ethan being adopted?" Margaret queried as they pulled up to Maude's place.

"Is it really something that matters anymore?" Matt explained that Ethan had been his brother for twenty-three years, and he'd processed through the loss enough to move on each day. "Just because we don't have DNA in common, or we aren't blood brothers, that doesn't erase everything we went through together as kids."

Margaret rested a hand on his thigh. "I'm glad you see it that way. Everything your mother said explains a lot now. I cannot imagine what she was going through last summer."

"When she visited all of us after the attorney read Dad's will?"

"Yes, exactly. She must've been suffering so much."

Matt agreed. "My mother is the strongest woman I know. She lost a child and never knew it happened. Twenty-three years later, she lost the son who took his place."

"And now, just when Olivia began to recover, excited about spending more time with her sons and with Emma, the poor girl is killed because of a misunderstanding."

Matt cocked his head in the opposite direction, then indicated his desire to meet Maude. "It's almost come full circle with Dad's letter being shared finally. I can't believe this could've been avoided if Mom had told the truth back then."

"But if she did, maybe everyone would've gone their separate ways instead of embracing each other. If she revealed your father's secret, things might have turned out much differently."

"Meaning what?"

Margaret grabbed her husband's hand as they walked up the front pathway. "Your mother might not have realized you were hooked on pills. And we may have lost you or one of the kids." She pulled him toward her. "This is the last time we're going through this situation, Matt. We need to ask Maude for help, and I'm counting on you to be one-hundred-percent honest when we go inside."

"I've been a jerk. I promise to fix everything. After we talk to Maude, you and I will meet Warren Payne, and hopefully we can convince him to give me another chance." Matt wanted to ask Warren for forgiveness, in the hopes it would remedy the lawsuit so that Wittleton and David could focus on rebuilding his late father's firm.

For the next hour, Matt opened his heart to Maude with Margaret by his side. By the time he covered everything, including the truth about the money he'd stolen in the past and the pills he'd bought from Quinn, he began to feel better.

"We all make mistakes, Matt." Maude shared her own struggles with them, then told Matt that she'd broker a deal with him.

"I'm all ears. What's on your mind?" Matt glanced at his wife, a smile on her rosy cheeks assuring him their future was looking brighter.

"If you can convince me in three months that you haven't touched any pills or contacted any more drug dealers, I'll give you a part-time job in my company." She promised him that she'd watch more closely, and there would be several eyes on all his work when he finally started.

Margaret said, "What do you think, Matt? It's a generous offer. I know you wanted to go back to your father's firm, though."

Matt contemplated the opportunity. "I did want to go back. It was the only thing that made sense. I spent so much time building my career there, I couldn't see another future. But maybe it's time I moved on, began my own path without daily reminders of my past mistakes."

Maude and Margaret got to know each other a little better, and Margaret even convinced Maude to join one of her charities. Matt felt stronger about his future. He knew it was time to move on, but before he could do that, he needed to fix things with Warren Payne.

After leaving Maude's place, he and Margaret met Warren for coffee at his hotel. Warren sat in the corner of the lobby, sipping from his cup. When they approached, he immediately stood. "You must be Matt?"

Matt introduced his wife to Warren. "Before we discuss anything, you need to know how awful I feel. Not because you're Jake's brother and I hurt someone who's part of my extended family, but because I made a mess of your life too."

Warren laughed. "You did. Things got nasty for a while. But I think you also helped set me free in a way." He explained that when he and his partner fought over ownership of their company and the patent on their technology, Warren realized how many bad choices he'd made in his life.

"What can Matt and I do to fix this for you?" Margaret clasped her purse and lowered her head. "My husband made a huge error in judgment, and I want to support him. We intend to pay back any money that he stole, but the law firm shouldn't suffer because of his mistakes."

Matt apologized again, then confirmed everything Margaret had said. "Truly, this is something I need and want to fix. I'll consider any option at this point."

Warren leaned forward and placed his mug on the table. "My business partner and I worked out an agreement once. Based on an earlier update, he's agreed to back down from suing the firm if we can prove you've returned the stolen money and that I had nothing to do with it."

"I'll sign anything he wants, explaining you weren't involved." Matt's heart began to race. He felt terrible for all the damage he'd caused, but for the first time in a long time, by telling the truth and being open with everyone around him, he knew this was the right decision.

"It's a good thing you have so many people who care about you," Warren noted.

"What do you mean?" Matt looked from Margaret to Warren, confused at the man's words.

"Someone went to bat for you earlier today. I'm not at liberty to reveal who, but I'm willing to figure out how to find a resolution that works for everyone." Warren cocked his head, then shrugged.

"Thank you so much. What should we do next?" Margaret beamed.

"I'll talk to my partner tomorrow. We're meeting at the law firm's offices to settle it. Wittleton will send you the document you need to sign. It confirms the amount you stole, and apparently your brother Teddy has volunteered to represent your interests." Warren explained that no one wanted Matt to go to prison as they felt he'd suffered enough and had been ill. "You have a disease, and I've seen people with it before. Some get angry and abusive. They never change. I can tell you want to heal."

Matt looked at his wife with humility and sorrow, but also with acceptance and hope. "I do have a disease. And I want to heal. This is the best next step."

Warren stood and handed Matt a folded sheet of paper. "If you can pay this amount back by tomorrow morning, then perhaps we can come to an agreement quickly."

Matt waited for Warren to leave, then gave it to Margaret. "You read it first."

Margaret unfolded the paper and cleared her throat. "It's more than I expected, but that's pretty much what we have left from your father's inheritance."

"How will we survive without that money until I get a job?" Matt lowered his head.

"I'll ask your mother for a loan. She let us have the house, and we have a stipend to cover the expenses. We just need money for ourselves and the girls for a little while." Margaret convinced her husband that they would find a way to make it work.

Matt knew the only way to change his future was to start over again. When all was said and done that week, they'd have zero dollars to their name and his job wouldn't start for another ninety days, assuming he could stay clean and sober. As he considered his next response, Matt's phone chimed with a message from Caleb, asking him to participate in a brotherly fishing trip in two weeks.

Even after everything that had come out the previous day, his brothers still wanted to get together and repair their relationships. Matt knew he could handle anything thrown at him in the future.

"Yes, I think we can make this work. I'm so lucky to have you," Matt whispered in his wife's ears. He nibbled her cheek, then cradled her neck between his hands and kissed her lips. "Do you think you're ready for us to... you know...?"

Margaret pulled away from him, then scowled friskily. "I just had our fourth child last week. No, I'm not ready for what you have in mind. Besides... you need to sit on the bench for a few more weeks. Then we can discuss getting back to normal again."

Matt cast his best impression of a whimpering puppy dog. "Is this punishment for not telling you the truth about the lawsuit and the one pill?"

"No. I just think it's time you learned how to be patient and prove you can get back on the right track. Maybe then I'll consider how to best reward you, player." Margaret grabbed his hand and led him out of the hotel lobby.

"This is so unfair. I'm sick, remember?" Matt jested coyly, then shuddered when she threw her hands to her hips. "Okay, okay… let's do this your way. I've been bad. I need to listen more. I must get help. And I promise I will never do anything like this again. Does that sound better?"

"It's a start. And as soon as we get home, you need to focus on your new job." Margaret left him standing at the front entrance as she strolled to the parking lot.

Confused, Matt ran after her. "But Maude said it wouldn't happen for three months."

"I'm not talking about that job."

When they reached the car, Margaret unlocked the doors and sat in the driver's seat. Matt quickly propelled himself into the passenger seat. "What are you talking about?"

"If I remember correctly, you insisted that I hire Pilar as our maid. Yes?"

"Oh!" Matt's lips fell into a worried frown.

"Since Teddy ensured she won't be coming back to work for us, and I'm not ready to bring another stranger into our home…." Margaret stopped talking and let Matt figure out the rest.

"Are you saying I have to clean the house now?"

"And do the laundry. And cook our dinner. And run all the errands. It's a lot, and I suspect it'll keep you quite busy and unable to think about much else for a long while."

"That's so unfair!"

"So is life, husband. It'll be good for you to see what I used to have to do every day. Besides, isn't this what they call pinch-hitting in baseball?"

Matt loved his sports, but he loved his wife even more. "If it means everything works out between us, you've got a deal, babe. I'll take my turn. At least until I get that new job."

"And then what?" Margaret laughed.

"Then I can find us a new housekeeper, right?"

"No. I'll find us one. You have a poor track record." Margaret cautiously pulled out of the parking lot and headed home, one hand firmly on the wheel, the other reaching for her husband's arm.

Matt knew when he'd been beaten. "Yep, you're the boss. I never should've doubted it." He stared at his wife as she drove them home, astonished at how lucky he'd gotten when they met. "You are one in a million, babe."

Chapter 27 – The Following Day (Teddy)

When Teddy had returned home after the incident at the Glass estate, he had an awakening, an epiphany of sorts. Life was short. Shorter than people realized. In less than a year, he'd witnessed the death of four people who'd each held some significance in his life. Although he'd only known Emma for the last few months, she'd been genuinely kind and supportive of him whenever they were around one another.

Emma had once suggested to Teddy that people were like clocks. They came in all different shapes and sizes. Some were wound up; others needed a source of powerful energy to keep them running. In the end, they all functioned for the same reason—a slow and careful passage of time where events were recorded and marked milestones in a universe so large, it was as distinct and complex as the personality of all its inhabitants. When he asked Emma to share her opinion of him, Teddy never expected the three words she'd chosen—passionate, encumbered, and enigmatic.

Teddy always believed he was a simple man with a solitary purpose in life. When everything had been turned upside down the last year of his life, he began to explore other possibilities under duress. It was only when Emma died that Teddy recognized why she'd selected those words for him. He was passionate because he had the zest for life, but he buried it so deep it floundered for the entire time he was alive. Now, with the subsequent loss of his wife and child, the enigmatic characteristic became even more obvious. Although Teddy loved Sarah in his own way, they could never repair what'd broken between them. Too much time, anger, and pain had trampled on their marriage. The right thing to do was to let her go, to let Sarah move forward in her own manner to process her grief. He crafted an email from the heart, rather than his logical mind, and hit send.

As he lay in bed that morning, contemplating all the tasks before him, Teddy knew he'd been given a gift. Not every person could see through the heartache and tragedy that had befallen his family, but Teddy's unusual ability to see the forest for the trees won out. The attorney in him had always focused on the specific language and intent of a law or a person's words. The artist in him could see the creativity and expression meant by the symbol of the object or action before him. His life had a renewed purpose, and as he showered, he reviewed everything he needed to accomplish that day.

Teddy soon set out to complete a series of tasks. All six of them. Six goals that would alter the future of his family. Only, they no longer felt like tasks or obligations he had to address. Something inside him had changed when he awoke that morning, and he wanted to route everything on its proper course.

Teddy's first item was to contact Wittleton and Davis. Although he'd sold the family's interest to them months earlier, they still kept in touch to ensure a smooth transition for their clients. In his conversation with Davis, he implored her to let him speak with Warren Payne before their final meeting the following week to attempt to resolve the situation with Matt's theft and the technology patent. Wittleton was hesitant at first, but Davis told Teddy that she trusted his instincts.

Once Davis texted the number to Teddy, he called Warren. "I apologize for troubling you early on a Sunday morning. I know you're meeting with Jake and Caleb later today, but there's something else we should discuss."

Warren replied, "Of course. What can I do for you? I have some time before I see them. I'm anxious to meet my nephew, if they'll let me be a part of his life."

"I wish only the best for you. Repairing relationships is never easy." Teddy pulled up in front of the precinct for his next appointment. "Listen, things have gotten out of hand with my brother. I beg of you to listen to me."

When Warren agreed, Teddy resumed his plea to help Matt. Teddy accepted responsibility for being distracted the previous summer when Warren's lawsuit was being addressed. He explained that Matt had a personal problem that interfered in his job, and the firm should've noticed the issue sooner. Teddy implored Warren to recognize that people made mistakes, and often, apologizing and asking for forgiveness was the best way to open the door to change.

"I'm not sure I understand. What is it you want me to do?"

"I'm so sorry for what my family and I have done to impact you and your business partner's relationship. I personally take the blame, and I am willing to pay the cost of your legal fees to resolve the situation." Teddy promised to cover everything that the firm had charged Warren's company to address the patent ownership. All he asked in return was that the lawsuit against the firm be dropped. Teddy would guarantee that Warren would receive any stolen money if Matt couldn't produce the funds.

"I'll give it some thought. I know what it's like to abandon your brother when he needs you the most." Warren agreed to meet with Matt that afternoon, then disconnected.

Teddy felt proud and hopeful that he'd set things on the right path for one of his brothers. Before heading into the precinct, he sent a text message to Jake.

Teddy: *Check your email. I sent you an article about how to handle your son's biological father's request. You can't give him money, but here's an alternative option.*

Jake: *Thank you so much. I just read it. This might actually work. Why are you helping us?*

Teddy: *Because my brothers mean the world to me. And by extension, so do you now.*

Jake: *Brothers are supposed to be there for each other. Especially older ones.*

Teddy: *Give Warren a chance. I don't know what happened in the past, but time changes everything.*

Teddy tossed his phone in his coat pocket. Two down. Four more to go. He went inside and asked for the detective in charge of the incident that'd unfolded at his family's home the previous night. Twenty minutes later, someone proffered him a folder with a stack of papers. "This is everything I asked for earlier this morning?"

The desk officer nodded. "It's only the preliminary report, but it should be good enough for your purposes. We'll send you a copy of the final one later this week."

Teddy strolled out of the precinct and stopped at the local Staples. He made a photocopy of the report, scanned it on one of their machines, and emailed it to himself. He then forwarded a copy to another attorney and thanked the man for his help. The other attorney promised to address it immediately. Teddy knew that the sooner he acted on his instincts with this situation, the better chance he could protect one of his brothers.

On his way to his next appointment, Teddy's phone rang. He pulled to the side of the road and parked just outside the residence of the person he was planning to visit.

Sarah cautiously greeted him when he answered her call. "Hello. I received your email."

"I'm sorry for everything that happened between us. Can you ever forgive me?" In the email Teddy had written the previous night, he notified Sarah that he'd doubled the offer for their divorce settlement and would give her permission to move their son's grave to wherever she decided.

"Is this for real, Teddy?"

"Yes."

Sarah thanked him for his generosity and humanity. "I've been thinking about it all morning. Your words truly impacted me."

"I meant everything I wrote." Teddy knew that it was time for him to let go.

"I've changed my mind. About our son's final resting place."

"Are you sure?"

Sarah confirmed. "I don't think you and I are meant to be together anymore, but our son belongs there with his grandfather and his uncle. I'm not sure what the future holds for me."

"Maybe when you return to visit his grave, we could have dinner together. Or coffee. Whatever you're comfortable with." Teddy assured his wife that all he hoped for in the future was to maintain a friendship with her. "We've spent too much time together to walk away without the possibility of connecting again one day."

Sarah agreed to reach out to Teddy the next time she was in town. "I am here now, but my train leaves soon. I went to his grave yesterday afternoon to say goodbye. I thought I'd confront you again today. There's no need now. I'll be in touch."

"Goodbye, Sarah. I will always love you."

"I think I will always love you too." Sarah hung up.

Teddy exited the car and wandered down the path of the apartment complex. He knocked on the third door and waited for someone to open it. When the owner did, Teddy said, "Uncle George, it's great to see you. Been way too long. Mind if I come in?"

George backed up when Teddy pushed his way inside the sparsely decorated one-bedroom residence. "What do you want? I was just heading over to see your mother. We have a meeting this morning."

"This place looks like a pigsty. I guess your meeting with my mother means you were the one behind the original blackmail note, huh? I never really doubted it, to be honest." Teddy displayed a few photos and spreadsheets he'd collected from a private investigating firm the previous month. He'd also found the photos of Diane and Ira and the original blackmail letter in Pilar's bedroom earlier that morning. "If these are real, you're in a lot of trouble, Uncle George."

"You call it blackmail. I call it getting my fair share. After suffering through your family's drama for thirty years, I deserve a reward." George studied the documents in his nephew's hands and grunted loudly. "How did you get hold of those?"

Teddy smirked. After several conversations with his aunt over the holidays, Teddy had suspected George was cheating the government on his taxes. The man had run his own garage but funneled any income through foreign banks and secret accounts. While he hadn't gotten rich off the schemes, George had successfully avoided paying taxes for almost a decade.

"I doubt that matters. But I'll certainly be willing to look the other way."

George slammed his fist on a nearby table. "If I do what in return?"

"I think that's rather obvious. Aunt Diane is the most caring soul in the entire world. To think you would try to steal money from her future when all you ever did was rob her of a happy life for the last three decades... watching private videos you recorded inside her house after you moved out... well... there's certainly a name for men like you." Teddy tossed the photos in a garbage can and lit them on fire. He threw the tax documents at his uncle and sauntered back to the front door. "You will destroy any other videos or photos you kept of her."

"You expect me to sign the divorce papers and walk away from your father's inheritance?"

Teddy guffawed. "No. I expect you to sign the divorce papers and offer my aunt double what she's asked for alimony. My father's inheritance was never up for discussion. And that's just my starting offer. I've got other dirt on you. Wonder what might happen if I check out your garage? Evidence of foul play in my father's death?"

George stepped toward Teddy as if to attack him. "You little—"

"I wouldn't do that if I were you," Teddy warned, holding his hand up in George's direction. "Although I can't prove whether you engineered my father's accident, I will always believe you did. Copies of these documents are set to be released if anything happens to me or Aunt Diane. You have twenty-four hours to sign the divorce settlement. Goodbye, Uncle George. It's been a pleasure knowing you, but it's time for you to move on. And just to be sure we're clear about the options here, your alternative is a lifetime prison sentence for murdering my father and an innocent driver. I'll engineer the evidence if I have to, that's how little you mean to me right now."

"I never did anything to your father's car. I contemplated tinkering with the gas tank or adjusting the brakes. Maybe I could've punctured a hole in the line. But I didn't," George snarled at his nephew.

"Why should I believe you?"

"Because I might be a horrible husband, uncle, and brother-in-law, but I draw the line at murder. I knew Diane was too much of a chicken-shit to go to the cops. I thought I could scare her enough, that she might worry I was a little too crazy. Then she'd give me the money and leave so I could marry a real woman. A beautiful one. A younger one."

Teddy grinned. "At least your true nature came out in the end. Aunt Diane is the most perfect woman you could ever hope to meet, and you're worthless by any other standard. I hope you find some new girl who treats you as well as you deserve. And maybe she'll have the guts to kill you one day. It'd do the world a huge favor. I wouldn't have to get my hands dirty to seek justice this time."

Teddy exited the apartment complex and congratulated himself on completing four of his six tasks that day. The fifth had already been set in motion when he delivered the paperwork from the police precinct to the lawyer. He anxiously awaited confirmation that his plan was in progress.

To complete the last item on his schedule, Teddy needed to track down his mother. She still hadn't responded to his voicemail, which prompted him to drive to the cemetery. Perhaps she was visiting his father or brother. When Teddy arrived, he found two bouquets of fresh flowers on his son's grave. One had been from Sarah, the other from his mother. Teddy bent down to the grave and touched the headstone. "I will always remember you, son. The world will never know how good you could've been, but I believe everything has happened for a specific reason. Someday, I will figure out what that is. For now, I plan to become the man I always should've been, so you can still look up to me as the perfect father."

Teddy left the cemetery and drove to the Glass family home. Only Diane was there, and when she saw Teddy, she glowed. "Ira just called. George will sign the paperwork. He's finally doing the right thing."

Teddy embraced his aunt. "You deserve only the best. And I hope he agreed to give you more money too. I'm so glad he's out of your life now."

Diane stepped back from her nephew. "You arranged this, didn't you?"

Teddy kissed his aunt's cheek. "I didn't do anything except love you. Like you've always loved me. But now, I must find my mother. Do you know where she's gone off to?"

Diane shook her head. "No, and she's not returning my calls."

Teddy promised to update Diane. He had one more place to check, and when he arrived there, Teddy found his mother. Deep inside, he knew where she had gone, but he wasn't ready to go there until he finished all his tasks that day. He opened the door and entered, smiling at his mother as she sat in a chair in the building's main lobby. "Mother, we need to talk. I want you to hear something from me before you go ahead with your plans."

Olivia glanced at her eldest son. "Of course, Theodore. It's time I listened to my boys."

Chapter 28 – The Following Day (Zach)

When Emma lay dying in the ambulance on the way to the hospital, Zach experienced a weird out-of-body sensation, something unfamiliar but comforting all at the same time. If he hadn't known better, he would've thought his brother Ethan had assumed control of Zach's physical existence to usher Emma into Heaven with him.

After the emergency worker confirmed Emma had died from the location and impact of the gunshot wounds, Zach slumped in silence on a bench outside the hospital. He'd already signed paperwork to admit her body and notified his mother that she'd passed. He had no clue what to do next. Was he supposed to contact Emma's parents? Should he wait by her side and hold her hand until they got there? His body raged, thirsty for revenge.

Emma was twenty-two years old. She had an entire lifetime to live, and three strangers had descended upon the Glass house, leading to her unexpected death. Who exactly were Rowena, Flynn, and Nathaniel? Zach understood bits and pieces of the previous night's conversation, but nothing made total sense. Nor did he want it to make sense.

After wandering around the neighborhood, Zach finally called his Aunt Diane to ask her to look after Anastasia for the night. He wasn't sure when he'd be home, but he couldn't go back to the house until he had answers. The only problem was that he didn't know what questions to ask.

Emma was just a friend. He had fallen for her, but the same level of love would never be returned. She belonged to his brother, and now they were together forever. Zach couldn't decipher his feelings from his desires. All he knew was that a beautiful woman had died a tragic death, and there were so many secrets that led to it happening. How could women like Katerina live when one like Emma died? Was there no balance in the universe to right a wrong?

Zach laid low in a dive bar for most of the night until they kicked him out at four o'clock in the morning. He hung out at the bus station, pretending to wait for the next bus to arrive. When each one did, he ignored it and stared at anything but his own reflection in the building's windows. When the sun began to rise, Zach realized he'd completely forgotten about Tressa. He called to thank her for all her support. "I hope you stayed at the house. My family knows who you are, it's okay."

Tressa assured him she was fine. "I rented a hotel room. After leading them to Katerina and Quinn in the garage and talking to the police, it was the middle of the night. I didn't want to start asking everyone where I should sleep, so I drove to the closest place."

"I'll give you money next week. I'm sorry."

"Don't be an idiot. I got to meet a hot police chick with real handcuffs this time! This was some crazy shit, papi."

Zach laughed. "I'm not even sure how to explain it all. She's gone, Tressa. Emma was alive and breathing twelve hours ago, telling me she couldn't make it to the party. Now she's dead."

"Were you able to find out why she showed up?"

Zach explained the snippets he could remember. "I need to find my mother. Maybe she knows more about the people who crashed the party."

Tressa told Zach what she'd learned by hanging around the house. Between the two of them, they reasoned out that Rowena and Flynn were Ethan's biological parents, and Nathaniel and Pilar had been seeking revenge against the Glass family for the death of their son and husband.

"When I left, all four of them were taken to the local precinct. Your mother went up to her bedroom after the detective finished questioning her." Tressa asked Zach if he wanted to meet for breakfast, but he declined.

"I need to figure out how to get hold of Emma's parents. I have to go back to the hospital to do something, I guess." Zach refused to cry. It had nothing to do with being a man or too strong to show his emotions. He just couldn't cry when he understood so little of the downward spiral twisting him in knots.

Tressa volunteered to look after Anastasia while he took care of everything else, but he confirmed Diane wanted to be with the kids that day.

"Papi, you should talk to the police too. Maybe they plan to call Emma's parents. If the hospital has her personal information, they might call too. You can't let this go much longer."

"I know. I just don't know if I can be the one to call them. I have no idea how to do this. My mother would know what to do." Zach thanked Tressa and promised to seek her out the following day when his head was in better shape.

He stopped by the police precinct and talked to the primary detective in charge of the investigation. They'd already reached out to the hospital and arranged for notification to Emma's parents. Olivia had told them she wasn't the right person to call Emma's family, but she would follow up with them to discuss how to proceed.

Zach understood. He asked if he could speak with Flynn or Nathaniel, but the police wouldn't allow him to talk with either man. "They're with their attorneys right now. We're still getting statements, confirming everyone's understanding of all the events. You can check back again in twenty-four hours."

When Zach left the station, he found Rowena sitting on a bench outside. He approached her and studied the woman's face. She looked so much like his brother. "Excuse me, you're Rowena Hector, right?"

Rowena confirmed, then slid further over on the bench. "Please, sit. You're Zach? Olivia told me all about you last fall."

Once Rowena filled Zach in on everything that happened in the last month, he began to process the news. "Emma was keeping this a secret from me?"

Rowena nodded. "I believe she cared very much for you, but this was something she had to do herself. Emma never recovered from Ethan's death, and this was her only way to connect with him."

Zach and Rowena shared a few memories of Emma, then Ethan. Before long, they realized how much they liked one another, how tragic the entire situation had truly been. Zach grabbed her hand. "I'm sorry you never got to know your son."

"Oh, but I did. I have a lifetime of memories from talking to your mother and to Emma." Rowena assured Zach that she'd seen so much heartache in her life. She knew the grieving process better than anyone else. "Time is the only thing that will help you decide how to move on. You will never be the same again, but you will also learn how to be happy and enjoy life."

Rowena revealed that Flynn suffered from PTSD. "He's devastated, but I only spoke with him for a few minutes before the police locked him in his cell."

"What happens next?" Zach thought about his own situation with Katerina, wondering whether she was also in a cell nearby.

"We've gotten him an attorney, someone who understands his background. I don't know yet. But I will support him through this." Rowena stood and thanked Zach for listening to her story.

She also shared with him Emma's desire to support Ethan's and Ben's dreams about the veterans and POW projects.

Zach volunteered to help make it happen. "I owe her that much."

Rowena tapped his chest, where his heart was racing. "Love will be yours again. Don't seek the thing you crave the most, and in return, it will find you when you least expect it."

Zach smiled. "I understand. I just need to accept what happened to Emma."

"Please remember, Flynn is not a dangerous man. He only wanted to protect everyone when he saw the gun." Rowena prepared to leave for the institute where Flynn would meet with a doctor.

"I know he didn't mean to kill Emma. I blame Nathaniel and Pilar for everything they've done to hide the truth from us. I blame my ex-girlfriend for stealing the gun."

Rowena added, "She's here somewhere. I saw them walk her to another room, away from that young guy she was with. Maybe she will be punished for the damages she's caused."

Zach returned inside with Rowena and asked for an update on Katerina, but the detective wouldn't provide him with any details. "I'm sorry, but there's nothing else I can offer at this time."

Zach's anger grew, but he convinced himself not to cause a scene. When he returned outside, he called for an Uber as his car was back at the Glass house and he needed to get home. Before he could arrange for one, the attorney handling his custody case called.

"I'm so sorry about everything that happened last night, but at least we have some good news."

"What do you mean?" Zach waffled between curiosity and suspicion.

"We received the police report from your brother. Apparently, Katerina was arrested and will be formally charged on several counts." The attorney confirmed that Katerina had been in possession of drugs, stolen the gun, trespassed on private property, and broken several laws pertaining to indecent exposure. "And those are just the top of the iceberg. Once we speak with her roommate and your mother, they could press further charges."

Zach hung up with the attorney, grateful for all Teddy had done, even after he'd slept with his brother's wife. Zach planned to contact his brother later that day, but he needed to find his mother and his daughter before he could do anything else. He called and arranged to meet Olivia at the hospital, where she helped him decide how to say goodbye to Emma. After Zach's heartfelt discussion with his mother, an Uber dropped him off at home, where he rushed to his daughter's room. Zach held Anastasia for several minutes before letting her go. "Everything's going to be okay, penguin. I promise you."

"You're silly, Daddy. I'm always okay with you." Anastasia smacked her lips against his cheek, then dragged him to the den to watch cartoons with her. "Can I have some juice?"

"No juice. We've had enough juice this weekend, baby girl." Zach sat with his daughter until she became so absorbed by the show, he sneaked into the hallway and contacted Emma's parents. He'd remembered their names and hometown from a previous conversation, and they were listed in an Ohio directory. He spoke with them for several minutes, grateful that they'd known who he was.

"Our daughter mentioned how much you comforted her after Ethan's death. We're forever thankful you could be with her in such a devastating time."

Zach's heart skipped a beat knowing she'd told her family about him. Even though she had a strained relationship with them in the weeks before her death, the fact that she talked about him convinced Zach that what they'd felt was genuine.

Emma's parents explained that they planned to have her body shipped to Cleveland, but if the Glass family wanted to hold a small ceremony beforehand, they understood. "Emma found a home with your family. We know you're hurting just as much as we are."

Zach and Emma's family worked out the details for him to plan the service in Connecticut the next day. Once it ended, Emma's body would be flown to Cleveland and buried in a cemetery in her hometown. Zach promised to call them with any questions later that evening, but in the meantime, he wanted to spend the afternoon with his family, especially after Caleb's text message about scheduling a fishing trip in a couple of weekends.

As Zach walked toward the staircase, Diane exited her room and approached him. "Honey, remember the caterer who was here last night?" She explained that the caterer had left before Nathaniel, Flynn, and Rowena arrived and wanted to collect her check. "Pilar never paid her, so I told her to swing by in an hour. I need to meet with the detective and won't be around. Can you handle it for me?"

Zach nodded, recalling the caterer's sexy pigtails. "Sure, happy to help."

"Okay, good. Besides, she mentioned something about how attractive you were. Apparently, you two work out at the same gym, and she wants to get your number." Diane handed him the check, pecked his cheek, and sneaked away with a wide grin. "Good luck with that one!"

"Are you trying to set me up already?" Surprisingly, Zach was beginning to feel stronger, and the day suddenly looked brighter. Although he would always treasure his connection with Emma, he realized she was with Ethan now, which meant he should focus on his future. "Eh, she was kinda hot. Any chance you know how she feels about piercings?"

Chapter 29 – The Following Day (Olivia)

Throughout the night, Olivia wrestled with her own conscience, falling short of assigning blame to any one person for the events that had led to Emma's death. By divvying it up among everyone involved, she crafted an acceptable way to move forward. Had she assumed responsibility for the entire situation herself, Olivia might never have left the Glass home again. Too much had occurred there, and when she considered what life would be like the next day, it was more than she could handle.

Ben had been guiding her as she addressed all her responsibilities in the last few months since leaving for Italy. The letters he'd left behind were never meant to stay hidden. Rowena had been just as much a victim as Olivia had been in the past. When Ben died in the car accident the previous spring, Olivia's life had changed in more ways than she understood. It was almost as if Ben had reached beyond his grave to pressure her to make the correct decisions. And when she didn't, he found a way to make it happen. She was mistaken by believing Ben had approved of all she'd done since his death. He might've agreed with some of her actions, but he'd also intended to rectify his poor past choices.

After accepting Emma's death was partially her fault, Olivia focused on her own set of priorities. Although Margaret and Matthew had been awake and taking care of Madison, they were too preoccupied to hear her walk through the hallway and down the stairs. Diane appeared to be sound asleep in her bedroom. Olivia didn't want to bother her, so she grabbed her sister's car keys from a hook in the mudroom. She sneaked out of the house very early, as she did the day before, and drove to the cemetery. She spent several hours talking to Ben, Ethan, and her grandson who'd died minutes after he was born, just like her own son so many years ago.

Olivia ignored her family for most of the morning, needing the time to push herself forward and decide what to do about George's potential role in Ben's death. She'd already responded to Caleb's text message about where he could fix things with Jake, only because she knew her son needed her help. They all did, but each one would ask for it in time, when they were ready. By lunchtime, Olivia called Emma's parents to tell them how sorry she was about everything. At first, Emma's parents were quiet, as they'd only spoken to the police briefly about the conflict. They listened to Olivia's entire explanation and chastised her for allowing their daughter to get caught up in the mess, but later relented and indicated they understood it was all a horrible accident.

Olivia promised to visit them in the coming days as she wanted to be there when Emma was buried in Cleveland. Olivia initially thought Emma would want to be with Ethan in his grave, but Emma's parents objected to the decision. Nothing had been in writing, and Emma's parents were technically her next of kin. Olivia had to let them make the decision, even though she disagreed with their choice. Once they said goodbye, she grabbed lunch at an out-of-the-way restaurant, quietly eating her meal alone in a corner booth. That's when Olivia had her revelation, the most logical and acceptable outcome for everything that'd occurred.

After meeting with the detective in charge of the case that afternoon, providing her official statement and decision not to press charges against anyone other than Katerina and Quinn, she begged him to provide the address where Flynn and Rowena had been released. The detective explained that he'd dropped them off at an institute a few towns away for a psychiatric evaluation of Flynn's current state-of-mind. He wasn't being formally charged with murder, nor was he considered responsible for Emma's death; however, the state of Connecticut wasn't comfortable releasing him back into the public without having undergone a thorough medical evaluation.

The detective noted that he wasn't allowed to provide her with the name of the institute, but he left her alone in his office when he went to pour a cup of coffee. Upon returning, he said, "Did you learn everything you needed to today? My desk is such a mess. I hope I didn't leave anything out that I shouldn't have."

Olivia nodded, then thanked him for his kindness. "I'm sure you wouldn't do such a foolish thing." She held the institute's name and address in her closed fist as she left the office.

"I'm glad I could be of service today. Please see that he gets all the help he needs."

Olivia drove to the institute and asked to see Rowena Hector, indicating she was a family member there to support Flynn and Rowena during their stay. Moments later, Rowena emerged from a waiting room and embraced Olivia.

"I'm so sorry." They were the only words exchanged between the two women as they comforted one another over their shared loss.

Olivia and Rowena discussed all the details of their mutual losses in the preceding months. "If only Emma would've come to me and told me the truth. If I knew Ethan wanted her to have the money, I would've given it to her. She'd be alive right now."

"You don't know that," Rowena advised, offering Olivia her handkerchief. "Everything happens for a reason. We cannot live our lives worrying or wondering about what could have been. We only have what is in front of us today. We must learn from the past and strive for a better future."

"That's the same conclusion staring me down in this rear-view mirror redirecting my life." Olivia promised Rowena that she would cover all of Flynn's medical expenses and help them figure out their futures.

"Emma had an idea. I think it's a good one." Rowena explained the project that she, Emma, and Flynn had discussed the previous day. "Maybe we could use some of Ethan's money to make that happen."

Olivia replied, "We can use all of his money. I want to be part of the project. Emma and I talked about this before. I just wasn't ready to accept that my son was gone at the time. The three of us can do this together. We can grieve for Ethan's and Emma's deaths as a family. You. Me. Flynn." She reminisced about the many times Ethan had told her all about his discoveries… all the family war heroes and veterans.

The two women agreed to touch base the following day. Rowena wanted to focus on Flynn's psychological evaluation, then decide next steps. Olivia left the institution and checked her phone. Zach had reached out. When she returned the call, he begged her for help. Olivia met him at the hospital and assisted him with addressing all the plans for Emma's upcoming funeral. By the time they finished pulling everything together, Zach was ready to head to the family estate to see his daughter. He hugged Olivia goodbye, then said, "A boy will always need his mother. I'm so glad you are mine."

Olivia's soul finally began to heal. As each son checked on her, she confirmed his road to recovery was one that wouldn't veer off course anytime soon. "My son, we will all grow from this experience. And you will find love again… when you least expect it to happen."

Once Olivia reached the precinct, she asked to see the detective in charge of Emma's case. While waiting for him to appear, Teddy arrived and approached his mother. After a few moments discussing the tragedy, he said, "Mom, it's my job to take care of this family. You deserve a break. I took care of Uncle George. For what it's worth, I believe he didn't actually do anything to Dad's car. I think he was attempting to scare Aunt Diane into giving him the money." Teddy explained what he'd done to help his brothers and his aunt and how it was time for them to truly move on. "My last gift is to you. I found you the perfect house." He handed her his phone so she could scroll through the photos.

"It's gorgeous!" Olivia exclaimed, viewing a replica of the house she and Diane had been raised in sixty years ago. From the traditional English garden in the backyard to the gabled roof, the Tudor-style home was exactly what Olivia hoped for in her remaining years. "You've changed so much, my son."

"Because of your influence, no doubt. Thank you for being my mother and encouraging me to find the real me," replied Teddy, before embracing Olivia and preparing to leave the precinct. "Let's meet for dinner tomorrow. We can talk about both of our futures."

Olivia watched her son leave, proud of all he'd done that day. She then met with the detective to confirm how to post bail for Nathaniel. She waited for Nathaniel to meet her in the lobby when processing was done. Pilar also showed up moments before he was released, eager to comfort her father-in-law. Olivia asked if she could take them out for a cup of coffee, so they could discuss everything that'd transpired. They agreed, noting their fears that Nathaniel would face several charges, specifically related to his picking up the gun and threatening several members of the Glass family.

At the café, Olivia assured him that she wouldn't press charges, and she'd do her best to convince the rest of her family to let Nathaniel and Pilar get off without going to prison. "I'm so sorry that I didn't attend your son's funeral," Olivia said to Nathaniel. She listened to him praise his deceased son, grateful to know more about the late chauffeur, then asked Pilar to share her favorite things about her husband.

Pilar offered a few memories of their marriage and first year together as newlyweds. She also apologized to Olivia for the death of Emma as a result of their actions.

"You were hurting just as much as my family. Only, you cared enough to check on us. We failed to check on you." Olivia relayed that she partially blamed them for Emma's death, but grudges helped no one. "My brother-in-law was the reason all this started. It needs to end with George too. We must move on and accept the future we all deserve."

"Pilar and I will figure this out together," Nathaniel stated as they rose from the table. "You've been most kind and generous, Olivia. How can we repay you?"

"By letting go of the past." Olivia directed him to wait a minute longer, then handed him an envelope from inside her purse. "Oh, and this belongs to you."

Nathaniel opened the parcel, then turned to Olivia. "This is a check for one-hundred-thousand dollars. Why? After our blackmail attempt, I'd think you wouldn't feel the need to do anything for us anymore."

"I do. I must atone for my sins. This money belongs to your family, for your loss." Olivia walked with them toward the entrance of the café.

Pilar and Nathaniel embraced one another, appreciative of the gift she'd given them. "Olivia, it seems Destiny has a formidable opponent. You've surprised us all this time."

"I surprise myself sometimes too." She smiled at them both, confident she'd begun a step in a more positive direction. Olivia pushed open the heavy glass door and sighed expressively as she left them behind to catch a cab.

Two parents and their five sons strolled by her on the sidewalk, laughing and teasing one another, reminding Olivia of all the uplifting times from her past. As they reached the corner, the family disappeared like ghostly apparitions... but in the process, Olivia recognized them as Ethan, Emma, and all the children they'd once been meant to bring into the world. Her heart swelled to witness such happiness.

"In less than nine months, I've come full circle. I thought everything was on track after the last family disaster. But I was clearly wrong. Not the first occasion either. This time, I'll know when I'm right." Olivia concentrated on an eagle soaring high above her in the sky, impressed by its giant wingspan and confidence in flight. "I'll be with you again in the future, my darling Ben. Just don't count on it being anytime soon... it's my time to live now. I'm ready to handle whatever Destiny has in store for me. She's one fickle bitch, but don't ever underestimate who taught her how to do it with such style!"

Dear Reader,

Thank you for taking time to read *Hiding Cracked Glass*. Word of mouth is an author's best friend and much appreciated. If you enjoyed it, please consider supporting this author:

- Leave a book review on Amazon US, Amazon (also your own country if different), Goodreads, BookBub, and any other book site you follow to help market and promote this book

- Tell your friends, family, and colleagues all about this author and his books

- Share brief posts on your social media platforms and tag the book (#HidingCrackedGlass or #PerceptionsofGlass) or author (#JamesJCudney) on Twitter, Facebook, Instagram, Pinterest, LinkedIn, WordPress, Tumblr, YouTube, Bloglovin, and SnapChat

- Suggest the book for book clubs, to bookstores, or to any libraries you know

About the Author

James is my given name, but most folks call me Jay. I live in New York City, grew up on Long Island, and graduated from Moravian College, an historic but small liberal arts school in Bethlehem, Pennsylvania, with a degree in English literature and minors in Education, Business and Spanish. After college, I accepted a technical writing position for a telecommunications company during Y2K and spent the last ~20 years building a career in technology & business operations in the retail, sports, media, hospitality, and entertainment industries. Throughout those years, I wrote short stories, poems, and various beginnings to the "Great American Novel," but I was so focused on my career that writing became a hobby. In 2016, I committed to focusing my energies toward reinvigorating a second career in reading, writing, and publishing.

Author

Writing has been a part of my life as much as my heart, mind, and body. At some points, it was just a few poems or short stories; at others, it was full length novels and stories. My current focus is family drama fiction, cozy mystery novels, and suspense thrillers. I conjure characters and plots that I feel must be unwound. I think of situations people find themselves in and feel compelled to tell the story. It's usually a convoluted plot with many surprise twists and turns. I feel it necessary to take that ride all over the course. My character is easily pictured in my head. I know what he is going to encounter or what she will feel. But I need to use the right words to make it clear.

Reader & Reviewer

Reading has also never left my side. Whether it was children's books, young adult novels, college textbooks, biographies, or my ultimate love, fiction, it's ever present in my day. I read two books per week and I'm on a quest to update every book I've ever read on Goodreads, write up a review, and post it on all my sites and platforms.

Blogger & Thinker

I have combined my passions into a single platform where I share reviews, write a blog and publish tons of content: TRUTH. I started my 365 Daily Challenge, where I post about a word that has some meaning to me and converse with everyone about life. There is humor, tears, love, friendship, advice, and bloopers. Lots of bloopers where I poke fun at myself all the time. Even my dogs have had weekly segments called "Ryder's Rants" or "Baxter's Barks," where they complain about me. All these things make up who I am; none of them are very fancy or magnanimous, but they are real. And that's why they are me.

I love history and research, finding myself often reaching back into the past to understand why someone made the choice he or she did and what were the subsequent consequences. I enjoy studying the activities and culture from hundreds of years ago to trace the roots and find the puzzle of my own history. I wish I could watch my ancestors from a secret place to learn how they interacted with others; and maybe I'll comprehend why I do things the way I do.

Websites & Blog

Website: https://jamesjcudney.com/
Blog: https://thisismytruthnow.com
Amazon: http://bit.ly/JJCIVBooks
Next Chapter: https://www.nextchapter.pub/authors/james-j-cudney
BookBub: https://www.bookbub.com/profile/james-j-cudney

Social Media

Twitter: https://twitter.com/jamescudney4
Facebook:
https://www.facebook.com/JamesJCudneyIVAuthor/
Facebook:
https://www.facebook.com/BraxtonCampusMysteries/
Facebook: https://www.facebook.com/ThisIsMyTruthNow/
Pinterest: https://www.pinterest.com/jamescudney4/
Instagram: https://www.instagram.com/jamescudney4/
Goodreads: https://www.goodreads.com/jamescudney4
LinkedIn: https://www.linkedin.com/in/jamescudney4

Genres, Formats & Languages

I write in the family drama, suspense, and mystery genres. My first two books were Watching Glass Shatter (2017) and Father Figure (2018). Both are contemporary fiction and focus on the dynamics between parents and children and between siblings. I wrote a sequel, Hiding Cracked Glass, for my debut novel, and they are known as the Perceptions of Glass series. I also have a light mystery series called the Braxton Campus Mysteries with six books available.

All my books come in multiple formats (Kindle, paperback, hardcover, large print paperback, pocket size paperback, and audiobook) and some are also translated into foreign languages such as Spanish, Italian, Portuguese, and German.

Summary of Books

Father Figure (Contemporary Fiction / Family Drama)

Between the fast-paced New York City, a rural Mississippi town and a charming Pennsylvania college campus filled with secrets, two young girls learn the consequences of growing up too quickly. Amalia Graeme, abused by her mother for most of her life, longs to escape her desolate hometown and fall in love. Contemplating her loss of innocence and conflicting feelings between her boyfriend and the dangerous attraction she's developed for an older man, Amalia faces life-altering tragedies. Brianna Porter, a sassy, angst-ridden teenager raised in New York City, yearns to find her life's true purpose, conquer her fear of abandonment, and interpret an intimidating desire for her best friend, Shanelle. Desperate to find the father whom her mother refuses to reveal, Brianna accidentally finds out a shocking truth about her missing parent. Set in alternating chapters two decades apart, the parallels between their lives and the unavoidable collision that is bound to happen are revealed. FATHER FIGURE is a stand-alone emotional story filled with mystery, romance, and suspense.

PERCEPTIONS OF GLASS SERIES

Watching Glass Shatter (Contemporary Fiction / Family Drama)

The wealthy Glass family lost its patriarch, Benjamin Glass, sooner than expected. Benjamin's widow, Olivia, and her 5 sons each react to his death in their own way while preparing for the reading of his will. Olivia receives a very unexpected confession from her late husband about one of their sons that could shatter the whole family. Prior to revealing the secret to her children, Olivia must figure out which boy Ben refers to in the confession he left her in his will. While the family attorney searches for the mysterious Rowena Hector whom Ben says holds the answers, Olivia asks her sons to each spend a week with her as she isn't ready to let go of the past. When Olivia visits her sons, she quickly learns that each one has been keeping his own secret from her. Olivia never expected her remaining years would be so complex and life-altering, but she will not rest until her family is reunited after Ben's untimely death. We all need family. We all want to fit in. We're all a mix of quirky personalities. Will Olivia be able to fix them, or will the whole family implode? What will she do when she discovers the son behind Ben's secret? Check out this ensemble cast where each family member's perspective is center stage, discovering along the way who might feel the biggest impact from all the secrets. Through various scenes and memories across a six-month period, you'll get to know everyone, learning how and why they made certain decisions. Welcome to being an honorary member of the Glass family where the flair for over-the-top drama pushes everyone to their limits.

Hiding Cracked Glass (Contemporary Fiction / Family Drama)

An ominous blackmail letter appears at an inopportune moment. The recipient's name is accidentally blurred out upon arrival. Which member of the Glass family is the ruthless missive meant for? In the powerful sequel to Watching Glass Shatter, Olivia is the first to read the nasty threat and assumes it's meant for her. When the mysterious letter falls into the wrong hands and is read aloud, it throws the entire Glass family into an inescapable trajectory of self-question. Across the span of eight hours, Olivia and her sons contemplate whether to confess their hidden secrets or find a way to bury them forever. Some failed to learn an important lesson last time. Will they determine how to save themselves before it's too late? Each chapter's focus alternates between the various family members and introduces several new and familiar faces with a vested interest in the outcome. As each hour ticks by, the remaining siblings and their mother gradually reveal what's happened to them in the preceding months, and when the blackmailer makes an appearance at Olivia's birthday party, the truth brilliantly comes to light. Although everyone seemed to embrace the healing process at the end of Watching Glass Shatter, there were hidden cracks in the Glass family that couldn't be mended. Their lives are about to shatter into pieces once again, but this time, the stakes are even higher. Someone wants to teach them a permanent lesson and refuses to stop until success is achieved.

BRAXTON CAMPUS MYSTERY SERIES

Academic Curveball: Death at the Sports Complex (#1)

When Kellan Ayrwick, a thirty-two-year-old single father, is forced to return home for his father's retirement from Braxton College, he finds the dead body of a professor in Diamond Hall's stairwell. Unfortunately, Kellan has a connection to the victim, and so do several members of his family. Could one of them be guilty of murder? Then he finds a second body after discovering mysterious donations to the college's athletic program, a nasty blog denouncing his father, and a criminal attempting to change student grades so the star baseball pitcher isn't expelled. Someone is playing games on campus, but none of the facts add up. With the help of his eccentric and trouble-making nana weeding through the clues, Kellan tries to stay out of the sheriff's way. Fate has other plans. Kellan is close to discovering the killer's identity just as someone he loves is put in grave danger of becoming victim number three. And if that's not enough to wreak havoc on his family, everything comes crashing to a halt when his own past comes spiraling back to change his life forever. In this debut novel in the Braxton Campus Mystery Series, readers discover a cozy, secluded Pennsylvania village full of quirky, sarcastic, and nosy residents. Among the daily workings of Braxton College and the charming Ayrwick family, Kellan weighs his investigative talents against an opportunity to achieve a much sought-after dream. When this first book ends, the drama is set for the next adventure in Kellan's future... and it's one you won't want to miss.

Broken Heart Attack: Death at the Theater (#2)

When an extra ticket becomes available to attend the dress rehearsal of Braxton's King Lear production, Kellan tags along with Nana D and her buddies, sisters-in-law Eustacia and Gwendolyn Paddington, to show support for the rest of the Paddington family. When one of them appears to have a heart attack in the middle of the second act, Nana D raises her suspicions and asks Kellan to investigate who killed her friend. Amidst family members suddenly in debt and a secret rendezvous between an unlikely pair, Kellan learns the Paddingtons might not be as clean-cut as everyone thinks. But did one of them commit murder for an inheritance? Kellan is back in his second adventure since returning home to Pennsylvania. With his personal life in upheaval and his new boss, Myriam, making life difficult, will he be able to find a killer, or will he get caught up in his own version of stage fright?

Flower Power Trip: Death at the Masquerade Ball (#3)

Braxton College is throwing the Heroes & Villains Costume Extravaganza to raise money for renovations to the antiquated Memorial Library. While attending, Kellan stumbles upon a close family friend standing over a dead body that's dressed as Dr. Evil. Did one of Maggie's sisters kill an annoying guest at the Roarke and Daughters Inn or does the victim have a more intimate connection to someone else on campus? As Kellan helps the school's president, Ursula, bury a scandalous secret from her past and unearth the identity of her stalker, he unexpectedly encounters a missing member of his own family who's reappeared after a lengthy absence. When all the peculiar events around town trace back to the Stoddards, a new family who recently moved to Wharton County, the explosive discovery only offers more confusion. Between the special flower exhibit that's made an unplanned stop on campus and strange postcards arriving each week from all around the world, Kellan can't decide which mystery in his life should take priority. Unfortunately, the biggest one of all has yet to arrive at his doorstep. When it does, Kellan won't know what hit him.

Mistaken Identity Crisis: Death on the Cable Car (#4)

A clever thief with a sinister calling card has invaded Braxton campus. A string of jewelry thefts continues to puzzle the sheriff given they're remarkably similar to an unsolved eight-year-old case from shortly before Gabriel vanished one stormy night. When a missing ruby is discovered near an electrified dead body during the campus cable car redesign project, Kellan must investigate the real killer to protect his brother. Amidst sorority hazing practices and the victim's connections to several prominent Wharton County citizens, a malicious motive becomes more obvious and trickier to prove. As if the latest murder isn't enough to keep him busy, Kellan partners with April to end the Castigliano and Vargas crime family feud. What really happened to Francesca while all those postcards showed up in Braxton? The mafia world is more calculating than Kellan realized, and if he wants to move forward, he must make a few ruthless sacrifices. Election Day is over, and the new mayor takes office. Nana D celebrates her 75th birthday with an adventure. A double wedding occurs at Crilly Lake on Independence Day. And Kellan receives a few more surprises as the summer heat settles in Wharton County.

Haunted House Ghost: Death at the Fall Festival (#5)

It's Halloween, and excitement is brewing in Braxton to carve jack-o'-lanterns, go on haunted hayrides, and race through the spooky corn maze at the Fall Festival. Despite the former occupant's warnings, Kellan renovates and moves into a mysterious old house. When a ruthless ghost promises retribution, our fearless professor turns to the eccentric town historian and an eerie psychic to communicate with the apparition. Meanwhile, construction workers discover a fifty-year-old skeleton after breaking ground on the new Memorial Library wing. While Kellan and April dance around the chemistry sparking between them, a suspicious accident occurs at the Fall Festival. Soon, Kellan discovers the true history and dastardly connections of the Grey family. But can he capture the elusive killer - and placate the revenge-seeking ghost.

Frozen Stiff Drink: Death at Danby Landing (#6)

A winter blizzard barrels toward Wharton County with a vengeance. Madam Zenya predicted the raging storm would change the course of Kellan's life, but the famed seer never could've prepared him for all the collateral damage. Nana D disappears after visiting a patient at Willow Trees, leaving behind a trail of confusion. When the patient turns up dead, and second body is discovered beneath the snowbanks, Kellan must face his worst fears. What tragedy has befallen his beloved grandmother? Kellan's brother Hampton learns essential life lessons the hard way after his father-in-law accuses him of embezzlement. While trying to prove his innocence, Hampton digs himself a deeper hole that might lead to prison. Sheriff Montague wants to save him, but she receives the shock of her life as the past hurtles forward and complicates her future. Between locating Nana D and solving the scandalous murder of another prominent Braxton citizen, Kellan and April's worlds explode with more turmoil than they can handle. Too bad neither one of them knows what to do about the psychic's latest premonition. The suspicious deaths happening around town aren't ending anytime soon.

Lightning Source UK Ltd.
Milton Keynes UK
UKHW021847280121
377874UK00010B/549/J